GROWING UP FOR
BEGINNERS

CLAIRE CALMAN

For Kathy —
thanks for reading and
for the delicious
Provençal tart!

Claire
x

B

Boldwood

First published in Great Britain in 2020 by Boldwood Books Ltd.

A CIP catalogue record for this book is available from the British Library.

Paperback ISBN 978-1-83889-505-1

Ebook ISBN 978-1-83889-499-3

Kindle ISBN 978-1-83889-500-6

Audio CD ISBN 978-1-83889-506-8

MP3 CD ISBN 978-1-83889-503-7

Digital audio download ISBN 978-1-83889-498-6

Boldwood Books Ltd
23 Bowerdean Street
London SW6 3TN
www.boldwoodbooks.com

For our wonderful son, Leo –
you will always be my favourite.

The Untold Want

The untold want by life and land ne'er granted,

Now voyager sail thou forth to seek and find.

— WALT WHITMAN

1

ELEANOR

For as long as Eleanor can remember, she has snuck a look at the end of a book before reading it. In her head, it was rather like when you go swimming and you want to know exactly how deep the water is before you get in. She was embarrassed by her need to do this – and it was unquestionably a *need* – realising that other people might find it an odd thing to do, foolish even. When she was little and her father was reading to her at bedtime, even then she would reach out and peep at the last page to see. She could still recall his saying, 'Well, it's *your* book, little thing, so you can read it any way you choose.'

She wanted to know that the terminus would definitely be there before embarking on the journey. When she read a novel, which was only rarely nowadays, she liked to turn to the final page at once, read the very last sentence, then the whole of the last paragraph, then the final page and perhaps a paragraph or two of the penultimate page. If dissatisfied – the ending seemed ambiguous or inconclusive – she abandoned it; if intrigued, she felt it was safe to commit to it. She was sure that this peccadillo must reveal something deep and meaningful about her warped psyche but she didn't care. Why shouldn't she read a book back to front, upside down, or perched on the branch of a tree if she so chose? It didn't harm anyone else, after all.

Before she married Roger, he used to tease her about this habit, often mentioning it to other guests at parties or dinners if ever the conversation turned to books. Eleanor flushed and tried to redirect the subject away from herself and back onto what people liked to read, which was surely much more interesting anyway.

But his remarks were limited to teasing at that point, even if at times she thought the teasing had a note of something else that she couldn't quite put her finger on. The first occasion he went further was while they were on their honeymoon, over twenty years ago now.

* * *

Roger has booked a fortnight for them in southern Italy. It is July and Eleanor is looking forward to it, of course, but with some reservations, chiefly about the fact that it would be so very hot. She does not function well in heat and feels like a wilted flower unless she can skulk in the shade, while Roger basks and stretches in the baking sun like a freshly sated lion.

Anticipating that she might spend a fair amount of time sitting beneath a tree, she has packed eight books, all novels she had been saving up for their trip. Roger is clearly taken aback when she unpacks their suitcases and sets out her book stash on top of the bedroom chest of drawers.

'You do know we're not relocating, just here for a fortnight?' he teases, and she laughs.

He has brought just two books: a thick thriller and a political biography.

'Darling,' he says, pulling her to him, 'I do hope you won't spend the entire time reading?'

'Of course not.' She smiles invitingly and stretches up to kiss him.

'And you're not going to be a naughty little wifey and read the ending first, I hope?' His tone is still teasing and she assumes he is joking.

'No, I'm planning to read it upside down.'

They go off on long excursions the first two days and return exhausted, so in fact it isn't until the afternoon of the third day that she opens one of the novels to begin it. Roger has gone to lie by the pool while Eleanor has opted to rest in their room for a little while, desperate for time out of the heat. As usual, she turns to the end. Odd. The last sentence seems... not final. Intermediate, not conclusive. She reads the last paragraph. Disappointing. It doesn't even seem like a proper ending at all. She really dislikes books where the story simply peters out or stops. And the reviews were so glowing, too. She sets it to one side and selects another. This one she picked up at the airport, read the last paragraph right there in the bookshop and found it irresistible. But still she wants to refresh her memory.

She jolts back as if she had been slapped. That isn't the right ending. How can that be? Besides, now it breaks off mid-sentence. It makes no sense at all.

A horrible thought strikes her but she pushes it away and drops the book with a bang as if it has burned her. Thinks for a minute, recalling her husband's expression, that strangely knowing smile this morning when she came out of her lovely long shower. No. *No.* Slowly then she picks up the book and turns to the final page again; cracks the spine to open it as wide as she can. It couldn't be true surely? And yet it is: the last page has been excised from the book. Now fully spread, the remaining tell-tale stub is visible. It has been cut with something very sharp: a razor blade or – her mind racing now, breath catching in her throat, imagining – a *knife*. A penknife, to be precise. She thinks of the ever-present bulge in Roger's left-hand pocket: his red Swiss Army knife, with its useful corkscrew, nail file, scissors, pliers, and blades. She swallows and blinks, a rabbit noticing the yellow glint of the fox's eyes suddenly very nearby.

No doubt Roger means it as a joke of sorts. Sometimes his sense of humour is really rather different from her own. She has no problem with being teased, but this is different. There is something very deliberate about it that unsettles her. Still, she would tell him that he has upset her, albeit inadvertently, and he would understand and never, ever do such an awful thing again.

She wonders how best to broach the subject. Roger could be a bit... prickly at times if one happens to catch him at a bad moment, rather like her father in that way, so she knows how to manage such a man. Perhaps a teasing comment would be best, showing she understands that it is clearly no more than a misguided joke that has overstepped the mark?

Out on their bedroom balcony, having an aperitif before dinner, looking out to the sparkling sea, she steels herself.

'Such a curious thing has happened in this heat,' she says, clinking her glass against his.

'Oh, yes?' Roger leans back in his chair and stares out at the view.

'Yes. Some of the pages in my novel seem to have melted away! But only the last one or two – isn't that odd?'

He smiles and pats her leg.

'You'll thank me soon enough.' Behind his sunglasses, his expression is unknowable. 'Go on and read it in the normal way. You'll love it, I promise you.'

'But I already love reading *my* way.' She sits more upright. 'Roger?'

'Oh, *darling!*' He waggles her leg to and fro with his hand. 'Come along now. It's so peculiar to read the end of the book first. Don't you realise it's abnormal behaviour?'

'I don't care if it is. It's not bothering anyone else.'

'Well, it bothers *me*, as you very well know.' He takes a long swallow of his gin and tonic. 'And I think you ought to care about that, if nothing else. I am your husband, after all.'

'That doesn't entitle you to... to... defile my things!'

'Oh, don't be so ridiculously emotional! That's inflammatory language. No one's *defiled* anything. So I temporarily removed a page or two from the books so you'd read them normally, like everyone else. Big bloody deal. It's not as if I chucked the pages away. For God's sake!' He stands up and marches into the bedroom and comes back a minute later with a sheaf of pages scrunched in his fist. He drops them from a height into her lap.

'Have them now if you're really such a baby you can't manage without them.' He sniffs and turns to go. 'I'm going down to the terrace to have my drink and a cigar. I'll see you at dinner in twenty minutes. Don't be late.'

The bedroom door slams.

Eleanor's whole body is shaking. She picks up the pages from her lap, the table, the floor and does her best to smooth them out, crying uncontrollably now, great gulpy sobs lurching out of her body, tears splattering onto the crumpled pages. She takes them into the bedroom and looks through all the books she has brought with her: all eight of them have been cut. Tries to tuck the shorn pages back into position, telling herself perhaps she could buy some tape in the morning and it would be OK, everything would be OK.

* * *

Later, back at home, at first she simply tucked her book out of sight, in her bedside cabinet or in her underwear drawer, but that proved to be insufficient. Instead, she settled on short stories, biographies, travel journals. These she was happy to read in the 'correct' way, and Roger left them alone. But if she read a novel, she had to secrete it very carefully, put out a decoy book to allay his suspicions, and only read it while he was out.

She kept the honeymoon books up in her studio, all together on a shelf. Whenever it happened again, she added the brutalised corpse to the others, a sad, strange sort of shrine. She needed to keep them as some sort of record for herself, so that she would never think, even for a passing moment, that she had imagined it. It was silly, of course – why give yourself further pain by reminding yourself, after all? – but she couldn't bear to throw them away. It would seem a second violation. The loose pages had been returned by Roger and she had smoothed them out and blotted away any stray tears and tucked them into the back of their amputee parents. After that first time, she chose never to tape them; that would merely offer some illusion that they were whole and fine.

Sometimes Eleanor ventured into bookshops and stood in the fiction section, guiltily reading the last page of a novel, sneaking a glance over her shoulder as if she might be caught indulging in this secret pleasure. Then she turned her back on all those stories just waiting, longing for her to immerse herself in them, and headed instead for Memoir or Travel or Poetry, or treated herself to a sumptuous cookery or gardening book. Only very occasionally, when she could not resist, did she buy a novel. She would take it home, bury the bag at the bottom of the rubbish bin, and slip the book itself into the linen cupboard, between the sheets and pillowcases for the guest room, where Roger would have no cause to look.

Once, she had what at first seemed a rather clever idea of buying a hardback novel and switching the loose dust-jacket with a biography of the same size at home. She curled up in an armchair, entirely lost in the story, but something must have triggered Roger's radar because he suddenly asked some odd, specific detail about the book. She flushed and looked guilty and he took it from her hands, unpeeled it from its dissembling cover and read to himself for a minute while she sat there feeling stupid, like a child who has broken some precious ornament and been found trying to hide the pieces. He sighed and reached into his pocket for his knife.

'Oh, no, no, please *don't*.' She stood up to face him square on. 'I hate it when you do that. It *is* my book, after all, and it doesn't affect you how I choose to read it, does it? I don't understand why it bothers you so much.'

'*I* really *hate* it when you behave in an embarrassingly eccentric way *for no reason*, Eleanor. Perhaps you should think about that for a minute?' He stood very close to her. 'And it is not *your* book. I believe you paid for it from our joint account – i.e., with the money *I* worked extremely hard to earn.' He set the book down on a side table and, as she left the room and ran up the stairs to be on her own, Eleanor heard the quiet click as he slid open the blade.

* * *

October 2012

It was not the first time that Roger had moved his wife's birthday, so she told herself that perhaps she was just being silly to mind so much. This year, the date happened to clash with an important work function he couldn't avoid; these things were inevitable sometimes. Roger pointed out how much better it would be to celebrate just a couple of days later instead, on the Saturday; then he could wine and dine her in the evening at their favourite restaurant. It was infuriating anyway, wasn't it, having to open presents in a mad rush before dashing off to work? Yes, better by far to shift it to the Saturday, have a lie-in, breakfast in bed, the whole kit and caboodle, and bask in her birthday all weekend long if she so desired.

It certainly made good sense in a way, Eleanor could see that. But she only worked two days a week, never liked to lie in, and considered breakfast in bed overrated, as the bed ended up full of scratchy toast crumbs and you couldn't move if you were hemmed in by a tray. Perhaps, the thought crossed her mind, she would have been quite capable of enjoying her birthday on the day itself.

'But Saturday is Hannah's last day,' Eleanor said in response. Their daughter was about to embark on a trip to India and south-east Asia as part of her gap year before going to university the following autumn.

'So? Her flight's at six: plenty of time for you to take her to the airport and be back for dinner.'

'Won't you come, too? I thought perhaps it would be nice if we both saw her off?'

'No, darling. That would be overkill. You do it. Then you can both be soppy and snivelling into tissues together. As she'll be away nearly five months, I hardly think she'll mind doing without my company for a couple of extra hours, do you?'

'I suppose not.'

'Good, good.' Roger turned back to his newspaper.

Eleanor thought that she should just clarify about her birthday; maybe Roger only meant that her birthday dinner would be on the Saturday, as they had done a couple of years ago? Yes, that made sense, of course. She went back through to the kitchen to clear away the breakfast things.

On Thursday morning, her birthday, Roger turned to her and kissed her and said with a laugh, 'Happy not-proper-birthday, darling! I've got you a little unbirthday gift for today, because I know you'd be a sad little kitten if you had to wait another two whole days until your proper birthday and would feel hard done by!' He handed her a small gift bag. Inside was a bottle of the extremely expensive perfume he always bought her; he was very thoughtful, making sure she never ran out, although she had in fact not yet opened the bottle from the previous year.

Eleanor suppressed the urge to point out that today *was* her proper birthday and she had her birth certificate neatly filed away so she could prove it.

* * *

Saturday. Out there, somewhere, there were, no doubt, many women who would be thrilled with a pair of fluffy sheepskin slippers as a birthday present. For Eleanor, however, relishing the promising rustle of gold tissue as she opened her present, there was a moment of silent revulsion, followed by sagging disappointment that her husband could have so little idea of her taste. She imagined how her father would view the slippers, as further proof of the decline of civilisation. What could she say, other than, 'Oh dear God – take them away! Bury them in a pit, far from human view.' Externally polite as always, however, she installed her feet in the slippers, wondering how quickly she might reasonably remove them again. Beneath the svelte black legs of her elegant trousers, the bulky beige slippers looked absurd, as if the feet were no longer her own.

'They're so comfy, you'll want to go everywhere in them, you'll see.' Roger, in grey cashmere sweater and weekend cords, was clad in a pair of identical sheepskin slippers himself, but in a darker brown.

In her head, Eleanor amended the word 'comfy' to 'comfortable' automatically. That word, along with many others, made her feel queasy, she disliked it so much. It was a word for people who were 'roundy corners', as her sharp-cornered father labelled them – people who had no edge, no bite, people who followed up any opinion with 'on the other hand', scared to formulate a view and stick to it, people who were beige on the inside. In fact, Roger was not usually 'roundy corners' at all; he was rarely devoid of a strong opinion on most matters, but there were certain words he favoured that Eleanor could not bear. There must be *something* nice she could say about the slippers. Think, *think*.

'Gosh, they're certainly very warm. Thank you, darling.'

'I knew you'd love them.' Roger smiled. 'We'll be snug as two bugs in a rug.'

'Yes, won't we?' Eleanor shucked off the slippers with what she hoped didn't seem like unseemly haste. Seeing Roger's face, she said, 'I'll just give them a spray with fabric protector... while I think of it.' She picked them up firmly, trying not to look as if she were removing two large turds, and bustled out towards the kitchen.

'Good thinking. And you don't mind about not having jewellery this year, darling?' Roger called out.

Normally, he gave her a necklace or earrings that she had picked out herself – something quietly elegant and unfussy, something Eleanorish. This year, as well as the perfume and the slippers, he had bought a Joint

Membership of the National Trust for them both, the perfect gift to remind a woman of forty-seven that she was getting older and had better set aside any thoughts of wild carousing and instead turn her mind to the exploration of the stately homes and enviable gardens of England. But, after all, they did enjoy visiting National Trust properties, so really, it was a very good choice. And the perfume was lovely. And the slippers were certainly intended as a kind thought.

Perhaps the problem was partly in having an autumn birthday? In October, no one thought to buy you a chiffon scarf or a silky camisole. Everything was woolly or fleecy or snuggly; all presents were, at heart, roundy corners at this time of year, in the run-up to the full-on chunky knitwear-fest of Christmas. It wasn't that Eleanor really wanted to receive scarlet satin lingerie; she would never have worn anything so obvious, and scarlet would have made her look horribly washed out. It was just that, sometimes, it would be nice to think that the person you lived with, had lived with for twenty-one years of marriage, might still – even for a mad, impulsive moment – think of you that way, as a vibrant, passionate woman. Even if you didn't see yourself that way, even if you never had. And, when she had first seen the plump tissue parcel, clearly not jewellery, hadn't she thought for a second or two that it would be something silky – or lacy – or maybe a velvet scarf in burgundy or purple, the colour of ripe plums?

It was highly possible that she might not have heard Roger's enquiry about whether she minded not having jewellery. The acoustics were often unreliable in this house, so that at times one simply failed to catch what the other person was saying.

She placed the slippers in the hall closet.

'Oh, and I said I'd pop over to see my father,' Eleanor said as she came back in. 'He has a present for me.'

'Must you go today?' Roger checked his watch. 'It *is* Hannah's last day before the off.'

'I won't be long and she's not even up yet.' Eleanor dropped her gaze. 'And... I believe the conservator is returning Dad's painting this morning. It's been reframed, too. I offered to help hang it.'

'Oh, that bloody painting!' Roger thunked down his coffee mug. 'How much did all this faffing about cost? And why has it taken all this time? There was barely a mark on it. If he hadn't tried to pick the broken glass out, it would have been fine. Honestly, it's ridiculous – so much fuss over a picture! It's not even as if it's especially valuable.'

'No one's asking you to pay for it.' Eleanor picked up her handbag and started fingering through the contents as if she were looking for something in particular. 'It's fine.'

'But I *did* offer to pay for the stupid thing.' He stood up then and marched over to the window to glare out into the garden.

'I know you did. My dad doesn't mind about the money. Really.'

Roger snorted. 'Exactly – that's so bloody typical of Conrad. He's insisted on paying for it just so he can relish the pleasure of resenting me.'

'I'm sure he doesn't resent you at all.' Eleanor's voice took on the soothing tone she had used to comfort her children when they were small.

'It was his own stupid fault in any case. He's impossibly stubborn. I *had* it safe. If he'd just let me carry it instead of trying to grab it—'

'I'm sure he accepts it was an accident.' Eleanor re-zipped her bag. 'And, as you say, it's ages ago... Well...'

'I really ought to put in some time in the garden.' Roger half-turned to look at her like a cartoon bloodhound, his face comically freighted with woe. 'You can hardly see the lawn for all the fallen leaves.'

Eleanor knew he was wondering just how wet it was out there. If the leaves were sodden, there would be no point using his all-time favourite toy, a leaf blower, which he had come back with a few weeks ago after visiting the garden centre unaccompanied. Lately, Eleanor often caught her husband looking up at the mature trees at the far end of their garden as if mentally willing the leaves to fall so that he would have a reason to get out the leaf blower. When he used it, Eleanor retreated to her small studio right at the top of the house, the only place where the noise could barely be heard.

'It's all right, you don't have to come, too.' She tapped him lightly on the shoulder. 'I hereby release you from the onerous and perilous under-taking of visiting my father.'

'It's just the leaves, you see.' He faced back to the garden again. 'You know I don't *mind* having to visit him sometimes.'

'No, I know. You're very noble to put up with me and my irascible parent.'

2

CONRAD

1945

At last, the huge coils of barbed wire have been partly rolled back, allowing access to the longed-for beach, a scant quarter-mile from the big house up on the hill where he lives. There, down at the water's edge, the boy plays alone. No, not quite alone as his playmates are two dogs, who are watching him intently. The boy, though perhaps only seven or eight years old, is clearly born to command. In his hand, he clutches a short stick. The dogs wait, poised, ready to run. The larger dog, black and white, has a shaggy coat, tail flicking with excitement. The other – smaller, smooth-haired, the colour of sand – has one ear half-cocked.

Sometimes his mother comes too, with his little sister, to stand looking out at the waves. Or Cook walks down with him and sits on a bench, puffing, exhausted from the exertion, as he tears up and down the promenade with the dogs. Occasionally, as today, he is allowed to take them on his own as it's only a few minutes away, down the hill and cross one road, easy-peasy.

Then he draws his arm back and flicks it forward fast: the stick shoots out along the beach. Both dogs yelp and they're off – racing down the shoreline. The bigger, longer-legged dog gets there first, but not by much. Triumphant, he lollops back to his master, tilts his head up in offering, with pride.

The boy takes the stick, then reaches down and pats the dog generously. The boy hunkers down now on his haunches, extending a hand to the smaller dog, turns his hand over, palm up, beckoning. He holds out the stick and the dog lifts its head a little. Now the boy stands up but leans in to hold the black-and-white's collar. He nods at the small dog, then hurls the stick. The dog pauses a moment then hurtles off, practically flying along the beach. The black-and-white barks in protest, tugs against the boy's restraining grasp... but the boy stays firm. Back comes the victor, trit-trotting the last few steps with head held high. The boy showers him with pats, then suddenly plonks himself down on the sand and draws both dogs close, stroking and hugging and laughing.

Back at home, he rubs the dogs down with an old towel outside the back door, and comes tumbling into the kitchen, ready to beg Cook for homemade cake and lemon barley water, he can't possibly wait hours and hours till lunchtime because he is starving, literally starving, has never, ever been so starving in his whole, entire life.

'Cook, Cook, can I have... I mean please, please *may* I have, dear, lovely Cookie—'

'Conrad. Not now.' Her voice is serious, the way it is when she wants him out from under her feet, only not cross, just... strange. Her face is pale as the flour sprinkled on the table, ready for pastry-making.

'But can I just—'

'Oh, my dear, dear child...' Cookie puts her arms around him and crushes him against her enormous bosom. As ever, she smells of good things, of gravy and pastry and syrup. The cloth of her apron rasps against his cheek and, after a minute, he tries to pull away, but still she clamps him there and so he submits, sinking into this vast pillow of a woman. Eventually, she releases him and he looks up at her. She takes a tea-cloth from the table and rubs at her face. 'Och, silly old Cookie. And the lunch not even on yet.'

'They said on the wireless that the War's nearly over, Cookie – did you hear?'

She nods and sniffs.

'That means Daddy can come back now. He can put on a suit and go and be important in an office again. Like before.' Conrad doesn't remember those days, of course, but he has made his mother tell him about them often enough. He thinks about Daddy a lot, a lot, a lot, and prays for him at bedtime every night. Last time he came home on leave, he brought Conrad a harmonica and Mummy was all smiley again and singing as she went about the house and Daddy promised he'd be home soon for good.

Cook says nothing, but shakes her head and gathers him to her again, then covers the top of his head with floury kisses.

'My poor, poor boy,' she says. 'It's not fair, it's just not fair...'

'What's not fair?' Conrad looks up at her dear, wrinkly face, and stretches up to kiss her powdery cheek. 'Mummy says I shouldn't complain when things aren't fair, that you just have to knuckle down and get on with it.'

She takes a big sniff and holds him out at arm's length now, her eyes all watery like when she's chopping onions.

'Now, Conrad, you're going to have to be a very brave young man,' she says. 'Something very, very bad has happened.'

* * *

Mummy says now that he is growing up and becoming a fine young man, he must go away to proper school, one of the best in the whole country, she says.

'But who will look after you and Flora?' he asks. 'If I'm not here?'

Mummy does that smile she does now: not a proper smile like she used to, the sort of smile you do when you fall over and scrape your knee and you're trying to be brave and not cry.

'Cookie,' she says. 'I'm sure Cook will take very good care of us. So you mustn't worry.'

Conrad shifts from one foot to the other and stuffs his hands in his pockets to fiddle with the length of string he has there, and the mouth organ Daddy gave him the last time he was home on leave. *Before.* He runs his finger over the smooth metal of it, dabs into the little square windows along its side.

'Why doesn't Flora have to go away to school?' He doesn't say, *It's not fair*, but he is thinking the words so hard that he is sure they must be charging across the gap from his own head to his mother's and knocking bang-bang-bang so she must definitely hear them.

Mummy explains very slowly, as if he is just a small boy, that Flora is still only little, and a good education is not so important for girls as it is for boys because when she is older she will find a nice husband and will not have to go out and make her own way in the world as he will. And anyway, he will have a wonderful time because the school has lots and lots of space and squillions of other boys just like him and, best of all, a really big library so he'll have as many books to read as he likes and won't have to mope about the house saying he's run out of things to read. Mummy will write to him every single week and Cookie has promised to send him some fudge. If she can get enough sugar.

Conrad will not cry because he is a big boy now. He bites the inside of his lip on the right-hand side and tries to think of something else. You can stop yourself crying that way.

He wants to ask his mother lots of questions, but now the words are all crowded and muddled in his head like the black ants crawling over each other that time he and Henry poked their sticks into that nest: *Won't you miss me? – I'll miss you! – Who will tuck me in? – Who will kiss me good night? – What if I have a bad dream? – Can I take Squire Teddy? – What if I don't like it? – Can I come back? – Will you visit me? – What if it's really and truly horrid, horrid, horrid? – What if no one wants to play with me? – Please, Mummy, don't make me go – please, Mummy, please...*

There are too many words, all at once, trying to clamber and struggle up to the surface. He bites his lip again and pushes them back down.

His mother puts her hands on his shoulders and does the not-proper smile again.

'Look at you,' she says. 'Growing up so fast.' Her eyes are all shiny, like his glass marbles with the blue bits in. She leans forward and kisses the top of his head. 'You really are starting to look so like—' She makes a funny little noise then, as if she is choking on a piece of crusty bread, and she stands up suddenly, clasps him close for a moment, then tells him to run along.

* * *

Conrad is in the dining room, listening at the serving-hatch that goes through to the kitchen. There is a narrow gap where the two little doors don't quite meet, and if you stand right there, you can listen and even peep through but you must be super-duper silent, like a spy. His mother is in the kitchen, talking to Cookie, but her voice is too quiet to decipher. *Decipher* is his new word this week and he is using it at every opportunity.

Then Cookie says, 'I don't think it's right. He needs his mother. Even more now.'

'I can't—' His mother's voice, suddenly loud. 'Don't. He's just the spit of him, Martha – don't you see? It's just... I can't... it's too hard...'

Through the gap, Conrad sees Cookie fold his mother in her huge floury arms and tuck her in close to her the way she does with the big mixing bowl when she is stirring the ingredients for a pudding or a cake.

'I know, my duck, I know. Have a good cry now.'

He does not understand what his mother said but he will go upstairs later and look in the big dictionary, the one in Father's study. It doesn't make sense – you're not supposed to spit, everyone knows that. He would ask Mummy or Cookie, but then they would know he was listening at the hatch and he'd be told off for eavesdropping. Cookie would say, 'Them as listens at keyholes never hears no good of themselves.' But all spies have to eavesdrop otherwise they'd never find out anything and they'd be pretty hopeless as spies, wouldn't they? Honestly, grown-ups could be awfully daft sometimes.

3

THE WOMAN IN THE WINDOW SEAT

It was a little after 11a.m. when Eleanor arrived at her father's flat, in an imposing mansion block in Bloomsbury near the British Museum. The door opened wide to admit her, as usual, as if her father were expecting a procession of visitors rather than only his daughter.

'Ah – Eleanor.' Conrad nodded, unsmiling, and stood back. He had never been in the habit of saying hello.

'Daddy.'

Her father's brows lifted at the rarely used, affectionate 'Daddy', but he said nothing, merely bending to proffer his cheek for her to kiss.

'Happy birthday for Thursday. I hope you received my card? And I have a gift for you.'

'Thank you. Yes, lovely card. So, how are you?' Eleanor hung up her coat.

Conrad waved away the enquiry with a dismissive hand. Even now, at seventy-four, he was an imposing, handsome man. He stood six foot two in his socks – not that Conrad would ever pad about just in his socks (or, worse, slippers) while receiving a visitor – good God, whatever next? His posture was that of a considerably younger man, though on occasion Eleanor had spotted him wince when he rose from his chair. His eyes were still fiercely blue, bright and beady, assessing.

'Come through to the study. Andrew's just on his way out. He brought back my painting. Very decent of him to deliver it.'

The flat was more than large enough for a person living alone, although the principal bedroom had been made into Conrad's study, while he slept in the much more modest second bedroom. The study was a gracious, handsome room, with a high ceiling, the original fireplace, and tall sash windows framed by faded green velvet curtains transferred from the old family house when he'd moved over a year ago. The walls were lined with bookshelves, even in the space above the door. The only gaps were for the windows and above the fireplace, opposite Conrad's desk, an empty space, waiting. A man stood awkwardly by the fireplace, with his hands in his pockets.

'Andrew. Have you met my daughter, Eleanor?'

'Yes, at the Museum once, I think.' He came forward to shake her hand. 'How do you do?' His voice was quiet, unassuming.

'Yes, of course. How are you?' He had a rather forgettable face, so Eleanor was not actually sure if she had met him before or not. There was something vague about his features, as if he had been sketched with a very soft pencil.

The painting was still on the floor, leaning against the bookshelves.

'But this is incredible.' Eleanor crouched down to see the restored area. 'I can't see any damage at all.'

'It wasn't too bad, not really – just that abraded area from the broken glass and a couple of blood spots.' Andrew smiled. 'It was only tricky because the medium is egg tempera and not all conservators have worked with it, that's all. I think it's having a decent frame that's made the biggest difference really.'

'Don't be so modest. Oh, and there's no glass now! That's why it's so different. Is that OK? You can certainly see the painting much more clearly.'

'Honestly, with tempera, there's really no need for it to be glazed. It's not in a public gallery where there might be a risk of damage. And the reflections are always annoying so it's better without, I think.'

'Me, too.' She peered at it closely. 'It's wonderful without, nothing between the viewer and the woman at all now. It feels quite different... more intimate. Don't you think, Dad?' She turned towards him.

Conrad nodded but said nothing.

'Shall we hang it, then?' Eleanor and Andrew lifted the painting together. 'Dad, tell us when it's straight, will you?'

In the family, this picture was always known, as far as Eleanor could remember, as *The Woman in the Window Seat*. The subject, her face half in light, half in shadow, seemed to be turning towards you, as if you had just entered the room. One had the odd sense of being not quite sure that she was pleased to see you, and the effect was strangely disconcerting.

It was painted using the very old medium of egg tempera on board, where the powdered pigment is mixed with an emulsion based on egg yolk, and the paint had been applied in very thin layers over a white gesso ground, giving it a radiant, translucent quality. The colours were predominantly greens and blues, against which only the moon-pale oval of the woman's face and the bright flame of her hair stood out. Her green eyes glinted jewel-like, with points of light reflecting some unseen lamp. Her red hair hung forward over her shoulder in a plait, a brilliant snake charmed into submission. The woman sat with her knees tucked up in front of her, her arms looped round them as if hugging some strange secret to herself. She gazed out at you, seeming like a magical marine creature, watching you from beneath the cool, glimmering depths of the sea. Sometimes her gaze seemed knowing, sometimes sad, but now, today, to Eleanor it looked something akin to pity.

It was undoubtedly a wonderful painting, not just technically accomplished – though that brought pleasure enough on its own – but atmospheric, haunting. Eleanor had always loved it, the way it seemed as if the woman were looking at *you* in particular, as if she wanted to understand you. After so many years of seeing it, both here and in her father's much grander study in their familial home, Eleanor found she could barely think of her father without imagining the painting at the same time. Conrad had always said that he had happened to spot it in a gallery in to which he had darted to escape a sudden downpour. He had joked that, if he had only spent a few pounds on an umbrella instead, he'd have saved himself quite a bit of money.

Eleanor's mother, Marcia, had been rather less in love with the painting, saying it had been an utterly pointless extravagance, quite unjustifiable. As it was, with so many books, they had not enough wall space free of shelves to hang all the pictures they already owned: innumerable antique prints and maps, a handful of unarresting landscapes.

Andrew headed for the door.

'Well, I'd better be off now. See you at the BM.' He stood there for a few moments. 'OK. Conrad...? Bye, then.'

'Hmm?' Conrad was standing close to the picture, inspecting the restored area once more.

'I'm just going...' Andrew waved. 'I'll see myself out.'

'Oh. Hold fire.' Conrad pulled himself away and crossed to the desk. Took out a sealed envelope from the top drawer and handed it over. 'Thank you very much, Andrew.' He held out his hand to shake. 'You've done an excellent job, really first rate. I'm very glad I entrusted it to you. I knew I was right to wait until I found the best person for the job.'

'Well, thank you, too. It was entirely a pleasure. There's really no need...' He tapped the envelope Conrad had given him.

'No, no. I insist.'

'I'll show you out.' Eleanor came over. Her father returned to the painting.

'She's lovely, isn't she?' Andrew gazed back at the painting. 'I mean *it*, I suppose.'

Eleanor smiled. 'Yes, *she* really is.'

'I think I'll miss her, having had her all to myself for a while.' He laughed at himself. 'I guess that sounds daft?'

'Not at all. I've always loved that painting. There's something about her that draws you in. I almost feel as if I know her, or have met her in a dream. Now who sounds daft?' Eleanor watched as her father stood there, looking at the picture. 'I'm sure my father hated letting it out of his sight.'

In the kitchen, Eleanor filled the kettle and began to make tea: Darjeeling for her father, limeflower and lavender for herself; she kept a selection of herbal teas there for when she visited; her father would never have bought such a preposterous thing of his own accord. He referred to it as 'hippy tea'.

'Are you pleased to have her back then?' Eleanor said, teasingly.

Conrad gave a small nod, then looked out of the kitchen window.

'So, Hannah is trotting off in search of the other end of the rainbow this evening. What next?'

'What next for who?'

'*Whom*. For *you*, of course.'

'What do you mean?' Eleanor crossed to the fridge to fetch the milk for her father.

'I mean: have you given any thought to this next stage of your life?'

'Empty nest and all that?' She shrugged. 'You mean will I be bored because I'll have less laundry to do? Hardly. Anyway, they'll both be back soon enough.' Eleanor's son, Daniel, had just begun his second year at Bristol University. She laughed, her tone breezy, unconcerned. 'I still have work – such as it is – plus the choir, swimming, print-making. Friends.'

'And Roger.' Her father's expression was unreadable but she thought she noted the smallest twitch of his lips.

'Well, of course, Roger. But he's not in nappies, Dad; looking after a grown-up husband is hardly a full-time occupation.'

'No indeed.'

Eleanor ignored his tone and the implied jibe – *not usually.*

'Hannah will be OK.' Telling herself as much as him. 'Won't she?'

Conrad nodded, then said, 'Sensible girl, on the whole. Still, it's normal to worry. You're a mother.'

'Hmm.' Eleanor picked up both mugs, raised her eyebrows – a tacit question.

'Back to the study, I think.' Conrad stood back to let her go first. 'Marginally warmer.'

Eleanor set her father's mug down on a folded newspaper on his desk and took her own over to the green velvet chaise longue. Conrad eschewed any kind of coaster or drinks mat, regarding them as near-iconic symbols of bourgeois pretension.

'But *you* didn't worry about me much, did you? You and Mum, I mean.' Eleanor shucked off her shoes and curled her legs up to one side in her favourite position.

Conrad sat at his desk and swivelled his chair to face her. He looked down into his mug then shook his head slightly.

'Not about *you*, certainly. Never needed to. You seemed to know what you were about even when you were just a tot of four or five.'

Eleanor made a face. 'Hmm. I don't remember Mum fussing about my safety. Ever. That time I fell out of the willow tree into the pond, she was only upset because I trailed mud the entire length of the hall.'

'Well, perhaps she didn't need to fuss because you could usually be trusted to be sensible.'

'For which read dull.'

'Hardly. Still, it's an underrated virtue, perhaps.'

'I didn't choose to be the sensible one. Maybe I would have liked a day off every now and then to be wild?'

'Maybe.' He nodded. 'Though you're still young – perhaps your wild days are ahead of you?'

'I doubt it. Talking of *wild*, I'm sure I saw that bonkers woman in the street the other day, the anorexic blonde one who lived with him for a while. I wondered if I should ask her if she'd seen him, but she looked quite feral. Do you remember her?'

Conrad did not need to ask which 'him': Benedict. Always Benedict: her younger brother.

He shook his head, met her eyes for a moment, then looked away again. There was nothing to be gained by discussing Benedict. Neither of them had seen or heard from him for over five years; what more was there to say?

'Oh – present, *present*.' He started patting the various piles of paper on his enormous desk. 'Where did I – ah, here it is.' He held it out to her and she came to receive it. It was still in its paper bag. She didn't think her father had ever been known to wrap a present; of course, he hadn't needed to until five years ago, when Eleanor's mother had died. What on earth would be the point in wrapping something in silly patterned paper when it would only then be unwrapped and the paper discarded?

She started to open it, then spotted something peeping out from beneath a stack of papers.

'Oh, did I leave my sketchbook here?' She reached for it. It was dark red, hardback, spiral-bound, the same type she always used.

'*No*.' His hand pressed down on the pile. 'No. It's just an old notebook of mine. Very old. I was looking for some notes on something.'

Eleanor withdrew her hand and opened the bag her father had given her. It was an early hardback edition of Daphne du Maurier's *Rebecca*, bearing the legend: 'Price unchanged in spite of war'. Perfect.

'Thank you very much.' Eleanor bent to kiss him, still seated in his chair. 'You know I will treasure it.' She looked at her watch. 'Don't let me stay too long... Roger...'

'And you can tell him the painting is perfect now.' Conrad gave a small smile as he silently removed the spiral-bound book from the pile in front of him and slid it into a desk drawer. 'I mean, just in case he's been fretting about it.'

'Now, now, Father-dear, play nicely. In fact, Roger was very concerned, and he offered to pay for the restoration and reframing, as you know.'

'I don't need his money.'

'But you're not cross with him any more? You promise?'

'Cross? Why should I be cross? I'm sure he can't help being a clumsy oaf—'

'Dad! Come on now – that's hardly fair.'

'Ah, dear Eleanor, always so desperate to keep the peace. I promise to behave myself. Really.' He looked at her and arched one eyebrow. 'It'll be fine.'

They both smiled at his echoing of her most familiar phrase. She couldn't remember exactly when she had first started saying it, almost as punctuation, but it must have been more than thirty years ago. Benedict had been the first to point it out, joking that it would make a perfect epitaph for her gravestone: 'Eleanor Marriott', her dates and 'It'll be fine'. How bad would things have to be, after all, for Eleanor to admit that they were not fine?

Conrad leaned right back in his chair, stretching his long legs out straight in front of him.

'And how is the dear old BM?' Eleanor asked, moving on to safer territory. She copied her father's habit of referring to the British Museum this way, as if it were a much-loved friend of long acquaintance. Conrad had been Keeper of Prints and Drawings, in charge of the collection there for many years, but had retired nearly ten years ago.

'Wonderful and infuriating in equal measure. As ever.' He had been working on his third book – an academic tome on early copper engravings – for nearly four years, so still went into his old department at least a couple of times a week for research purposes, but also, Eleanor suspected, because he couldn't bear to leave it. 'And *your* work?'

Eleanor wrinkled her nose. She did voluntary work two days a week at a local conservation organisation, but she knew her father was asking about her print-making: Eleanor sometimes made small wood engravings of rural scenes based on sketches she drew on country walks or while on holiday – trees, hills, tiny cottages, grazing sheep – but it was hard to find the time to fit it in.

'I haven't done any for ages.'

'And why's that, do you think?'

'Because I've been *busy*.'

Her father looked at her but said nothing.

'What? I know you think that's a feeble excuse.'

'Not at all. I have no doubt that you are extremely *busy*. The question one might ask oneself is, *is* one being *busy* doing things one really wants to do? And if not, might one do better to make some alterations to one's schedule? Perhaps lose any inessential distractions?'

'Don't go all impersonal pronoun on me, Dad, I can't bear it. You mean *one* should just shove aside all *one's* other commitments, tell *one's* husband to iron his own fucking shirts, and barricade *oneself* in to *one's* studio?'

Conrad raised his eyebrows a fraction, but whether at her rare employment of a swear word or the idea of her asserting herself in such a way, it was hard to tell.

She sipped her tea.

'Roger's talking about taking early retirement.'

'Is he now? He's, what, only fifty-five, fifty-six? Why the rush?' Conrad had retired at sixty-five, and then only extremely reluctantly. Even now, he was still asked to give occasional talks on his particular area of expertise, plus he sat on the boards of two important charities and was working on his book.

'Fifty-eight. His work can be very stressful, as you know.' Her husband was a senior partner in a law firm, and he specialised in property development law. 'He needs a rest. He wants us to go on a long cruise.'

'How perfectly hideous. Rather you than me.'

Eleanor made a face. 'Some people would love it.'

'So?'

She shrugged and said nothing.

'Eleanor. *So?*'

A tiny shake of the head.

'Time, if I may say, to water your own garden. For your own benefit and pleasure. For *you*.'

'But Roger wants—'

'For you alone.'

'You're not instructing me to be *selfish*, surely?'

Her father, who throughout her entire childhood and teenage years, had usually backed up her mother, Marcia, every time she reprimanded Eleanor for wanting her own way or being disobedient or showing off. While her younger brother, who lost his books, flunked his exams, got fired with increasing regularity, who couldn't say no to drink, to drugs, to whatever, whoever was up for a laugh, a jaunt, a tumble, got away with everything – the golden boy who could do no wrong.

'A little, yes. Why ever not?'

As if on cue, her mobile rang: 'ROGER'. Summoned, she rose to her feet.

4

ANDREW

When he returned home from Conrad's flat, Andrew found a wall of boxes and bulging black bin bags like a barricade across the end of the drive. Vicki appeared as he got out of the car and, at the same moment as he was thinking: Ahh, she's come out to meet me, that's sweet, she folded her arms and said, 'It's time to move on, Andrew.'

For a few moments, he imagined she was suggesting that they move house, perhaps buy a place together at last. Clearly, she had been making a start by packing things into boxes. But then he realised that what she actually meant was, 'It's time for you to move out.'

He stood there, hands in pockets and droopy-mouthed, like a child who knows he's done something wrong but hasn't a clue what it might be, while she set out the situation – there was no one else, it was just that she couldn't envision a future for them long term, going forward, as a couple, together. Andrew disliked any kind of change; he didn't even like it when someone else took 'his' mug at work. So he found himself saying things that didn't sound like him just so all could carry on as before.

'Is it that you want to get married, is that it? Let's get married!'

Vicki compressed her thin lips so that they disappeared into a line.

'Please don't do this – we're good together, aren't we?' He reached for her hand but she withdrew it after a second as if he had slipped a clammy, dead fish into her palm. 'But where am I supposed to go?' A

whining note had crept into his voice, which even he realised was
unlikely to make him seem irresistible.

'Not really my problemo, Andrew, is it?' The lips disappeared from
view once more. 'Call a friend. Go round your mum and dad's. You're a
big boy now – work it out.'

That stung. It wasn't the first time he had heard it from a girlfriend –
soon-to-be-ex-girlfriend. At first, perhaps it was that touch of the little
boy lost that was part of Andrew's appeal, but after a while a woman
always started wanting him to 'man up' or 'grow a pair', when he
couldn't get the waiter's attention, or was last to be served at the bar, or
let another man nick the parking space he had been waiting patiently
for.

So, he bit the inside of his lip, yanked open his car boot, and began
jamming in the boxes and bags any old how, just to annoy her. Even
watching him hurl boxes in – on their sides, at an angle, jabbing his foot
down on one to make it fit – must be killing her. She gave a small sniff,
told him he could stack – neatly! – any boxes that he couldn't manage
now in the garage and collect them at a later date.

'Where will you go, then?'

'Not really your *problemo*, is it?' Andrew twirled his car key in what
he hoped was a devil-may-care manner, and attempted to curl his lip in a
sneer. God, she could be a pretentious twat, he thought, getting into his
car and slamming the door. He clung to this thought as he drove round
north London, trying to decide where the hell to go. Not Mike's (really
not in the mood for three screaming children this minute); not Gabriel's,
as he was away; not Dave's, as he had a brand-new girlfriend so was still
in the must-shag-every-spare-second mode and would not appreciate
having Andrew appear on his doorstep. He mentally listed all the things
that annoyed him about Vicki. He had reached Number 14: *Sighing when
I sit on the couch in an 'untidy' way*, when he realised he was already
round the corner from his parents' house. They would welcome him – of
course they would – but still... Andrew speeded up and instead drove
back north again to his favourite café, the one he usually went to when
Vicki wanted him out from under her feet. He could spend ages reading
the papers there; she didn't like newspapers in the house because they
made such a mess. It made her beautiful home look like a rubbish tip.
And you could always watch the news on the telly if you wanted to but it

was the same things mostly, wasn't it, bearded men being angry in the Middle East, children in Africa with flies on them, and fussing about money and the banks in Europe, and there was nothing you could do in any case, so why make yourself miserable over it?

After spinning out three mugs of tea, toast, and an omelette and chips for nearly two hours, and checking his mobile every other minute for a text from Vicki begging him to come back, Andrew drove to the station and took the tube into town. He'd felt so good earlier, when he'd taken that painting back to Conrad's. Looking at something that had been spoiled and knowing that you had made it perfect again was the best feeling in the world. Even Conrad had pronounced the restoration 'excellent', and he almost never said anything nice about anyone or anything. They all respected him, absolutely, but they made jokes, too, pretending that old Marriott slept in the Museum and was part of the European Antiquities collection. Must be sad to be like that, no life really apart from the dear old BM, wife dead, nothing to do or think about other than his prints and his next book he'd been working on for God knows how many years now.

As he walked along Great Russell Street, Andrew could see the vast grey bulk of the British Museum behind its high black railings, its size and solidity immediately reassuring. This was his true home. So what if Vicki had chucked him out? This was where he really belonged. He made his way to the key pound. Officially, people couldn't just show up at the weekend and get into the Conservation Department. After all, his section was housed within Prints and Drawings and the collection was priceless. If you were there on a Saturday unattended, theoretically you could roll up a Raphael and shove it down your trousers and be off with it in a heartbeat. But he was Andrew, good old, harmless Andrew. He knew most of the guys at the key pound where he went each morning to collect his keys for the department. It would be OK.

It was one of the guards he barely knew, the very chubby one with cheeks so shiny they looked as if they'd been buffed with a fine cloth. He was playing a game on his phone and had a half-eaten doughnut next to him. Robert? Rob.

'Hey, Rob. Good morning, good morning! Sorry – good afternoon, I should say! How's tricks?' Andrew could hear himself adopting an atypically matey tone; could hear the falseness of it, as if he were pretending to be a different kind of person. 'Hello,' he added lamely, looking down, suddenly embarrassed by himself.

'Andy, is it?' Rob nodded.

Andrew fought the urge to correct him.

'Yup. Thing is...' Andrew laughed lightly, showing how relaxed he was, 'I've only gone and left something up in Conservation and I'm kicking myself about it. I wonder if I could just pop up briefly to retrieve it?'

'Sorry, mate, no can do. You know the rules.' The guard looked back down at his phone as if the conversation were now ended.

'Yes, yes, absolutely – I totally know the rules and all that – very much – but, see, what it is... is... see, I've left my wallet in the department and it's got all my cards and everything, and what I was thinking was... I could just nip in and grab it – in and out.' He shifted from foot to foot. 'It wouldn't take a minute.' His wallet was sitting snugly in his back pocket as usual; he could feel the thickness of it digging into his left buttock like a reproach.

Rob glanced up from his phone, apparently surprised that Andrew was still there.

What was the point in all this, he wondered. He didn't want to nip in and out anyway, did he? What did he want? He wanted to sit in his department for a bit, that was all. Maybe do some work, nothing too demanding. There was that lovely Ardizzone pencil drawing with a bad tear on one side that he was about to mend, the kind of thing he could do in his sleep. He'd be working on it on Monday morning anyway, so why now? There was no rush for it. He wanted – he fumbled with the coins in his front pocket as a comforting distraction – he wanted to just *be*, be in the quietness, that particularly calm space that was like nowhere else, with the vast windows and the massive press in the corner, a fixed presence, solid as an oak tree.

'It's my wallet, you see.' He thought of taking it out of his back pocket to show Rob just how many things were in it that he really couldn't manage without: his credit and debit cards, some cash, his loyalty card at the local car-wash – one more wash and he'd be entitled to a free one – postage stamps. Vital stuff. He started reaching towards his pocket then stopped himself.

'I'm not exactly your average master criminal!' Andrew's tone sounded more and more artificial to his own ears. And what was an average master criminal anyway? Surely a master criminal was, by definition, not an average one at all? Shut up. Just say never mind and leave.

'Nothing personal. Sorry, mate.' Rob shrugged. 'If you're really desperate, you'd have to get written authorisation from your Section Head. Can't you borrow a tenner off a mate or something?'

Andrew smiled and took a step back.

'I've got a few quid, I'll get by. Sorry.' He patted his trouser pocket and his coins jingled. 'Sorry about that. See you. Cheers.' He nodded goodbye and backed out, so that Rob wouldn't see the wallet-shaped bulge in his back pocket.

Now that he was here, well, perhaps he'd go and see some of the collections he never had time to see normally. He passed through the main entrance with a throng of others. The Great Court was abuzz with people; they really were just like bees, jostling appetitively around the shops, the café, the information desk: Japanese teenagers, organised groups clustering around a guide, elderly out-of-town couples perching awkwardly on the low, hard stools to unpack their cheese and chutney sandwiches brought from home.

He walked up to the huge map of the Museum to study it. Of course, he knew parts of it very well indeed: the Prints and Drawings exhibition space just outside his department – Rooms 90 and 91 – the Japanese Galleries, as they were so close, Ancient Greece and Rome as they were his favourites, and the route from Conservation all the way over to the other side of the museum to the staff canteen where they collectively headed for coffee most mornings, but he'd barely visited the rest of it, not since he was at school. His parents were never keen on museums. There was an astonishing amount to see. His eye fell on Ancient Egypt. He'd popped in briefly once the first week he worked here, but it was a weekday and packed with groups of schoolkids, pressing their noses to the glass and shouting, 'That's your *mummy*, that is!' Papyri in need of conservation work came into his department; they had a specialist who did nothing else. He wouldn't mind taking a look now.

He made his way there, taking the stairs two at a time, suddenly eager to be at the heart of the museum, to be surrounded by things that had lasted for thousands of years. The first room was very busy but just about bearable. He stood looking in at an exquisite sarcophagus, its interior covered with hieroglyphs. Someone had dipped a brush in pigment and painted those pictographs, knowing what they meant, forming each line with exquisite care, brow furrowed in concentration – someone patient, dedicated – someone possibly not unlike himself. It was extraordinary. An image of Vicki standing on the drive in her clackety pink sandals suddenly came into his head. He swallowed and forced himself to concentrate on the information caption instead. It didn't matter. In four thousand years, no schoolkid would want to come and find out about Andrew's crappy relationships or Vicki's garish footwear. It was the collections that mattered: the vast, extraordinary array of treasures here in the Museum, some of which were entrusted to your care. And even though you were nothing – you would be dead and turned to dust soon enough – some of these astonishing objects and artefacts had passed through *your* hands and *you* had helped safeguard their existence. You were like a *shabti* really, a servant ensuring that they would be preserved forever.

Afterwards, Andrew went to a pub and sat in a corner sipping a pint and reading his book for a while. At a little after 7 p.m., he straightened up and accepted the inevitable. He decided not to call first: that would make too much of it. Better to swing by casually, say he and Vicki had had a bit of a row and could he stay for a day or two? No big deal. He imagined giving a little laugh, showing his parents how unbothered he was by it. The timing would be perfect. By the time he got the tube back, then drove to their house, he should get there at about 8.30 p.m., late enough for them to have finished their evening meal, but not so late that his mother would have conniptions at the sound of the doorbell.

5

DEPARTURE

Eleanor did not cry at the airport; she found public displays of emotion a little suspect, as if they had been put on and played up for an unknown audience. Besides, it would only distress Hannah, and would benefit no one. If children really understood just how much their parents worried about them, they would probably be freaked out. She silently reminded herself for possibly the thousandth time that Hannah was mostly very sensible, that she would be with her two friends for the entire trip, and that all three girls had been repeatedly briefed on how to stay safe. At that moment, Hannah's friends appeared with their parents and backpacks, and the three girls fell into an ecstasy of shrieking and hugging.

'Here's a little extra something for the journey.' Eleanor handed over a bag of homemade lemon shortbread, her daughter's favourite, tied with twirly gold ribbon.

'Oh, yummy – thanks, Mum.'

'And this is for once you get there...' It was a spiral-bound sketchbook, the same type she used herself. 'I know you haven't had time to draw so much recently, but...'

'I know, I know – *always* keep a sketchbook with you. *Always.*' They laughed together at the rare piece of advice Eleanor had offered. 'Thank you.' Hannah hugged her mum. 'It's really nice to have a proper one. I promise to use it.'

Finally, kisses and cautions were dispensed all round and the girls were waved off outside the Departures gate.

Still Eleanor did not cry, even when, at the last moment, Hannah suddenly turned and ran back and threw her arms around her mother in a final hug – 'Oh, Mummy, I'll miss you lots and lots!' – sounding like a little girl again.

Eleanor had squeezed her daughter tight, unable to speak.

'Don't cry, Mum.'

'But I'm *not*, silly. I'm fine.'

'Just because I can't see any tears doesn't mean you're not crying, Mum. I'm not two.'

Eleanor clamped her lips shut and just gathered her daughter close for a few precious moments more.

'Have fun, sweet pea. Plenty of texts and emails, yes? Otherwise, I will follow you out there and say I've come to bring you your little snuggly bunnikins as I know you can't sleep without him.'

'Funny. I'll email and text and send you lots of pics, OK? And we can FaceTime or Skype or whatever. Have a fab dinner out tonight.'

'Thank you.'

'And promise not to worry. Repeat the family mantra – one, two, three...'

'It'll be fine,' they said together.

Once Hannah had gone, Eleanor suddenly felt starving. She bought a takeaway tea and a croissant from a café on the concourse and slowly went back to the car park.

She sat in the car, taking small sips of her tea and tearing off pieces of croissant. Glanced at her watch. There was really no need to rush home this instant. Conceivably, she could well be at the airport for at least another half an hour as they'd allowed so much time, and she'd still be back in time to change for dinner. Roger would not approve of her having a croissant so close to eating out at such an expensive restaurant; it was silly of her really, she could see that. She should just have waited. Tore off another flaky fragment and pushed it into her mouth.

She let her mind drift, pleased she had thought of the sketchbook. Hannah used to draw all the time when she was younger, on any scrap of paper she came across, but there was something special about having a really good-quality sketchbook. Eleanor remembered when she'd been given her first proper grown-up one – by a total stranger, too. It was such a nice memory that she'd carried on using the same kind ever since: the same type she'd given Hannah, the same type she had even now in her handbag. She wasn't much younger then than Hannah was now...

* * *

Feeling suddenly overwhelmed by the pressure of her looming A levels, after school, Eleanor goes into Central London on her own. She wanders around the shops for a bit but doesn't have enough money to buy anything anyway. Looking up at the ugly monolith of Centrepoint at Tottenham Court Road, she decides to go to the British Museum as it is so near. She could go and visit her father for a few minutes, if he is free; he always knows just what to say when she is getting herself het up about homework or revision. He will put it all into perspective.

But when she gets there, he isn't in his department. A colleague in Prints and Drawings explains he has had to leave for a meeting elsewhere.

Feeling flat, Eleanor goes to sit in one of the Ancient Greece galleries. There is a beautiful statue there she has always loved: a woman reaching for something unseen, yearning.

Eleanor gets out a pencil and a lined A4 pad from her schoolbag. Drawing always makes her feel better. She begins to sketch the statue, losing herself almost at once in the act of intense concentration, looking, really *seeing*.

A flicker of movement catches Eleanor's eye. She stops and turns: another woman, drawing standing up a little further away. She is wearing very baggy dungarees smeared with what looks like brown paint, or perhaps clay, and a bright blue and yellow headscarf tied Caribbean-style covering her hair.

'That's very good,' the woman says, stepping nearer. 'Are you at art school?'

'No, I'm still at school. I'm sitting my A levels in a couple of months. I should be at home, revising really.'

'Well, I can't imagine you'd have any problem getting into a decent art school if you draw like that.'

'I've applied to university to read English. I don't think my parents would be happy for me to go to art school.'

'Oh, *parents*! What do they know?' The woman laughs. 'Still, I'm sure you'll enjoy that too. Here, would you like some better paper?' She tears out a couple of sheets from her sketchbook. 'It's awfully annoying drawing on lined paper, I always think.'

They sit in silence for a while then, side by side on the bench, just drawing. Then Eleanor stands up and says she'd better be heading home and thank you for the paper.

'I come here quite often to draw,' the woman says. 'Sometimes I draw exhibits, but also the people looking at them. It's a good place as people often stand still for ages.'

'My dad works here so I sometimes come just to see him. He works really hard so he's not at home much.'

'Oh, *men*! Honestly. That's a shame.'

'Mmm. It's really not the same at home when he's not there.'

'What does he do here – your dad? Which department?'

'Prints and Drawings. He's the Assistant Keeper.'

'Oh. Is he? How – how *grand*. Well, that's – that must be very interesting, I'm sure.'

'Yes, he's hoping to be made Keeper soon, when the current one retires. I'm sure he will be. He's very clever.'

'He – I'm sure he will. Well, I must be off. Nice to meet you.'

'Can I just ask, what make is your sketchbook? The paper is lovely.'

The woman shows her the cover, then looks down for a few moments, appraising her sketches.

'Hang on a tick.' The woman tears out the two pages she'd just covered herself with quick-fire sketches and hands the blank sketchbook to Eleanor. 'Take it.'

'Oh, no, I couldn't.'

'Yes, you could. Every artist needs a decent sketchbook.'

'But I'm not an artist!'

'Every *artist* needs a decent sketchbook,' she repeats. 'And you should always keep a sketchbook with you. *Always*.'

* * *

Funny how a stranger could do something or say something that left its mark on you. Like always using the same type of sketchbook, as if it were a lucky talisman because it had been given to her by some random woman who told her she was an *artist* probably just to be kind. Silly really.

Eleanor drained the last of her tea, then leaned her head back against the headrest and closed her eyes. What would it be like to stay here, in her car, in the car park all night? There was an old blanket in the boot, a bottle of water in the cup-holder, and a tin of travel sweets in the glove box, her sole vice. She could probably manage at least a couple of days... more if she popped back to the terminal for food. Then she could last a week... a month... the rest of her life... Maybe she could just live there, eating and sleeping in her car, and no one would ever find her? But no, she was already uncomfortable and Eleanor was highly pragmatic. She shook the thought away – how silly; what a peculiar thing to think of. Funny to think of Hannah's not being at home. Or Daniel. Just the two of them now. Well, people made such a fuss about empty-nest syndrome but it was fine really. As she'd told her father, it wasn't as if she'd be drifting about the house off her head with boredom. There was always plenty to do, always plenty of things to occupy her time and her head.

She turned the key in the ignition, and put on the radio. It was time to go home.

6

THE DEVIL TREE

Mr and Mrs Tyler's house was a 1930s mock-Tudor semi, with a pebble-dashed exterior painted white, and fake timber framing. As he walked up the front path, Andrew averted his eyes from the recently installed uPVC windows as if from a particularly unpleasant scene in a horror film.

The bell rang *ding-dong*, insistently chirpy regardless of your mood. After a few moments, the distant hum of the hoover stopped and he heard his mother's voice bellowing down to his father.

'Ron! *Ron!* Can you not hear the bell? I'm doing the *hoovering*! Do I look like I can be running up and down the stairs every two minutes?'

His father's footsteps, shuffling and apologetic. Thank God.

'Hey, Dad.'

'Son.' His father looked down at the holdall in Andrew's hand. 'You'd best come in, then.'

'Who is it?' His mother from on high. 'We don't buy from people at the door.'

'It's Andrew.' His father's voice was at its usual volume, barely audible, but his mother's hearing was the stuff of legend.

From the hallway, Andrew could see his mum's legs on the landing above, clad in her 'hoovering trousers' – navy-blue velour tracksuit bottoms, hems flapping above her pale pink quilted slippers.

'I'm nearly done with Colin's room!' Notify the press, thought

Andrew. Let's all light a candle and sing Allelujah. Colin's room had barely changed in nearly twenty years. There was a shrine-like feel to it, as if his older brother had died and due reverence must be shown, even though he was alive and well, and living in Canada. Pictures of Colin, his family, his whacking great house on the outskirts of Calgary, even his gas-guzzling 4x4, were displayed in annoying matching modern frames on the mantelpiece. There were only two of Andrew: one on his first day at grammar school in his new grey blazer, the other in his graduation gown at the end of university.

'No need to rush, Mum!' Andrew called up the stairs.

'Shoes!' came the command from above. Andrew imagined she would demand that single word as her epitaph.

Andrew duly filed his footwear in the under-stairs cupboard. God forbid his shoes should be left out on display for anyone to see and perhaps realise that the occupants of the house were in possession of feet and wore shoes on them. He paused to bestow his customary glare at the keyboard on the back of the cupboard door, which proclaimed 'Keys' in Tudor-style lettering, as if otherwise you might not be able to fathom just what those metallic objects hanging from the hooks were. It was the kind of thing that set Andrew's teeth on edge. He wanted to shout at it, 'Yes, I can see they're fucking keys, thank you!' And if people wanted to hang something else on the hooks – kitchen utensils, cups, Christmas baubles – well, why the hell shouldn't they?

He instinctively drew himself in as he walked down the hallway to the kitchen at the back. There was something about this house that always made him feel large and ungainly, even though he was boringly average in height and weight. Wherever you turned, tiny tables appeared to jab you in the shins or trip you up. If you gestured while speaking, you would send some much-prized knick-knack hurtling across the room – a miniature crystal cat, a porcelain weeping child (and who wouldn't want a crying infant to decorate their living room?), a tiddly trinket box. The safest bet was to navigate your way to a seat – trying not to mess up the cushion configuration by leaning back, or slouching, or moving – and stay there, out of trouble. This had been his father's strategy for decades.

In the kitchen, Andrew filled the kettle and clicked it on.

'Best let your mother do that, eh?'

'It's only putting the kettle on, Dad.'

His father darted a look towards the kitchen doorway, and stuffed his hands deep in his pockets, perhaps to demonstrate that he was in no way complicit in the kettle-filling debacle.

Mrs Tyler bustled in.

'Well, this is a nice surprise.' She crossed to the worktop. 'Oh! Kettle's on! You'll be doing me out of a job in a minute!'

'Sorry, Mum. Just trying to help...' Andrew dug his hands down into his pockets.

''Course you were.' Mrs Tyler banged her way in and out of cupboards, clanking cups, thunking down the biscuit barrel, clattering teaspoons. 'Milk, Ron! I've only the two hands, you know.'

His father roused himself and retrieved the milk from the fridge, opened a cupboard, then stood there, contemplating the four different milk jugs with something akin to terror. Andrew watched his father but elected to remain at a safe distance. Would the 'family' jug be the correct choice, or would he be classed as 'guest – ordinary' as his visit was unscheduled. It was a tough call.

As ever, delay of any kind prompted Mrs Tyler to move up a gear to Full Speed Ahead: she steamed past her husband, stretched up on tiptoes and plucked the 'family only' stainless-steel jug from the shelf. Removed the bottle of milk from his hand.

'Go on through to the lounge. Ron, be a love and take the tray. I'll bring the biscuits.'

Andrew led the way, stumbling only once on the fringed corner of a lozenge-shaped rug, neatly side-stepping a floorstand bearing a ceramic duo of fairies apparently sharing a mischievous secret – *Shall we get the fuck out of here when she's not looking?* Andrew smiled at the thought and carefully positioned himself in one corner of the sofa.

There were lemon puffs, jam sandwich creams, and – an unexpected interloper – dark chocolate biscuits with stem ginger in them.

'Ooh, these are posh, Mum. Expecting royalty?' God, he'd barely been here ten minutes and already he was starting to sound like his parents.

Mrs Tyler's head quivered and she gave a loud sniff. Andrew, unsure of the source of the outrage, threw a covert glance at his father.

'They're from her with the apple tree,' Ron said, not one for long speeches.

'Well, that's nice of her...' Andrew could feel himself walking into quicksand but had no idea how best to retreat.

Mrs Tyler's head trembled again as if he had said, 'It's nice to crap on the carpet,' and she nodded at her husband to continue.

'Will I show Andrew in the morning in the light? Would that be best? See it for himself, like?'

Blimey – three sentences in a row. Practically a record for his father.

'*In the morning?*' Mrs Tyler's head swivelled round like a Dalek. 'What's going on? Andrew?'

'Well... I wondered if maybe I...' Andrew hung his head. 'Vicki. She...' He looked down at his feet in their grey socks, tipped with yellow at the toe end. Vicki had given him these socks. He didn't even like them, so why did staring at them now make him feel as if he might cry? He shook his head and stared into his teacup.

'You can stop here with us,' his father said, unusually decisive. 'Can't he?'

''Course. It's your home too, Andrew.'

One good thing about his parents: at least they wouldn't want to sit round in a circle and talk about his feelings. Have a cup of tea, have a biscuit, do some hoovering: there was no problem in the world that could not be bypassed by Mrs Tyler's strategy for life.

She set her cup and saucer down with a clink. 'We'd best go up and check your room, Andrew.'

* * *

Andrew perched on the single bed. God, it was going to be a snug fit, this bed. He swivelled round and swung his legs up to stretch out. If he let his arm flop out to the side, as if in sleep, it went right off the bed. Still, it wouldn't be for long, would it? He let that thought roll around his head for a minute. What if Vicki didn't beg him to come back? What if she really were done with him, with them, and he was now alone?

His mother marched back in with a new toothbrush and tube of toothpaste, a guest flannel, and a clean pair of his father's pyjamas: the old-fashioned sort, striped, with buttons down the front.

'Oh, no, thanks, Mum. It's OK.' At home, with Vicki, he usually wore just a T-shirt and mismatched PJ bottoms in bed.

'Do you have pyjamas with you?' She held them out, averting her gaze as if they were possibly something sexual or dirty, or both.

He looked round at his holdall, realising he'd left most of his clothes in the black bin bags still in the car and he'd no idea what was in each bag.

'Erm... well...' He took them from her. 'Thanks, then.'

'You'll just have to make the best of it,' Mrs Tyler said, apparently addressing the curtains.

'Yes, Mum. I know.'

'At the end of the day, you have to put it all behind you and move on,' she instructed the wardrobe.

'Yes, Mum. You're right.'

'Make a fresh start,' she told the rug as she bent to comb out the errant fringe with her fingers. 'There's plenty more fish in the sea.'

'Yes, indeed.' Andrew looked down, making a conscious effort not to keep a tally of his mother's clichés; that way lay madness. 'I'm really tired...'

'Good night then, Andrew, love.'

''Night, Mum.' He bent to kiss her cheek. She was a kind soul really. 'Thanks for everything.'

'You're more than welcome. Sleep tight.'

Mrs Tyler made a final tour of the room, tweaking the bedspread, plumping up the mathematically aligned cushions, and looking round for any rogue piece of fluff or speck of dust that might have dared to enter the room in ignorance of her zero-tolerance policy.

Andrew got himself ready for bed, slipped under the covers, and lay there, looking at the green numbers on the bedside clock: it was 9.42.

* * *

He awoke to the irresistible smell of frying breakfast.

At the kitchen table, Andrew asked his dad about the apple tree and the mysterious invasion of the posh ginger biscuits. Mrs Tyler, having eaten her own, more modest, plateful at impressive speed, was up and burrowing in the broom cupboard – her favourite part of the house – in quest of Brasso so she could assault the fittings on the front door.

'We'll pop out to the garden when you're done,' his father said without elaborating further.

'I've washed my hands of the whole sorry business. Your dad's promised to sort it out, Andrew. He'll show you, won't you, Dad?'

Out in the back garden, Ron nodded towards the far end where a mature, magnificent apple tree grew just on the other side of the fence.

'That's the devil tree then.'

Now in early October, it was still well endowed with huge, shiny green apples, like something from a child's picture book.

Andrew laughed.

'Go on, fill me in. Why does Herself want it put down, then?'

'Stealing our light, son.' His father shrugged, resigned to the tree's inevitable fate. 'And blocking her view onto the allotments.'

'Dad, you're never going to let her have her way on this, surely? I mean, it's a wonderful tree.'

'You can't argue with your mother. Might as well hope to hold back the tide.'

Andrew sighed. 'And what part do the biscuits play in all this?'

His father explained that, after repeated promptings from his wife, he had gone round to the other house, whose garden backed onto their own at an angle, and spoken to the owner, or rather attempted to.

'And?'

'So I says my piece about the tree and about how Herself wants it out, and the woman says, quite posh you know, "Ohhhhhh, nooooooo, I couldn't possibly. It would be a sin against Nature," she says. And I'm stood there on the front step feeling like a right pillock and she picks up this packet of biscuits from her hall table, puts it in my hands, and says to tell my wife she's sorry.'

Andrew laughed.

'God – and what did Mum say?'

'I'll leave you to imagine.'

'So now what?'

His father stuck his hands deep in his pockets.

'We'll have to do something otherwise *She'll* be over the fence of a night-time and at it with the breadknife.'

Andrew offered to go round to see the owner again. Perhaps he could persuade her to have the tree thinned a little to let in more light instead?

'Would you, son? You're better at all that clever talking. I'm no good with this kind of thing.'

* * *

One street away, Andrew rang the doorbell of the house with the apple tree. He stood there, hoping it would indeed be the little, posh lady his father had described and not a large and aggressive man who might say, 'It's our tree, what the fuck's it got to do with you, you tosser?' He retreated a step. With any luck, they would be out and he could say he'd tried. He waited a minute, then rang the bell again, very lightly this time. No answer. He started to turn away, then sighed and patted his pockets, looking for a pen. Andrew scribbled his name and mobile number and a brief, very polite note on the back of an old envelope, and poked it through the letterbox, thinking, God, this place could do with his mother on a cleaning jag for an hour or two. The windows were dusty, the front hedge towering and ungainly, the brass door fittings neglected and dull.

As he reached the corner, he noticed a very attractive woman laden with shopping bags coming towards him. For a moment, he thought she looked familiar but he couldn't place her. He smiled and gave a small nod, thinking how embarrassing it would be if he ignored her and then she turned out to know him. She returned the smile but walked on without speaking. He was sure he had seen her somewhere before. Perhaps one of Dave's innumerable exes? Or maybe on telly? He'd done that before, said hello to someone, thinking he knew them, only to click a minute later that it was a newsreader or an actor. He turned right round to have another look as she walked away from him. Hard to tell from the back – tall, slim figure, hair tucked into a woolly hat, extraordinary long green scarf trailing right the way down behind her almost to the ground. At that moment, she turned suddenly as if she knew he was watching her. Andrew jerked round to face front... and walked straight into a cherry tree.

The woman laughed – he could hear her from thirty paces away – and, mortified, he scurried on without turning round again.

7

CECILIA

It was not that Cecilia was lonely, or that she minded living alone, but in the morning, when she was woken by the light, in those drowsy moments, the memory of *him* bringing her a cup of coffee was dreamy and delicious. She lay there for a while, savouring the flurried twitterings of the birds battling at the bird-feeders, the faint rumble of the trains, and, most of all, the weight of the covers on top of her. She slept beneath an eclectic millefeuille of layers: a brushed cotton sheet, topped with a much-loved 'get-better' blanket composed of multi-coloured knitted squares, her grandmother's ancient feather eiderdown, and an embroidered bedspread lugged back from Marrakech many years ago, swirled in shameless pinks and reds with glimpses of gold and lapis lazuli. The top layer consisted of spread-eagled books, half-read sections of the newspaper, Cecilia's long, hand-knitted, green cardigan, and a changing assortment of disparate items: scarves, clean washing, free-range scraps of fabric, a tangle of tights en route to the laundry basket, and, more often than not, a crumb-crusted plate.

Cecilia slunk out of bed sideways so as not to disturb the layers and tugged on the long cardigan over her nightdress. The girls had bought her a dressing gown, of course – more than one over the years – but there was something so dispiritingly homely and resigned about a dressing gown that, even now at sixty-six, Cecilia couldn't bring herself to become the kind of woman she pictured would wear one, and so the cardigan still reigned supreme. She pulled on a skirt over the bottom of her nightie, and poked her feet into a pair of pointed leather slippers from Istanbul. Madeleine, her younger daughter, referred to them as 'your conjuror shoes', while Olivia, the elder, merely glanced downwards at them, then gave that funny, Olivia-ish half-smile that seemed to Cecilia like a mixture of affection and amused acceptance of her mother, though why Cecilia's choice of footwear... or clothes... or food... or anything should bother anyone else remained one of life's great mysteries.

'Morning, Puss.' The cat leaped up onto the counter-top and stroked its face against her hand.

Cecilia opened a tin of food for the cat and spooned some out into its dish before setting down a bowl of fresh water.

'There you go, Pusskin.'

She filled the kettle and rummaged in the bread bin. She really ought to go for a quick walk or a swim, but there wasn't much time as the girls were coming for brunch. No doubt Olivia would arrive laden with 'proper' food, but Cecilia needed something to keep body and soul together for now. She made some brutally strong coffee in a red enamel pot and drizzled honey onto a stale scone she had unearthed among the unloved ends of bread.

It was already cold for October. The radiators were sluggish in the mornings, probably in need of flushing or sluicing or bleeding, or whatever it was that was of little interest to her. Cecilia shuffled through to the hall and plucked her long winter coat – a tweedy, over-large relic of some long-forgotten ex – from the hallstand and put it on.

She opened the French windows onto the garden and looked down at the patio. Just think how lovely it would be to have a little sunken pool with a fountain out here. Lined with mosaic, though it would be awkward to work on if sunken – she'd have to lie full-length on her front. Could look incredible, though. Maybe something wild and strange – the Kraken, one eye open, watching you from the depths?

The scone was too stale, even for her, so she crumbled up the rest of it and scattered it onto the patio stones for the birds. Then she pottered down to the far end of the garden with her coffee, and sat on the battered old bench by the apple tree to watch a robin.

After a while, the doorbell rang, but Olivia had a key so she could let herself in. On a Sunday morning, if it was anyone else, it could hardly be important anyway. Cecilia ignored it and looked at the robin as if it might hold all the answers.

But in fact Olivia arrived a minute or two later, giving her usual light ding-ding on the bell before using her key, and calling out hello just as the old grandfather clock was chiming the half-hour. Olivia was punctual as always, definitely not a trait inherited from her mother. Cecilia called out and came back into the house. Her daughter leaned down to hug her, unwound herself from her long green scarf, then strode through to the kitchen with her bulging shopping bags.

'So, how are you doodling, Ma?' A phrase from when Madeleine was little, long since incorporated into the family lexicon. 'Mads is coming separately. She stayed at Ben's last night.'

Cecilia patted one of the radiators as if it were a misbehaving puppy.

'The heating doesn't seem to be very hot... but I don't mind really.'

'Ma, you're wearing a coat in the house. Would you like me to organise someone to look at the radiators?'

'Well, it is a bit awkward trying to do anything in this coat. The sleeves are too long.'

'I wish you'd let us get you one that fits you. You look like a child who's raided the dressing-up box in that.'

'I could afford a new coat...' Although her mosaic commissions were now very few and far between, Cecilia had no penchant for extravagance and she had managed to buy a flat some years ago, which she now let to her two daughters and largely lived off the proceeds. 'I just don't want one.' She slipped off the coat and threw it onto the chaise longue. 'Anyway, I'm warm enough now.'

Olivia rinsed out a cloth, wiped the table and worktop, then – with a certain amount of sighing and tugging – extricated a broom from a tangle of things in the cupboard and swept the kitchen floor. Then she unpacked the shopping. Cecilia disliked shopping unless it was for art materials – who could resist those? Then she was like a small child, transfixed by the delicious treasures in the sweet-shop window, wanting everything all at once. But buying eggs and bread and loo paper – where was the pleasure in that?

'I did call from the shop to see if you wanted anything. You must answer the phone sometimes.'

Fresh eggs, thick-cut smoked bacon, orange juice, a crusty sour-dough loaf, mushrooms smelling of darkness and clean earth, bulging tomatoes, properly plump and deep red. A thick thud of the Sunday papers as they were disgorged onto the worktop. Colombian coffee, smelling of Heaven. Despite her ostensible lack of interest in food, Cecilia's mouth started to water.

'You hungry, Ma?'

'I think I must be.'

'Have you got coffee on the go?'

The pot was nearly empty, so Olivia refilled the kettle to make more.

'Did Mads ring?' Olivia started slicing the mushrooms. 'Is she on her way at least?'

'No... oh, she might have called. I don't know. The phone may have rung.' Cecilia looked round vaguely. 'I was just in the garden...'

'She's probably texted.' Olivia dug into her jeans pocket and pulled out her mobile to check. 'Yes. "Round the corner", i.e., ten minutes away, probably. I'll start anyway.'

Olivia opened the fridge for milk.

'You *are* eating properly, aren't you?'

'Of course. Don't fuss.' Cecilia tipped the coffee dregs into the compost bucket below the sink.

Olivia began removing items from the fridge and ranging them along the worktop.

'They're fine! I just bought those.'

'I'm just having a quick look at the dates, that's all.' She carried on taking things out. 'Good grief, that's practically *vintage*. And that. *And* that.'

'Supermarkets just put those dates on so you'll throw them away and buy more. You're playing right into their hands.'

'Why don't you buy less, then? Buy one packet of ham, not three.'

'They were on offer – three for two.'

'Now who's playing into the big bad capitalists' hands, Mum? And it's not a bargain if you leave two of them to become a breeding-ground for botulism.'

'Oh, nonsense. I've never had botulism from eating anything in this house.'

'It's probably too scared to enter. Can't you hear the noxious bacteria huddling by the fridge door, whimpering: "Help, help! Let us out! The maggotty brie is coming for us!"'

Cecilia laughed appreciatively.

'Oh, you girls, you're spoilt rotten. And so cautious. When I was your age, I never worried about food or the electricity bill or boring things. I thought only about my work and love – and sex, of course. Live a little! Take risks – where's your sense of adventure? Ah, there was this time in Rome—'

'God, please not up against the wall at the Colosseum again.' Olivia pressed her hands over her ears and began to hum loudly.

The doorbell rang: Madeleine's signature insistent triple ring. Always late herself, she was nevertheless impatient to get stuck in the second she arrived.

'I'm starving. What have we got?' Madeleine planted kisses on her mother and sister. 'Ma, I found this note on your mat.' She waved an old envelope in the air and deposited it on the hall table.

'*We* have got bacon and eggs, etcetera. Do you want the whole shebang?'

'Fab, yes, yes. Tons of everything for me, please.' Madeleine shucked off her grey military greatcoat, like her mother's, way too big for her. 'God, why's it so cold in here? Can't you turn up the heating?' She went and stood right next to the radiator. 'That's an... um... *interesting* item of clothing, *Mother*. What is it exactly?' She cast a glance sideways at Olivia.

'Feel free to mock – I don't give a damn.' Cecilia hitched up her long cardigan, then walked up and down as if along a catwalk. 'Lilian made it for me and *I* love it.' It was a skirt with an asymmetric flounce that bulged out at the bottom and a wavy hemline, though whether this was by accident or design was unclear.

Lilian was one of Cecilia's numerous 'artistic' friends, sometimes referred to by Cecilia as 'the coven' – all women in their sixties, like Cecilia, and single, widowed or divorced.

'Hmm, I rather thought I detected the distinctive hand of Lilian in it,' Olivia chipped in, while cooking the breakfast.

'It makes you look like a lampstand,' Madeleine pronounced.

'It's *jacquard*.' Cecilia enunciated the word with relish as if it were the name of an unusually attractive man. 'Very good quality.'

'It looks like a recycled sofa-cover.'

'But a good-quality sofa-cover,' Olivia added.

'It's not sofa fabric,' Cecilia said. 'Lilian was given Mrs Reynolds' curtains – yards and yards of fabulous material. She's made such wonderful things—'

'—and also your skirt,' said Olivia.

'Isn't that the horrid old woman at the big house on the end? The one who *died*?'

Cecilia ignored the questions. Madeleine made a face at her sister and mouthed '*Dead woman's curtains!*' at her.

* * *

'Who was that man I saw on your doorstep just before I arrived?' Olivia asked, fork poised in mid-air, as the three of them sat around the table.

'Hmm?' Cecilia, though she rarely bothered to cook for herself, was an appreciative recipient when it came to food. She wished she could somehow paint the taste of these tomatoes... intensely red... sweet... those lovely burnt bits on the cut side... 'What?'

'That man. As I was coming along the road, there was a man turning away from your door, or perhaps it was your neighbour's? I was too far away to be sure.'

'Oh, that's what it was! The doorbell did ring earlier, I think.'

'Mum!' Madeleine scooped up the last of her mushrooms and stuffed them into her mouth. 'You have to answer the door, you know.'

Cecilia shrugged and swigged her coffee as if draining a tumbler of Scotch.

'Why do I?'

'Well...' Madeleine turned to Olivia. 'Why does she?'

'Because people *do*.' Olivia neatly cut the rind off her bacon. 'Otherwise, why bother having a bell? Besides, perhaps it was something nice. Maybe he was a lawyer, come to tell you you've been left thousands of pounds by your eccentric aunt Amelia?'

'Who's Aunt Amelia?'

'Not a real aunt, you noodle.'

Cecilia waved away the question. 'All aunts deceased now, thank the Lord. Think the last two were probably poisoned by do-gooders wanting to show the other occupants of the home a degree of mercy in their final years.'

'He had a nice face.' Olivia tilted her head to one side, the way she did when she was picturing something specific.

'Ooh, Liv's got the hots for the lawyer!'

'Grow up, Mads.'

'Nooooo – but I'm really happy for you. Can I be a bridesmaid?'

'No. We're going to run away to Mull and get married at Calgary Bay. *On our own.*' Olivia terminated the conversation by standing up and clearing the plates.

The smears of egg yolk were brilliant on Cecilia's plate, paint on a palette. *Sunflowers.* Darker than daffodils. Almost enough to make you believe in God, a colour like that. Almost.

Cecilia looked up from her plate.

'*Who's* getting married?' she said.

8

MARRYING MARCIA

Marcia was not the kind of woman you fooled around with. If you'd made it as far as a fourth date, you'd better start saving for an engagement ring and preparing your bank statements to show her father. Conrad thought he detected the slightest slowing of her footsteps when they passed the window of an estate agent or a jeweller, but perhaps he was imagining it. Still he held off, although he wasn't quite sure why as there were no obvious objections to the match. It was all most satisfactory. He was twenty-seven, not too young to settle down, Marcia a couple of years older, but there was nothing wrong in that. She ticked all the boxes. She was educated, more than adequately intelligent, composed, and – on the whole – a rather rational creature not unlike himself.

Their dates – though Conrad never named them to himself as such, thinking of them (if he thought of them at all) more as pleasant enough time spent with a companion who shared his interests – were usually cultural: museums and galleries, classical concerts, music for the mind rather than the heart perhaps (German or Austrian, not Russian), occasionally the theatre or cinema. Marcia was admirably capable and efficient, what in the past might have been termed accomplished: she could cook, sew, sail, swim, play the piano, etc., all to a high standard and without a trace of fuss or even pride. She never drank more than a single glass of wine, rarely raised her voice, and would not embarrass you in front of your friends. There was no history of madness or serious illness in the family. And, Conrad reminded himself, they never argued. She was not unattractive, though perhaps a little angular – as if she had been drawn with the aid of a geometry set – but nothing to complain about. Not a woman of ardour, but then not someone who would be swayed by raging passions this way and that – unlike his previous amour, who had spent an inordinate amount of time crying over the fact that Conrad never told her he loved her (and why would he? He would never lie just to get a woman into bed).

* * *

In the end, he doesn't need to ask.

They are by the river one day, walking, when Marcia says, 'My mother thinks a June wedding is best. That way, one can honeymoon during the long vac without taking off extra time.'

At that time, they are both living in Oxford: Conrad employed at the Ashmolean Museum, Marcia on the administrative side at the University.

It is late February now. June is barely four months off.

Conrad pauses for a moment, then carries on walking as Marcia continues: 'I dare say we could use one of the college rooms, if we like. For the reception. Registry office for the ceremony, yes? Keep it simple.'

It sounds modest, unthreatening. No overblown church fandango with endless fussing and fretting about the dress and bridesmaids and cars and all that nonsense. Something manageable. And yet...

'I wonder...' Conrad turns so that his body is facing her but he looks out over the river. 'I wonder if...'

'I'm pregnant,' she says.

'Ah, I see.' He glances at her face, then back to the river. 'Well, June then, yes, that sounds sensible.' Conrad nods. 'Very few guests on my side, so we can keep it small.' It seems he has assented then. Well, why not?

And so it is. The four months scoot by and, if Conrad considers applying the brakes, there is no outward sign of it. A registry office ceremony, with just immediate family and a couple of friends apiece. Marcia wears an empire-line dress and matching jacket in a rather unfortunate shade of light green, a colour that leaches her skin of any note of warmth it might have. As a concession to the occasion, she applies some make-up, but – unfamiliar as she is with the art of it – the effect is somehow very slightly askew. It is hard to pinpoint exactly what is not quite right; perhaps there is a little more eyeshadow on one eyelid than the other, or maybe her lipstick is straying just a fraction beyond the boundary of her thin lips in a minor act of rebellion. Still, no matter – it is really a jolly day, and surely hardly anyone notices it at all.

Conrad looks very much himself, only somewhat smarter, in a grey suit, rather than his usual academic's tweed jacket, with a new silk tie and a crisp blue shirt. A modest drinks party for their small circle of friends is followed by a formal dinner at the Randolph Hotel. Marcia's father makes a moderately amusing speech and toasts 'the happy couple'. For a moment, Conrad glances round, then realises that this refers to him and Marcia. Well, they are a happy couple. Marcia seems extremely happy today. And he is content. It is a clichéd phrase, not the kind of language he would ever use, other than as a mocking aside, but he is not unhappy about the marriage or the day so far, so it is all good. Conrad's own speech is a source of pride to him – clever, pithy, gracious, witty; he has spent quite some time honing it and practising the pauses to seem natural when there might be responsive laughter.

The newlyweds spend their wedding night at the hotel. And if their nuptial coupling is perhaps a little lacking in bells and whistles, it is none the less perfectly satisfactory: lights off (as always), new wedding nightgown duly lifted, a moderate amount of foreplay, and proceed to the main event.

Before their wedding night, they have gone to bed together on a small number of occasions. It is the sixties: if the magazines are anything to go by, people are expected to rip each other's clothes off at every opportunity. Conrad and Marcia do not go in for ripping off clothing, of course, but their activities between the sheets are usually reasonably effective, at least for him. Early on, Marcia instructed Conrad 'not to concern yourself about it' on the matter of her orgasm. Occasionally, she grinds herself to climax, eyes tight shut, rocking regular as a metronome against him, but her absolute silence and minimal facial expression mean that it is easy to miss it. The only clue, Conrad notes, is an intense pursing of her lips as she comes, as if something very slightly unpleasant has occurred, like when she passes by a rubbish bin that is in need of emptying and there is a lingering whiff of fish bones or old cheese.

In the early days, despite Marcia's diktat, Conrad does his best to be an imaginative lover, inspired perhaps by notions of romantic love absorbed from art and literature, or from the mysterious cogs and corners of his own mind. Surely women like that sort of thing and, in any case, he has never had any complaints. He initially pays a great deal of attention to Marcia's bosoms, thinking of Marvell's line about spending two hundred years to adore each breast, but she frowns and moves his mouth away from her nipple - 'That's for babies surely?' – and opens her legs so far and no further so that he can proceed to insert his erect penis which, after all, was the point of the thing, was it not?

9

INSUFFICIENT DATA

Andrew went to make himself a cup of coffee in the cramped, grimly lit kitchen used by both the Prints and Drawings department and his own section that was housed within it, Conservation – Western Art on Paper. He was too busy to go all the way over to the staff canteen again this morning just for a quick coffee. If there was someone in the kitchen already, he usually went away and came back later, otherwise you felt obliged to make conversation. It wasn't that he didn't like talking to other people, not at all; it was just he didn't want to have to do it if he wasn't in the mood. Of course you couldn't take your drink back into the department, where you might accidentally spill it over an irreplaceable work, but had to stand in the flat fluorescent light or perch on the lone wobbly stool or cold stone steps and drink it there. He poked his head round the doorway, as if he were just passing, hoping it would be empty. Conrad was there. Ah, well, he was safe enough. Not a man for small talk either. He was standing by the worktop, waiting for the kettle to boil.

'Andrew.' Conrad nodded.

'Good morning, Conrad. How are you?'

'I'm well, thank you.'

Andrew paused for a few moments, waiting for Conrad to ask him how he was, too, but he did not.

'I enjoyed meeting your daughter the other day. She seems very nice. What does she do? I mean, does she work or...?'

'I suppose these days one might call her a "homemaker" – repellent though that is – as the term "housewife" seems to have become *verboten*, for some reason.'

Andrew checked the coffee jug in the filter machine, but it was nearly empty. Some bright spark always left just a tiny, irritating amount in it; if you finished it, you had to make a fresh batch. He sighed and reached for the coffee jar.

'Well, these things change, of course.' Andrew gestured towards the machine. 'Coffee?'

'Tea, I think. Yes. Earl Grey, if there is any.' Conrad watched while perched on the stool as Andrew foraged in the cupboards, looking for the tea. 'And I'm doing my daughter a disservice, in fact. She's also a print-maker. Wood engravings,' he added, anticipating Andrew's next question.

'Sort of a family tradition then?' Andrew turned round.

'In what way?'

'Well, you know, you... here... being an expert on prints... and your daughter... making them.' It sounded childish, simplistic. Conrad's particular area of expertise was actually early Italian engravings, but of course he had acquired an encyclopaedic knowledge of the collection over the thirty-odd years he had worked there. Even now, in his supposed retirement, the man was in two or three times a week, researching material for his next book.

'I am merely an observer then; my daughter, by contrast, a creator. Not, I suggest, in the same tradition. Though perhaps different sides of the same fence, shall we say?'

'Yes.' Andrew was keen to agree. 'And is she successful?'

'In what sense?' Conrad tilted his head a fraction to one side in that way he had of looking at you as if you were an intriguing but clearly defective object, like a drawing with a bad tear across it.

'Well... in the sense of... of... being... er... successful, I suppose.' Conrad was possibly the most intelligent, erudite person Andrew had ever known, but no one else had such a gift for making him feel like a blithering idiot.

'Financially? Artistically? Does her work make my daughter fulfilled? All of the above?'

'Er... yes... well. All of those. I mean, any. Not all. Any of them. One of them. I guess.'

Conrad raised his eyebrows, and leaned back against the wall with his hands in his pockets, entirely at ease.

'Hmm. Well, financially, I *guess*...' Conrad lingered a little too long on the word as if he had come across an unusual yet ugly little stone at his feet and was curious to examine it for a few moments before discarding it with contempt. 'Not. Artistically – yes, certainly. Her work is of a consistently high standard: technically accomplished. And the prints are definitely attractive, charming and so on and so forth. My daughter is highly professional and capable at whatever she turns her hand to. From a personal satisfaction perspective?' Conrad paused for a long time. Although he was someone who rarely spoke without forethought and due consideration, it seemed to Andrew that this was a lengthy pause, even for him. Conrad frowned, apparently puzzled.

'Insufficient data, I'm afraid.'

'Sorry? Data?'

The kettle came to the boil and clicked off automatically, but Conrad didn't move. Andrew would have to lean right past him to get to the kettle.

'Er... shall I...? The kettle...? Sorry – may I...?' He manoeuvred awkwardly around Conrad for the kettle.

'I mean I have no information on that score.'

Andrew thought he must have missed a step somewhere, but didn't want to feel even more stupid by asking for clarification, so he simply said: 'Oh. I see.'

'I have no data.' Conrad took his tea with a nod of thanks. 'My daughter...' He looked down into his mug. '... is something of a closed book. Impossible to read.'

'Emotionally opaque?' Andrew offered.

'Quite so.' Conrad nodded in acknowledgement. He looked slightly surprised that Andrew did indeed seem to understand.

Well, there's a surprise. Like father, like daughter, Andrew thought. It was possible – probable even – that Conrad did occasionally experience some sort of emotion, but who knew what on earth went on behind that impregnable façade?

'Hmm. And do you have other children?' Andrew thought it best to move on from what was clearly an awkward area.

'No,' Conrad said immediately, then after a moment, 'Yes. I mean, yes, a son – but he's – he's away at present.'

It was so unlike Conrad to change his mind or to say something that came across as an unforced error that Andrew was quite shocked.

'Ah. Travelling. For work, is it?'

'Not as such.'

Andrew held out the milk, a question, and added some at arm's length in response to Conrad's nod.

'My son does not.' Conrad stopped. 'Is not.' Usually, even Conrad's most casual utterances were exemplars of grammatical perfection, so Andrew was struck by these odd, amputated phrases. He glanced at Conrad's face but, as ever, could read no indicator there – those glittering blue eyes like polished glass, that high forehead, that erect posture even while seated born to command. 'Benedict has been. Away. For a considerable period of time. In fact, it would be true to say that we are not certain when he will return. Or.' He inhaled and jutted out his chin. 'Or *if*.'

'Oh. I see,' said Andrew, though he wasn't sure he did see at all. 'I'm very sorry.'

Conrad snorted as if Andrew had suggested they pop out to the forecourt and do Morris dancing.

'Nothing to be sorry about. Things are as they are.'

'Yes, but still... you... it must be—'

'*Things are as they are.*'

Clearly, this was a thorny topic. Andrew poured himself some coffee and looked for safer ground.

'Oh, if you have another minute, I meant to say how much I enjoyed working on your painting. It really was such a pleasure. It sounds silly, but I've missed having it around.'

The cloud lifted from Conrad's face and his lips curved into something akin to a smile. It was such an atypical expression for him that Andrew didn't quite recognise it straight away. The man looked suddenly ten years younger.

'It certainly is a fine painting.' Conrad nodded. 'In my opinion. And you did an exceptional job, Andrew. *Exceptional*. Not a word I use often, I assure you.'

'Well... um... thank you very much.'

They sipped their hot drinks in companionable silence for a few moments.

'It has an irresistible atmosphere. I find myself thinking about it at odd moments, wondering who she was, your flame-haired temptress...'

There was a pause.

'Temptress?'

'Yes, the woman. In the painting.' Perhaps the old fellow had been thinking about something else; he seemed to have lost the thread rather.

'Why do you refer to her as a temptress?' Conrad stood up then and turned to face Andrew, unsmiling. He drew himself up to his full height. God, he really was a tall bugger.

'Well, I... you know... she's beautiful and... well...' Andrew felt himself flush, as if he had been caught lying or stealing. 'And alluring... so, it was just...' He shrugged.

'Ah.' Conrad looked down at him. 'I see.' He turned, apparently to look out of the window, though it gave only on to a blank brick wall a few feet away. His expression was unreadable. Insufficient data, Andrew thought.

Andrew shoved his hands deep in his pockets, wishing he'd never embarked on this conversation. Conrad did this sometimes: took some completely nothingy, unimportant, passing remark and worked it to death until you wanted to curl up in a corner, whimpering.

'Well... not "temptress" then... It was just, you know, shorthand for an attractive woman.' Andrew took a cautious sip of his coffee. 'So anyway, I was wondering who the painter was. The signature's a bit of a scrawl.'

Conrad shrugged. 'Philip – something, I think.' He paused. 'Actually, no. Perhaps Peter. It's a long time ago. Why do you ask?'

'I'm just interested. Thought I might Google him, see if he's still painting. Maybe even find out who the sitter was – the woman.' Andrew looked down into his coffee. 'Are you sure you can't remember? It's just—'

'Of course, it's many years ago, as I said. Well, I'd better crack on. Good talking to you, Tyler.'

Had Conrad really just called him by his *surname*? In earnest? God, no one had done that since the miserable afternoons of football or rugby in the wind and rain at his grammar school. One of the games teachers had previously taught at a private school and was in the habit of calling boys by their surnames, usually at a volume audible even if they had been in a different county, and in his case always accompanied by injunctions to pull your socks up, get a move on, pick up your feet, move your bloody backside, run, weave, kick, or for Christ's sake, Tyler, just bloody pass it to someone who knows what to do with it.

Andrew took out his mobile and scrolled to the before and after close-ups he'd taken of his restoration work on the painting. He zoomed in on the signature. It was illegible but true, the initial letter did look like a P, then a dot, the scrawl of the surname, possibly beginning with – was that an N? Or maybe an H? Still, it didn't solve the question of the hidden initials on the back. He'd discovered them when he'd removed the damaged frame and was very keen to ask Conrad if he knew about them. Oddly, they were in single quote marks. Very odd, really. Perhaps they were the initials of the woman, the title of the painting, or some sort of private joke by the artist? 'ML' – like that. Conrad would be unlikely to know anyway, Andrew reasoned. Maybe he'd ask him another day when he was in a better mood. He turned to the sink to wash out his mug. Conrad's tea remained where he had abandoned it on the worktop, undrunk.

10

GETTING AWAY FROM IT ALL...

'*Must* we go?' Roger sighed and put down his pudding spoon with a clatter.

Clearly, the invitation to spend next weekend at their friends' seaside cottage was less alluring than she had hoped. Eleanor offered him another slice of homemade *tarte tatin* and topped up his coffee cup.

'Honestly, I've never understood the *point* of a country cottage. Why on earth do relatively sane people with a perfectly comfortable, warm house in London think nothing of slogging through appalling traffic for .three, four hours to go and stay in a much smaller, darker, colder, less well-equipped house where there's sod all to do other than walk in the rain, sit about talking and eating too much or – with you two – waste hours at the farmers' market, fondling the vegetables.' He laughed.

'But I love it there. It's so cosy and I really like—'

'Cosy! Hardly, darling. Last time, you kept your dressing gown on in bed!'

'Well, I was feeling a bit... but it's—'

'And what kind of person buys a place in *Suffolk*, for God's sake? The Cotswolds are miles nearer! That's where *we'd* have a second home if we had one, isn't it, darling? Decent restaurants, good road links, charming villages and all that sort of thing.'

'But Sarah and Mark's house is so close to the sea. You can walk to the beach in five minutes.'

'You funny thing. It's not been transformed since the last time we went, has it?' He tilted his head on one side and took off his glasses. 'I mean, it is still a cold, rainy, windy, *English* beach, with no sand, no palm trees, and no clear, turquoise ocean?'

Eleanor's voice was quiet: 'I just really love being by the sea. I don't mind about it being cold and grey... it's so beautiful there. The sky is incredible. It changes all the time.'

'I'm not sure it's ideal timing. I'm bound to have some work to do next weekend.'

There was no point trying to push Roger into anything he didn't want to do; her shoulders sagged, then a small thought struck her: 'Sarah mentioned that Mark would... um... really appreciate your expert advice about some problem he's had at work with a supplier... if you wouldn't mind...?' She fought the urge to emphasise the word 'expert'.

Roger nodded. 'He's a bit of a babe-in-the-woods when it comes to business, isn't he?' He stood up and took his dirty cafetière over to the worktop, and left it there. 'Well, I suppose we've nothing more exciting on. And you'll only be hankering after it if I say no. Tell her we'll come then.'

'Thank you.' Eleanor went over, kissed him on the cheek, and made a mental note to tell Sarah to brief Mark about his supposed work problem.

'And you can fondle as many vegetables as you like at the market. I promise not to rush you. I can sit in that surprisingly good coffee shop with the paper while you ogle the cauliflowers to your heart's content.'

* * *

On the Friday, Eleanor was ready by half-past three, as agreed, as Roger had said he would come home straight from his lunchtime meeting. She had packed their bags, and set them in the hallway, ready to transfer into Roger's car. It would be simpler to use her own car, of course, but Roger was voluble on its shortcomings in terms of size, comfort, lack of under-seat heating and so on. He'd better come very soon, otherwise they would be caught up in the weekend exodus from London. She sat on the stairs in her coat, waiting, so that they could leave the moment he returned.

Quarter to four. If she went and relaxed with a cup of tea and a book, he'd be bound to come through the door that very minute and catch her. In the kitchen everything was clean and tidy; it would be a shame to start making a mess by having a cup of tea. Still, he *was* late and hadn't called. She put just enough water in the kettle and clicked it on. The phone rang then, making her jump. It was Roger, saying his meeting had overrun but he'd be back in half an hour and could she please have everything *ready*.

Eleanor drank her tea standing by the sink, then she zipped round the house, double-checking the lights, the window-locks, and the back door.

When she heard Roger's car pull in forty-five minutes later, she quickly opened the front door to greet him. He deposited a kiss on her cheek, and swapped his dark cashmere overcoat for a padded jacket, his black business shoes for tan loafers.

'Right,' he said. 'Let's get this show on the road then.' He nodded at the bags in a neat row, with his pillow lying on top in its own sealed bag. 'Well done, you remembered my pillow. And my phone and laptop chargers?'

'Yes.'

'Water, etc., for the journey?'

'Yes.'

'Good, good. Now, bring me the bags, starting with mine, then – let's see – that one, my briefcase, the pillow, then yours. I'll go and open the boot.'

Roger positioned the bags in the boot as Eleanor ferried each one out to him. He tucked tartan picnic blankets around everything with care, something akin to affection even, to minimise movement during transit. Eleanor popped a bottle of wine into each of her wellies, which were wedged in one corner, pleased with the efficient use of space.

'Darling! Whatever are you doing?'

'But it's saving space...'

'You funny old thing.' Roger shook his head and laid his hand on her shoulder. 'Do you actually *want* your wellingtons full of glass and wine? Do try to think, darling.'

'But the bottles are protected by—'

'Darling, we don't want you ending up in casualty with glass in your foot, do we?' He sighed. 'Let's do things properly, eh?'

'Shall I get some bubble wrap?'

'No, no, we don't want to be faffing about all night. I'll do it.' He stomped up the front path.

'There should be some in the cupboard under—' she called after him.

'I do live here too, you know.'

Roger returned to the house a final time to double-check that Eleanor had set the lights on timers and double-locked and bolted the back door, as she had claimed. It was now well after five. Perfectly timed to hit the exodus at its peak.

'Oh, did you remember new blades for my razor?'

'Yes, of course.'

'And my slippers?'

'I did.'

'And yours? Your birthday ones?'

'Mmm, I think so.' She frowned, as if trying to remember, although she could picture them clearly in the hall in the closet under the stairs, where she was hoping that with any luck they might biodegrade in the darkness. 'I'm not one hundred per cent sure...'

His hand was on the ignition key.

'You'd better go back and check.'

'I can manage without them. I don't want to hold us up.'

'It won't take a minute. You know how much you hate being cold. Go on.'

She went back to the house. Maybe she could accidentally leave them behind at the cottage? She had a sudden image of dormice nesting very happily in them, luxuriating in their snuggly new home.

'I can't believe you forgot them.' Roger laughed. 'You dozy thing!' He patted her leg beside him. 'Think of that freezing flagstone floor in the hallway!'

When on her own, Eleanor loved to listen to music when she drove, or to sing. She would practise whatever they'd been working on in the choir or sing along to anything she chose – blues, musicals, opera. When Roger drove, which he preferred when they travelled together unless he intended to drink, he opted for Radio Four or a talking book. Roger liked music, too, but he preferred to listen in the comfort of his own armchair, via his outsize headphones. He did not like his music unfettered, free range, loose in the air very much. Occasionally, they went to a concert together, but Roger was vehement on the subject of why it was a waste of time and money when you could hear the same music at home and put your feet up while you were at it. No doubt he was right. Saying that when she was in the same room as the orchestra, it made her heart beat a little faster, her skin fizz with goosebumps – she shrugged the thought away – well, it was ridiculous, of course.

* * *

Now, finally skirting the fringes of Ipswich to head towards the coast, Roger sighed. Again. Eleanor had the strangest sensation that, somehow, the traffic congestion was her fault, even though she'd been ready to leave the moment he arrived.

'If we'd left even ten minutes earlier, it would have been fine,' he said.

'It's generally pretty bad even by four, though,' she pointed out. 'I suppose we could have used my car instead so I—'

'Don't be ridiculous. The boot's the size of a matchbox.' He sighed and fiddled with the radio knob. 'It would have been helpful not to have to faff about hunting high and low for bubble wrap at the very last minute.'

'I don't think the wellies idea was *so* bad.'

He laughed. 'Oh, *darling*.' He turned to smile at her.

'I'm sorry,' she said automatically.

Eleanor looked out of the window. It was properly dark now, and she caught glimpses into lit-up windows where people had not yet drawn their curtains – fragments of lives: a woman reading a newspaper, a man standing on a chair to change a lightbulb, a mother with a child on her lap; other lives. She wondered what it would be like to be that mother, that child even, to be small again, held safely by someone bigger than you. Earlier, there had been a beautiful sunset, with glowing orange streaks merging into pink in a delicious discordance, and long banks of dark grey cloud. Roger had declared that it was an especially fine one precisely because of this juxtaposition of the dark clouds and the brighter colours, that was what made it so effective, you see. He was almost certainly correct; no-one could analyse a sunset quite like Roger.

* * *

At last, the car pulled smoothly onto the rough gravel parking area beside Sarah and Mark's ancient Citroën.

'Hello, hello!' Sarah came running out, her wild curls bouncing, like an eager spaniel. She hugged Eleanor tight. 'I won't ask how your journey was because it must have been hellish at this hour. Forget about it and come in. The wine is open, the roast chicken is done or even over-done, but please, please will you do the gravy because mine is always crap.'

Mark ambled out and greeted them.

Sarah and Mark were very different from each other. Sarah was like some extraordinary bundle of energy and passion that had been condensed and contained in her compact frame, while Mark was tall and stooping and as laid-back as it was possible to be without actually being in a coma. Still, Eleanor thought they were a very good fit; there was something about the way their different temperaments dovetailed together that made the two of them cohere. Mark was like a perfectly calm, reflective lake, and Sarah a manic duck constantly zig-zagging and flapping around him. He soothed her; she enlivened him.

Roger started to unpack the car. Eleanor started to help but he pressed the two bottles of wine into her hands and waved her inside, telling her to go on in and get warm.

'Are you OK?' Sarah peered up at Eleanor's face as if trying to decipher exceptionally small print.

Eleanor raised her eyebrows a fraction.

'I'm fine.'

'Hmm. Fine, fine? Or Eleanor-fine?'

11

HAPPY FAMILIES I

1965–1972

'Do you mind about its not being a boy?' Marcia's voice sounds grey and cracked. She looks exhausted after the long labour and, in the end, a forceps delivery.

'No, of course not. Why would I?' Conrad moves to sit by his wife's bed and pats her hand. 'She's healthy, she has all her limbs – what else matters?' He dislikes misogyny, not because he believes he ought to support the feminist cause but because it's simply illogical. Women are physically weaker, clearly, but there is no *evidence* for their being lesser beings in any other regard as far as he can see. Looking down on women just because they are women is a perfect example of lazy thinking and, therefore, he has no truck with it. Ergo, why would the arrival of a female child be a cause for disappointment?

'Daddy's *desperate* for a grandson, you know.'

Marcia's two older sisters have produced only girls and seem to have called a halt to breeding.

'Well, let him adopt one then, if he wants one!' Conrad laughs.

'Oh, don't be so silly, darling!' Marcia has a tendency to be very literal at times, especially when she is tired. 'Still, we can always try for another, can't we?'

'Let's not worry about what to have for pudding when we've yet to take a bite of our hors d'oeuvres, yes?'

'What?' She closes her eyes.

She is tired, he knows, and perhaps now is really not the time for one of his foolish quips.

'No rush, I mean.' He reaches out and pats her hand again. 'One chapter at a time, dear thing, yes?'

Marcia is a more efficient mother than he had expected, capable of attending to the infant's needs without undue fuss. The baby, Eleanor, is a placid little thing, who gurgles with delight when Conrad dangles his jangly keys for her to clutch at. As a rule, Conrad does not find babies of any great interest, as they can neither converse nor read, but still, when he holds his finger out and his little daughter clings onto it like a lifebelt, he notes an indefinable feeling in his chest that is hard to label. He detests inarticulacy so it is most frustrating not to be able to name this strange stirring in the core of him. He laughs at himself and supposes it is simply part of the biological imperative, the necessity of feeling protective towards one's offspring, to preserve one's genetic line. Entirely selfish therefore. Nothing to crow about.

* * *

Less than two years later, they are back in the same hospital. This time, it is a boy – sing Allelujah! – and Marcia insists on calling the child Benedict – 'Blessed one', although Conrad had favoured Leo as being short and unpretentious and impossible to reduce to an undesirable diminutive. Still, there are times when one can see that the victory would not be worth the battle, so he gives way. At the news of the baby's arrival, Marcia's parents hotfoot it down from Harrogate as fast as they can, rather than, as had been the case with Eleanor, after two days due to 'previous engagements'. They bring expensive presents for the baby: a silver rattle, an engraved napkin ring, a white cashmere cardigan. Standing in the doorway of his wife's private hospital room (paid for by Daddy, of course), witnessing the family scene, Conrad is struck by the resemblance to the Adoration of the Magi – serene Madonna, blessed infant, acolytes worshipping and bearing costly yet useless gifts. All it needs is a donkey in the corner...

* * *

Marcia has bought black cherry yoghurt for the children to try, still a rather exotic treat in the early 1970s in England. Conrad, musing on his forthcoming trip to accompany another exhibition to Florence, wanders into the kitchen to see if there is any coffee going. He watches his daughter peel back the foil lid of her yoghurt and just look into the pot. Most children would probably either dig their spoon in at once or refuse it altogether, but Eleanor likes to take her time over things. Benedict is struggling to open his yoghurt and immediately starts to get into a strop about it instead of asking for assistance.

Marcia, ironing on the far side of the room, sighs, 'Oh, do help him, Eleanor. Don't just let him sit and suffer.'

'I will in a minute,' Eleanor is already halfway across the room en route to the Welsh dresser. 'I want to have my special spoon.'

Conrad pats the side of the coffee pot and, finding it still warm, tops up his mug, then goes to the fridge for milk.

Eleanor takes her time, standing by the drawer and slowly clinking through the spoons, presumably trying to find her favourite one with the rosebud on the handle. She closes the drawer quietly, then returns to her seat.

Benedict hits her on the arm and shouts, 'Open it now!'

'Say please, Benedict.'

'Oh, Eleanor, just do it for him, will you?' Marcia has her hands full, folding and turning a large tablecloth to press it.

'All right, but I always have to say please.' She opens the yoghurt, and plonks it in front of him.

Benedict picks up the yoghurt then reaches up and tips it upside-down over his sister's head. She lets out a yell and shoves him, and he roars with rage.

Oh God, not more of this, for crying out loud. Conrad takes his coffee and backs out of the room to the hallway.

'Oh, for goodness' sake!' Conrad hears Marcia thunk down the iron and march across the room. 'That's very naughty, Benedict. You're not to do that.'

Conrad frowns. It is odd, hearing his wife's voice without seeing her face. The words are an admonition, true, and yet the tone does not fit somehow. Why is that? She sounds... hmm, not cross, not really... she sounds as if she is reading something from an instruction manual, as if she knows that is what a parent is supposed to say.

'You provoked him!' Now she *does* sound cross. Oh dear, poor Eleanor seems to be bearing the brunt of her mother's displeasure. 'Why did you make him wait? Honestly, Eleanor, you've only yourself to blame.'

'It's not fair!' Eleanor is crying now. 'You *always* take his side.'

'Don't be silly. Go and get cleaned up. Take off your blouse and bring it straight back to me to wash.'

Conrad sits halfway up the stairs, waiting for her.

'It's not fair,' she repeats, snivelling. Her hair and face are smeary and clown-like with the yoghurt, her white blouse blotched with purplish-pink gunk.

'Ah. Life's not fair, little thing.' He digs out his cloth handkerchief and dabs at her face and hair. 'He's just a tot who doesn't know any better – you know that. Go up and wash it off and you'll feel better.'

'Can't you help me?'

'You're a big girl – you can manage. Daddy's got to work. Trot along now.'

Back downstairs, he pokes his head round the kitchen door. Marcia has Benedict cuddled on her lap and is singing to him: *'Dapples and greys... pintos and bays... all the pretty little ponies...'* He has his thumb in his mouth and is curled into her; he looks like a cherub, all soft and sweet and golden.

'I think Eleanor might need a hand in the bathroom getting that stuff off,' he says.

'Can't you help her, for once?'

'I have a lot of work to get through.'

'Well, she'll just have to manage, then.' Marcia rests her chin on top of her son's head. 'He's very upset.'

Conrad nods but says nothing further, then turns and leaves the room.

He stands, undecided, in the hallway for a minute. Checks his watch. Sighs. Then bounds up the stairs two at a time and knocks on the bathroom door.

'You all right, little thing?'

There is no response so he opens the door. Eleanor is standing at the basin in her vest and skirt, face scrubbed, hair still clogged with yoghurt. She does not speak but he meets her eyes in the mirror. Her mouth is clamped tight shut and he can see that she is doing her damnedest not to cry, and it is this, more than anything else, he finds hard to bear.

'Come on,' he says, fitting the shower attachment to the bath taps to wash her hair. 'Let's get it off. Crikey, what a horrid mess. Let's not use that stuff as shampoo ever again, eh?'

12

THE WEEKEND IN SUFFOLK

Eleanor loved this cottage. It was not that it was decorated or furnished exactly as she would have done it herself. Sarah's taste tended towards the ethnic and the rough-hewn, so there were more fringed hangings and lumpen coffee mugs than Eleanor would have chosen, but it was very cosy and welcoming, and she would not have changed the cold flagstones for fitted carpet. She liked the unevenness of them, the way their dips and hollows were a map of so many footsteps over the last two hundred years.

The guest room was small, with a standard double bed, which felt cramped compared with the superking-sized one Eleanor and Roger had at home. The sloping ceiling of the eaves made it impossible for an adult to stand upright on the far side by the window. Roger deposited his bag on the side nearer the door, saying, 'I know you like to have the window side.'

'Thanks.'

'Aren't you going to unpack?' Roger swapped the pillow on his side of the bed for the one they had brought from home, as Eleanor turned to go straight out again.

'I said I'd help Sarah in the kitchen.'

'Honestly, she shouldn't make you do all the work. You're a guest.'

'It's only the gravy. And I'm not a proper guest, more like family.'

Roger snorted but turned back to his unpacking, tutting at the jangling of the wire hangers as he hung up his trousers and shirts.

Back down in the kitchen, Sarah poured Eleanor a huge glass of wine.

'Good grief. I was only wanting to drink it, not swim in it.'

'You looked as if you might be in need.'

Eleanor nodded without comment and rolled up her sleeves.

'Now, gravy. And tell me what you've been up to.'

As she stirred the gravy, Eleanor could hear the rumble of male voices in the sitting room; she wasn't sure what Roger and Mark might talk about on their own but Mark seemed equally happy talking about business or gardening or sport or the cryptic crossword as he was discussing people and books and films and politics, or indeed anything at all.

'And how did the seasonal sex go?' Sarah asked, handing her a jug.

'Sssh! It's not seasonal... will you please sssh?'

'I am shushing, I promise, but I know it's pretty much bang on every three months because you told me. You can't deny it now.'

'I'm not but it's not seasonal. Ah, the Spring Equinox, time to get my knickers off...' Eleanor took a deep swig of her wine. 'It's just gradually settled into that sort of pattern, that's all: his birthday, our anniversary, my birthday, and either Christmas or New Year. Nothing odd about that.'

'No, not at all odd. "Darling! It's October the fourth – I must ravish you!"'

Eleanor laughed in spite of herself.

'You're very cruel. Come on, let's get the food on the table. You know how Roger gets when he's hungry.'

* * *

Later, up in their room, Eleanor changed into her nightdress while Roger was in the bathroom.

'Did you leave your slippers in the car?' he said, looking down at her bare feet as he came in. 'I can fetch them for you.'

'Don't worry, I can get them in the morning.'

'I don't mind. I'll get them now.'

She knew he wanted to go outside anyway. Roger often liked to smoke a cigar last thing at night.

Eleanor went over to the window. The moon was almost full – just a whisper off it, a near perfect disc of silver light against a black sky. It was so much darker here than in London. She could see hundreds, thousands of stars; at home, all you could see in the night sky were the blinking lights of aeroplanes. She turned off the bedroom lights and opened the window to see better. The darkness was exquisite, scattered with stars, as if a child had spilled glitter over black velvet. She leaned against the sill and drank in the night and the moon and the stars, trembling a little in the cold and the vastness of it all.

Below, the front door opened and Roger emerged. He paused briefly on the step to light his cigar, then moved onto the front path. She thought he would look up at the moon, wondered if he would notice – as surely he must – how much clearer the sky was here. But instead, he took out his mobile and looked down at it, scrolling through his emails. Now she could see his expanding bald spot gleaming in the moonlight. She suddenly had the mischievous thought that she could drop something onto his head, just for fun: a flowerhead plucked from the sweet little posy of flowers Sarah had placed in their room? She turned round to look. The heavy brass candlestick on the chest of drawers caught her eye. An image of herself letting go of it directly above Roger's head came to her. She imagined it thunking into that target zone of his shiny patch of scalp, his collapsing without a sound, blood pooling across the path into the roses by the front door. God, she really was losing the plot. Honestly – she shook the thought away, then shut the window as quietly as she could and went to brush her teeth.

Whenever they were away from home, Eleanor read non-fiction, usually a biography or travel memoir or a collection of letters. She rarely read novels any more unless Roger was away for work. Over the years, she had tried various strategies to address 'the problem'; she tried not to think about it at all, but when it came slinking into her head unbidden, she kept it framed by crisp quotation marks as if it were simply a bothersome practical difficulty she had to deal with. An e-reader seemed the obvious answer, but she found it an unsatisfactory experience. For Eleanor, holding a book, the feel of it in her hand, turning the pages, the ink, the paper, the smell of it, even the turning back a page or two to check something – these small pleasures, which might sound foolish if she were to try to describe them, were part of the deep, quiet enrichment that sinking into a book provided.

As always, there was rarely anything to be gained by confronting Roger over areas of disagreement. One had either to accept his way or find a path to circumvent him without his having even the slightest suspicion that you were defying him. Or fume silently, of course.

Roger came in and handed her the slippers.

'Thank you.' Eleanor smiled. 'It looks like a beautiful night out there.'

'What? Oh, yes. Nippy, though. Winter's just around the corner, you can tell.'

'Mmm, I suppose so.'

'Good book?' He nodded at her paperback and started to undress.

'Yes, I think so. It's a collection of poems by—'

'Poetry!' He snorted. 'Well, whatever turns you on, darling. So long as you don't expect *me* to read them!'

'Of course not.' She looked away. 'Did *you* bring a book?'

'Plenty on my tablet. Plus some work, inevitably.' He reached for his pyjamas, then stood looking in the mirror for a minute or two, examining his gums.

'You work so hard.' She smiled at his reflection. 'I hoped this weekend might give you a bit of a break.'

He turned to face her. 'I'd rather crack on than have a backlog to clear on Monday a.m.'

'You're right.'

'Still...' He transferred his tablet from the bed to the bedside table and turned towards her. 'Perhaps we could...? After all, we didn't on your birthday as usual, did we?'

If necessary, they deferred their seasonal sex for a few days. Eleanor was just at the end of her period on her birthday, so it had not taken place, and midweek sex had never been on the agenda as Roger always had to get up so early for work.

'But these walls are awfully thin.' Eleanor patted the wall next to her. She dropped her voice to a whisper, 'They're right next door...' She herself was almost completely silent when they had intercourse; Roger's grunts were, by contrast, really quite loud.

'Well, perhaps you're right.' He leaned over and planted a kiss on her face somewhere between her mouth and her cheek. 'Sunday evening then, once we're home.'

'Mm. Think I'll turn my light off now. Good night.' Eleanor put down her book, took a minute to insert her earplugs with care – Roger couldn't help snoring, but it was always wise to get a head start otherwise the sound drilled into her head – then snuggled down beneath the quilt.

* * *

After breakfast, Eleanor and Sarah drove to Woodbridge for the farmers' market, while Roger helped Mark conquer a wild corner of the garden.

'So how's it been with Hannah gone? Did you cry at the airport? God, I'll be a mess when the time comes.' Sarah and Mark had one son, Tom, aged fourteen, away staying with a friend for the weekend.

'I was a model of restraint.' Eleanor gave a small smile.

'There's a surprise.' Sarah paused by a stall selling meat and game. 'What shall we do for supper?'

'Venison? Duck breasts?'

'Ooh, that reminds me – Julia and Roland are getting divorced.'

'How on earth does that remind you? Isn't Julia the one with the long face like a horse?'

'Neigh-neigh,' Sarah whinnied. 'The tall one with the smeary spectacles.'

'Oh, I know, with the husband who always talks to your bosoms and it makes you think you've spilled something on your top?'

'Yes, them. Shall we go for the venison?'

'Good idea. So why are they getting divorced, then? God, aren't other people's marriages so much more fun to discuss than—' She turned to the stallholder. 'Can we have two packets of the diced venison, please?'

'Because they stopped loving each other.'

Eleanor gave a snort. 'Well, that's hardly a reason! God, you'd have no married couples left at all if everyone threw in the towel just because they'd stopped adoring each other.'

Sarah said nothing, just rummaged in her bag for her purse.

'Oh, well – you two, sure, but you're not normal. Ordinary mortals, I mean.'

'Come on, Mark and I argue and get on each other's nerves.'

They drifted on to a stall piled high with autumn fruit. 'Have you considered having an affair?' Sarah said.

'Sssh!' Eleanor dropped her voice. 'I barely let Roger see me without my nightie done up to the top button – I'm hardly going to let a total stranger ogle my cellulite and greying pubes, am I?'

Sarah patted her own tummy.

'Mark can't even see my greying pubes because my tummy is in the way, lucky him!'

Eleanor laughed.

'Anyway, now promise me you'll do more wood engravings with Hannah gone? I love our two: the one of the pond with the ducks, and that one with the huge oak arching over the path. People always ask about them, you know.'

'Thank you. I was hoping to have more time with them both away...'

'Could you ease up on the gourmet meals for Roger every evening so you'd have a bit more time and energy left for yourself?'

'But he works so hard; he likes to have proper food when he comes home.'

'Ha! Mark considers himself lucky if his ready-meal isn't still frozen in the middle.'

'Well, he's very lucky to have you for a thousand other reasons – who cares about the catering?'

'So your logic is what? That Roger's not so lucky to have you, therefore you must make perfect banquets to compensate him for his sub-standard wife? Bonkers!'

'Yes. No. I don't know.' Eleanor tried to think. 'You know how I was brought up. My mother took charge of all things domestic. Not that my dad even noticed really – he would quite happily live in a tent as long as it had bookshelves.'

'But that's *their* generation. Most men we know at least cook supper once a week or empty the dishwasher or something.'

'Roger tames the garden. I wouldn't expect him to cook as well.'

'El?' Sarah's face looked suddenly very young and anxious. 'Do you think it'll be OK, with just the two of you...? Sorry, should I not ask? It's none of my business – tell me to sod off if you like.'

'Don't be daft. Ask away.' Eleanor fiddled with her zip. 'Look, I'm not pretending that everything's perfect. Every marriage has its problems—'

'I know.'

'It's just...' She burrowed down into the upturned collar of her coat. 'What's the point in working oneself up into a state about it? Roger has plenty of merits: he's generally very reliable, he mostly means well and he does love me. Plus, he's not mad, alcoholic, or a wife-beater. What more is reasonable to expect?'

'Well, personally I think that's a fairly low standard to have to meet. Can we go for coffee yet? I'm freezing.'

'I'm so glad you cracked first. I need cake.'

'It's not self-indulgence – we're supporting the local economy.'

'The business rates are bound to be horrendous round here. Should we have a cream tea, maybe, just to help them get by?'

'You're very thoughtful that way. Come on.'

Just outside the tearoom, Sarah turned suddenly and hugged Eleanor.

'I'm just worried about you, that's all.'

* * *

Suppertime. The combination of delicious food, good wine and the pleasant tiredness earned by a long afternoon walk slowly worked its magic. The conversation ambled easily this way and that, with no particular direction or focus, just an unhurried ramble along a network of meandering and criss-crossing paths.

'*Where* did you say you bought this wine?'

'... read about it in the *Sunday Times*...'

'... well, while they're not strictly speaking a legitimate expense, one could...'

'... those brambles at the back of the garden...'

'... should have bought there fifteen years ago...'

'... really wish she'd do more wood engravings, don't you, Roger?'

'... she actually put the bottles in her bloody wellingtons!'

'Did Tom call earlier?'

'I wonder what Hannah's up to.'

'... give more of your hard-earned cash to the Government than you have to?'

'Daniel loves it there, but we've no idea if he's doing any work ...'

'... any more mash?'

'... very good investment...'

'You can Skype Hannah from here if you like.'

'Don't be a complete pig, Markie. Save some room for pudding too.'

'...she sent these incredible photos...'

'The cream's in the fridge.'

'Was that really the second bottle?'

'What's the time difference?'

'Should I put it in a jug or do we not care?'

'Who wants coffee? Eleanor, herb tea?'

As they sat in a mellow daze of wine and candlelight, Eleanor said, 'Sarah and I were thinking we might take a quick dip in the sea tomorrow.'

'Yes, care to join us, chaps?' Sarah squeezed Mark's arm. 'Or are you too chicken?'

'Cluck, cluck.' Mark flapped his elbows. 'Way too chicken. It'll be freezing.'

'Have you *completely* lost your marbles?' Roger reached for the coffee pot and topped up his mug. 'It's not a matter of being "chicken", it's a matter of common sense.'

'We thought it might be fun.' Eleanor sipped her herbal tea, looking down into the depths of her mug.

'Fun! What's fun about catching pneumonia?'

'You know Sarah and I used to swim in the Hampstead ponds every weekend, and it won't be—'

'*Exactly. You *used* to swim there. Fortunately, sanity has prevailed and you haven't been for months.'

'Ah, don't rise to it, Roger. They're having us on. They'll jump about on the beach shrieking, then run off to the tearoom.'

'No, we won't!' Sarah gave him a playful shove. 'That's so unfair.'

'Not unfair.' Mark put his arm around Sarah's waist and pulled her close. 'Mean but accurate.'

'You're practically fifty years old, darling. You'll give yourself a heart attack.' Roger removed his glasses and started to polish them. 'It's sheer folly.'

Eleanor stood up and started clearing away the coffee cups.

'I'm sure there's a perfectly adequate heated swimming pool somewhere nearby,' Roger called through.

Sarah came into the kitchen.

'Well, I'm still up for it if you are.' Sarah lowered her voice. 'But I'm not fussed if it's... awkward or whatever for you.'

'I think...' Eleanor's voice sounded detached, almost robotic in her ears, '... that I would *really* like to go for a swim in the sea.'

They came back into the dining room.

'We're definitely going.' Sarah laid her hand on Mark's arm. 'If you don't believe us, you can stand on the shore and watch.'

'I'm certainly not encouraging you both by being an audience.' Roger stood up and gave a massive yawn.

'Still, you have to admit they're brave at least, Roger?' Mark leaned back in his chair. 'Crazy, yes, but brave.'

Roger snorted. 'I've never understood why reckless behaviour is so often considered to indicate courage.'

In the kitchen, the dishwasher door slammed shut.

* * *

Sunday morning. Eleanor and Sarah stood on the shore. In the end, the husbands had elected to go to a nearby pub for a pre-lunch pint while the women braved the ocean.

'If we're shivering now, how cold will we be once we get our clothes off?' Sarah said.

'You stay here if you like, but I need to do this. I don't know why really, but I *need* to.'

'Right, come on then.'

They tugged off their boots and jackets, jeans and jumpers until they were down to their swimsuits underneath. Eleanor looked at Sarah in her bright blue costume with white polka-dots and a small frill of a skirt around the bottom, then down at her own functional black Speedo, devoid of frivolity.

'Oh my God!' Sarah cried out as a small wave splashed over her bare feet. 'Shit, we may be about to die. Roger was right.'

Usually Eleanor took her time getting in, but now she simply ran straight into the sea and launched herself headlong. The cold slammed into her, snatching her breath away. She surfaced with a gasp and struck out with strong strokes away from the shore, then turned to swim parallel to the beach, letting the waves lift her body, swimming fast to try to keep warm.

Sarah, not such a strong swimmer, swam a few token strokes, then quickly scrambled out again and scurried over to their pile of towels and clothes on the deserted beach.

Eleanor trod water for a minute, and turned to look out to the open sea and the steel-grey sky stretching to the horizon in a vast arc. She was no more than a speck in the scheme of things, of no greater significance than a single, sea-smoothed pebble or a tiny seahorse. The thought held no fear for her, no disappointment even. It was as it should be. The sea would keep rolling in regardless of whether she were there or not; the sun would set, the moon rise; the world would turn. Around her, the waves rose and fell. She could just keep going, until the cold and the weariness got too much... then let go... surrender to the sea... descend to the cool, blue-green depths. Her body would be embraced by tendrils of seaweed; limpets would cling to her; sea-creatures would colonise her. The images swam into her head, oddly comforting. Already, the cold was making her numb but it wasn't unpleasant. There was no need to think any more, no need to try. She took a deep breath, then leaned forward and started to swim away from the shore.

'El!' Sarah was shouting from the beach. '*Eleanor!*'

Eleanor stopped and turned round, lifting her head up to see what was the matter. Sarah was right down by the water's edge, waving and beckoning frantically. 'Come in! El, come back! Come *back!*'

Eleanor looked at her friend for a long moment. She looked suddenly very small, hunched in her towel, her wet curls hanging round her head. It reminded her of taking the children to the beach when they were little, wrapping them up in towels, cuddling them close, the smell of salt and suntan cream on their skin, their lovable little faces close to hers. The *children*.

'Come in *now!*' Sarah yelled.

Eleanor swam back in quickly and picked her way up the stony beach to Sarah.

'What's the matter?' Eleanor asked. 'Why all the shouting? Are you all right?'

'Yes. I thought – you – sorry – I...' Sarah tried to put a towel round Eleanor but her hands were shaking. 'I was worried you – you seemed – I thought you – you must be getting too cold. El?'

Eleanor could feel her friend looking at her but she didn't meet her eyes as she briskly dried and dressed herself, then together they hurried back up the beach.

* * *

After a pub lunch, Roger said they had better be making a move. The journey had been so bad on Friday evening, and he was anxious not to endure a repeat performance.

It was grey and drizzly on the way home and the traffic was foul anyway, despite their early departure. Eleanor could feel Roger's irritation expanding, filling up all the available space in the car until she could barely breathe. She imagined opening the car door and stepping outside, saying casually that she had decided to walk to London instead, picturing the expression on his face. Disbelief? Anger? Scorn?

Roger fiddled with the radio, giving each station barely more than a second before moving on to the next one.

'Would you rather listen to your audio book?' Eleanor suggested.

'You haven't heard the beginning. You won't know what's going on.'

'I'll catch up. Go on if you'd like to.'

'Well. Thank you. Yes.' He smiled at her. 'But could you...?'

'I promise not to ask annoying questions about who anybody is or what's happened so far.' She smiled back.

'Good girl.'

True, she had no idea who was who or what was what, and it was a thriller with what seemed to be a gratuitously convoluted plot. Still, the actor reading it was very good, with a warm, mellow voice; it was like listening to a cello piece if she just let the sound and timbre sink into her. She relaxed back into her seat.

'It was a good weekend.' Roger patted her leg. 'I'm glad we went.'

'Me, too.' She rested her hand on his for a moment.

Back at home, they had supper on trays in front of the TV, an occasional treat they allowed themselves. At ten o'clock, they watched the news headlines, then Roger clicked off the TV.

'Let's go up then, darling?'

'It's still early. Don't you want to watch the rest of the news?'

'Well. I thought we might... you know.' He raised his eyebrows. 'Remember?'

'Oh, of course. Yes. That's right.' She stayed on the sofa a moment longer. She really had hoped to see the full weather report for tomorrow at the end of the news.

Eleanor took their plates through to the kitchen and loaded them into the dishwasher. Poured two glasses of water to take up. Went to the freezer to take out two portions of a homemade casserole for supper tomorrow. Set out cups and plates and cutlery for breakfast. Cloth napkins from the dresser drawer. Watered the houseplants on the kitchen windowsill. She really ought to trim that little weeping fig – the shape was awfully lopsided...

'Darling? Are you coming?' Roger called from upstairs.

'Just coming now! Sorry!'

She checked the front and back doors were locked then slowly climbed the stairs to bed.

13

PARTS OF THE PUZZLE

Even now, after so many years, Cecilia was loath to admit that she rather enjoyed making mosaics. It appealed to the less obvious facets of her character, that diligent, clever, rather painstaking schoolgirl she had once been before she had rebelled against her conventional parents. She liked the puzzle-making and solving elements of it, seeing the fragments come together in her mind then, tangibly, before her eyes – pointillist patches of colour and tone coalescing into an image. She had always been rather dismissive of her own mosaics, though whether this was pre-emptively because she feared other people would dismiss them as mere craft rather than Art with a capital A, or because they had been her only lucrative creative endeavour over the years, she could not be sure.

Outwardly, she had always championed the value and significance of crafts. How typical it was, after all, that the fruits of women's creativity should be undervalued, relegating all those exquisite patchwork quilts, lace so fine and intricate it looked as if it had been worked by angels, beautiful embroidery... tapestries... basketry... all dismissed as merely decorative, or perhaps useful yet devoid of meaning. Men's work, by contrast, was exalted for its epic themes, its seriousness, its scale – the giant canvases of Turner, the lumbering bronzes of Henry Moore. Small wonder that men's work survived when it was kept in the hallowed, hushed halls of national galleries while women's work gathered moth-holes, cobwebs, mouse droppings in dusty drawers and mouldered, forgotten, in old cupboards.

While she banged the drum for the cause, a bit of her also believed that mosaics were 'not proper Art' or, rather, only felt of value if they were ancient. No one dismissed Roman ones for being just attractive tiled floors, did they? Once an artefact had been buried and then unearthed two thousand years later, it became something else altogether, uplifted by the patina of age and history.

At her friend Ursula's, over a cup of rooibos tea and a regrettable wedge of worthy flapjack, Cecilia attempted to resist her urgings to take on a mosaic commission for a wealthy friend-of-a-friend; apparently, the woman had been wowed by the large frieze of Adam and Eve on the end wall of Ursula's patio, which Cecilia had done some ten years before.

'I'm very busy. I'm not sure I could take on anything large,' Cecilia said. They both knew this wasn't true but Ursula, good friend that she was, let the remark slip by unchallenged.

'Go and take a look, at least. She lives in this unbelievable house in Hampstead. Pots of money from her divorce settlement.'

'She'll want something ostentatious and vulgar, won't she?'

'Almost certainly.' Ursula shrugged. 'Go and see her. Think of a figure then treble it. If she says no, you're no worse off. And you can have a good nose round her art collection. She's got an original Hockney. A Lynn Chadwick sculpture in the garden.'

So Cecilia had gone and had a tour of the house and the art, while sipping some incredible wine. The woman wanted a mosaic of Poseidon on her bathroom wall. Cecilia had nodded in a thoughtful way, while thinking: God, how naff, what a shame money can't buy you taste. Still, the bathroom could be beautiful. Would be if she could keep bloody Poseidon out of it. If she wanted mythical marine clichés, she ought at least to go for mermaids... hmm... yes... strong female icons... sexy... powerful... triumphing over poor, pathetic men... that ought to appeal to a newly divorced woman...

Cecilia walked over to the wall in question, then turned to face the woman.

'I wonder...' she scrabbled in her bag for a small sketchbook so she could draw what she had in mind, 'I wonder if something more female and sensual in here might be more intriguing?' She found herself talking very animatedly about what would work... perhaps a ragged edge as if the mosaic had been only partially excavated from the wall behind?... Colours ebbed and flowed in her mind... she swept her hands up and over the wall, weaving a picture of the mermaid – beautiful, solitary, victorious... perhaps the shore here, snaking into the foreground... the waves... the rocks... and over here possibly some suggestion of a semi-drowned man...

Still, she had no intention of taking it on. It might take a month or more and she couldn't be bothered really. She'd ask for some ridiculous sum and the woman would say no, and then Cecilia could go and have a nice proper coffee in one of the innumerable cafés in Hampstead, then maybe cut through to that side of the Heath and sit by one of the ponds to draw the birds or the children feeding the ducks.

'The thing is,' Cecilia began, 'it is a large area and I don't use an assistant, you see, so it would probably take a good six to eight weeks.'

'It's fine. There are three other bathrooms. But this is my en-suite so it needs to be fabulous.'

'Right. Um... good. I meant, you see, that it would therefore be quite, er, costly...' God, how she hated this bit. She tried to tot up in her head roughly how much it should be if she calculated it at, say, four days a week for six weeks, though actually she was pretty fast once she got going.

'Well, whatever. Ballpark figure?' The woman named an extremely large sum.

Cecilia paused. Blimey. What a thing to have so much money to throw around. Well, in that case, maybe she should do it? She tried to think what she might do with the money, standing there mute.

The woman must have assumed that Cecilia was affronted by the offer so she amended it upwards by a sizeable chunk.

'That should be fine,' Cecilia said quickly, before she could change her mind. It was *thousands* of pounds. More money than she had made in the whole of the previous two years. She'd give some of it to the girls to buy a second-hand car to share.

'Do you want some up front? For materials and so on? A third?'

'Yes, that's usual, thank you. Do you want to see preparatory sketches first?'

'Sure. Just email them to me.'

'Er...' Cecilia had no idea how you could email a sketch. Perhaps the woman thought she drew on a computer? Yeuch. 'I don't actually use a computer. I don't do email.'

'You don't have email?' The woman looked at her as if she might be mentally defective, then she laughed. 'Oh, you artists! I suppose it's a distraction from being creative or something, is it?'

'Something like that.' Cecilia nodded, though in fact it was nothing to do with that. Some while ago, Olivia had brought round her laptop to teach her mother how to use one, but Cecilia had ended up feeling horribly inept and stupid, like when she'd had to learn about logarithms at school. She couldn't apply herself if it was something that she found completely devoid of interest. The on button didn't even say 'ON', for goodness' sake, just had that silly circle with the line like a partial clock face. It was ridiculous. What sort of designer had come up with that? In the end, she had given up. It wasn't as if she needed a computer, after all. If she had one, it would just be another technological thing – like the cordless phone, the DVD player, even her bloody digital radio that she didn't understand – to go wrong.

After her coffee, she walked through to the Heath, found a bench by the first pond and sat watching the ducks and the coots. Her thoughts spun and wove in a delirious tangle, first diving into a succession of colours plucked from sea and sky – cerulean, turquoise, aquamarine, peacock, lapis lazuli, kingfisher, sapphire – then, with a flush of guilt, thinking about what she could do with the money. She wasn't very *au fait* with how much things cost, but she was pretty sure it would be enough to build a simple studio-shed in the garden with a good sum over for the girls. She wouldn't admit it to them, of course, but she was finding it harder and harder to use her studio at the top of the house. Her left knee made a noise like a creaking cellar door in a horror film and she feared it might be arthritis. Arthritis! Like old people have. If she told the girls, Olivia would have her on the waiting list for a knee replacement, and there was really no need. Bollocks to all that.

14

THE MAN WHO WALKS INTO TREES

Saturday morning. Andrew had already had tea and a bowl of Weetabix ('It's important to keep yourself regular,' his mother said, prompting Andrew to bury his head in his bowl as if he needed to examine his cereal in extreme close-up) at home with his parents but had managed to extricate himself – 'Just popping to the library to do some work' – to go to a café to read the papers in peace. Fortunately, as his mother had never got to grips with exactly what his job involved, she did not question how he might accomplish much work in a library; his father, surely, had twigged that Andrew just needed time out. Andrew told himself that he was merely imagining the beseeching look in his dad's eyes – *Take me with you!* – and managed not to do a hop, skip and a jump in the hallway as he headed for the front door.

Already, after only a couple of weeks, he had elected a particular café nearby, called simply Froth, as his favourite. Although it was trendier than he would usually go for, the coffee was excellent, it had deep, squashy sofas you could sink into, and plenty of free newspapers. He disliked the bobbly modern lamps that descended at different heights from the ceiling like a gathering of UFOs hovering in space, and the orange Perspex stools you got stuck with if you didn't manage to get there in time for a sofa or a proper chair. But this morning he woke up thinking about their banana muffins and, while he told himself he was a sad sod to be having a fantasy about food rather than sex, still, food was unquestionably easier to obtain and, in the absence of sex, a banana muffin was about as good as it was likely to get.

Ah-ha, a covetable corner of a sofa was free at one end of a big table and he colonised it immediately, marking out his turf with his jacket on one side and his laptop on the other, though he might not even open it. It was just a prop, he knew, as he was here on his own: look, I am a busy, important person who needs to check my emails and stay on top of my jam-packed life at all times, not a sad git who has no girlfriend to come out with me for coffee on a Saturday morning.

Andrew tried to catch the eye of the pretty Spanish waitress who sometimes served him, but she was covering the other side of the room today, and it was the annoyingly good-looking designer-stubbly waiter who came over instead. His blond hair was swept forwards and to one side as if he had stepped out of a cartoon in a high wind and been left stuck that way.

'Yuh?'

'*Good morning*,' Andrew said pointedly. 'Could I have a cappuccino, please? And a banana muffin.'

'Not a problem!'

Andrew tried not to grind his teeth in annoyance. Why would it be a problem? It's a café, serving food and drink. I haven't asked for anything problematic, have I – a pot of yellow paint and a stepladder? He went and fetched a newspaper and sat back down.

The door opened and *she* came in: the woman he had seen in the street a couple of weeks ago when he had impressed her by walking into a tree. She hesitated, scanning the room – luckily, it was pretty packed this morning – then took a step towards him. He smiled encouragingly in what he hoped was a friendly yet unintrusive way.

'Are these two seats free?' She gestured at the orange stools at the end of the table.

Two seats. Bugger.

'Yes. Help yourself. Please.' He wondered if he should offer her his prime corner seat on the sofa, or would that be too much? It might scare her off. Besides, any moment now, surely her ultra-tall, ultra-handsome boyfriend would come in and then Andrew would be perched awkwardly on a stool while she and her boyfriend snuggled cosily in the corner together and he'd feel like a right prat.

'God, these stools are just ridiculous, aren't they?' she said. 'Fine if you're an eight-year-old boy; hopeless if you're a woman with hips.'

'Oh, sorry. Would you like to swap?' He started to gather his belongings.

'No, no. I'm sorry, I wasn't hinting, honestly. Just... you know... whingeing pointlessly.' She smiled. 'Number One leisure activity for the English.'

He laughed appreciatively and she smiled again.

And what a smile. He looked back, drinking it in. She was not just attractive, as he had first thought, but beautiful, with creamy skin and green eyes. He looked away suddenly, aware that he had been staring at her gormlessly.

'I suppose the stools are to deter customers from lingering too long?' he said, attempting to stay in the ring.

The waiter bounded up to take her order, and set down Andrew's coffee and muffin with a cheery, 'There you go, mate.'

'Well, good morning, good morning! And how are *you* today? Haven't seen you in here for a couple of weeks.' He took his time, Andrew noted, with a range of unnecessary questions and comments: would she like extra hot water with her tea, what type of milk would she prefer, excellent choice, the almond croissant, they were especially good today and not long out of the oven so still warm, was there anything else he could get her? That's a lovely scarf, really suited her, brought out the colour of her eyes.

He hadn't bothered with any of that friendly chit-chat with Andrew. The penny dropped. He was chatting her up. What a creep. Honestly. Men. No wonder women were always complaining about being harassed. Couldn't a woman even go to a café without some smug lothario hitting on her? At least *he* wasn't like that. No, he respected women, knew when to give them a bit of space, not to keep bothering them when they clearly just wanted a few minutes' peace. Yes.

Still, he had seen her before, albeit only in the street. He could perhaps mention that: Excuse me, you do look slightly familiar. I wonder if...? It sounded lame, a contrived chat-up line. For God's sake, he was thirty-five, why wasn't he better at this by now? He'd barely progressed since he was fourteen. What do other men say? Her scarf *was* nice, but he couldn't compliment her on that. She'd think he was just copying the waiter. He wished he'd thought of it first, then dismissed that idea. Besides, then she might think he was gay.

He caught her eye, smiled, then quickly looked away and stirred his coffee, trying to think.

'Excuse me,' she said, 'this is going to sound like an awful line, but you do look incredibly familiar. I wonder if...?'

'Yes!' He grinned as if he had just won the lottery. 'I saw you in the street the other day. In Eastern Avenue?'

'That's it! I knew I'd seen you somewhere. You're the man who walked into a tree.' She smiled.

Great. I'm the man who walks into trees. Still, at least she remembers me.

'Yup, I've been practising it as a comic turn. It's nearly perfect now.'

'I thought you had it nailed pretty much. You could probably take it on tour.'

'Coming soon to a venue near you...'

She laughed, then turned to the waiter, who had begun putting down her tea with an elaborate degree of care, repositioning her teapot, milk jug and cup in front of her. He left, then scooted back after a second and a half with her almond croissant.

'And here's an extra napkin for you, Beautiful.' He set the napkin on the table as if delivering a crown on a velvet cushion. 'Enjoy your almond croissant.'

My God, the man was practically drooling into her cleavage. He was completely shameless.

'Thank you.' She beamed up at the waiter. 'I intend to.'

Bloody hell – why hadn't *he* called her 'Beautiful'? After all, she was. Look at her: she was practically glowing with pleasure. He could have made her feel like that with a single word. There was no copyright on the word. But he hadn't said it... because... because... it would have sounded contrived and kind of creepy, and it wasn't the sort of thing he would say to a woman he'd only just met. Still, no sign of handsome boyfriend yet so he could say something else, something that wasn't too obviously flirtatious, something low key and normal, yet sparkling with wit and cleverness. Or, in the absence of that, just something. Anything. He returned to stirring his coffee. Anything at all, Andrew, but say something.

'So, do you live around—' he began, and she turned towards him, smiling.

A swirl of bright pink coat and clashing scarlet scarf and red leather satchel swept in through the front door and straight up to their table.

'Hello, hello, yes, I know I'm late.' The woman in pink bent to kiss the beautiful one's cheek. You could see at once that they must be related, although this one had dark hair and was shorter. 'Can we move? I hate these stools. Here—' There was a man on the other side of the café turning round to gesture for his bill, though he was still seated. She swooped in like a hawk, and with a huge smile and a, 'May we? Thank you so much. That's so kind', commandeered the table. The man found himself standing up and heading to the counter to pay, his half-drunk coffee still in his hand, looking both pleased and bewildered as if had been kissed and slapped at the same time. 'Liv! Liv! Over here. Come on.'

Beautiful turned and smiled at Andrew with a shrug.

'My sister.' She gestured with a nod of the head. 'An irresistible force of nature.'

'Have a nice... croissant,' he said. Is that *it*? Is that really your best chat-up line? Dear God, man, get a grip.

'It was nice talking to you.' She nodded. 'Um... see you around?'

'Yes.' He attempted to lever himself upright, but the low, squashy sofa defeated him and he subsided once more rather than mortify himself further by an undignified scramble to his feet. 'Yes, you will. I will. See you around. Definitely. Yes.'

She gave a half-laugh then, though whether because she liked him or felt sorry for him and his hopeless ineptitude, it was impossible to tell.

15

MOSAIC MERMAID

Sketches approved, here Cecilia was in this huge house in Hampstead, working away. Best of all, the owner had explained she'd be back in Florida for most of the winter – Cecilia tried not to think of her as a goose flapping across the ocean in her horrid leopard-print leggings – but the housekeeper would pop in every day anyway to clean the house and water the plants and feed the cats, so she would prepare something simple for Cecilia's lunch. Cecilia had said, ah, yes, good, as if this were a perfectly normal thing: a housekeeper coming in to leave her a blissful roast beef sandwich or a chicken salad with a clingfilmed platter of perfect, sliced fruit for afterwards as if she were in a fancy hotel.

She'd had a field day choosing the tesserae, had floated round her supplier buoyed on a delicious cloud of cash, knowing that for once she could choose anything she fancied.

The girls, bless them, seemed almost more excited about the commission than she was, and not just about the money.

At brunch, Olivia had said, 'Good for you, Ma,' and kissed her on the top of her head as if Cecilia were the achieving daughter and Olivia the proud mother. She'd given them all the advance money left over once she'd bought the materials; the studio could wait until spring. So nice to be able to give them something without having to go back to her ex-husband with a begging bowl.

At six o'clock each day, she stopped. Partly because, even though she rarely started much before noon, still it felt like a long day as the work was so intense, and partly because, even after all these years, it was at this time of day that she allowed herself a brief reverie about DH. It was almost like a prayer, a telling of a rosary – this interlude on the cusp of day becoming evening when she succumbed to the bittersweet temptation of remembering. She allowed herself only a few moments for each thought, pausing at each image: the first time she ever saw him, being in bed with him, the way he lit up like a little boy when he was talking about something he loved, his deep, wonderful voice in her ear, his strong hands hot on her skin, his unexpected tenderness, and, at last – unbearable – his tears.

As always, after a minute or two, she let the memories flit away, like a child releasing a butterfly back into the summer breeze.

* * *

On Sunday, the girls came to brunch. After they'd eaten, Maddy asked if she could rummage in her mother's stash of wool and fabric scraps. Madeleine made knitted and appliqué cushions with quirky, stylised animals on them, which she sold online and at various craft fairs across London. She said she was looking for something in a very particular shade of green, partway between eau-de-Nil and chartreuse, she thought. Olivia took the opportunity to excavate the hall table, which was a repository for unopened post, unwanted takeaway menus and fliers, and stray items that Cecilia hadn't got around to returning to their proper places. She held things up from time to time for Cecilia to pronounce judgement.

'Broken Javanese shadow puppet?'

'Ah, yes, that's going to Thalia. She's promised to mend it for me.'

Olivia sighed and set it down again.

'Note on old envelope about your apple tree?'

'Hmm? What note?'

'From someone wanting to talk to you about your apple tree at the back. Have you dealt with this already? Presumably not?'

'Oh, don't think so. Someone came round a while ago. I presumed the problem had gone away.' Cecilia returned to the basket of wool.

Gosh, she'd forgotten she had that undyed Jacob sheep wool. Glorious. Perhaps there would be enough to knit a beret or something?

'So, do you want me to deal with this, Ma?'

'Would you really?' Cecilia stroked the hank of wool in her hand. 'You know I'm hopeless with that kind of thing. Thank you.'

Olivia came over to peer into the basket.

'God, what a tangle. Doesn't it drive you mad having to disentangle it every time you want to extricate something?'

'Oddly, I think I rather enjoy it. I do have my methodical side, too, you know.'

'Ha!' Maddy snorted. 'That's a well-kept secret, for sure.'

'I don't know. Like with your mosaics, I can see there's a sort of cross-word-puzzle element to it alongside the creative bit.'

'Exactly. I'm really enjoying making my mermaid one. There is great satisfaction in creating an orderly whole out of chaos. Bringing disjointed fragments together to find meaning. Very *Gestalt*.'

Her daughters exchanged a look. *Gestalt* was one of those words that would set them off into an oh-mother! alliance, along with many others, such as Jungian, Kleinian, loom, intercourse, miso paste, rooibos tea, soy milk, evening primrose oil... Ah, well, let them have their fun – she didn't mind.

'Well, I wish you'd employ your methodical side to sort out the kitchen,' Olivia said. 'I'm struggling to see an orderly whole in the midst of the chaos.'

'Oh, *you*. Life's too interesting to waste it in tidying up.'

'That sounds like a platitude you'd find printed on a tea-towel,' Olivia said.

'I hate tidying up.' Maddy tugged out a skein of wool.

'Really? I had no idea. I've barely noticed, despite sharing a flat with you. I always thought all that mess was caused by leprechauns making mischief in the wee small hours.'

'Still, you take the point, Olivia? Tidying is not inherently interesting.'

'No, it's not. But I like knowing where my things are. I don't think I'm especially tidy, but I find being around too much clutter and chaos unsettling. It's not relaxing.'

'I wonder if perhaps you have OCD?' Cecilia said.

'Oh, Mum, come on. She's not that bad.'

'Of course I don't have OCD. I'm just averagely tidy.'

'I wouldn't want to be averagely anything,' Maddy pronounced.

'You know what I mean. When I lived with Alex, our flat was pretty tidy. It was nice. You could actually sit down without having to shift a pile of papers from the chair first. It was restful.'

'Ah, Alex – he was a lovely boy. Whatever happened to him?'

'Mum! Sssh!' Maddy frowned at her mother and mouthed 'Remember?' at her. Oh yes, he was the one who'd dumped Olivia for someone else and made her move out as his parents had paid for the flat. Well, these things happen. She'd grown up a lot since then. Life was all about learning really.

'Anyway, I've got to be off now, Ma. Anything in particular I should know about the tree?'

'What tree, dear?'

'This! The apple tree.' Olivia was waving a scrap of paper. 'I'll call them.'

'I'm not cutting it down! I'll camp out in the branches if I have to!'

'Remain calm, Swampy. Good luck with your mosaic mermaid.'

16

A PROPER PERSON

After she had seen Roger off to work, Eleanor zipped round the kitchen, loading the breakfast dishes into the dishwasher, wiping the kitchen table and worktops, giving the enamel sink a scrub. Then she rushed back upstairs to tidy the bedroom, fold Roger's pyjamas, wipe his tooth-paste spittle off the bathroom mirror, and apply her minimal make-up before leaving for work. Today, it was one of Eleanor's volunteering days at the Conservation Trust, a small charity that offered expertise and guidance to residents and architects wanting to adapt or extend local period buildings. There was no compulsion for her to arrive at a partic-ular time, as she was unpaid, but she liked to get in early anyway and was always one of the first ones in.

This morning, as soon as she arrived, the Director, Rachel, asked Eleanor if she could pop in to see her.

'Of course. In five minutes?' Eleanor's heart sagged as she took off her coat and hung it up. She supposed Rachel was going to say they didn't really need her any more. Or maybe it was to do with that report she'd drafted on the area's hedges; Eleanor had spent ages on it, but now she worried that she must have got the wrong end of the stick and it wasn't at all what was wanted. She'd been working there for the best part of a year and had gradually been given more and more complex tasks, not just admin any more but attending site meetings and writing reports and doing research. Truth was, she loved it there: the work was fascinating and she liked the people, who were not unlike herself – quiet, meticulous, thorough – who saw nothing tedious in discussing the detailing of a front door for forty-five minutes; people who understood the deep satisfaction in working hard to arrive at something that was exactly right. Roger found it puzzling, this devotion to work that wasn't even paid, so no doubt he'd be relieved when he came home and she had to tell him they no longer wanted her.

Eleanor nipped to the loo to check her face in the mirror. It looked pinched, as if she were trying to be brave in the face of bad news. Well, that was right. She suddenly had the awful feeling that she might cry when Rachel told her, that she might sob uncontrollably and beg to stay. She cranked a smile to her face – don't be so *silly*, Eleanor – and went and scooped up her notebook and pen, and knocked on Rachel's office door.

Rachel came out from behind her desk and gestured for Eleanor to join her at the round meeting table. Clutching her notebook in front of her like a shield, Eleanor smiled tightly, already biting the inside of her lip.

'Now, you know that Siobhan's going off on maternity leave in February?'

Eleanor nodded.

'Well, we wondered if you'd be interested in covering for her? As a paid position.'

'*Me?*'

'Yes. The thing is – and feel free to say no, of course – but we'd need you three days a week really, same as Siobhan does now, not just two. And I could only offer it to you as a maternity cover position as Siobhan is entitled to come back later if she decides to.'

'But why would you want me? I mean, aren't you advertising it? For a proper person?'

'Oh, Eleanor, you are funny. I don't think I've ever encountered anyone before so refreshingly devoid of ego.' Rachel smiled at her with affection. 'Do you really not think you are "a proper person"?'

'But I'm not being modest. Surely I don't have enough experience?'

'Eleanor, trust me. You understand the work, you're efficient, capable, precise and never get flustered. And you're extremely diplomatic, which, in this place, counts for gold bars. It's invaluable with prickly home-owners, architects, planning officers – you must know that? You help us get the right results, and everyone comes away feeling that they've scored some sort of victory. It's a rare gift.'

'But... but...' Eleanor knew there must be plenty of other objections but, for now, she couldn't quite put her finger on what they were.

Rachel briefly outlined the pay and other benefits.

'And, of course, there are one or two short training courses we could send you on, if you'd like to do that. It might give you more confidence.'

'Well.' Eleanor could feel herself flushing. 'Yes, then. Yes, please. I'd love to do it.'

'Wonderful.' Rachel stood up to return to her desk. 'And is the timing OK? You mentioned you might go on a cruise in the New Year?'

The *cruise*, oh God, the bloody cruise. Roger had started rhapsodising again about the supposed joys of a cruise yesterday, but she'd deflected him by pointing out a squirrel in the garden starting to dig up his precious hyacinth bulbs and he'd dashed out to chase it off.

'Well, my husband is very keen to go on one, but we'd be back by then, I'm sure. Anyway, it's not booked yet. With any luck, he may change his mind!' Eleanor laughed.

'Don't you get any say in it?'

'Oh, yes.' Eleanor felt herself blush and looked down at her notepad as if a better response might be written there. 'Yes, of course he lets me have a say. I mean, I do have a say, of course I do.'

'Good. I'm very pleased you want the job, Eleanor. We all think a great deal of you, as I hope you know.'

'Thank you.' She turned to go, then had a thought. 'Oh! I suppose I should... I ought to... to, ah, run it by my husband, shouldn't I?'

Rachel raised her eyebrows. 'I'm afraid I have no idea about these things. I've always managed very well without a husband, but I suppose some people like to have one around the place.'

Eleanor laughed appreciatively.

'Well, I probably should ask him. Tell him.'

'Up to you. Let me know on Monday then?'

'Yes. Yes, I will.'

* * *

She mustn't let herself agonise about telling Roger. It made no difference in the end anyway. Either he'd be fine with it or he wouldn't. Tying herself in knots and fretting about how best to sell it to him would just make her more anxious. And waiting wouldn't help either, tempting though it was to stave it off till the last possible moment on Monday morning when he'd be heading out the front door to drive to work. She had visions of standing in the hall and saying, 'By the way, the Conservation Trust has offered me a proper job. Three days a week. Paid. And I've said yes. Have a good day!' And slamming the door.

Still, as she put the final touches to supper, sprinkling the beef stroganoff with a handful of chopped parsley as if she were light of heart, she thought perhaps she might wait until dessert. By then, Roger would have had two large glasses of wine and, if she waited for the influx of sugar from the poached pears to kick in, it should all be fine.

She poured his coffee and pushed the little jug of cream towards him, as if tentatively offering an unworthy sacrifice at an altar.

'And what about you, darling? Did you do anything nice today?' Having run through the minutiae of Roger's own day over the course of supper. 'Was it a conservation thingy day? I can never remember.'

'Yes, it was. And guess what?'

'Oh, darling, I've no idea. Somebody wants to put a hot tub in their back garden? Pull out a hedge and erect a fence? Something that set you all spinning in circles of indignation, no doubt! Honestly, I can't see what all the fuss is about half the time. If someone wants to enhance their property, stick on a conservatory or whatever to maximise their investment, so what? An Englishman's home is his castle, etc., eh?'

There was no point in having this sort of conversation with Roger. She had tried before, on more than one occasion, but he didn't really understand why you might want to encourage people to keep their front hedge rather than grubbing it out to replace it with a wall. For him, a house was solely an owner's business; thoughts of context, history, wildlife, the whole streetscape were entirely irrelevant.

'They've offered me a job. Part-time. Paid.'

'A *job*? Whatever *for*?'

'Well.' Eleanor fiddled with the corner of her napkin on her lap. 'Rachel said she thought I'd be good at it. It's only three days a week and it wouldn't start till February. I'd still have lots of time to... to take care of the house and everything.'

'I've no doubt you'd be *good* at it, darling. Of course you're very competent. That's not what I meant. I meant – what *for*? It's not as if we need the money, is it? Am I not giving you enough? Honestly, darling, you should have said. I know women's little needs are expensive – hair salons and toiletries and all that sort of thing. I want you to be able to treat yourself to a nice dress, a silk scarf, whatever you like. What say I up the amount I transfer to the joint account for your personal expenses each month? I'm very happy to.' He raised his coffee cup to his lips, smiling.

'No, it's not that.'

Roger stopped smiling and lowered his cup.

'I mean, thank you for the offer – that's very kind – but it wasn't about the money really. It's the work itself. I like it there. And it's only three days a week, so barely more than I'm doing now.'

'Is it that you're a bored little bunny?' He patted her leg and made his mouth into an exaggerated pout. 'What with both the kids away now?'

'Well, a little, I suppose.' Digging her fingernails into her own palms; wishing she were brave enough to reach across and pinch him instead.

Roger sniffed.

'I trust you warned them you'll be away in the New Year for a while on our cruise?'

'Of course. And I said I needed to speak to you first before I could give them an answer.'

Roger nodded.

'I suppose it's all right then. If you must. I presume the pay is an absolute joke?'

She told him what the pay would be and he laughed.

'Charities! Honestly, they're hopeless, aren't they? No wonder these places are always staffed by bumbling amateurs! Oh well, you go and have fun with them, darling, bossing people about their extensions and their windows if it makes you happy.' He shook his head, laughing, and drained his coffee.

17

HAPPY FAMILIES II

1973–1977

When Benedict is six or seven, he pushes another child down the garden steps that lead from the terrace to the lawn.

The screams ring round the garden and Conrad springs out of his study to see who is murdering whom. Marcia and the other boy's mother are fussing over the child – Conrad can't remember the woman's name; she is an irritating, fluttery sort of a woman, all eyes and giggles and pretending to be even dafter than she actually is, though Lord knows she is not over-burdened with intelligence so why she feels the need to assume this mantle of absent-minded silliness, he has no idea. The child does seem to have quite a bit of blood on his nose, mouth and on his T-shirt, but Conrad is aware that these things often look more dramatic than they really are.

Marcia calls to him, 'Could you bring some ice, darling? Wrapped in a cloth. Quickly.'

He strides back towards the kitchen. Marcia has become quite good at giving specific directions rather than uttering vague pleas for assistance.

He returns with the ice, wrapped in one of their finest damask napkins, which is all he could find.

'Oh, I meant a tea-towel or something! Not this.' Marcia looks at the white damask as if at a dying bird then at the child's bloody face. Conrad pulls out his cloth handkerchief, fresh this morning at least, tips the ice into it and hands it over without comment. Marcia clamps it firmly to the bridge of the boy's nose.

'He p-p-pushed me!' says the bloodied boy, between sobs. 'On *purpose!*' His outrage is unmistakable.

Marcia directs the fluttery mother to hold the ice in place, then draws Benedict to one side.

'Benedict, you *didn't* push him, did you?' She takes him by the arms. 'You would *never* do such a thing, would you?'

'I didn't do it, Mummy.'

'Do you promise, my darling? You wouldn't do anything so *wicked*, would you?'

'No, Mummy, I wouldn't.' Benedict puts his hands behind his back. Conrad spots him crossing his fingers. God, but he's convincing. 'We were just playing. On the terrace. Then he fell down.'

The temptation to shop his own offspring is very strong. Conrad wonders what Marcia would say if he said to the other boy – what *is* his name? – 'Poor you. Very sorry and all that. Perhaps you'd like to shove Benedict down the steps, too?'

'I see,' she says. 'Well, then.'

'You do believe me, Mummy, don't you?'

'Of course I do.' She leans forward to kiss him on the forehead. 'Please promise me to be more careful next time, won't you?'

'Yes, Mummy.' Benedict bestows one of his winning smiles on her and she echoes it back to him.

Conrad thinks, after a time, that the other child never did come back to play, but he couldn't swear to it. They are all rather interchangeable at that age: mostly a source of noise and irritation. Not a huge loss, then, but Benedict's willingness to lie is another matter. Conrad will attempt to speak to him later, explain the importance of telling the truth, especially to one's parents. He would rather know the truth, even if unpalatable, than be told a lie. He is not entirely sure that the same holds true for his wife, but surely she will understand that they must present a united front over something like this?

Eleanor, by contrast, is admirably self-governing on the whole. At bedtime, she stretches up to kiss each parent good night and takes herself off to bed. When she was little, he read to her almost every night, and she was an appreciative audience, begging him to do different voices for the characters, pleading for 'just one more page, Daddy, one more page,' but once she could read well herself, he considered it better to encourage her rather than have her listen to him. She often reads while drifting about the house, driving Marcia into fits of exasperation as the child is not looking where she's going and will surely cause an accident. When Eleanor can get away with it, she has a book open on her lap during meals, something that Conrad aches to do himself but accepts that children need a good example to follow when it comes to social norms. Still, he turns a blind eye until Marcia spots that Eleanor is not eating because she is glued to a book yet again and whisks the offending volume away to a high shelf until Conrad retrieves it at bedtime. When he pokes his head round his daughter's bedroom door each evening, more often than not she is still reading, even if she can barely keep her eyes open. He dips to kiss the top of her head, whispering 'Good night, Small Book,' and gently taking her book to place it on the bedside table. 'Good night, Big Book,' she murmurs, slipping into sleep.

* * *

When Eleanor and Benedict fight, Conrad is sometimes called upon to intervene if he is unfortunate enough to be at home at the time. Marcia would knock and enter his study in the same beat, without waiting for his imperious, 'Come!' as she usually would. He knows it would be unreasonable to bar her from his study altogether but he wishes he could somehow explain that having her there sets his teeth on edge and makes him feel as if all the calm, rational molecules in the room have been shaken about and are now whirling around in pointless circles.

'It's the children,' she'd say. 'You have to *do* something. You can't hide in here all day. Come out and be a father for once!'

Conrad would physically separate them, direct them to chairs on either side of the room, then deliver what amounted to a sermon on whatever he felt to be the heart of the matter.

'Every human being has these base impulses,' he says on one occasion after an especially ferocious battle. 'It is entirely natural to want – at times – to hurt, punch, strike, even kill, another person. I am not asking you to pretend to be a saint when you are not.'

'How on earth is this helping?' Marcia appears in the doorway. 'There's a time for philosophical deliberations, darling, and a time for laying down the law surely?' She sighs and returns to polishing her family's silverware.

'My *point*,' he continues, 'is that one of the key characteristics that distinguishes humans from other animals is our capacity to make conscious choices. We may *desire* to kill our sibling; we are able to *choose* not to do so. I leave that thought with you.'

Benedict, who has been rolling his eyes and making faces at his sister throughout, slouches off, leaving the words unabsorbed behind him.

Eleanor sits in silence for a while, then asks, 'Is it really all right that I sometimes think my life would be nicer if Benedict didn't exist?'

'Ye-e-e-e-s.' Conrad wonders if perhaps his wife is right and he should simply have given them both a sharp smack and told them not to do it again. 'But...?'

'But it would be wrong to try to harm him?'

'That's correct.' He looks at her, trying to read her. She is a funny little thing, rather serious and sort of... opaque. Self-contained. 'Do you understand why?'

'Is it because I could be sent to prison?'

'Well. That's one very good reason, certainly. But not the only one. And I think most prisoners would tell you that going to prison has ruined their lives. But also, if you hurt another person, you might injure them irrevocably and—'

'What's irrevocably?'

'Irreversibly. Something you can't undo.'

She nods and he sees that she has squirrelled it away for future use, a word worth saving, like a beautiful shell found on the shore.

'Also, you would be lessening yourself.'

'Why would I?'

'Because...' He draws up a chair and sits down close to her. 'Because if you act in a way that is... hmm... not just bad but significantly worse than *your own* idea of yourself, you will sacrifice your self-respect, your sense of yourself as a worthwhile, decent person. I believe self-respect is very important and it is not something I would choose to give up just to satisfy a passing whim to hurt someone else.'

A little frown crosses her face and he can tell that she is mulling it over, turning it around in her head to see it from all sides.

Then she gives a small nod and says, 'I see.'

* * *

The children are absolutely forbidden to come and bother Conrad in his study if the door is closed, as it usually is. Nor are they to enter if he is not there. There is, he reminds them, nothing they could need that could not be obtained elsewhere in the house. Scissors, pencils, paper, sticky tape, interesting books, etc. – all are available for their use but not from his study.

Early one Saturday morning, however, he comes across Eleanor sitting in his office chair, twisting this way and that, gazing into one of the drawers in his desk. She doesn't seem to be looking for anything in particular and when he asks her what on earth she thinks she is doing, what part of the word 'private' does she fail to understand, she looks up at him with puzzled brows and a sad mouth.

'But I want to know what it feels like to be *you*.'

Although this is clearly just a fanciful childish notion, her words surprise him and defuse his anger, so he simply nods and tells her to run along now and not to come in again without permission. Afterwards, he sits in his chair and looks into the drawer at the jumble of pens and paperclips, as she had done. He regrets having barked at her and wishes instead he had thought to pause and observe her. The thought strikes him that she is really quite an interesting child. No. An interesting *person*. It has not occurred to him before that children might be intelligent, amusing or diverting companions, people with whom you might choose to converse or spend time. He looks down into the drawer again, and twirls playfully this way and that in his chair. He shuts his eyes and suddenly spins the seat in a complete circle. For a few moments, he lets his mind spin, too, and wonders what on earth it might feel like to be Eleanor.

18

DEEP WATER

Sunday was usually a pottering sort of day. Sometimes Eleanor went to a farmers' market or an antiques fair, with Hannah tagging along when she'd still been at home, or with Sarah if she were free, while Roger stayed at home to work on the garden. Periodically, Eleanor helped in the garden, too, attending to the tasks Roger disliked: dead-heading the spent flowers, clipping the dwarf box hedges that flanked the path in the front garden, tying in the clematis and roses to the trellis – a fiddly job more suited to someone with patience and fine fingers. Today, however, Roger said he really ought to put in a couple of hours at the gym. Then he might go to a pub for a pint while he checked his emails before heading home for lunch. Eleanor fancied a swim. The chicken was already prepared with lemon and herbs, sitting in its roasting tin, and the potatoes were peeled and par-boiled ready to roast, so it would be easy to shove it all in the oven when she got back. She dashed upstairs to put on her swimsuit under her clothes.

Eleanor usually swam a couple of times a week in a public pool, but on a Sunday morning, it was likely to be very crowded. Today, the sky was bright and the temperature mild, almost spring-like. The bare trees looked as if they might be about to burst into leaf rather than ready to hunker down for the winter. Suddenly, the prospect of the pool seemed less inviting: the tang of chlorine in her nostrils; the antiseptic footbath you had to walk through between the showers and the pool, which always made her feel like a ewe being corralled through a tank of sheep-dip; the men hogging the fast lane even when they were poor swimmers. How lovely it would be to swim outside today, to hear birdsong and feel fresh air on her face. She didn't want to plough up and down a soulless tiled rectangle.

She started the car and drove to the narrow, tucked away side road where those in the know parked for the eastern side of the Heath and the swimming ponds.

Some time ago, she and Sarah used to swim once a week here at the Ladies' Pond on Hampstead Heath, but on every occasion Roger had made such heavy weather of it, asking what was so special about swimming in that muddy hole anyway, for God's sake, and wasn't it all just a bunch of men-hating dykes, they might as well call it the Lesbians' Pond and have done with it? And then a woman had died of a heart attack at the pond and Roger had put his foot down and forbidden her to go again, saying it was ridiculous, absolutely ridiculous, this obsession with the pond, it was far too cold for a normal person. Sarah, never quite as keen in the first place, hadn't wanted to carry on without her.

Now Eleanor took out her mobile and sent Sarah a text:

Sorry I haven't called. At the heath now. Going to swim in our pond. Wish you were here. Come if you can. Much love – E x.

In the past, she had first swum in summer, then as the water gradually cooled through autumn, it prepared you so that you could carry on right the way through winter, if you had the will and the nerve to do it.

She hovered outside the entrance to the pond for a minute. It was silly really. What did it matter either way? Eleanor felt almost guilty, as if Roger might be observing her via some hidden CCTV camera. She darted a look along the path in each direction, then took a breath and went towards the changing room.

There were three or four women there already. Eleanor quickly took off her clothes down to her swimsuit and pinned her hair up. She didn't bother with goggles here because the water was rather murky and you couldn't really see anything. Anyway, it was a pleasure to swim with your head above the water, so you could see and hear the pond and its environs: ducks waddling along the bank, the occasional heron poised absolutely motionless, the sound of women talking and laughing by the steps.

She checked the water temperature, which was chalked up each day on a blackboard by the changing room: 11°C. Much colder than a swimming pool, of course, but by now she was determined to go ahead. Eleanor sat on the edge of the platform by the metal steps and inserted one foot. Yikes! Still, after the first shock, the hideousness as the cold hit your waist, your breasts, your shoulders, if you got in and got moving you soon warmed up.

She slowed her breathing, then turned and lowered herself in. The first thirty seconds or so were always a bit of a horror, more so these days as she so rarely swam outdoors other than that time in Suffolk with Sarah a couple of weeks ago. Just as she was thinking – well, maybe Roger was right; this is daft really; I should just go to the swimming pool as usual – she noticed another woman, who looked familiar, hovering by the steps. Ah, yes, the swim-cap lady! She was wearing a plain navy swimsuit and a memorable swimming cap absolutely covered in three-dimensional unashamedly clashing fake flowers: yellow and pink and lime green and orange.

'How hideous is it today?' she called down to Eleanor.

'It's just balmy! Practically like a bath.'

The woman laughed.

'Oh, well, nothing ventured, I suppose...' She climbed down via the steps with a sharp intake of breath then trod water next to Eleanor. 'You look familiar – didn't you used to swim here?'

'Yes, I'm sure I've seen you before. I do love your hat.'

'Thank you. Why did you stop? Just too grim when it's cold?'

'Hmm. No, it wasn't that. Shall we swim to warm up?' They struck out side by side in a steady breast-stroke. 'Actually, my husband got freaked out by that awful case of the woman who had a heart attack here and he forbade me to come again.'

'*Forbade* you? What's it got to do with him? And anyway, she had a pre-existing heart condition, you know. If you're healthy, you should be fine.'

Eleanor glanced across at her and said nothing.

'Sorry, I'm very blunt. It's always getting me into trouble.'

'No, it's fine. You're right, though. I'm not sure that it is to do with him really.'

The woman smiled.

'And so what will the husband say when you tell him you swam in the forbidden pond today? Is he like Bluebeard? "Wife, you have broken the sacred eleventh commandment: Thou shalt not swim in the Ladies' Pond. I shall lock you up in the attic with the bodies of all my previous wives! Heh, heh, heh!"'

Eleanor laughed.

'I was thinking of getting round the problem by not telling him I've been here.'

The woman made a face but said nothing.

'What?'

'Nothing.'

'No, go on. You said you were blunt. What do you think? I'd like to know.'

'Really?'

'Yes. I'm... well, I'm not good at this sort of thing. With conflict, I mean. I hate arguing. I kind of had my fill of shouting and door-slamming when I was growing up and I can't bear it.' Funny how effortless it was at times to be truthful to a stranger. 'If I think he won't like something, I usually try to get round it somehow...'

'By doing it in secret so he won't know?'

Eleanor thought of the novel she was reading, now tucked in right at the back of the airing cupboard in the middle of a stack of laundered bedsheets.

'Yes.' She felt tears prick her eyes and she turned away for a moment. 'I realise that must sound awfully silly. It's just that I've got used to it being that way so I do it automatically, but now I hear myself saying it out loud, it sounds ridiculous.' Eleanor smiled at her. 'So, tell me then?'

'Well, you said it yourself. It is a little ridiculous. You're an adult. You're not seven years old. Presumably, he's not actually going to lock you up in the attic, is he? If I were you, I'd be asking myself if this was really how I wanted my life to be.'

Eleanor met her gaze, then looked away.

They swam one more circuit in silence. The trouble with other people is that they didn't understand. It was all very well to stand on the sidelines, making judgements about people and their lives and their marriages, and telling them how to make it better, but it wasn't the same as being *in* it.

'I'm sorry, I fear I've offended you.' The swim-cap lady said, following Eleanor as she pulled herself out. 'I really am a bull in a china shop.'

'No, it's fine. I was just getting too cold.'

'Me, too. I'm going for a hot chocolate to warm up. Care to join me?'

'Thank you.' Eleanor grabbed her towel to head for the showers. 'But, well, I should be getting back, really. I have to get the lunch on.'

'Right. Of course. Well, sorry again. I enjoyed talking to you.'

In the shower, Eleanor heard someone call out from the doorway of the changing room.

'Yoo-hoo! Are you in there?'

'Is that the swim-cap lady?'

'Yes. I just wanted to say, I'm really sorry I'm such a clod and I hope you come back soon. Whatever Bluebeard thinks.'

'I will!' Eleanor called out. 'I'm Eleanor, by the way.'

'Good to meet you! See you soon. I'm Cecilia.'

* * *

On the way back to the car, Eleanor's skin felt tingly and alive, her whole body fizzing as if her veins were rushing with clear lemonade. She had forgotten this feeling, how amazing you felt a few minutes after you got out of such cold water, as if every cell were dancing at the thrill of simply being alive.

She tugged out her mobile from her bag. There were a couple of texts: one from Sarah and one from her son, Daniel – a simple 'hi' followed by a question mark, his usual shorthand to see if she was free for a quick chat. They usually ate lunch quite late on a Sunday so there was no desperate rush to get the chicken on. Daniel almost never phoned home these days, in case his father answered. There had been a falling-out over his choice of degree: Roger had tried to steer him towards science, whereas Dan had wanted to study history. 'What's the use of it, for God's sake, Daniel? You're young – you should be looking to the future, not the past. Or go and do accountancy training. Something with some sort of relevance to today's world, at least!' In the end, Daniel had stuck to his guns, taken out a student loan rather than accept any money from his dad, and the two – never close at the best of times – were now stuck in a stand-off.

'Hey, Mum. How are you doing? And how's the *Gauleiter* behaving without us there to look out for you?'

'Now, now. He's fine. Anyway, tell me what you're up to and when will you break up for Christmas?'

'Oh yes, I can give you my dates and all that, but first, do you promise me you're really OK?'

'Of course I am. I'm absolutely fine.' Her conversation with Cecilia in the pond rose to the surface. *If I were you, I'd be asking myself...* Well, you're not me. Eleanor pushed the thought back down. It really wasn't at all helpful. 'We pootle along together in our middle-aged way perfectly well.'

'As long as he's not bullying you?'

'That's a bit harsh.'

'Is it? Really?'

'Well, I think it's just that your dad doesn't handle... dissent terribly well. He can't understand it when other people don't see things exactly as he does. It's more of a slight shortage of imagination and empathy, perhaps, than a deliberate intention to bully.'

'That's complete crap, Mum, and you know it. Only you could possibly put such a generous spin on it. He absolutely has an intention to bully. Look how you always end up going on holiday to hot places even though you hate the heat!'

'That's not true. We went to Yorkshire once.'

'Exactly – *once!*' And I remember he moaned about the weather almost the entire time we were there, so he spoiled it for the rest of us anyway.'

'Well, never mind that now. Tell me what you've been up to.' And then they talked happily about Dan's current flatmates, his fabulous girl-friend, Alice, and the band he'd just joined as a singer. At the end, he rang off with a cheery, 'Love you, Mum!' and left her feeling happy.

She opened the text from Sarah then, wondering if she might be annoyed as they hadn't spoken for a couple of weeks.

Nothing to be sorry for. I've missed you. Can't swim now but supper next week? Much love, S x

* * *

At lunch, Roger asked briefly if she'd had a nice swim and she said yes, then the conversation inevitably turned back to him and his workout at the gym and how he'd talked to one of the personal trainers about devising a targeted programme because honestly, darling, he didn't know if she'd noticed at all but he was really getting quite a paunch these days. Then he detoured onto assorted inadequacies of the gym, shocking, given how extortionate the membership fees were, how the lockers should include those fixed-in hangers, given that some members, such as himself, obviously wanted to hang up their jacket properly, and then onto how disgusting some men were, failing to wipe their sweat off the machines with their towels after use even though there were clear, laminated signs indicating that you should do precisely that. Eleanor agreed that it was certainly a very poor show and indeed people so often didn't follow reasonable standards of behaviour, did they, while wondering if she might have some laminated signs made herself to pin up around the house: 'Please hang up your towel after use', and 'The dishwasher is not merely ornamental – feel free to put your dirty dishes in it', and 'Please rinse out your cafetière before I hurl it at your head', and offered him some more roast potatoes.

It wasn't until much later, as they were getting ready for bed, that Roger suddenly called from the bathroom where he was flossing his teeth, 'Was the pool crowded this morning?' She could hear the little click-click sound as he flicked the floss between his teeth. 'Full of rowdy kids jumping in and peeing in the water, etc.? Really, darling, join a proper gym! The pool's not large at my one, but at least it's clean and isn't teeming with the great unwashed British public all the time.'

'I don't mind the public pool...' She paused. Really, she was being daft. She'd been mulling over what the swim-cap lady had said that morning and realising she was right: Eleanor was a grown-up. How silly to be hiding something so trivial from her husband.

'Actually, I went for a swim in Hampstead.' She pulled on her dressing gown over her nightdress and glanced towards her husband in the bathroom. 'At the pond.'

'The pond?' Roger stopped mid-floss, looking at her via the mirror. 'But we agreed that you weren't going to go there any more.'

'Well...' Eleanor tied the cord on her dressing gown, looking down as she made the bow as if she needed to see what she was doing. 'You weren't keen on it, I know, but there was no real reason not to go.' She straightened up again. 'And I just fancied it today. So I went.'

'But I'd *told* you not to. I was extremely clear about it, darling. That woman had a heart attack. It's just not safe. Especially at this time of year. It's practically freezing. Another few weeks and it'll ice over, I should think.'

'No, it was fine.' There was no point in telling him that the water had been pretty cold as that would rather prove Roger's point. 'Besides, she had a heart condition, apparently.'

'I can't believe you went there after I'd expressly told you *not* to, Eleanor. It's most unlike you. What on earth were you thinking of?' Roger stood in the doorway of the bathroom, holding the floss taut between his hands, as if he might suddenly lunge forward and attempt to strangle her with it.

'I just felt like going. I know you're only concerned for my welfare, but I don't see why it's such a big deal.' Eleanor slumped onto the stool in front of her dressing table, defeated, and reached for her cleansing lotion and a cotton-wool pad.

'It's a "big deal", Eleanor, because we had discussed it and you agreed not to go. You knew I would only worry about you if you went. It's just so selfish. You're *my* wife, the mother of *my* children. I need to know I can trust you to be safe and sensible.'

Eleanor felt her face flaming. She accepted that she was far from perfect but she didn't believe she was selfish.

'I think that's unfair. And you didn't worry in any case, because you didn't even know I was there until just now.'

That was the trouble with people like the swim-cap lady. Life was easy for people like that: they just went ahead and did whatever they felt like, and to hell with the consequences. Eleanor knew now she should have stuck to her original plan and not told him. Her tactics had been honed over years and usually worked perfectly well; what was to be gained by suddenly dragging the truth into things? Where was the benefit?

Roger turned away from her and retreated further into the bathroom.

'I think that's the *end* of this conversation, Eleanor. There's to be no more swimming in the pond.' His voice had a slight echo as it bounced off the cold, hard tiles of the bathroom. 'I, for one, do not want to have to explain to my children that their mother has dropped dead from a heart attack because she refused to see sense.' She could hear him tugging open the mirrored cabinet above the basin once more, then a clatter as he presumably tried to shove the floss back and some items fell into the basin.

'For crying out loud, this fucking cupboard is full of crap we never use. Eleanor, if you have a *minute* tomorrow, could you possibly – if it's not too much *trouble* –' his tone openly sneering now, '... see your way to clearing out some of this shit in here so that a person might actually be able to find something without having half a pharmacy jump out at him. That would be marvellous. *Thank you.*'

Then the sound of his nostril-hair trimmer started up and he banged the door shut.

Eleanor looked in the mirror and smoothed on her cleansing lotion and started to wipe it off. She leaned forward a little, noticing another line on her forehead, the slight sag around the jawline. Dragged the cotton pad over her face once more, and again. She had a sudden vision that perhaps she could just keep on, wiping and wiping, until she had erased not just her make-up, but everything, her wrinkles first, then even her skin, her flesh, her entire self, until there would be nothing left and Roger would emerge from the bathroom, his nose now pristine and perfect, and see nothing but her dressing gown, empty and lifeless, pooled on the floor.

19

THE SCARLET LETTER

Sunday morning. The birds were singing, the sun was shining, and Andrew was full to the brim with one of his mother's outsize breakfasts and multiple cups of tea. He leaned back in his chair and let his mind wander. Vicki has had over a month without him – long enough, he hopes, for her to have missed him. After all, didn't he bring her a cappuccino in bed every morning? Didn't he take out the rubbish and sort the recycling without needing to be asked? Didn't he check her tyres and even fill up her car with petrol? And there were plenty of other things, too, like rubbing her feet while they watched telly together, or going downstairs to confront a possible intruder when Vicki heard a strange noise. It was long enough for her to have missed him but not so long that she might be used to it and starting to think she really was better off without him.

Vicki was always in a good mood on Sunday mornings. She'd probably be meeting friends for lunch later at the local gastro-pub, as they usually did, though it was getting harder to find other childless couples. Andrew and Vicki had lived together for less than two years. When he'd tentatively raised the topic of marriage and children, Vicki had said that, while those things were absolutely on her long-term schedule, they didn't feature on her near-time horizon as she was only thirty-two. When Vicki didn't want to talk about something, it was as if a heavy blackout curtain had been drawn across the subject, with not a glimmer of light remaining. Andrew, now familiar with this approach, knew better than to attempt to fling open the curtain once it had been closed, and he had let the matter drop.

By now, Vicki would have had time to think again. She would be feeling his absence as a noticeable hole in her life and in her house (it was, unquestionably, Vicki's house; he had moved in, he paid for all the food and half the bills, but it was her domain). Who would deal with any spider that dared to scuttle across the gleaming kitchen floor? Who would change the halogen bulbs in the kitchen, which she couldn't reach, even teetering on tiptoes on a kitchen chair? Who would bolt the top bolt at night (she couldn't reach that either)? Who would carry the heavy shopping in from the car or mow the lawn? Yes, she would surely be missing him by now. He smiled at the thought, allowed himself to muse on her pretty face, the funny way she ran when she went jogging with her feet flopping out at an angle, the way she was so sweetly appreciative when he prepared the fruit for her breakfast smoothie each day.

'Fabulous breakfast, Mum.' Andrew put his dirty plate and cutlery in the dishwasher and kissed his mother on the cheek. 'That's set me up for the day.'

'Well, I do like to feed my boys properly, don't I?' Mrs Tyler wrung out a cloth and began spraying and wiping the kitchen table with a degree of vigour appropriate for removing an influx of the plague. His dad, enclosed behind the wall of his Sunday newspaper, murmured his assent.

'I'm just popping back to see Vicki.'

'Hmph!' She removed the butter dish and set it down with a clunk on the worktop.

The newspaper was folded back to one side.

'She expecting you?' his father asked quietly.

'Not especially. Why?'

'Maybe best give her a call first?' The newspaper spread out again so Ron's disembodied voice drifted over the parapet. 'Show her you're considerate, like.'

'It's no biggie. I'll say I've only come to pick up some of my stuff.'

Mrs Tyler sniffed and started returning the breakfast accoutrements to their allotted places at some speed and with perhaps more force and sound effects than strictly necessary.

'If she's any sense at all, she'll be begging you to come back,' Mrs Tyler told the mixer tap. 'She doesn't know when she's well off, that one.'

There was a small rustle from his father's newspaper but no comment.

'She'd better hurry up before someone else snaps you up.'

Andrew put his arm round his mother and gave her a squeeze.

'Aw, Mum, that's really sweet. Thank you.'

'Not at all. It's just a plain fact. These days you're a good catch, Andrew. You've a steady job, and that's not to be sniffed at. Be glad you don't work for a bank: you might be put out on the street tomorrow like a bag of rubbish.'

'Well...' There was no point attempting to converse with his mother about the banking crisis. 'You're right,' he conceded. 'It's very steady.'

* * *

On either side of the front door, two ornamental urns had appeared, planted with crisply clipped balls of box encircled by assertively yellow pansies. The urns were large enough and fancy enough to merit taking up residence outside a grand old pile in the country, but were possibly a tiny bit over-ambitious for a red-brick semi in Whetstone, albeit one with a through-lounge, a leather corner suite, and enough space for three cars on the front drive. Or, rather, there would normally be space for three cars, but now, next to Vicki's metallic purple Mini, was a large convertible Mercedes in gun-metal grey straddling two spaces.

Andrew parked his own dusty Renault on the road and got out slowly. The Mercedes glimmered in the feeble sunshine. Andrew had less than zero interest in cars, but even he could see that here was a thing of beauty. There was not a scratch on it. Who in London managed to keep a car completely free from dents and scrapes? He cast an eye down at the number plate: COOL 1.

The side-gate through to the back garden was wide open and Andrew could hear the heavy drone of the lawnmower. Surprising. Vicki didn't generally like doing that sort of task because you could so easily break a nail and it left your hands oily or dirty. He supposed he ought to ring the doorbell, but of course she'd never hear it from the back with the mower going. God, this was ridiculous – only a little while ago they'd been living together, sharing a house, a bed, a coffee-maker – it's not as if he'd come to nick the garden furniture. He walked down the side path and called out a cheery hello so as not to give her a fright. The buzz of the mower had stopped. He came face to face with a man in navy chinos and a bright orange polo shirt. Not just a man. Vicki's boss, Ian Sutton.

'Oh. Ian? Er, hello. Hello again.' Andrew had met him a few times at office parties or if he'd occasionally picked Vicki up from work. 'I was looking for Vicki.'

'Andy, isn't it?' Ian clasped his hand firmly and clapped him on the back as if they were good mates. 'How's it going?'

'Andrew. Is Vicki here?'

Ian nodded towards the house and rolled his eyes.

'Making herself beautiful upstairs. Women, eh? What can you do?'

Andrew found himself grinning and nodding in agreement, chaps together. True, it had always taken Vicki an age to get ready, but Andrew felt he was missing something, as if he'd come in when the movie was already halfway through and he'd skipped some critical piece of the plot. Maybe Ian's business wasn't going well and he had taken on part-time gardening work to... to... supplement his income? Maybe Vicki was already finding it all too hard without him and Ian had kindly offered to help her out a bit? The way you do... pop over and mow a subordinate's lawn.

Ian had dazzling white teeth and a year-round tan. Vicki had said ages ago that all 'the girls' at work found their boss 'a complete and total hottie', but that he was also 'a perfect gentleman' and never stepped out of line. Andrew stood on the patio, hands in his pockets, wondering what to do. Should he recline on one of the sun-loungers, to show how very much at home he still was? Or perch casually on one of the unfeasibly heavy teak chairs? Ian's leather jacket was hung on the back of the nearest one and Andrew poked it with a finger as if he were a small boy intent on provoking an animal.

Ian brushed himself down to remove any stray bits of cut grass.

'I'll go and see what she's up to,' he said. 'How long does it take to powder your nose, for Chrissakes?' He laughed and clucked his tongue, then slid open the patio door, slipping off his annoyingly perfect loafers as he did so. Andrew sidled over to the gap and poked his head in. Hmm. Still looked the same. Everything perfectly neat and tidy. Fresh flowers –

stiff yellow roses – in that grotesque orange glass vase, though. Vicki wasn't a fan of fresh flowers, with their tendency to drop leaves and petals and pollen all over her shiny surfaces. He could hear footsteps on the stairs and he sprang back from the opening and stood surveying the now striped lawn. Ian reappeared and they stood there side by side.

'Nice job.' Andrew nodded at the lawn. He said it as if he were an authority on such matters, as if in fact he often went round the country judging lawns and the quality of the finish. He thought about shoving Ian to the ground and pounding his head to a pulp on the patio.

'Cheers. Soon knock the garden into shape, I reckon.'

What the fuck was that supposed to mean? It was already in shape under Andrew's attentive curatorship, extremely in shape.

'Take up this patio.' Ian tapped his foot on the paving slabs. 'Get some decking down instead. Decent bit of hardwood.'

Andrew tried to think of something clever to say about decking but all he knew was that it seemed to feature on every single gardening makeover programme he had ever watched with Vicki, and he hadn't really been watching, not properly; he had usually been reading the paper at the same time because he hated makeover programmes. He thought about running Ian over with the lawn-mower and making nice stripes across his fucking horrible polo shirt.

'Bit last year though – decking – isn't it?' Andrew employed his mother's dismissive sniff. He gave a knowing laugh. 'I rather think garden design has moved on a notch since then.' He leaned back on his heels and nodded. Yes, he too could be a total arse when the need arose. Ian laughed, however, apparently completely unbothered by the put-down. He took a swig of his beer and didn't offer Andrew one.

'Well, I guess I'm no *expert*–' Ian paused over the word, allowing it to hang in the air, 'on –' he laughed again, 'ah, *garden design*.' He made it sound as if such an activity was fit only for lesser beings. 'Not much time for that sort of thing, I'm afraid.' The unspoken conclusion was as loud as if it had been bellowed across the now-immaculate lawn – *being a highly successful, well-paid fellow with a big fuck-you house and a spanking new Merc in your girlfriend's driveway. Ex-girlfriend's driveway.*

'And how is the – ah – "museum"?' Ian asked, making air-quotes with his fingers when he said the word, as if Andrew were really a spy or a drug-dealer, and being a museum conservator were merely a rather quaint cover story. Andrew toyed with the idea of crushing Ian's head in the sliding patio door while reminding him that the British Museum is the greatest 'museum' in the world, bar none, you perma-tanned creep. He pictured Ian looking up at him beseechingly while he, Andrew, Paper Conservator Extraordinaire, made air-quotes at him.

'It's fine,' he said, after a few moments.

Vicki appeared, looking all pink and perfect and neat and smelling of the expensive perfume Andrew had given her on her birthday.

'Andrew.' She nodded, and gave a very small, tight smile, as if she was doling out a strictly controlled ration.

'Vicki,' he responded. 'I've come for my stuff.'

'Of course. Come this way.' She click-clacked back along the path, gesturing at the garage, as if she were an estate agent giving him a tour of the property.

Any moment now, Andrew would say, 'So what the fuck's the deal with Ian, then?' He would tell her he's no fool, he can see what's going on, she can't pull the wool over his eyes. He would demand to know how long this has been going on. He would even raise his voice, if necessary, and be extremely firm with her.

Vicki pressed the remote and the garage door opened upwards. Andrew's remaining boxes were marshalled along one edge, each marked with a large red 'A' on a white label. It reminded Andrew at once of Hawthorne's novel *The Scarlet Letter*, in which the heroine, Hester Prynne, had to wear the letter 'A' stitched on the front of her dress – 'A' for 'Adulteress'.

'Ha!' he said, emitting a sound somewhere between a laugh and a snort. 'The Scarlet Letter! How very apt.'

But of course Vicki had never read it, or probably even heard of it, so the cutting reference just sat there pointlessly, cutting no one.

'Yes,' she said. 'The ones with the red "A" are yours. Obviously.' She looked at him as if he were ever so slightly stupid. 'Do you need a hand shifting them to your car?' She folded her arms and did not meet his eyes. He picked up the roll of white labels resting on top of a box to give himself something to fiddle with.

'No, thanks!' determinedly capable and cheerful now.

He dipped to lift the first box. Jesus, why was it so bloody heavy?

Books, no doubt. He tried to look as if his arms weren't about to snap in two from the strain and grinned at Vicki.

He was definitely going to say something. As he walked to and from his car, hefting the boxes, he tried out a series of nicely barbed gambits in his head: *So, I see Ian's got his smug loafers well under the table then?... So how long have you been shagging Ian?... Nice you've found a new hobby – fucking that smug Ian – did you give up on the Tupperware-collecting then? Just what was it that appealed to you most about him – his wallet or his car?* It had to be exactly right – sharp, wounding – something that conveyed that of course he knew exactly what was going on, had known for some time, in fact, but he simply didn't give a toss. He had such a rich, full life he was above fretting about such trivial things.

'How have you been keeping?' Vicki asked, as he settled a box into the boot.

'Me? I'm fine!' *La-la-la – why wouldn't I be? Sure, you've just ripped out my heart and kicked it around your stripy lawn like a deflated old football, but why wouldn't I be completely fucking fine?*

'Good. You're a decent man, Andrew.' She looked up and met his eyes at last. 'You'll find someone nice to be with, I'm sure of it.'

She said this as if his pet gerbil had just died but soon he would feel strong enough, hopeful enough, to toddle along to the pet shop and choose a new one and all would be well again.

'*I'm* sure of it.' He slammed the boot closed. 'Though I'm very much relishing being single actually. And there are – I have – very much – I have plenty. Plenty. Of things... happening. Irons in the fire. And so on. Yes, indeed.' He twirled his car keys with a cavalier recklessness and they spun off the end of his finger halfway across the drive. Shoulders slumped, Andrew walked over to retrieve them, and it occurred to him that perhaps turning up on a Sunday morning rather put paid to the idea that he was out wildly carousing with different women night and day.

'Well, I'm glad,' said Vicki. 'You deserve to have fun.'

Annoyingly, Vicki was refusing to be riled, for some reason. How very unlike her. Now he would bring her to her knees with a devastating one-liner. He would leave her feeling bruised and pathetic and, most important of all, guilty. It had to be perfect, though. He opened the driver's door and stood there, wishing he were sweeping into a chauffeured Rolls-Royce or at least a scratch-free Audi. There was moss around the window seals, he noticed. The footwell mat on his side was almost worn right through. For God's sake, surely he could at least get himself a new rubber mat? He would do that, yes, he would stop off at a garage on the way back and splash out on a new mat. Terrific.

'Leave any you can't fit in your car now,' she said, giving a small wave and moving out of the way. 'But please text before you come next time in case I'm busy.'

'Sure.' He nodded.

'Have a good day then. Take care.'

Here it comes. Verbal annihilation. He drew himself up tall, ready to deliver. He looked at her, at her neat hair, as she reached up to tuck it behind her ears, her tiny feet in her high-heeled shoes, her fingers fiddling with the gold chain she always wore round her neck, a present from her mother before she died. She looked like a child dressed up in her mummy's grown-up shoes.

'You too,' he said. 'Take care of yourself, OK?'

She nodded and waved and went back into the house.

He stood there for a moment. Thought about taking a leak down the side of Ian's smarmy car – God, that would be great! – then swivelled his head round and realised there was a fair chance of being seen by a neighbour and reported to the police. Still, he had to do something – anything – even a tiny gesture of... of... defiance.

He looked at the cocky yellow pansies in the urns and thought of ripping one up and leaving it right in the centre of Ian's gleaming car bonnet, letting sticky clods of soil mar the paintwork. Hmm. His eye caught the number plate again. God, of course. So obvious. Quickly, he went back to his car, rootled in the glove compartment for a black pen, and grabbed the roll of white sticky labels. A small amendment would clarify matters, he thought.

As he got into his car and started the engine, Andrew looked back at his handiwork, at the number plate now specially personalised for Vicki's perma-tanned paramour: FOOL I.

20

MOTION SICKNESS

She would tell Roger that she does not want to go on a cruise. Eleanor is a grown-up, after all, with her own opinions and wishes. Of course, many people would be thrilled at the prospect: staying in a comfortable suite with a sea view on a luxurious ocean liner for weeks. Gourmet meals and flowing wine, entertainment every night, cabaret, dancing, exotic destinations; it would all be absolutely delightful – if you liked that sort of thing. So why didn't she want to go? Eleanor rolled the question around in her head, like a marble in a maze, trying to find the exact spot where it might click into place. It's not as if she isn't fond of the sea, quite the contrary; she *loves* the sea, loves to swim in it, be part of its otherness for a spell, and she loves to watch it while sitting on the shore, is fascinated by the way it changes every second, the play of light on water, the power of it, the way it shifts from crashing against the rocks to the softest shushing sound as it strokes the sand. Perhaps it was simply that she suffered from motion sickness, so the idea of spending so long on a boat was unappealing? Although really it was nothing like as bad as when she was a child, and if she took a tablet an hour or so before, she was usually OK. But this was no ferry trip out to an island; this would be living on a ship every day and every night for weeks. Already she felt queasy at the thought.

Those vast ships are extremely steady now, she knew. Maybe it was the idea of being trapped with the same bunch of people night after night at dinner, whether you wanted to see them or not? She imagined the daily farce of ducking behind pillars and potted palms to avoid some awful man whose unstated mission is to bore her to death by explaining bloody hedge funds or some frightful woman with a braying laugh who wants to show off her Prada handbag.

But these were not proper reasons, reasons that had an empirical value, that would mean something to Roger. These were silly, Eleanorish reasons that would carry no weight. Still, surely it wasn't unreasonable for her to have a say in where and how she would like to go on holiday?

She would say to Roger, 'Darling, I've been thinking about the cruise. It's incredibly kind and generous of you but I've decided that I don't want to go. Can we discuss booking something else instead? A different kind of holiday?'

She picked the words over in her head, modifying the phrasing here and there. Was 'decided' too strong a word, perhaps? Should she focus a little more on Roger's generosity? Maybe amend 'don't want to go' to 'would perhaps prefer not to go' – adding a pause or two, so that she wouldn't sound too awkward or stroppy. Roger meant to be kind, of course. He wanted to treat her, to help her relax, give her a break. It's just that it was difficult for him, at times, to understand that... well, that not everyone is Roger, that another person might not have exactly the same likes and dislikes as he does.

So that is what she would say. The words cycled over and over in her head. The only difficult sentence really was the one about not wanting to go. She timed it. Four seconds. Four seconds out of a lifetime. She would say it and then the words would be out there, in the world, and she wouldn't be able to take them back and Roger might not be entirely happy and the infamous Cloud might descend – one of Roger's legendary black moods that engulfed the household from time to time – but then he'd let it go after a little bit... at some point certainly... and they'd book something else, a couple of weeks in Italy or something, and it would all be fine.

Roger came home from work late, at a little after half-past eight. She could tell he had had a bad day by the heavy thump as he slammed his car door in the driveway, and the excessive force used to shut the front door. Maybe this wasn't such a good day to raise the topic after all? He preferred it when she appeared in the hallway at once, but still she lingered, relishing these last few seconds of solitude. She waited a few moments more, pointlessly opening the oven door and shutting it loudly so that it sounded as if she were in the middle of some vital cooking task. Now he'd be taking off his stiff work shoes and abandoning them in the middle of the hall floor for her to tidy away while he put on his sheepskin slippers.

'Hello?' he shouted out, already sounding annoyed by her failure to be there to greet him at once. 'I'm home!'

'Just coming!'

Eleanor glided through to the hallway, paused to kiss his proffered cheek, hung up his coat and scarf, and said nothing as he went and plonked himself in his armchair in the sitting room, even though it was now twenty to nine and she was hungry and supper was not improving by being left in the oven all this time.

'Glass of wine, darling?' Her voice was bright.

'Yes.' He sank back heavily in his chair. 'Definitely. Is there any of that decent Beaujolais left?'

Well, no, she thought, because you finished it yesterday, so of course not, but no was not really a word Roger liked very much if someone else was saying it.

'I don't believe so, but there's a very nice bottle of claret. How about that?' She caught herself using her coaxing voice, the tone she would use to soothe a toddler out of a tantrum.

'All right. I really prefer Beaujolais. As you know. Claret can be so tannic.'

'This one is quite smooth, I think.'

'You don't even drink red!'

'No, but I read about it somewhere. It's supposed to be very good.'

'Oh, well, if the *Sunday Times* says it's good, then who am I – mere humble mortal that I am – to disagree with the experts?' He was mocking her because Eleanor was 'always' referring to things she had read in the newspapers.

She brought him a large glass and he sniffed it, then sipped it, gave a small nod.

'Um, supper's ready – any time you'd like it? Shall I...?'

'I'm barely in the door, darling. Give me five minutes, will you?'

'Of course. Sorry. I just thought you might be hungry as it's quite late.'

'Not especially. I had a huge lunch with a client. You go ahead and eat without me, darling. You know how you hate eating late. Go on. I'll have a snack a bit later if I want anything – some cheese or something.'

'Are you sure?'

'Yes, yes, you go on. Let me just chill here with the paper for a bit.' He picked up the folded newspaper from where it lay on the side-table waiting for him, stretched out his legs on his footstool.

The chicken breasts sat, shrunken and shrivelled, in their diminished pool of sauce. The gratin potatoes were cracked and dried out. On the kitchen table, a bowl of salad wilted. Eleanor stabbed a piece of chicken with a fork, added a spoonful of the potatoes and a pile of leaves. She tipped some homemade vinaigrette over her portion of salad.

She sat at the kitchen table and unfolded her cloth napkin, then got up again to fetch the book she was reading at present – a political biography. Roger could have called her to say he would be late, or that he wouldn't want supper after all. She could have eaten over an hour ago. She really hated eating late unless they were going out for dinner. She opened the biography and looked at the page. Her gaze travelled across the words, onto the next line, and the next. At the bottom of the page, she glanced back up the sheet of words and realised she had absolutely no idea what she has just read. Roger had pronounced the book fascinating and told her she really ought to read it, rather than silly short stories or poetry that don't tell you anything useful about the world, and so she had started to read it. But she did not want to read it. The thought struck her quite suddenly that she didn't care; she told herself that she certainly should care, surely most proper grown-ups would care, politics is so important, obviously, and no doubt it is extremely interesting how this man came to be an MP and then a member of the Cabinet, but really she didn't give a toss and she would rather hurl the book across the room, to hear the nice, resounding *whump* such a heavy hardback would make as it hit the wall.

I want to read a novel, I want to sink into another world and belong to it for a while. I'd like to be able to read a bloody book of my own choosing without lying awake in a cold sweat thinking that my husband will find its hiding-place.

A tear fell onto the page. And then another. No. Eleanor does not cry. It serves no purpose, after all. She snapped the book shut and quickly dabbed at her eyes with her napkin. She wasn't hungry any more. The chicken was stringy and dry, the potatoes parched and joyless. She poked a few salad leaves into her mouth and chewed them dutifully but suddenly felt like a sheep chomping on grass. Maybe she'd wait until tomorrow to say about the cruise? Maybe Roger would be in a more receptive mood tomorrow.

Do it now. Go on. *Now.*

She approached the doorway to the sitting room; hovered at the entrance.

'Would you like some more wine? Or anything?'

'Yes, a top-up would be good.'

She started to turn away.

'And have we got any nuts or anything? Nibbles? Those cheese crispy things I like?'

'There's still the chicken for supper if you're peckish?'

'I don't fancy all that, really. Anyway, you can have it for your lunch tomorrow, can't you, so it won't go to waste.'

'Mmm.' She retreated to the kitchen and returned with the wine and a small dish of salted almonds.

'Oh. No cheese crispy things?'

'Sorry, there aren't any.' Eleanor could picture them in their plastic tub in the kitchen cupboard. A tiny act of defiance.

He picked up his wineglass and shut his eyes.

Do it. Say about the cruise.

'Um... ' She came further into the room and perched on the arm of the sofa several feet away from him, suddenly realising that her prepared script would not do, would not do at all.

'You know, I was just wondering about the cruise... thinking about it a little bit... and... I mean, I happened to be thinking about it today and I—'

'No need to worry at all, darling.' Roger opened his eyes and glanced at her. 'It's all sorted. I was just about to tell you. Booked and paid for.'

'You've *booked* it?'

'You are a funny old thing, always fretting about everything.' He rested his head back again and smiled. 'You know you can rely on me, darling. I booked it today from work. Got Linda to do it, actually, as I was so busy. Just as I said. Suite with an ocean view. In fact, Linda managed to wangle us an upgrade so we've even got our own big balcony. She really is marvellous. Eight glorious weeks. I can't wait.'

'*Eight* weeks?' She felt faint.

'Yes, I know we thought four or five but might as well make the most of it while we're at it. And the longer one gives you such an incredible itinerary. Jolly lucky I can take so much leave, but I'm so on top of everything, of course, and Jake can follow up where necessary. Best time of year to go climate-wise – Jan, Feb – though obviously I know you'll miss the delights of the British winter.' He laughed. Roger liked to tease his wife about her love of crisp winter days and thick snow. 'Just think, we'll be able to sit out on our own balcony every night, sipping cocktails looking out to sea.'

'I thought we were still discussing it?'

Roger turned to look at her, perhaps unsettled by the unfamiliar tone of his wife's voice.

'We have discussed it. And I left the brochure out for you so you could peruse it at your leisure, with all the relevant pages correctly flagged.'

'I thought we would, I don't know, talk about it some more?'

'What would be the point in that?' Roger laughed. 'The only sticking point, remember, was over whether I'd be able to take so much leave. But Alan was fine with it. What else is there to discuss?'

'Well, it's just... you know... that's a very long time... and I have my – my own commitments – my work and the choir – and—'

'But it's not even a proper job, your conservation thingy, is it? More of a hobby, really.'

'But I said I'd take the paid position. It starts in mid-February. We won't be back in time.'

'Well, so you'll start in March instead. So what?'

'Because I *said* I'd start earlier.'

Roger sighed heavily.

'I can't imagine a couple of weeks either way will make a jot of difference, darling. And if they don't like it, you can always tell them to stuff their silly little job and get something else to amuse you once you come back from our trip, can't you?'

'It's not a "silly little job". It's important. And there's my print-making.'

Roger puffed out a sigh.

'Oh, that! Well, of course your "*Art*" must take precedence.' He took a deep drink of his wine. 'What it is to be an *artist*. Everyone else better just kneel at the altar of your creativity. For Christ's sake, Eleanor, take a fucking sketchbook or something. You'll have aeons of time with nothing to do, no house to take care of, no fiddling about in the kitchen, you can doodle away to your heart's content.'

There was a silence. She dug her nails hard into the palms of her hands. Tears pricked her eyes but she bit her lip to keep them in check.

'You see I thought I'd said that I wasn't sure... because of – of – well, partly the seasickness thing, I suppose... but not just that...' Her voice faded away.

'Oh, for goodness' sake, darling. How many times do I have to tell you? We're not talking about crossing the Atlantic in a pedalo! This is a state-of-the-art luxury liner. They have stabilisers. You would hardly know you were even on a ship. It's just like being in a top-notch hotel only with 360-degree views of the ocean. What's not to like? And there are plenty of excursions ashore. Honestly, it's not like you at all to be so ungracious. I thought you'd be over the moon. Anyway, you love the sea – you're always rattling on and on about how much you love it.'

'I'm sorry. I—'

'I work incredibly hard for the good of this family – for *you* – for this house,' he gestured around him at their capacious living room. 'You can hardly blame me for wanting a decent holiday every now and then.'

'No, of course not. You deserve a lovely holiday, of course you do.'

'Yes, I bloody well do.' He leaned back again and closed his eyes.

She withdrew silently. It was true: he had left the brochure out for her. She should have said something sooner, before he booked it. But she'd thought that he would talk to her properly first as it was so long a holiday and so expensive. They hadn't discussed it at all; he had talked about it a couple of times and she had listened. But she'd assumed he would raise the subject again and then that would have been the natural opportunity for her to voice any doubts she had. But he hadn't because...

because... well, because he was Roger and he wasn't prone to doubts. It must be wonderful to be so decisive all the time, always knowing exactly what you wanted without doubting your own judgement, your own feelings, just knowing.

Eight weeks. She put the leftover chicken and potatoes in the fridge for her lunch tomorrow, transferred the undressed salad leaves to a plastic tub. The leaves looked sad and tired, but they'd do OK for her. Eight weeks. She half-filled the kettle and clicked it on, her body going through the necessary sequence of movements like an automaton. Think of how quickly a single week zips by. Yes, that would be the way to manage it: one week at a time. Never thinking beyond the nearest weekend. *I don't want to go.* Sssh. Shut up, Eleanor, you're being silly. Lots of women would kill for a luxury trip like this. And Roger needs it, he works so hard. And then he would be so much more relaxed, wouldn't he, and easier, and everything would be nicer, so it was a good thing really, would be a very good thing, of course it would, of course.

'Would you like coffee?'

'Mmm.' He nodded, half-dozing now.

'So, um – when is the departure date then?'

'January the fourth. I'll get Linda to email you all the details and a link to the website. Take some time to look at it all properly, darling. They've got beauty salons and spas and so on, and you can book yourself some pampering – treatments – have your nails done. I know you ladies love all that. A cinema. Cabaret. Gym. Swimming pools, of course. Plenty of entertainment and things to do if you get bored of lying in the sun. I plan to barely move a muscle myself, other than the heavy lifting of a Mai Tai to my lips.' He laughed.

Eleanor has had precisely three facials in her entire life and perhaps half a dozen manicures. Even if she had a manicure every single bloody day on board, that would still leave her about twenty-three and a half hours to fill out of twenty-four. Roger didn't understand about sketching. She liked to draw the countryside. She liked to sit under a tree, completely still and silent, and draw sheep or cows sheltering by a dry-stone wall, ducks waddling towards a pond, a house hunkered down into the lee of a hillside.

She wanted to ask if he also thought to take out cancellation insurance but realised that 'wife doesn't want to go after all' was unlikely to count as a legitimate reason to cancel the trip.

Well, it was nearly two months away. Anything could happen between now and then. She tried to think of reasons why the trip might be cancelled but they were all things involving appalling catastrophes or disasters so she pushed the thoughts away and pulled on her rubber washing-up gloves. She wanted to talk to Sarah, and she didn't want to talk to Sarah; if she told her that Roger had gone ahead and booked the cruise, Sarah would be bound to give her a hard time for being so feeble. Eleanor knew it was feeble; she was an expert at holding a mirror up to her own shortcomings and berating herself for them, but she wasn't in the mood to hear Sarah getting exasperated with her. Anyway, it was fine. Or rather it would be fine once she'd had a couple of days to adjust to the idea, that was all.

* * *

Hannah usually did her best to call once a week from the school in a remote highland region of India where she, along with her two friends and two others, were teaching English to local adults as well as the children. There was no mobile signal but if you walked just a couple of miles or so into the village, there was a basic shop-cum-café that had a sporadic internet signal and you could make an internet call and download your emails if you didn't mind having half the village crowding round watching you while you did it. In another few weeks, the work part of the trip would come to an end and the three girls would travel to south-east Asia where there would be Wi-Fi in more places or at least internet cafés. So far, all their setbacks had been fairly minor: their bus broke down and they had to wait four hours for another, her friend Georgia's phone was nicked on the journey there; Hannah somehow lost her sleeping bag. But she sounded well.

'Hi, Mum. I just picked up your email. I take it you were having me on about the cruise, right?'

'No. Your dad's booked it. As a treat. Eight weeks. We'll get back not long before you do.'

'How is it a treat? He knows you hate boats! You get so sick.'

'Apparently, they have really good stabilisers now.'

'And all those awful people. Being trapped with them and feeling seasick at the same time! God, I'd go mad.'

Hannah's words were so exactly a perfect voicing of her own feelings that for a moment Eleanor wondered if she had spoken them herself.

'Well… they couldn't all be awful, could they?'

'As long as you are sure you're happy about going, Mum? Honestly, it doesn't sound like your bag at all.'

Eleanor shifted uneasily.

'I'm not saying it would be my absolute top choice of holiday, no, but your dad's been working so hard and he really needs a long break.'

'So send him on his own, then! Honestly, Mum, don't be such a bloody pushover! Did you tell him you don't want to go?'

'Yes. No. Sort of. Well, I tried to, but it turned out to be too late.'

'*Mum*. For God's sake. You know what Dad's like. He doesn't get subtle hints. It's no good being all sweet and polite about it. You have to look him in the eye and say, "I DO NOT WANT TO GO." Then give him a large gin and tonic and evacuate the building for a week for the fallout.'

Eleanor laughed, in spite of herself. Thank God her children were made of sterner stuff than she was herself.

'But it's all booked now.'

'And what about your job? And your engravings? You can't do those on a bloody boat, can you?'

'Well, not really, no.'

'Mum? Oh, Georgia, just sod off a minute, will you?'

'Yes, darling. What is it?'

'You sound sad, Mummy. Now I feel sad.'

'There's no need to be sad, sweet pea. I'm absolutely fine. I'll muster some enthusiasm and all will be well.'

'If it were me and my husband was trying to bully me into doing something I didn't want to do, I wouldn't let him.'

Eleanor laughed.

'I love it that you can stand up for yourself. I'm very proud of you. But marriage does involve compromise inevitably, otherwise one would never make it past the honeymoon.'

'I get that, OK, I get it, but look who makes all the compromises! When did Dad ever compromise about anything? And the point is,

Mum, that it's simply NOT FAIR for one person to get their own way all the time. Is it?'

'No,' Eleanor said, 'it isn't.'

'I have to go, Mum. Georgia has to make a call too. Speak to you soon. It'll be easier when we leave here because there'll be internet cafés once we hit the well-worn backpack trail.'

'Take care, Hannah-banna. Love you lots.'

'Love you, too, Mum. Love to Dad and tell him not to be so pig-headed.'

* * *

That night, she has the dream for the first time, and after that it comes almost every night. Always the same. She is on a huge ship, so vast that it blocks out most of the sky. Every window, every porthole is blazing with light; loud music blasts from every orifice. People are shrieking as they splash and cavort in an unfeasibly large number of swimming pools. There are pools by the bar, in the cinema, even in their suite, but all full of hysterically happy holidaymakers. She watches herself from above, sees her head leaning out over the deck rail to look into the sea far below. The ocean looks dark, dark blue, almost black, frothed with choppy waves. She is wearing a long evening dress, covered in black sequins. She kicks off her high heels, thinking how odd, I never wear high heels and I would certainly never wear a dress covered in sequins. Climbs unsteadily up onto the deck rail. Far below, the ocean waits for her and a wave of pure fear surges through her. Still, she stands, feeling the rail solid beneath her. A breath. She raises her arms then and spreads them out wide for a swallow-dive. As she lifts up onto her toes and launches herself from the rail, her dress suddenly shimmers into a swirl of silver, scintillating in the light. And she *soars*, a bird in flight, sweeping low over the water, laughing at the surprise of it, glittering with life, with relief, with joy. Glances back at the ship for a moment, but falters then, plunging into the icy water. Alone now and freezing in the black ocean, looking up at the huge liner so close it threatens to drag her below to the depths. She wakes up, clammy, breathless, terrified.

21

HAPPY FAMILIES III

1976–1979

Conrad likes to think that he has been a good husband on the whole. He has always provided for his family, taken out the rubbish (except when he forgot), escorted his wife to innumerable functions and dinners (even when he had really not wanted to go), and allowed her to have her way on most matters relating to the house, holidays and children (although sometimes he had subtly seeded his own idea first so that Marcia could have the satisfaction of feeling she had held sway). Conrad dislikes discord. It drains him. It is an annoyance and a distraction. Although he has an extremely analytical mind, he would not turn that keen spotlight to shine its penetrating beam onto the dark conundrum of his inner life. He desires only his work, his books, his museum or his study; he likes thinking and reading and conversing with other people who are not embarrassed to be serious or clever or erudite. For him, argument means debate – the civilised trading of differing views, using evidence, citing sources to support your stance, assessing the contrary viewpoint, wondering if there might be some merit in it. Arguing over domestic matters – *You promised you would mow the lawn... You shouldn't have left your keys out where Benedict might see them... Do you really have to have the light on half the night to read?* – was simply tedious and unproductive.

Better to give in, or at least seem to do so, then navigate along a different path next time to pre-empt the point of potential conflict. Conrad, after years of expert manoeuvring in the surprisingly political world of museums, is remarkably adroit at that sort of thing. If he is unable to head off a brewing argument with his wife, his response is usually either to go out for a walk, or to appear to accede by remaining silent.

On the question of how good a father he has been, however, his steely-eyed judgement is less forgiving. He believes he has always acted with good intent and tried to do his best. The children have never had to go short of anything important certainly: the family lives in a handsome detached house with a very large garden; they have clothes, good food, books, music lessons, holidays, etcetera. They attend decent schools, and he has supervised or helped with homework on request, indeed often prompting Eleanor to think in a deeper, more complex way about her school topics. He has listened attentively to piano practice, and taken them on visits to museums, galleries and historical sites of interest until Benedict's increasingly wild behaviour stripped such outings of any pleasure.

Over the last year or so, the volume inside the house seems to have been turned up several notches. Benedict is a door-slammer. When he comes in – slam! Then thundering up the stairs to his room – slam! Thundering down again to the kitchen, demanding fizzy pop – of which Conrad heartily disapproves, other than for high days and holidays – and cake or biscuits. The boy's appetite is prodigious. The children seem to have become even more polarised in their behaviour and manner. As Benedict has become louder and more obnoxious, Eleanor has become... Conrad can't quite put his finger on it. There is something elusive about his daughter. More than that – she is almost a ghost of a thing, flitting out of the kitchen, gliding up the stairs, appearing suddenly beside you without your noticing the moment of her arrival. When the family are all together, which is as little as possible, she is near-silent, limiting her speech to polite requests to pass the potatoes please, or asking her mother if she needs any help with anything. Conrad imagines that she would make a convincing heroine in a Victorian novel – patient, yielding, stoic – but he wonders if she is really content to spend her life in the background in this way. At school, by contrast, she glows, quietly excelling in most of her subjects other than sport – most of all English, history, Latin, art, and music. She is in the school orchestra, where she plays the viola, and sings in the choir. At last year's school concert, she played in the orchestra, then had to walk alone up the steps to join the choir on stage for a solo. Marcia had stayed at home, unfortunately, as Benedict wasn't feeling well, so he'd gone alone. He could see Eleanor blushing with embarrassment that people were looking at her as she had to take those steps alone, but then, two minutes later, she stood up and sang her solo without a tremor in her voice or body.

Marcia does not understand Eleanor or, it seems to him when he thinks about it, even like her very much, but still she is a competent organiser and she makes sure the child is fed, clothed, and diligent in the matter of homework, choir practice and so on. Benedict is another matter. From the first, Marcia has indulged the boy. She is... besotted with him. When he was naughty, she scolded him with a smile, so he believed that his actions pleased her in some way. When he pulled Eleanor's hair or threw her things out of the window, Marcia chastised Eleanor for not keeping out of his way or removing her belongings to a more secure place.

Now, looking back, as he finds himself doing increasingly often, it is horribly clear that, in the matter of Benedict, both he and Marcia have fallen woefully short. Marcia has indulged the boy and he had shamelessly manipulated his mother with his looks and his charm and his promises to do better. Conrad had largely left her to it. The children were primarily her domain and, when they were little, he frequently felt them to be an annoying distraction away from his work. His shoulders sag at the thought.

* * *

It is Eleanor's twelfth birthday. Marcia has ordered a rather expensive cake from the bakery, with waves of white icing lapping around the edge, and an edible plaque – marzipan, perhaps? – proclaiming '12 today' in fancy pink script as well as 'Happy Birthday Eleanor' in white on the chocolate icing of the cake. It is in the larder now, keeping cool. Conrad glimpsed it briefly as his wife transferred it there from the box. It really is a rather splendid-looking creation.

Cocooned in his study, he hears the doorbell ring multiple times, then a chatter of excited girlish voices and squeals and fussing over coats and scarves and where to put the birthday gifts and so on. He turns on his radio, tuning it to Radio 3.

There is a knock, then his wife sweeps in without waiting for a response.

'Darling, please come. I don't know what to do.' God, not more interruptions. It is so hard to get anything done in this blasted house with the constant noise and shouting and screeching. Still, there is no point in arguing. He clicks the lid on his pen rather pointedly and rises to his feet without comment.

Marcia leads him to the larder and opens the door.

'What's the matter?'

She gestures to the cake. The marzipan plaque has disappeared and the stiff white letters of Eleanor's name have been picked off and, presumably, eaten. Only the ghost of its snowy footprint remains.

'That bloody boy!'

Marcia lays a restraining hand on his arm.

'You don't know it was him. It might have been one of the party guests.'

'Don't be ridiculous – they're all in there, playing Murder in the Dark and so forth. Who else would have done such a thing? Rumpelstiltskin? Mice? Or was it an Act of God?'

'Now you're being silly.' Marcia looks him in the eye. 'Perhaps Eleanor did it herself. You don't know.'

'Now who's being silly? An Act of God is far more likely than Eleanor's sabotaging her own cake. Your excessive fondness for the boy is making you irrational.'

'What do you mean – "excessive fondness"? All mothers adore their children. It's only natural. It's only because you're such a bloody cold fish that you think anyone displaying an ounce of affection for their own child is peculiar!'

Conrad sniffs. There is no point in going down this fruitless cul-de-sac yet again.

'I suggest we focus our attention onto the matter of trying to rectify the damage rather than on examining my faults, which are, no doubt, innumerable and irreparable. Are you able to – to...' he waves a hand at the cake, '... repair it or redo the lettering, something like that?'

'No, I'm hopeless at that sort of thing. I don't even own any nozzles or anything. That's why I ordered the cake.'

Conrad is not sure what the relevance of nozzles might be and does not care, but he thinks that this is simply unfair. It is Eleanor's special day and it is about to be spoiled.

'Well, can't you cover that bit up at least? It will still say "Happy Birthday".'

Marcia scans the larder shelves.

'I don't even have any icing sugar. What on earth can I use?'

This is not the type of problem that Conrad is used to fixing. If he were at the BM, no doubt some helpful soul in Conservation would appear with a fine paintbrush and some special something or other and make the problem magically disappear. But he is here at home, with a flapping wife.

'Do we have any chocolate? To match the surface.'

Marcia finds a bar of chocolate and grates fine flakes of it over the damaged area. It looks, in truth, a little peculiar, but Marcia says it will have to do and, in the absence of any alternative, Conrad has to accept that she is right.

* * *

Benedict, barely thirteen, is in trouble at school. Again. Conrad is determined to talk some sense into him.

'Don't bring it up now. He has two friends here to play in the garden,' Marcia says, not looking up from the piece of embroidery she is working on. 'It really wasn't his fault. He's too easily influenced by those other boys. He can't help it – it's just his easy-going nature.'

Conrad cannot bear to engage in this self-deluding bunkum any more, so he turns and leaves the room, digging his fingernails into his palms in annoyance.

Down at the far end of the garden, round the corner of its odd L-shape where an ancient shed has half-subsided, crumpled among the nettles and mare's tails, he finds Benedict. He is with two older boys, smoking cigarettes and swigging from bottles of beer. For a moment, there is absolute silence. Then Conrad explodes, his rage erupting hot and sudden as a volcano. The other two boys look terrified and simply drop their bottles and run, scrabbling over the back fence as if being pursued by a mad dog. Benedict stands there and slowly stubs out his cigarette on the shed wall then flicks the end into a clump of nettles. He stares at his father, unflinching, defiant.

'You little shit.' Conrad gives the boy a hefty shove and he stumbles backwards into the nettles. 'Pick it up! You could start a fire, for God's sake. You're grounded for the foreseeable future.'

He turns and walks away then, ignoring the gasps as the boy tries to get up from the bed of stinging plants. As he marches off, does he hear a sob? If so, no matter, serve the boy right. He's a bloody disgrace.

* * *

Conrad has not been entirely faithful, although the couple of liaisons he has had are too insignificant in his mind even to be labelled as affairs. They were merely brief episodes while abroad, looking at foreign collections or overseeing the loan of exhibits – once in Paris, once in Vienna, twice in Florence. The Italian woman in particular returned to his mind for some time afterwards.

But they had not *mattered*. He had never fallen in love with any of them. God knows, he had loved the sex, which had been lights on and noisy and sweaty and altogether a different species from the orchestrated manoeuvrings that took place in his marital bed from time to time, but no one had captured his heart. That desiccated, disregarded part of himself he had never considered other than as a necessary pump, pushing the blood round his body, keeping him alive. He had read love poetry, of course, novels too; he considered himself rather knowledgeable about love in theory: that it drove people crazy, made them act foolishly or impulsively. Intellectually, he could dissect it and pronounce it very interesting, often rather comical or curious, but undoubtedly fascinating, but he did not *know* it. It was as if he had read about peaches his whole life, understood that the skin is downy and soft, that the flesh is juicy and sweet, but had never leaned his face in close enough to take a bite, to sink his teeth into one and feel that glorious first taste, let the juice run down his chin, laugh in surprise that at last he really *knew* what it was – not just in his head but in his mouth, his stomach, his being.

It is an extraordinary fact that, until he was forty-one, Conrad had never been in love. And so, when it eventually happened, it hit hard.

22

UNDERNEATH THE SPREADING APPLE TREE...

Ding-dong. Hearing the hoovering come to a halt on the landing above, Andrew called up the stairs: 'Don't worry, Mum! I'll get it. It'll be the people about the tree. You remember they called me back the other day?'

'Are you sure, Andrew, love?' As ever, Mrs Tyler was on the alert for possible callers whose mission might be to take advantage of her in some way – by trying to sell her overpriced dusters or tea-towels, for example, when she had enough of them to last her, and possibly the entire street, for the rest of her life.

'It's fine. Leave it with me!' Nothing would be gained by involving his mother in the proceedings.

It was *her*, the woman from the café: the beautiful one.

'Oh, hello, it's *you*!' She sounded surprised, but not unpleasantly so. The annoying sister who'd dragged her away that time at the café seemed to be in tow again, too. 'Um, we're here about the tree. It's in our mum's garden. I mean, I'm not stalking you or anything.'

'Pity,' he said. 'Hello.' He tried not to smile too much. 'It's good to see you again. I'm Andrew.'

'I'm Olivia.'

'What do you mean *again*?' the other one said.

'Oh, we – he – I—' She sounded flustered and then she blushed, she

unmistakably blushed. 'We met in the café recently, that's all. You know.'
A look passed between them.

The sister peered at him as if he were an abstract sculpture she didn't
understand.

'He's not the one you said you—'

'Mads!'

'Oh. Right. Really?' She looked at him again. 'I'm Madeleine, by the
way, not that anyone's interested, apparently.'

Olivia stared down at her feet for a moment then looked around the
hallway.

'Gosh, these houses are so different from the ones in our mother's
road.'

Andrew was suddenly acutely aware of the décor in this house, of
the old-fashioned, textured wallpaper in the hallway, the clear plastic
runner protecting the hall carpet, the collection of miniature crystal
animals on narrow display shelves near the door.

'Wow, these are so kitsch! Fab. Or are they serious? Oops. Aren't you
a bit old to be collecting glass animals?' the sister said, making no
attempt to remove the sneer from her voice.

'I'm terribly sorry. My sister has no manners. Please excuse her.'

'They're not mine. Obviously.' Andrew was desperate to get the two
women out of the house quickly. 'Do please go on through to the
garden.'

'Hey, I do have manners. That's so unfair.' Madeleine puffed out her
cheeks. 'Why have you got this weird plastic thing on top of your
carpet?'

'Mads.' Olivia covered her face with her hands for a moment. 'I really
am sorry. Normally, I leave her tied up in the attic, but she promised to
be good if I let her come out for some air.'

Andrew laughed.

'Well, let's go and take a look at the tree and get you some air, then.
You can run around the garden, too, if you like, stretch your legs a bit.'

Olivia giggled and smiled at him.

'Oi, she can take the piss, she's my sister. You can't.' Madeleine folded
her arms and stomped out to the garden.

'Sorry.' Andrew stole another glance at Olivia and she smiled back.

The garden was impeccably neat, the lawn as level and weed-free as a bowling green, the edges trimmed to perfection, the borders bright with purple pansies and white cyclamen. This was his father's realm, though perhaps turf might be a more appropriate word as the idea of his father's being in charge of anything, even this modest patch, seemed sadly preposterous. Still, it was the one area where his father mostly held his own. Usually. But when it came to the tree, Mrs Tyler had the persistence of a battering ram, saying it was making that end of the garden dark and spoiling her outlook onto the allotments, i.e., she couldn't observe her husband when he was working on his allotment and make sure he wasn't getting up to any mischief among the cabbages.

'It *is* a wonderful tree,' Andrew said.

'So, leave it alone then. End of problem.' Madeleine sighed.

'Look, if it were up to me, of course I'd leave it alone.' Andrew shoved his hands down into his pockets. 'But you can see it does cast pretty deep shade at this end and it blocks the view of the allotments.'

'We're not cutting it down, you know.' Madeleine crossed her arms.

'No one wants to cut it down,' Olivia and Andrew said at the same moment.

'Jinx!' they said together, suddenly both grinning ridiculously at each other. Andrew feared he must be blushing, as Olivia was.

'Oh God, get a room, why don't you?' Madeleine shook her head.

Andrew moved away towards the tree.

'Maybe we could just thin it a little? Cut out a couple of branches – say, here and here?' He pointed. 'And possibly that one?'

Olivia moved closer to the tree, too.

'That should be fine, I'm sure.' She looked briefly at him then back at the tree. 'So... you mentioned you were visiting your parents? Where do you usually live?'

'Oh, well, I'm staying here, actually. But just for a visit, really. I mean, it's not for long; it won't be for long.'

'Ah?' A flicker of a frown crossed her face and she said nothing else, as if waiting for him to continue. Andrew noticed her turn towards her sister and give the tiniest flick of her head.

There was no response from Madeleine, but then Olivia said, 'Weren't you supposed to be meeting Humphrey soon, Mads? I'm fine here if you need to go?'

'Oh, yeah. *Humphrey*. Right. I'll call him and tell him I'm on my way.'

She took out her mobile. 'I'll see you later, Liv, OK?' She looked down at her phone, then at Andrew. 'Nice to meet you. I'll see myself out. 'Bye.'

It was just the two of them. And the tree. Olivia peered over the fence into her mother's garden.

'So...' she said. 'It's always funny seeing something from another point of view, isn't it? Mum's garden looks kind of mad and jungly from this side of the fence, but it's rather wild and beautiful from her side.'

'I like it. This one's a bit over-manicured for my taste.' Andrew looked at her, then up at the tree again. Ask her. The crisp late autumn light shone through the golden leaves. Ask her. Just coffee. Speak. Even the tree seemed to be waiting.

'So...' he echoed. Stop being a twat, Andrew, get on with it. 'Um, I was wondering if you might fancy going out sometime,' he said, all in a rush. 'I mean, just for coffee or whatever.'

There was a brief pause.

'Or not. Not if you're busy. It was just a thought. You know, in case you wanted to discuss the tree a bit more. About... about, you know, exactly which branches... and... and so on. And the... the arrangements. Timing. Logistics.'

'You want to go out for coffee with me to discuss the tree?'

'Er... well... we wouldn't absolutely have to discuss the tree. Unless you wanted to. In which case, we absolutely could. We could talk about the tree. I could happily talk about it for hours.' Shut up, for crying out loud. Know when to stop.

Olivia stuffed her hands into her coat pockets and smiled, though once again he couldn't tell if she liked him or was amused by how hopeless he was.

'Well, what say we go for coffee and, if we can't help ourselves and feel utterly compelled, then we will discuss the tree, but if we can fight the urge, then we can just talk about anything that pops into our heads? Would that do?' And now she did smile at him, properly, and he smiled back.

'That would do very well. When can you do?'

She glanced at her watch.

'Well, I could manage a coffee now. We could walk over to the café where we met before, or do you have other... trees to discuss elsewhere?'

'Now?'

'Not if you're busy. We can make another time.'

'No. Now is good. Now is very good. Let's do it.' Now was brilliant. Now meant there was no extra time in which to get nervous or start worrying about what to wear and what to say and what not to say.

He just had to smuggle Olivia out past his mother without becoming waylaid in the hallway by the usual interrogation procedure: where was he going, what time would he be back, did he have his keys, had he remembered to pop on a vest as it was getting ever so nippy now winter was just around the corner.

'Here, why don't you go out through the side-gate and I'll just grab my jacket and meet you round the front in a tick.' He unbolted the gate and gestured towards the side path.

'You're never going out now, Andrew?' Mrs Tyler suddenly appeared halfway down the stairs while Andrew was in the hall picking up his jacket.

'Yup.'

'But it's nearly dinner-time. I've a nice bit of beef.'

'Not till one o'clock, though, Mum, eh?' He looked at his watch. 'There's loads of time.'

'But where are you going?' She stood in the hallway between him and the front door. 'Dad's got the newspaper already. There's no need to go out.'

'I won't be long. I'll be back in time for lunch.'

'I saw people in the garden looking at the tree with you – just girls, really. Dad said it was an older lady when he went round.'

'Yes, it was her daughters.' He manoeuvred awkwardly around her and reached for the front door latch.

'Are you going to look at the tree in their garden now? Is that it?'

Dear God, why wasn't he allowed just to leave the building like a normal person?

'Yes, that's it. I'd better go.'

'Stop a minute, then, and Dad can go with you.' She laid a hand on his arm. 'Ron! Ron! Andrew's off out to look at the tree from the other side.'

'What, love?' His father emerged from the living room, clutching his newspaper.

'Andrew's got to – to – inspect the tree from the other garden, he says. You'd better go too.'

'No, no! I can manage. There's no need.'

'Andrew's got it all in hand, love.'

'That's right, Mum, it's all in hand.' He wanted to open the door but was worried Olivia might be right outside on the front path and over-hear him having this ridiculous conversation.

'But what if you need a – a – witness, Andrew? It's only your word against theirs, you know.'

A witness. For crying out loud.

'I really don't think it'll come to that, Mum. I'm sorting it out.'

'The lad knows what he's doing. Leave him be.'

'But you'll be back for Sunday dinner, won't you?'

'Almost certainly.'

'You'll not miss your dinner, Andrew?'

God forbid. The sky would fall in.

'I'll be back. But please don't wait for me, just in case I'm a bit late.'

'Dad and I'll wait for you, won't we, Dad?'

'No, please don't.' Andrew opened the front door. 'See you later. 'Bye.' He stepped smartly out onto the front path and closed the door behind him, hoping that she wouldn't open it again to continue the conversation, her voice tugging him back as he attempted to flee along the road, screaming.

No sign of Olivia. At least she couldn't have heard the latest episode of The Great Escape, thank God. He came out of the gate and looked to right and left, but she was nowhere in sight. Maybe she had heard and had done a runner? Or simply given up on him as he'd taken so long? Bollocks. But who could blame her? He stuffed his hands down in his pockets. Maybe she'd gone ahead to the café? Had she, in fact, said that's what she'd do and he'd misunderstood somehow? He knotted his scarf, then looked ahead and saw her, almost directly opposite, perched on a low front wall, her green coat merging slightly with the hedge behind her.

'I thought you'd forgotten me,' she said.

He apologised for taking so long.

'I thought you must have gone.'

'One more minute and I'd have abandoned ship.'

'Sometimes it's difficult to extricate myself.' He shrugged.

'I have the same problem. My mother has a knack of starting up some long, elaborate – but entirely pointless – story about one of her bizarre friends the moment you attempt to leave, so it makes you feel you're being rude even though she only started the story to stop you leaving.'

They walked slowly to the café, then lingered there for over an hour, drinking coffee and talking about books and films, before she said she'd better head off, she was meeting friends out for lunch.

'Ah, yes, me too.' It would sound too pathetic to say he had to get back to his parents' house.

'Where are you meeting them? Are you heading over to the tube?' She nodded in that direction.

Shit. He must remember never to lie; he was so utterly useless at it.

'Um, just, you know, er, going to a friend's house for lunch.' He was aware that he sounded shifty, as if he were covering something up. 'Um, locally.'

'Oh. OK. Well, have fun. It was nice to meet you.' Her tone seemed to have cooled somewhat. She took out money for her coffees and stood up.

'No, I'll get this.'

'No, it's fine, I'd rather pay for my own, thanks.'

'Really, let me get it.'

'Well, OK then. Thank you.'

He stood up and helped her on with her coat, for once managing to hold it without dropping it on the floor or forcing her to dislocate her arm to put it on.

'So...' This was the bit he hated, where you had to ask someone for their number. But the tree! Hurrah for the tree. 'We forgot to talk about the tree in the end. Should I email you perhaps about the pruning? Or if you want to give me your number...?' He took out his phone.

'It's OK. I'll remember which branches we decided should go. I think I can make Ma see that it's fair enough. I can organise it.'

'I can contribute to the cost of—'

'No, it's OK, thanks.'

'Oh. Well, this was nice.'

'Yes.' She smiled at him, but she looked suddenly rather sad. 'It was.'

'Er, look, I'm not much good at this, but would you like to come out again with me? I mean properly – for – for – supper or something?'

'Hmm. Well...'

What on earth did that mean? Still, it wasn't a straight no. He quickly paid the bill and came out onto the street with her. She stood there, slowly winding her scarf around her neck and fiddling with her coat buttons.

'What do you think?' he said, as if asking for her opinion on a technical matter.

'It's not that I don't like you.'

'But...?'

'But...'

'I know – don't tell me – you've just started seeing someone so it's bad timing, I get it.'

'No.' She looked straight at him, frowning. 'That's not it at all. I thought you were seeing someone else, actually.'

'What?'

'Look, I don't want to sound at all heavy when I've only just met you, but the last man I was with cheated on me and I don't want to waste time with someone who's going to be like that.'

'But I'm so *not* like that. What on earth makes you think that?'

'When I asked about your lunch, you were kind of evasive...' She looked embarrassed now. 'I presumed you must be meeting a girlfriend. You looked so guilty. It's none of my business, I know, because I barely know you, but if you are seeing someone, it would be better if you could just tell me straight. It's fine.'

'I am not seeing anyone else, I absolutely swear it. I was living with someone, but she – we – *we* decided to call it a day, and I'm moving on with my life. The lunch thing – I can see I must have sounded suspicious. Look, no big deal. It was just that my mum's expecting me for lunch and I thought... I thought it sounded a bit pathetic and uncool, having lunch with my parents rather than doing what you're doing – heading out somewhere trendy with your mates. I was embarrassed, that's all.'

She smiled then, and the smile radiated across her whole face.

'Not pathetic at all. My sister and I go to our mum's for brunch most Sundays. It's a nice thing to do.'

'So it's OK then?'

'It's OK.'

'And I can call you?'

'Please do.' She reached into her bag. 'Here's my card then.' It said Olivia Herbert, Private Tutor, with a small drawing of an acorn with an oak leaf. And, more to the point, her landline, mobile, and email details.

'Nice drawing. You said your mother is an artist – did she do it?'

'No, I did that one. It's just a scribble really.'

'It's very good. Anyway...' Andrew held the card up as if it were a winning raffle ticket, 'thank you. And I'll see you soon.'

'You will.' She smiled once more, then turned and walked away. He watched her for a minute, until she half-turned and waved, and he waved back and managed not to walk into any trees as he headed towards home.

23

BEING NORMAL

'Mmm, that was *so* good.' Cecilia pushed away her plate and scrunched up her paper napkin. 'I've no idea how you've managed to turn yourself into such a good cook, Olivia. You certainly don't get it from me. It's lovely to be cooked for.'

The girls had come over for a midweek supper.

'It's only practice – there's no magic secret. Talking of which, may I take some of your cooking apples? I want to make a crumble.'

'Take, take – of course. Please take lots. There might be a few still on the tree if you can reach them, or there are plenty stored in boxes up in the spare room. Help yourself.'

Olivia went upstairs and returned with an armful of apples, individually wrapped in newspaper for storage.

'Ursula made an... interesting salad using some of them with linseed and alfalfa sprouts... but it wasn't quite...'

'God preserve us from the Ursuline salads, especially the "interesting" ones,' Madeleine said.

The girls had long been in the habit of turning the names of their mother's friends into adjectives: Ursuline for any dish that contained too many seeds or sprouting ingredients, Thalian for basketry and woven horrors, Lillianic for items of clothing that might be inventive but more suitable for fancy dress than for popping out to the shops.

'Well, not perhaps her finest hour in the kitchen.' Cecilia filled the kettle to make some coffee and turned to speak over her shoulder. 'So, are you making crumble for a *young man*?' She did her camped-up Lady Bracknell voice so that Olivia would know that she was only joking and not actually being nosy about her daughter's love life.

'Oh, *Ma*.'

'I was only asking. Many daughters might be *pleased* that their mothers show an interest in their love lives.'

Olivia sighed and rolled her eyes.

'Liv only doesn't like it because if she tells you about her boyfriend—'

'*Mads!*'

'—then she knows you'd be bound to ask her if he's any good in bed,' Madeleine continued.

'Oh God, spare me, please. He's not my boyfriend, anyway.'

'I can't understand why you're such a prude, Olivia.' Cecilia scraped out the old coffee grounds into the compost bucket and reached for the coffee jar. 'I tried to raise you to be completely relaxed and open about sex. What could be more natural, after all?'

'At least *I'm* not uptight about it,' Maddy said.

'I'm *not* uptight. And I'm not a prude, Ma. You're deliberately missing the point. As usual. Just because I don't particularly want to talk about that stuff—'

'That *stuff*! You're resorting to euphemisms! Surely you can at least utter the word "sex"?'

'Good grief. *Sex, sex, SEX*! – OK? But just because I don't want to talk about sex with my mother does not make me a prude. It's called having boundaries and it's completely normal in other families, I assure you.'

Cecilia rolled her eyes.

'Oh, normal. Thank goodness for that. God forbid you should ever depart from convention.'

'That's so unfair. Just because I don't feel the need to show off my eccentricity like a bizarre badge of honour, you dismiss me as conventional. And, anyway, what if I like being *normal*? Maybe I want to have a *normal* life and get married to a *normal*, straight man and have two children by the same father and have a *normal* sofa with proper cushions instead of this stupid chaise longue, which is all saggy in the middle, and this bloody throw that's always falling onto the bloody floor!'

Olivia crossed the room and picked up the throw and dumped it on the chaise in a heap instead of spreading it out neatly as she usually would.

'I really *like* the chaise longue,' Madeleine said.

'Bigger picture, Mads.'

Cecilia was silent for a few moments, then said, 'I didn't realise you girls minded so much.'

'What?' Olivia had inevitably picked up the throw again and was carefully arranging it over the chaise to hide the rather worn upholstery.

'About having different fathers.'

'I don't think about it really.' Madeleine shrugged. 'We've never met them so at least we're in the same boat.'

Olivia came and sat back down at the kitchen table.

'I'm sorry, Mads. You know I think of you as my sister not my half-sister. That bit doesn't make any difference to me. And Dad is *Dad*. I'm not saying I would ever wish he were someone else, it's not that...' Olivia fiddled with an abandoned toast crust on her side plate. 'Sometimes it's hard, wondering if *he* might be out there somewhere, that's all. He must be quite old by now and I hate the thought that he might be ill – or dying – and that I wouldn't even know. I don't even know what he looks like. At least Mads has that photo of her dad.'

'I'm sorry. You know I don't have a photo.' Cecilia pushed the coffee pot towards Olivia, as if to compensate somehow.

'I do know. It's just that it's difficult to imagine someone when you've never even seen them. It's all so abstract – just this idea of a man you once had a bit of a fling with.'

Cecilia stood up to forage in the cupboards for some chocolate.

'Maybe neither of your actual fathers would have been very good as fathers – did you ever consider that?'

'Of course.' Olivia nodded. 'I accept that. And it's not as if I'm fretting over it day and night. I love Dad to bits, anyway; you know I do. I'm better off than some of my friends who do see their actual fathers but find them really hard to talk to. That's kind of sad.'

All three sat in silence for a few moments, then Madeleine turned to her sister and asked, 'Anyway, so is thingybob good in bed, or not?'

'Oh, Mads, for goodness' sake. I've just met the man.'

'Ooh.' Cecilia perked up. 'Is *who* good in bed?'

'Now look what you've done.' Olivia glared at her sister and stood up to clear some things from the table. 'Not helpful.'

'Sorry, sorry! I won't say another word, I promise.' Cecilia drained her coffee and sat back. 'Boundaries, boundaries. I accept that it's your prerogative if you prefer to be secretive.'

'Not secretive, Mother – *private*. Not the same thing.'

Cecilia waved the assertion away.

'Of course it's the same thing.'

'No, it really *isn't*. I've *just* met someone recently and I reserve the right not to offer the poor man up to be picked over by you two prurient vultures.'

'I'm not prurient.' Maddy swung round to face Olivia at the sink. 'I just want to know if he's a good fuck.'

Olivia snorted with laughter and briefly covered her face with her hands. 'I rest my case.'

'Now, Madeleine, you must allow Olivia to keep her secrets if she chooses to. Not everyone is equally comfortable with the unrestrained, animalistic side of sexual intercourse—'

'Aaaaargggh!' Madeleine covered her ears. 'I hate the word "intercourse". You couldn't come up with a less sexy word if you tried. Horrors.'

'For crying out loud, Mother, I'm perfectly comfortable with myself sexually, thank you very much. I just don't want to talk about my sex life with my mother and sister, OK?'

'And to be fair, you've hardly had a sex life for ages, have you?' Maddy chipped in. 'Not since Jeremy with the awful earring, really?'

'Not everyone feels the need to leap into bed with every man who crosses their path.'

'Ouch. Bit harsh, Olivia. Be kind, girls.'

'You know what I mean. There's nothing wrong in waiting a bit.'

'But if they're good in bed, better to crack on with it so you get the benefit. Or, if they're crapola, you might as well know it sooner rather than later so you can jump ship and move on.'

'Well, I wouldn't quite put it that way...' Cecilia began.

'So you haven't even slept with whatsisface yet?'

'*Andrew*. No, strangely enough – because we have only had coffee together *once* and talked on the phone. We haven't even had our first date yet, though obviously I will call you both to consult with you beforehand about where we should go, what we should talk about, and which pants I should wear because, clearly, these things all fall within your joint jurisdiction.'

Cecilia laughed.

'Lord, that reminds me of the time I went to meet this chap without any knickers on and I—'

'Ma, I'm sorry to have to interrupt you but I really have to make a move now. I've got some work to prepare.'

'Of course, dear. I didn't mean to make you uncomfortable.'

Olivia sighed and went and put on her coat.

'Why don't you bring him here for tea or brunch or something? I promise to try to be as "normal" as possible. He's very welcome. We can have cake. Bought, from a proper shop – not homemade – so no need to panic.'

'And I'll come too. I can be normal, I promise.'

'Well, we'll see. I don't want to frighten him off.'

'Ooh – Liv's in love!'

'No, I'm not. There's no rush, that's all.'

'Livvy's in luuuuuurrrvve.'

'Oh, grow up.'

'Madeleine, don't tease her about this sort of thing. You know your sister likes to keep her love life under wraps.'

'I give up.'

24

ELOPE WITH A DWARF

Every few weeks or so, Roger had to fly over to Jersey to pay court to some of his most important, i.e., wealthiest, clients. He often travelled much further afield for business – to Dubai, Moscow, Beijing – but it was his Jersey trips that he seemed to relish the most, and he rarely resisted an opportunity to regale Eleanor with the many pleasures on offer there: the yachts, the clay-pigeon shooting, the piled-high platters of *fruits de mer*, the vintage Krug Champagne.

'Don't get me wrong – it's not that I think there's anything terribly wrong with *this* house, darling,' Roger said, half-reclining on the bed while his wife packed his suitcase, although she had not commented much beyond the occasional 'Gosh!' or 'Really!' 'It's perfectly adequate for our needs, after all, but really you should see Robert's spread over there. Or Alec's: eight guest suites – eight! Robert has two pools, indoor and outdoor, of course.'

'Of course.'

'Grass tennis court. Just think of the maintenance costs alone!'

'Awful.'

Roger rattled on in this vein for some time and Eleanor let her thoughts drift elsewhere while she checked that there was enough deodorant and shaving foam in his sponge bag, and neatly folded his clothes. She was wondering about going away herself for a few days, perhaps even a whole week, to have time to draw and work on her wood engravings. Back to Suffolk maybe, or to North Yorkshire, where they had once had a family holiday some years ago but never returned. Roger was voluble on the shortcomings of holidaying in the UK, and he snorted when Eleanor enthused about dry-stone walls or the silhouette of an ancient oak. She supposed it was a little ridiculous; it wasn't as if she were a proper artist, after all, just pootling about with it when she had time. She would love to do more but what was the point? As Roger always said, it wasn't as if you could earn a decent living from it, so why bother?

She glanced over to see her husband staring at her, unsmiling.

'You've gone off into one of your daydreams again,' he sighed. 'You know how irritating I find it when you don't listen to me properly.'

'I'm sorry, but I was listening really. You were telling me about Robert's house and his two pools and his grass tennis court.'

'And what did I say after that?'

Bollocks. I've no fucking idea, darling, because I was losing the will to live…

Eleanor hesitated. Who knew? Leather floors? Kitchen with crystal worktops? Brand-shiny-new trophy wife?

'Um… I know… it was about his—'

'I *knew* you weren't listening!' Roger suddenly sat up straight.

'I'm very sorry. It was only for a moment or two. I was concentrating on the packing. I know you like it done properly.'

He sniffed and went and stood looking out at the garden.

'We could afford a larger house ourselves, you know. With a pool, at least. Or we could excavate a basement here and put one down there – and a gym – maybe a cinema room too.'

'Whatever for?'

For a moment or two, Eleanor thought she had simply voiced the words silently in her head as she so often did when talking with her husband. It was only Roger's reaction that made her realise she must have spoken aloud.

'There's no need to be so bloody-minded about it, Eleanor. It's incredibly ungrateful. Most women would jump at the chance to live somewhere grander and enjoy a better lifestyle.'

She tried not to wince at the word 'lifestyle', one of her pet hates.

'I only meant we have more than enough space as it is,' she said softly, gesturing at their sizeable bedroom. 'And with the children away now, we don't need—'

'It's nothing to do with *need*. It's a reflection of who you are, your status and so on. I work extremely hard and earn a damn good living. Why on earth shouldn't I enjoy the fruits of it?'

'I'm not saying that at all. Of course I want you to reap the benefits and be comfortable and—'

'And you love swimming! I was only thinking of you.'

'Well, thank you, that's very thoughtful. But...' She paused for a moment.

Roger sighed. 'There always has to be a "but" with you, darling. I can't imagine there's another wife in the world who wouldn't be thrilled to bits at the thought of having their very own pool. I just don't understand you sometimes.'

'I was going to explain.' She bit the inside of her cheek to stop herself snapping at him. 'It's just that when I go swimming, I often see the same two or three women at the pool and we chat in the changing room and sometimes have a quick cup of tea afterwards. It's sociable.'

'You could have friends over to swim, then have coffee right here.' He shook his head and looked back out to the garden again. 'Go on, then – what would be your dream house? If we didn't live here. Money no object.'

It was rare for Roger to ask her view on something then pause long enough for her to answer, so she was caught unawares for a few moments. 'No, let me guess. I know: a draughty old ruined castle with ridiculous turrets and crumbling stone staircases – romantic and completely impractical, with open fires and no central heating!' He laughed.

Eleanor laughed, too.

'Well, that does sound lovely, but actually... I think my dream house would be a small, weatherboarded cottage by the sea—'

'A cottage! I couldn't live in a cottage. They're always so dark and poky. In England, people gush about them in such a preposterous way: ooh, it's so charming, so cosy – how delightful – how picturesque! For charming, read too bloody small to swing a cat in. There are never enough bathrooms so you spend half your time hopping from foot to foot on the landing in a draught, queuing for the toilet. And with stupid low ceilings – think of Sarah and Mark's place: I bump my head on that bloody beam every time we go – houses built for midgets. You won't catch me living in one of those, I'm afraid, darling. You'll have to elope with a dwarf from the circus if that's really your secret fantasy.' He laughed again, tickled pink with the craziness of the idea.

Eleanor said nothing but focused on finishing the packing. She had always packed for Roger ever since they got married. Sometimes he liked to watch her as she did it so neatly, crossing off each item on a checklist, placing his shoes into cloth bags so that the soles wouldn't mark his clothes, folding everything with care and precision.

He would be off first thing in the morning, the taxi coming at 5.30 a.m. to take him to City airport. Usually, Eleanor would get up to make him coffee and see him off, but this time she said, 'Would you mind very much if I didn't get up early with you tomorrow, darling? You know I haven't been sleeping so well since Hannah left and I'm awfully tired.'

'No, it's fine. I'm meeting Jake at City for breakfast before our flight, in any case. Sleep in the guest room tonight, why don't you? Then I won't wake you up in the morning with my "crashing about"!' This was a teasing reference to the time when, some ten years ago or more, Eleanor had murmured, half-asleep, 'Oh, please don't crash about, darling. I'm asleep.'

Roger found this evidence of his wife's hyper-sensitivity highly amusing and often referred to it.

* * *

Morning. Although she had slept in the spare bedroom, Eleanor had woken at around five, when Roger got up and showered and then clumped downstairs with his suitcase and clattered off the chain and thunked the bolt across and shouted back upstairs that he was off now and to have a nice lie-in.

Still, she dozed on and off for a couple of hours, relishing the acreage of crisp, fresh bedlinen all to herself. When she got up, she went downstairs and made herself a pot of proper leaf tea and cut two thick slices of walnut bread to spread with butter and lavender honey. Roger did not like walnuts, disapproved of them even as if they had been put on the planet solely to vex him, so she always seized the chance to have this bread when he was away. And how lovely to have the chance to read at breakfast. Eleanor ran back upstairs to fetch her book, a new novel she had bought in expectation of Roger's trip away. Now there was a whole hour in hand before she needed to get ready to leave for work. She stretched out on the sofa, snuggled under a soft cashmere throw, and shivered with a *frisson* of pleasure as she turned at once to the back of the book to read the ending first. She smiled at herself, telling herself it was silly to take so much pleasure in this small peccadillo, no longer sure if her delight was still in reading the end first or in her sense of victory over her husband. Well, it wasn't so bad, after all. Plenty of women do far worse: shag their personal trainer or the man next door, drink vodka during the day, or spend thousands of pounds on shoes and handbags. As vices go, this one struck her as pretty harmless.

After an hour, Eleanor went back upstairs to get ready, then set off for work at the Conservation Trust.

* * *

After a busy morning, Eleanor went out to eat her lunch in the park. It was unexpectedly mild for November, and the remaining golden leaves on the trees glowed in the bright sun. She perched on one end of a bench and unwrapped her sandwich. A little way off, she noticed a woman sitting on another bench – actually, not sitting but almost lying, with her legs stretched out in front of her and her head tipped back, basking in the late autumn sun. There was something captivating about this particular pose, a sense of unabashed abandonment, that caught Eleanor's attention. She set aside her sandwich and dug into her bag to find the small sketchbook she always kept there.

Eleanor quickly sketched in the principal lines of the bench, then concentrated on the woman – that dynamic diagonal of her body with her feet out on the path, her head and neck stretched back. It was funny, she rarely included people in her drawings, other than in the background. She usually drew trees, houses, landscape, occasionally intimate fragments of an interior – a windowsill with a jug on it, a table set for breakfast – but the urge to draw this woman had proved irresistible. Eleanor loved this feeling, the absolute focus on what you were doing as if nothing else mattered any more. The rest of the world – your worries, doubts, fears – all receded into the background instead of gnawing at you all the time.

After work, Eleanor decided to walk home rather than take the bus. The woman in the park appeared in her head again. Perhaps it would even make a good subject for an engraving. She found herself reimagining those lines and shapes, how she would stylise the drawing as she worked into the woodblock. Her mobile rang then. It was Hannah, bubbling up with everything she'd seen and done since they'd last spoken – how friendly the people were, how the children wanted to touch Georgia's hair because it was blonde.

'And is Dad behaving himself or is he being annoying?' Hannah asked.

'He's fine. Actually, he's in Jersey again till Saturday.'

'Good. I'm glad you're getting some time off.' And then she asked if her mum could send her out some of her favourite erasable pens plus refills, because she'd given all hers away as they didn't have anything like them out there. They chatted happily all the way until Eleanor was home.

* * *

Every other Thursday, Eleanor sang in a choir. As a child, she had sung in the school choir and always loved it, but she'd only found her way back to singing a few years ago. It was odd, because at home she only sang if she was alone – just as she had when growing up. Back then, if she had a solo to practise, it was impossible: her brother, Benedict, had always made fun of her, doing warbling impressions of her and singing a completely different tune much louder so that she couldn't hear her own voice, and her mother told her off for provoking Benedict when surely she could practise at school.

In recent years, she sometimes sang softly while she cooked, but then once too often Roger had come in and clicked on the kitchen TV for the news or the weather while she was singing; it wasn't that he was trying to shut her up, of course, it was just that it made her feel that her singing was surplus to requirements.

Choir was enjoyable as usual, but demanding as they had just embarked on a challenging new piece and they were struggling with it. Afterwards, Eleanor allowed herself to be persuaded to go to the pub for once as Roger was away so wouldn't be impatient for her return to keep him company.

Several of them squashed in round a table in one corner.

'And how are you, Louise?' Eleanor asked one of the other women.

'Only so-so. My husband's away for a whole fortnight.' She took a sip of her glass of wine. 'You know what it's like. Your husband travels a lot for work, too, doesn't he?'

'Yes, yes, he does. He's away now, in fact.'

'Aw.' Louise pantomimed a sad face with downturned mouth. 'What are we like – missing our lovely hubbies, eh?'

'Spare me, please!' Stella chipped in. She was recently divorced. 'I wish *my* husband had travelled for work. It was spending so much time with him that I couldn't stand!'

Stella offered Eleanor some more wine.

'So tell us, Eleanor, are you pining for your absent spouse or – sssh! – secretly enjoying the time without him?'

Eleanor sensed everyone was suddenly looking at her and she could feel herself flush. She hated being the centre of attention.

'He's only away for three nights and we have been married for over twenty years so I'm just used to it, I suppose. I really don't give it much thought.'

Was that true, that she really didn't think about it?

'Hmm, nicely side-stepping the question, I notice. I'll winkle it out of you, though. Let's order another bottle and make a night of it, shall we?'

Eleanor was tempted to expand and say, OK, since you're so nosy, yes, I do think about it. Not only do I think about it, sometimes I flick forwards through my diary, counting the weeks until his next trip – happy now? But that would sound mean-minded, maybe even a little mad. Anyway, it would only be misinterpreted. It didn't mean that she didn't miss Roger when he was away, it was simply that she enjoyed her own company, that was all.

'Not for me, thanks, as I'm driving.' She put down her glass, though it was still half-full. 'I ought to be getting off home anyway. Enjoy the rest of your evening.'

That night, she read in bed until her eyelids were drooping. It was lovely to let the book slip from her hands onto the bed beside her rather than having to put it away properly again.

25

AND DON'T CALL ME MADAM...

1979

Perhaps Conrad and Marcia's marriage would have trundled on well enough on its tracks, their two lives parallel and apart, if he had been either a minute earlier or a minute later that day over thirty years ago now, a day in July when the sky was so blue it dazzled his eyes, and the sun was warm on his hair and shoulders, and the soft, green grass beckoned him to forget his work and come and lie down.

* * *

Backing out of an angled parking space near the British Museum, he feels the sudden jolt and metallic crunch as his car hits another. He swears and gets out, only to be confronted by a rather small but extraordinarily angry woman who seems not the slightest bit daunted by confronting such a tall and imposing man.

'What on earth were you thinking?' she shouts at him, apparently oblivious to the passers-by pausing and turning round to stare. 'Are you *blind*?'

He might very well ask her the same question but he stands erect and simply waits for her to run out of steam.

'Madam.' His tone is calm, authoritative. 'You reversed. I reversed.

Clearly, neither of us was paying sufficient attention. I do not believe it was my fault.'

'Well, it sure as hell wasn't mine–'

'Madam, I—'

'And don't call me madam. It makes me feel about seventy-three.'

'I apologise for that. Sincerely.' Conrad takes out his business card, with the Museum address on it and his title and direct line.

She doesn't have a business card but scribbles her name and number on a scrap of paper from her bag with the stubby end of a pencil. He looks down at it: Pauline Barnes. The name – down to earth, ordinary, rather flat – seems unlikely for this fizzing firework of a woman. She looks as if she should be called Zenobia or Titania or some name he has never even heard before.

'I know,' she says, although he has not voiced his thoughts. 'I hate it. It sounds as if it's been moulded out of mud or hewn from granite. No one calls me Pauline, other than my mother, and she only does it to annoy, of course. What's yours?' She looks at his card. 'Good Lord. Assistant Keeper of Prints and Drawings at the British Museum.' She covers her eyes with her hand for a moment. 'I ought to be worshipping the hem of your garment, not crashing into your car.' Unabashed, she looks him up and down as if wondering whether to purchase him. 'You certainly look the part. Academics, museum bods – you have no idea how to dress, do you? Even the ones like you whom you'd expect to be more arty. It's practically a uniform – the tweed jacket, the faded cords, the shiny brown brogues. Jesus, woollen tie – you really are clad according to the Museum manual. You must be boiling in all that. Why not live dangerously and remove your jacket? Look – sunshine!'

Conrad, unusually, is speechless. He is tempted to say something cutting about her clothes. After all, she is wearing a most peculiar lime-green dress, jewellery of the sort that might diplomatically be described as 'bold', and glittery shoes in the daytime – as if she is about to step out on stage.

At that moment, she turns slightly and her hair is caught in the sun. It seems spun from red gold, lit from within. He swallows.

'And are you... you are... what do...?' He gestures around him towards the Museum, the park, the pavement, as if her job title might be found there.

She smiles suddenly then, and it is so unexpected and such an astonishingly generous smile, that he is silenced once more. Her broad lips curve with pleasure at – what? He couldn't say; he only knows that he would like to see it happen again, and he would happily stand here on the pavement all day, waiting for it, if needs be.

'If I had a business card, I suppose it would say – Jesus – I hate calling myself an artist. Makes me feel like a fraud. *I'm an artist!* I don't know. I don't have a grown-up normal job like other people, if that's what you mean.'

He forces himself to speak.

'You paint?'

She shakes her head.

'Rarely nowadays. I make large ceramic pieces that, apparently, no one wants to buy.' That smile again. 'And, in the interests of eating more than once a month, I teach clay sculpture evening classes and pottery to anyone who will pay me. I take a class near here, actually, should you ever have the urge to learn to throw a pot.'

'I imagine people are always telling you you look as if you've stepped out of a Rossetti painting.' The words are out before he is even aware he is thinking them. He is not in the habit of flirting – flirting! – with strange women on street corners. He must stop looking at her.

'Nonsense!' She dismisses the idea without the usual attempt at polite agreement one might expect from a stranger, though the corners of her mouth twitch slightly, easy to miss unless you were looking at her closely. 'That's a lazy assumption, because of my red hair. I'm nothing like a Rossetti really. Nose too short, insufficiently defined cheekbones.' She launches into an analysis, at once passionate yet incisive, of the typical Rossetti subject.

He calls her the next day, making himself wait until the afternoon. He wastes almost an entire hour staring into space and instructing himself not to phone her until the following day, then countering this – using an entirely logical sequence of arguments – and telling himself that, in fact, the judicious course of behaviour would be to call today, as his insurance company would no doubt wish to resolve the matter as soon as possible. The Keeper of P and D is away at present, so Conrad borrows his office and shuts the door. Dialling her number, his hands are trembling as he looks down at the scrap of paper she gave him.

The sense of disappointment when her answering machine cuts in is overwhelming. He tries to sound calm but upbeat, slightly jokey, as he doesn't want to come across as a stiff, tweedy 'museum bod'. She picks up halfway through his opening sentence, saying sorry, sorry, she had been working, her hands were covered in clay, hang on, hang on a sec, don't run away. He waits, swivelling in the chair this way and that like a kid until she returns a couple of minutes later. They briefly talk insurance, scraped paintwork, dents, while thoughts swirl through his head. He doesn't want to talk about his car. Fuck the car. He wants to... say... to ask her... he wants... what? There is a silence. Now she will say she must go, no doubt the insurance company will be in touch, goodbye then. Another two or three seconds pass, feeling like an age.

'Oh,' she says at last, 'I knew there was something I meant to ask you. The exhibition of Blake engravings at the Royal Academy? Have you seen it yet?'

'Of course.'

'Oh.'

He curses himself for being the stupidest idiot on the entire planet.

'But I have to go again. Definitely. I wonder if perhaps...'

'Yes. Tomorrow. One-ish?'

'One o'clock.' His heart is thudding as if he has run up ten flights of stairs. 'Ish,' he adds.

And then it is the next day and he finds himself shaving with special care, showering for longer than usual, squaring his shoulders as he combs his hair in the mirror. All through the morning he feels as if his skin is alive, as if he can sense the blood thrumming through his veins. He is brimming with charm and bonhomie, greeting every assistant, every security guard with warm camaraderie. His colleagues laugh at his quips.

At last, at last, it is time, nearly time – but early, in fact, too early – feeling like a teenager, rushing through the rooms, berating himself for not specifying a particular spot, just somewhere in the exhibition, moving from room to room, looking for her, telling himself she wouldn't be there yet but still, still, scanning the darkly lit space for that brilliant flame of her hair.

And then he sees her. She is not looking round for him. In fact she seems unaware that there is anyone else in the room at all. She is leaning over a display case, utterly absorbed in its contents. Today, her hair is in a thick plait, which curves forward over her shoulder, its glorious colour lit up by the illuminated case below. He comes and stands beside her, somehow knowing not to break the spell with clumsy words. In silence, he rests his hand on the edge of the case near hers. She looks up sideways at him, smiles without speaking, then lightly brushes the top of his hand with her own.

After another few seconds, she straightens up and turns full on to face him. He is lost – completely, hopelessly lost – in those extraordinary glittering green eyes, flecked with points of amber. He can hardly breathe. He wants to speak, to say the wild, crazy things in his head out loud, he wants to reach out and touch her pale cheek. And yet he dare not speak in case he breaks this magic thing that is outside everything he has ever known or understood. How could he explain it to her, this woman he barely knows, when he cannot begin to explain it to himself? Her lips slowly curve into that smile.

'I...' he begins. 'You...' but he cannot frame it – this – into words. Conrad, Dr Marriott, who is renowned as much for his articulacy as for his expertise and erudition, Conrad of whom it was said when he was still a schoolboy that he must have swallowed a dictionary – Conrad is speechless.

'I know,' she says, looking into his eyes, unembarrassed. 'Whoever would have thunk it?'

They walk straight out of the exhibition then; they walk and talk all afternoon, stopping to buy a sandwich, which they eat sitting on a park bench. He is desperate to kiss her, thinks he may well go mad if he doesn't kiss her soon, but feels like the inept and gangly teenager he once was. Should he ask, perhaps? What do people do at this age? He's over forty years old, for Christ's sake. Should he just take her in his arms?

They wander north, up through the back streets, into Regent's Park. Fewer people now. He has no idea what time it is.

She stops then and looks up at him.

'Aren't you ever going to kiss me? You know you'll have to bend a bit or I'll have to hop up on a bench to reach you.'

He takes her hand and draws her behind a tree, gathers her to him, feeling her glorious curves fitting against him, the soft swell of her breasts, the delicious scoop of her waist. Her lips open and their mouths entwine. She is hungry for him – he can feel it in the way she pushes against him, hear it in her quickening breath, the pressure of her hands on his back pulling him close. He is worried she will notice his growing excitement. Embarrassed, he starts to pull away, but she smiles and pushes herself against him, utterly without shame. His hands slide further down her back, to the point where it curves outwards to her bottom. He traces a fingertip just beneath the waistband of her skirt, touching her skin.

'Come tomorrow,' she says. 'You have my address. After work?'

He nods.

'Six?' He clears his throat. 'Ish?'

'Sixish,' she confirms. She smiles once more, looking up at him, then suddenly frowns. '*Oh.*' She is staring intently into his eyes as if she can see right into the very core of him, as if there is nothing she does not know. 'You look as if you really need to be *held*. For a long, long time.'

She reaches up and lays the palm of her hand against his cheek.

He feels winded, as if all the breath has been sucked out of him. He cannot even muster the word 'yes', cannot even nod his head in agreement. He shuts his eyes for a moment, places his own hand over hers.

By the time he gets home, it is late. Fortunately, Marcia is so used to his losing all track of time when he is absorbed in his work or at the library that it arouses only a minor show of irritation as she removes his dried-out, crusty supper from the oven. He eats without protest, without noticing, in a dream of soft lips and emerald eyes and flaming hair. As he eats, he lets the words cycle through his mind, though his eyes prick with unshed tears, relishing them like a mantra, berating himself for not having noticed this extraordinarily obvious fact: he needs to be held. He cannot even remember the last time he was held – properly held – by someone who wanted to hold him.

He sleeps not one jot, images of her dancing in his head, her voice, unexpectedly low, in his ears, her soft palm against his cheek... her captivating eyes... her hair... her mouth, open to his – warm, welcoming, wanting, wanting him.

26

ENGRAVING

Friday. Eleanor did her main weekly shop, came back and unpacked everything, then put some cubed beef to marinate overnight in red wine, with bay leaves and juniper berries, to make a casserole the next day for Roger's return. She was looking forward to having a Chinese takeaway this evening while watching an old movie, the classic *Now, Voyager* with Bette Davis. Roger wasn't a fan of either Chinese takeaway – 'it stinks the house out' – or black-and-white films – 'I can't bloody concentrate because I keep thinking the TV's on the blink if there's no colour!'

Delving into her handbag to find a replacement button she'd bought for one of Roger's jackets, she came across her sketchbook. Eleanor turned to the drawing she'd done in the park the other day. It really wasn't at all bad – better than she'd remembered; it seemed to capture not just the woman's physical pose, but something more – her attitude perhaps. So often, women sat in a very closed way, their legs crossed or pressed together, taking up as little space as possible, apologising for their existence. But this woman was unashamedly a presence in the world, her legs extending onto the path, her head tipped back to drink in the sun and the sky.

If she were to make it into an engraving, it would need more detail, texture, differentiation of light and shadow in the areas around the woman – in the tree and the bench. Well, it was only late morning; she could go back to the park now. Of course, the woman wouldn't be there, but she could put in more work on the surroundings.

* * *

When Eleanor came back she went straight up to her studio with the sketchbook open in her hands, thinking. Already, as happened when she was excited about the prospect of turning a drawing into an engraving, she could picture the process. For her, there was great pleasure in the sequence and absorption of the work itself, not just in the final result: the finalising of the drawing, the transferring of it to the prepared surface of the woodblock, the satisfying feel of the tool easing into the block.

She liked the orderliness of wood engraving, its very particular combination of allowing you to be expressive yet incredibly precise. It was not something to tackle in a hurry: you needed to be calm and focused, and work with great care; you couldn't just grab your tools and start gouging out grooves in the wood. She liked the tools themselves, the feel of each one in her hand, and their names that sounded like characters in a story by Roald Dahl – the scorpers, the spitstickers, the gravers.

Eleanor selected a woodblock from her plan chest, then proceeded to go through the stages of transferring the drawing to the prepared, black-painted block – tracing it onto thin layout paper, putting sanguine paper on the block, then fixing the tracing above this red carbon and marking the drawing once more using a very hard, sharp pencil to leave a clear guide on the block itself once she removed the carbon paper. She decided to start the actual engraving the following morning when she'd be fresh and rested. She tidied up, then went downstairs to order her takeaway and set up the film.

* * *

Saturday morning. With Roger not expected back until the evening, Eleanor had no need to make coffee for him or prepare a proper breakfast. She checked the time as she took off her watch; she never wore it while engraving as it tended to catch on the edge of the sandbag. It was only a little after 9 a.m. – hours and hours before Roger would appear. The beef for the casserole was marinating; all she needed to do was put it in the oven at around 4 p.m. so it would be perfectly tender and ready for his return in the evening. She grabbed a quick slice of toast, ate it while standing up, then took her tea up to her studio.

Tentatively, Eleanor approached her work bench, where she had left out the prepared woodblock. There was a difference between a drawing that might be quite good in its own right and one that could work as an engraving. She looked at the drawing again, trying to assess it with a cold, clear eye. She was tempted to take a photo of it and send it to Sarah to ask her opinion but thought Sarah might think it ridiculous. Don't be so bloody feeble, make a decision yourself, for God's sake. Be a grown-up!

The boxwood she liked to use because of its lovely fine grain was expensive and it was extremely fiddly and laborious to correct any mistakes.

Still, if it turned out badly, at worst it was a waste of the woodblock and her time – hardly a disaster.

She put on some music – Bach – so that she could relax enough to work well. She set the woodblock on the small round leather sandbag she used to keep the block steady and easy to rotate while she worked.

There was always a hesitation before Eleanor began. It wasn't just a lack of confidence, the anxiety that she might make a mistake, although no doubt that was part of it. It had taken her a long time to realise that the hesitation also held excitement, the anticipation of something that was a curiously thrilling mixture of the known and the unknown, twisted together tightly into a single cord: the known – the feeling of each tool in her hand, the complete absorption in the work, the satisfying give of the grain as the metal incised into the wood; the unknown – how the drawing would translate into the engraving, what the final print would look like, whether you yourself would feel that it was good. No matter how clearly you thought you could visualise it, something would be different. For her, in whom the habit of keen self-criticism was so long ingrained she no longer noticed it, there would usually be at least one aspect that fell short of her imagining. Occasionally, however, when she made her first test print, she would peel back the paper from the woodblock and there would be a brief – almost guilty – flush of pleasure that she had produced something she could recognise as good. It reminded her of the feeling she had in the choir sometimes, the nervousness and excitement she felt when she had a solo part to sing as the moment drew nearer and nearer. And then, afterwards, that lovely quiet glow when she knew she had sung well.

Eleanor picked up her first tool, took a breath, and began...

At some point, she stopped and stood up, stretched and realised she was hungry and thirsty and in need of fresh air. She dashed downstairs, slugged back a glass of water and grabbed a hasty hunk of cheese with a couple of crackers, then went out to the back garden and ran up and down the lawn a few times as fast as she could. God knows what the neighbours would think if they happened to be looking out of the window that minute.

* * *

The block looked all right, but you could never know until you made a test print exactly what the result would be. She set up the press, inked the block. Made the print.

A pause. Again, that feeling of nervousness coupled with excitement. Eleanor peeled away the paper. Felt a smile fill her face, her body. Forced herself to frown at the print, to pick it over in minute detail, hunting for faults. Yes, there – the texture of one part of the tree in the background could be improved. She cleaned the block thoroughly and returned to the workbench, worked on the rogue area a little more, then took another print.

That was it. There came a moment when you had to fight the urge to fiddle with it. Like making pastry, you needed to know when to stop handling it or it would be static and dull, overworked. With an engraving, you could work the life out of it altogether if you did not find the right moment to step away and allow that it was done. Eleanor looked at it for as much as an entire minute, allowing herself this brief solitary indulgence. It was possibly the best she had ever done.

She was stiff and aching, though, having been hunched over her workbench for hours. She ran downstairs, put on the kettle and peeled a banana, which she ate standing up; contemplated whether to get her things and go for a swim to ease her stiff shoulders and back or perhaps just a quick walk round the block, though now she realised it had got dark some time ago. She checked the time on her mobile, still plugged into its charger on the kitchen worktop. It was nearly half-past seven.

She opened the fridge, as if hoping that the beef might magically have found its own way out and into a casserole dish and a hot oven. It took a minimum of three hours to be truly tender. She stood there for a moment, with no idea what to do. Then the phone rang. It was Roger calling from his taxi en route from City airport, saying good news, his flight was all on time and he'd be back shortly.

'Lovely!' In a panic, she called their local Italian restaurant, their standby they often used. They were full but as she was a regular, of course, Signora, they would squeeze her in – at 9 p.m.

She zipped round the sitting room, plumping up the cushions and adjusting the lighting. Opened a bottle of red wine and set a large glass beside her husband's chair; placed a dish of her homemade cheese nibbles alongside to keep him going as they would be eating late.

She stood poised in the hallway, ready to open the front door the moment she heard his taxi pulling up outside.

'Good journey?' She stretched up to kiss him.

'Fine, thanks, darling. Very full-on trip, though. I'm shattered. Grateful for a quiet night in, I must say.'

'Um, actually, I've booked Trattoria Mondello for a little later. I thought your flight might get delayed.'

'Really? Oh, well, I suppose it's all right. Is there time for a little glass of wine before we go?'

'Absolutely.' She gestured to the sitting room, his chair, the wine, the nibbles.

'Ah, perfect.' Roger settled back in his chair and closed his eyes. 'Thank you, darling.' He put his feet up on the footstool. 'There are a couple of rather fancy gifts for you in my bag. Help yourself when you unpack, won't you?'

'Lovely. Thank you.' She went into the hall to take his case upstairs, but Roger called out to her.

'No, I'll take it up later. No need to unpack this minute. It's awfully heavy, darling – let me do it.'

See, he could be kind and considerate. Now she felt guilty that she'd enjoyed having the house to herself so much. He was only really crabby when he was stressed and tired.

She perched on the edge of the sofa.

'And what have you been up to, darling?' Roger asked, eyes still closed. 'Singing, swimming, hanging out with your conservation buddies – all that sort of thing?'

'Yes to all of those. Actually, I also worked on a new engraving.' She paused, allowing herself a small flush of pleasure once more. 'I think it's really not bad.'

Roger opened his eyes and twisted his head a little towards her.

'You sweet thing.' He reached forward to pat her knee. 'It's great you have a little hobby to keep you out of mischief.' He picked up the folded newspaper from where she'd placed it at his side. 'Have you got a print you can bring down to show me – or do I have to slog all the way upstairs to your ivory tower?'

Suddenly, Eleanor was quite sure that she didn't want to show the print to him. Another time, perhaps, but not now, not while it was still so fresh and new.

'Oh, it's not finished yet, darling – I'm still working on it. I'll show you another time.'

* * *

At supper in the Italian restaurant, Roger expounded at some length on the wonders of Jersey.

The waiter handed him the wine list, as usual. As Roger opened it out like a book, it triggered a sudden flash of memory in Eleanor. Last night, when she'd been reading in bed, her book had slipped from her hands. And this morning, as Roger wasn't due back till the evening, she'd just left the novel where it was, knowing that she would come back and tidy up and plump the pillows and so on during the day well before his return. But then she'd got caught up in her engraving and the day had zipped by without her thinking about anything else. The thought of that horrible quiet click as he slid open the blade of his penknife made her shudder.

'All right, darling?' Roger happened to glance across at her at that moment over the top of the wine list. 'Happy with a Sauvignon?'

'Mmm.' She didn't really like Sauvignon but sometimes it was just simpler to say yes rather than have a pretend discussion of the merits of different kinds of wine when Roger would always end up ordering what he wanted anyway.

It was fine, she told herself, clutching her menu. There was nothing to worry about. All she had to do was dash upstairs to rescue the book the moment they got in after supper. Roger was hardly likely to race her up the stairs. It would be fine as long as she didn't allow herself to get distracted. Beneath the table, she pinched the skin on the back of her hand, reciting 'book, book, book' mentally to herself, trying to will the reminder into her body as well as her mind.

They ordered and, for the rest of supper, she did her best to focus on listening attentively to her husband and to ask interested-sounding questions and offer appropriate responses as required. She tried not to keep thinking about how desperate she was to get back to her engraving. She really couldn't wait to make a few prints. She'd give one to Sarah, one to her dad, perhaps even have one framed to put up at home, if Roger didn't mind. She took another sip of her wine, trying not to wince at its green, steely taste, and to keep at bay the image of her book lying out on the bed, vulnerable, exposed.

27

THE FIRST DATE

Andrew did not go on dates. The greatest plus point about being in a relationship was that it meant you no longer need to tie yourself in knots wondering what you should wear, what to say, what not to say, how to sit, how to stand without looking like a weirdo. True, with Vicki, he'd had to remember that there were certain subjects that were rather... unsatisfactory as topics of conversation: politics, books, the BM, art and antiquities in general, religion, ideas or anything philosophical, or technical conservation problems, which were of no interest to her. Vicki wasn't a massive fan of delving deeply into a subject and talking about it at length, though come to think of it, when she had her girlfriends over for a Cocktails 'n' Pampering evening and he had come back too early, he could hear them talking in unbelievable detail about handbags – size, style, shops, prices, 'new handbag smell', whatever that was, 'handbag charms', which were possibly those dangly things that now seemed to be attached to women's bags but for which he could discern no possible purpose. But... but... at least he could relax. She was used to him and he was used to her. If they were going somewhere smart, she'd simply instruct him what to wear – 'blue striped shirt, navy chinos, your loafers – no, not that jacket, your other one'.

Andrew was not at his best on dates. He found himself embarrassing on such occasions, and always had done. He did not know where to put his hands or his feet. He was neither tall nor fat, but on dates there seemed to be too much of him. He was prone to knocking over the salt-cellar or his date's wineglass. Should he open the door for her or pull out her chair or help her off with her coat? He would hover uncertainly at each stage, opening the door but then spoiling it by saying, 'Is it OK if I open the door for you?', or feebly reaching towards her coat as if to take it, then not taking it so it fell to the floor. He wasn't sure how long one should reasonably spend looking at the menu. Why couldn't one just bypass the whole dating stage and simply move seamlessly on to living together – then you could go out together for a meal and just be you and it was so much easier?

Andrew acknowledged that he could not simply say to Olivia that he'd prefer to crack on and move in together because then he could relax. That might make her think he was odd or something. And anyway, she might not even like him. But she had agreed to meet him. He'd texted her in the end because he was getting himself in a cold sweat at the prospect of phoning her. The thought struck him that perhaps this wasn't a date at all, that she was just agreeing to meet him to talk about the apple tree some more and they might as well eat something while they were at it. Well, he would take his cue from her. He wouldn't say anything stupid like, 'So, how do you think this date's going so far?' in case she said, 'What date? What on earth do you mean?'

He put on his best jeans and a blue cotton shirt and his suede trainers that his friend Dave assured him were reasonably cool. He added a chunky grey jumper – he felt it made him look more well-built – and his wool jacket. He suspected that the jacket was not at all cool but at least it looked more casual than his long winter coat. He looked in the mirror but – how disappointing – it was still the same old Andrew looking back at him. He stood up straight and squared his shoulders and smiled, but it looked creepy so he stopped. You're over-thinking, just stop it and calm down. Think about something else.

He popped his head round the kitchen door, hoping to say a brief goodbye to his parents without getting interrogated about his movements. He had tons of time but planned to go for a walk first, maybe sit in the pub with a pint and read a newspaper, chill out for a bit just to calm down and stop himself thinking.

'Just popping out, folks, OK? See you later.'

'Andrew, you're never going out without your evening meal?'

'It's fine, Mum, really – thanks. Do you remember, I did tell you a couple of days ago that I'd be out this evening? I'm having supper out.'

'Out?' his mother said, as if she must have misheard. 'But it's lamb chops.'

'Off out, are you then?' His father said, looking up from his newspaper. 'Have fun.'

'What, in a restaurant, you mean?' Mrs Tyler looked perplexed.

'Yes, in a restaurant.' Not in a swimming pool or a cement factory – a restaurant, a place where people go out to eat.

'Eating out's so pricey, though, Andrew. And the chops are lovely – look, see.' She pulled out the grill pan to show him the raw lamb chops on their rectangle of foil, ready to cook. 'They're ever so lean.'

'They do look good. Well, Dad, you have mine then, will you?'

'Sure, son.'

'But why do you have to go to a restaurant?'

'He's probably seeing a friend, love.'

'Kind of. New friend.'

'Ah.' His father nodded and returned behind the paper.

'A new friend? How do you mean?'

God, please just let me leave the building.

'You know – just a person I met recently.'

'I'll not let you go out without so much as a cup of tea, Andrew. What sort of mother would that make me?'

I don't know – one who believes her thirty-five-year-old son is capable of deciding if he is able to leave the house all on his own, perhaps? He felt himself deflate. She meant well. They both did.

'Well, just a cup of tea then. Thank you, Mum.'

'It's all made and in the pot anyway. It's no bother.'

'Right.' Andrew sat down.

* * *

The moment he entered the restaurant, he could tell he'd made a mistake. He had wanted to impress Olivia, make her think he had his finger on the pulse and knew the cool places to go, but he was not convinced that this was one of them, especially as it was completely empty. Obviously, he didn't know the cool places to go, so he had asked

Dave, who was the same age as Andrew but still living the lifestyle of someone ten years younger. Dave had said: don't do the whole clichéd Italian thing, mate – think Pacific Rim, think fusion. Or, hey, North African. He'd been a few times to this great Moroccan place recently. Really laid-back. You sat on these big floor cushions – you were practically lying down through dinner – it was Seduction Central. It was in north London so handy, too. All Andrew would have to do would be show up and try not to be a total tit, and even he could manage that for a couple of hours, surely?

'All that lounging on cushions, it'll get her in the mood. By the time you take her back to your place, she'll have her hand down your trousers before you're in the door, I bet you.'

Andrew tried to imagine it, but realised he couldn't take Olivia back to his place because he didn't have a place. He'd have to be demented to take her home to his parents, with his dad shuffling about looking apologetic for disturbing the pile on the carpet and his mum popping up and wiping round you every two minutes like a jack-in-the-box with OCD. Also, it seemed highly unlikely that Olivia would attempt to grope him. Not that he would shove her off or anything, but Andrew wasn't the kind of man who would try to sleep with a woman on the first date. When he had ended up in bed with someone, it seemed to happen more by accident than design, or because the woman had instigated it.

They had arranged to meet there. The booking was very early – for 7 p.m. – because that was the only time they had available.

As Dave had said, there were carved screens creating intimate alcoves and ornate lanterns flickering. No floor cushions, though – just normal chairs. Perhaps they had refurbished the place? It was quite a relief really; it was never easy to get up and down from a floor cushion with dignity.

'When I booked on the phone, they said you'd be full.' Andrew gestured at the empty room.

Yes, the waiter assured him, it would be full. Two big parties this evening – coming soon, soon – very full.

He was led to the far corner, then down a narrow spiral staircase.

'Oh, isn't our table on the ground floor?'

'No, no, special room. Downstairs. You ask for special table, yes?'

'Well, yes... but...'

'You meeting special lovely lady, yes?'

Andrew smiled at the thought.

'Yes, she is, but—'

'And you Dave's friend – this his favourite table. Very... sexy.' The waiter gave him a knowing wink and clucked his tongue.

Oh God.

The table was in an incredibly dark alcove tucked between the staircase and the toilets. Down on this level, there were indeed floor cushions. Andrew had never seen such a large gathering of cushions in one place; a cushion warehouse couldn't have had more cushions in it than this room. There were huge stuffed round pouffes in ornate leatherwork, and large square floor cushions in covers stitched from old hand-woven carpets; there were cushions with tiny round mirrors on them, and embroidered cushions, and extra red and black and gold cushions scattered here, there and everywhere with an over-liberal hand. It looked like a stage-set for an orgy.

'Um, I wonder... do you have a table upstairs? That might be better.'

'No, is all full. This very nice. Very good table.'

'It's just a bit...' Andrew indicated the empty room.

'I put music on.'

Andrew lowered himself onto a floor cushion and tried to get himself into a sustainable position before Olivia arrived so that he wouldn't be constantly fidgeting and trying to get comfortable. He had a feeling you were supposed to sit cross-legged, but these jeans were feeling oddly snug around his middle.

Suddenly, the sound of nasal singing filled the room. The waiter danced back across the room towards him.

'Is better now, yes?'

'Fine, thanks.' No doubt it would be very different once the place started to fill up.

After a couple of minutes, there was the clang-clang-clang of footsteps on the metal staircase.

'Hello.' Andrew struggled to his feet to greet Olivia, thinking: should I kiss her or would that be too much, and then realising that he would have to vault over the table to get to her and, given that the room was very dark and basically furnished like a harem, she might well take fright and flee.

'Hello.' Olivia smiled, then peered round the room. 'Well, this is... um... interesting, isn't it? Did you book out the entire restaurant?'

'I'm so sorry. The waiter promised it would fill up very soon.'

'Now, is there an elegant way to do this?' Olivia gestured to the cushion.

'There may well be, but I don't know what it is. I can avert my gaze while you flump onto it.'

Olivia lowered herself and attempted to sit cross-legged.

'Ah, possibly not such a good idea to wear a skirt.' She rearranged herself with her legs tucked to one side.

Andrew smiled then stopped as he thought maybe she'd think he was leering over the possibility of looking up her skirt.

'Goodness, no shortage of cushions.' Olivia craned her neck round to survey the room.

'I think they must have got slightly carried away at the Cushion Expo.'

She laughed. 'Or it was Buy One, Get Two Hundred Free at Cushions 'R' Us.'

Andrew laughed too.

They looked at the menus, aided by the lit-up screen of Andrew's mobile phone, and the waiter recommended they order soon as a large party was due in at seven thirty.

'But the party's upstairs, right? No party down here?'

'Yes, yes, party here and upstairs. Very good. Two birthday parties. Lot of fun.'

Andrew met Olivia's gaze; she looked as thrilled by the prospect as he was.

'I'm really sorry,' he said.

'Don't worry, it'll cheer it up when there are more people.' She studied the menu. 'And I love this sort of food. It was a good choice.'

They ordered and the conversation turned to East Finchley, the area where their parents lived.

'I really like those Edwardian houses in your mum's street,' Andrew said. 'They're much nicer than the inter-war semis where my parents live.'

'That's only because you haven't set foot across the threshold yet. My mother thinks if you ever tidy up then you're just kowtowing to convention, God forbid. To her, living in chaos is virtually a religion – and she's a devout keeper of the faith.'

Andrew laughed.

'Ha! My mum is the exact antithesis of that. She regards Dust as the earthly manifestation of the Antichrist. If you were to sit still for more than ten minutes, she's likely to spray you with Pledge and give you a quick polish.'

Andrew asked Olivia if her parents still worked.

'My mother still draws all the time, but mostly she did mosaics.'

'Mosaics? How unusual. Is she good?'

'Yes, she really is.' Olivia nodded. 'And she was very successful too. She mostly worked on private commissions – often in gardens but also in houses. The odd frieze in a restaurant or hotel. She even has a couple of smaller pieces in the collection at the V&A. Not so many commissions lately, but actually she's working on a project now.'

'And your dad?'

'Also an artist. His early stuff was particularly good, but he's currently into creating rather peculiar constructions out of sheet metal. I'm not quite sure what to make of them.'

'Intriguing. And are you tempted to do something like that yourself? With *two* artistic parents? Or does that put you off because it's a hard act to follow?'

'I draw a bit but... well... my dad's not actually my biological father so...' Her voice petered out.

Andrew fiddled with his bread and waited for her to continue.

'My real dad might not be remotely artistic. He could be an accountant, for all I know.' She shrugged as if the matter were of no importance to her and reached for her wineglass. 'Or a banker.' She made a face and drank some wine.

'Do you not see him then?' Andrew sipped his wine. 'Sorry, is it OK to ask? Tell me to butt out if I'm being too nosy.'

'It's OK.' She tore off a piece of bread as if ripping off a chicken wing. 'I've never even met him. Sorry, I don't know why I'm telling you; I don't normally talk about it much.'

'I'm sorry.'

'Nothing to be sorry about.' She shrugged again. 'Don't miss what you've never had and all that. And my dad – my other dad – he was around properly all the time we were growing up, so it was fine. And we both love him. I'm very lucky really.'

'And he and your mum are still together?'

'God, no – Dad's gay. He lives in San Francisco with his partner; they've been together for years. We talk and email, though.'

'God, my family are so boring. I wish I had an interesting family like yours.'

Olivia laughed. 'Believe me, you really don't. Anyway, I'm sure they're not at all boring. You're not boring, so why should they be? Or are you adopted?'

'When I was a kid, I used to think I must be a changeling because my parents and my brother are so different from me. I do love them, of course, but I've always felt really out of sync with them.' Andrew topped up their glasses. 'But back to you, please. Sorry, I'm fascinated by this. So, the sheet metal guy is your sister's biological dad but your adoptive dad or stepdad, is that right?'

'Nope, he's not Maddy's dad either.'

'The plot thickens. Who's her dad then?'

'Um, you see, when my mother was younger, she was... fairly wild, I think, for a time. She met this guy on holiday, came back to England, found she was pregnant with me, but she didn't even have a number for him. She didn't have any money then ... and Phil was a really good friend, so they got married and moved in together. Mostly, it worked very well and it suited them both. Then four years later, she got up the spout by another guy, and Maddy came along.'

'But aren't you curious about your real father?'

'Sometimes.' She looked down into her wineglass. 'I do wonder... anyway let's go back to your family,' she said, 'as, clearly, mine's a bit bizarre.'

Then, with a series of deafening clangs, a procession of people descended the metal stairs, talking and laughing. The group filled up the rest of the room, hurling themselves onto the floor cushions with much hilarity and shrieking.

The waiter danced across the room,

'Party, party! Everybody happy!'

The music was turned up high then, from behind one of the carved screens, a belly-dancer appeared, dressed in a turquoise nylon bra-top and translucent skirt, edged with jingly gold discs. She shimmied across the room then tugged at Andrew's sleeve and jiggled her midriff in his face, trying to get him to get up and dance with her. He politely attempted to ward her off.

'I can't. I broke my foot!' gesturing at his clearly uninjured extremity. She grabbed his hand and he stood up. 'You have to come too!' he called out as the dancer pulled him towards the centre of the floor.

Olivia remained on her cushion. Well, that was that then: if Olivia saw him dancing, that would be the end of it.

'Please,' he mouthed.

Olivia got to her feet and came over to join him.

'I can't believe I'm doing this. I feel ridiculous.' She swayed tentatively.

'Me, too.'

The belly-dancer was wiggling from table to table, pulling people to their feet. The waiter joined in.

'Everybody dancing. Happy, happy!'

And it was true. The space was packed with people dancing and smiling and laughing. Andrew had no idea how you were supposed to dance to this kind of music but he and Olivia just fell into the same kind of style, a sort of self-mocking pastiche of Arabic dancing, with sinuously moving arms and swaying hips.

Their food arrived then and they returned to the table, laughing and breathless.

'That was surprisingly a lot of fun, wasn't it?' Olivia looked into his eyes.

'It was. Thank God for all those years of belly-dancing classes. I knew they'd pay off in the end.'

As it was near impossible to hear each other during the meal, with the music and the jangling and the shouting of the party revellers, they ate fairly quickly and skipped pudding and coffee.

'We could have coffee somewhere else if you like? Or ice cream?'

Olivia gave him one of those smiles that made his heart go skippity-skip. They sauntered along, looking for a café that was still open. He wanted to hold her hand, but was never sure about that sort of thing. What if he took her hand and she shook him off or said, 'What on earth are you doing?' He shifted his hand slightly so it brushed the edge of hers. She didn't recoil as if she'd been given an electric shock, but perhaps she hadn't noticed even? Or had noticed but didn't want to be rude. He let it happen again, this time letting his touch linger a little longer. Olivia took his hand and turned to him and smiled.

'Shall we get a takeaway coffee? Then we can walk at the same time, if you don't mind. I could do with the exercise.'

'Sure, me too. Which way shall we walk? May I see you home? You're in Crouch End, you said?'

'How very gentlemanly of you. Yes, but it's about twenty minutes' walk from here – is that too far?'

They walked and talked. Andrew took pretend sips of his coffee; he never ordered takeaway coffees because on his last attempt he had removed the lid but then spilled it all down his shirt and had to go round the rest of the day looking like he should have been wearing a bib.

Olivia asked him more about his work.

'I'd love to see what you do. Do you take before-and-after photos when you mend something or restore it, as a record?'

'Mmm, yes, I do sometimes, if it's something a bit unusual or if the work is extensive or particularly tricky. Here...' He took out his phone and opened up the photos. Selected one showing just an extreme close-up of the bottom of Conrad's painting. 'This is the damaged part of a painting I worked on recently.' He held out the phone to show her, then flicked to the next photo. 'And this is the same area after I'd worked on it.'

'That's amazing. It looks perfect.'

'Well, it's not, but I was quite pleased with it. I showed you that one because it's colour. We don't usually restore paintings in my department – that's a whole different section. We work mostly with the Prints and Drawings department – works on paper: engravings, drawings in pencil, charcoal, pastel, that sort of thing. This one was on board. I've got more photos of it if you want to see?'

'Well, this is me.' Olivia paused outside a handsome old block of flats.

Andrew wondered if she might ask him in for more coffee. He stuffed his hands in his pockets and paused.

'That was a lovely evening,' he said. 'Thank you for coming out with me.'

'It *was* lovely.' She looked away then back into his eyes. 'And belly-dancing was an unexpected bonus, of course. I'm sorry, I would ask you to come up, but my sister will only grill you and I'd rather expose you to my family very gradually, if you don't mind.'

'It's fine.' Andrew moved a fraction nearer. 'So...'

'So...' Olivia smiled and moved nearer, her face slightly tilted up towards his.

He leaned in then, and put his hand on her waist and drew her to him. And kissed her. She seemed to melt against him and he put his other arm around her to encircle her.

They drew apart but stood still entwined, looking into each other's eyes.

'Will you come out with me again?' he said. 'If that wasn't too hideous?'

'I think I could force myself.' She kissed him briefly on the lips and took out her keys. 'Good night then.'

'Good night.' He drew her to him and kissed her again. 'Shall I call you? Or text? Email?'

'All of those.' Her face lit up with her smile again.

Afterwards, he stood outside the entrance door to the flats for a minute or two, just revelling in this unfamiliar feeling. He feared he must be grinning like a kid on Christmas morning. Then he turned and set off to walk all the way back to his parents, wanting some time and solitude in which to replay every single moment of the evening in his head.

28

THE CLOUD

Roger came into the kitchen and flicked on the kettle, then opened the cupboard to take out a cafetière. They owned three small ones, to save having to wash one every time he wanted fresh coffee. He stood looking into the cupboard. Eleanor watched him, and could see his registering the inexplicable lack of cafetières. It was extraordinary how long he stood there just staring into the depths of the cupboard, as if the cafetières might be playing some sort of mischievous prank on him and were deliberately hiding, hunkered down behind the sugar bowl or holding their collective breath behind the milk jug. Eleanor remained sitting at the kitchen table, apparently reading the paper, flicking glances in his direction. Her feet pressed down into the floor, willing her to stand up and go out. It would probably be better if she were to leave the room. Then he would have to work it out for himself. There didn't have to be a confrontation. But, for some reason, she remained in her seat. She couldn't quite fathom why she was doing this, engaging in this small, rather pathetic act of defiance. What good could come of it, after all? Her arms shivered with goosebumps.

All three cafetières were still by the sink – his one from yesterday morning, yesterday evening, and the one he used this morning. Usually, Eleanor would have washed them and dried them and returned them to the cupboard. Even if one were in the dishwasher, she would never have put all three in there; there would always be at least one clean and ready for him. But today, now, here they all were, unwashed.

'I can't see a clean cafetière.' Roger half-turned towards her.

Eleanor knew he must have seen them – dirty, their thick layer of coffee gunge still in place – at the back of the worktop. Admittedly, Roger's obsessive eye for detail had mysterious blank patches; he always left his empty wineglass by his chair in the sitting room, and his dirty mug on the desk in his study. After his shower, his towel would be dumped on the floor or flung over the side of the bath rather than returned neatly to the rail to dry.

Eleanor dug her thumbnail deep into the newspaper page and half looked up.

'None in the cupboard?'

'Apparently not.' Roger sighed and shut the cupboard door with a bang, no mean feat given its expensive soft-close hinges.

'Oh?' Eleanor drew her thumbnail back up the page, scoring a groove.

She could get up now, rise to her feet, walk across as if she were a normal person, a wife carrying out a very minor domestic task. She should just wash one of the cafetières. That's what a good wife would do. She should definitely do that. Why make a big deal of it? Eleanor was not the kind of person who made a big deal of things, really not. She was the kind of person who just got on with whatever needed to be done, without making a fuss about whose turn it was or if it was fair or any of that. So why so stubborn all of a sudden? It was just a dirty cafetière, after all. Only a bloody cafetière. But then Roger was actually standing right by the sink, and was it really so much harder for him to wash one just this once, rather than for her to come over and do it for him? Especially as he was the one wanting coffee, after all. Eleanor didn't even drink coffee.

'The ones by the sink are still dirty. Apparently.' Roger's tone, Eleanor noted silently, had shifted. It was – surprisingly – not accusatory. It was... she thought for a moment, assessing... puzzled.

'Ah.' Eleanor looked back down at the newspaper. Beneath her fingers, the photo of a smugly blissful couple – C-list celebs, she assumed, though she had absolutely no idea who they were – was scored with deep grooves from her thumbnail.

She looked up at Roger, facing him now, clutching the edges of the newspaper as if it might hold her up.

'You might need to wash one then,' she said.

He met her gaze for a moment, then he turned and walked out of the room.

*　*　*

Roger was not happy, and when Roger was not happy, the whole of north-west London sat under a raft of thick, grey cloud so dense that no glimmer of sunshine could break through. When it descended, the Cloud hung heavy over the house for anything from twenty-four hours to an entire week, until Eleanor's finely tuned strategies succeeded in gently blowing it away. Now, three days in, she was unusually impatient with the need to tiptoe round her husband. Roger could not be teased out from the Cloud or told to snap out of it. The only effective strategy was to softly, softly coax and cajole him into allowing the Cloud to lift with a succession of small offerings, little touches that reflected his importance as Head of the Household: a clinking gin and tonic set by his chair the moment he came in, accompanied by a dish of Eleanor's homemade crispy cheese nibbles; his business shoes buffed to a mirror-shine; his pyjamas pressed and warm, ready for him to put on. In the early days of their marriage, Eleanor could tease him about being the silverback gorilla, the leader of the pack, and he would laugh with her, but a while ago, perhaps a very long time ago, she was aware that somehow the balance had shifted and that it was no longer acceptable to tease him in this way, that it would merely serve to deepen his displeasure.

Tonight they had a work function of Roger's to attend: drinks and canapés on a boat sauntering down the river to Greenwich and back. Eleanor had been dreading it, knowing that, once the boat had departed from the pier, they would not be able to get off it for four hours. But now she was feeling cautiously optimistic: if the party went well, Roger's spirits would be bound to lift and, in any case, surely even Roger would hardly dare to be grumpy around his valuable clients or his boss? At least it couldn't possibly be any worse than the last two evenings where they had sat having supper in stony silence until Roger claimed he needed to check some figures and had sat there stabbing at the screen of his tablet computer while he ate.

It was understood that Roger would drive to the dock and Eleanor would drive them home again at the end of the evening, so that he could relax and have a few drinks. That was the way it always was. In fact, tonight Eleanor would love the chance to kick up her heels and have a second glass of champagne for once.

'I wonder whether we mightn't do better to take a taxi this evening instead?' she speculated while looking in her wardrobe to choose a dress. Suggestions to Roger were often better received if she were not looking at him directly and if couched in the form of a question seeking his expert view.

'I'd rather have the car there. I hate coming out to find you can't get a cab for love nor money.'

'Won't it be tricky to park round there, though?'

'No, it's not a problem.'

'I just thought I'd quite like to be able to have a second glass of wine if I fancied it.' Eleanor looked at him from around the side of her wardrobe door.

'Be my guest.' He shrugged. Roger would happily drive after two or three glasses of wine, but Eleanor wouldn't dream of having more than one small glass if she were driving. 'I doubt you'll be much over the limit. You'd have to be pretty unlucky to get caught. Makes no odds to me.' He turned back to the mirror and tweaked his tie into position.

'It's OK, I won't drink.' It was nothing to do with the risk of being *caught*. It was about being *safe* – surely he could see that? She sat down at her dressing table to apply her make-up.

'Do try not to take ages – don't forget the boat leaves at seven thirty sharp.'

She heard him thudding heavily down the stairs followed by the plink-plink of ice and the clink of a bottle as he presumably poured himself a drink.

On the way, Roger fulminated against 'the cretin who had organised a bloody boat trip in winter, for crying out loud.'

'It's actually a rather lovely evening, though,' Eleanor pointed out. 'At least it's not raining. And the lights will look magical, I think.'

'And it's going to be bloody sushi instead of normal canapés. Who wants to eat raw fish and cold rice while shivering on the river?'

'But lots of people love—' she began then cut herself short. Contradicting Roger when he was in this mood would merely extend it. 'Well, I suppose sushi is trendy now,' she said softly. 'Perhaps she thought the clients would like it?'

'Nonsense. The clients don't know anything – that's why they need us to advise them.'

Eleanor did not point out that perhaps there was a difference between needing expert legal advice and knowing which foods you preferred to eat.

'Maybe they'll have those little seaweed rolls with fresh tuna inside – you quite like those, don't you?'

'Not nearly as much as proper, cooked food.'

Eleanor turned and looked out of the window. Well, it was only one evening and they would get a good view of the buildings along the river. She was not usually keen on boats, as she was prone to motion-sickness, but the river was very calm, and it was better to be out with the opportunity to talk to other people rather than stuck at home eating supper in silence.

She spotted him glancing at her black dress and held her breath, hoping she had made a good choice.

'That's all right,' he said. 'Is it new?'

'Fairly. I've had it a few months.'

She had spent some time trying to choose the right outfit, something that would make her attractive enough so that he would feel she was a credit to him, but not sexy or too alluring, which might invite comment.

'Good that you didn't wear that purple one like last time. I don't want clients thinking you're some sort of... well...' He sniffed.

The purple dress was supremely elegant but rather low-cut; Eleanor had originally bought it for precisely this reason, as the neckline was low enough to show off a beautiful pearl and amethyst necklace she had, but Roger had spent the whole evening frowning at it on the one occasion she'd worn it.

Eleanor flushed. It wasn't a tarty dress at all. She tucked her hands under her legs to quash the impulse to jab him in the face with her elbow.

'Well, I'm not wearing it, and so long as I don't start dancing on the tables and flashing my knickers I'm sure I can trick them into thinking I'm perfectly respectable.'

Roger shot a look at her, but she stared resolutely forwards.

'There's no need to be snotty about it, Eleanor. *I* didn't force you to spend *my* money on an inappropriate dress that isn't fit to be seen in for anything other than a hen night in Essex. Did I?' He breathed out huffily through his nostrils.

Eleanor remained silent.

'Did I?' He repeated.

'No,' she said, turning to look out of her side window once more. 'You didn't.'

They drove in silence for the rest of the way. Eventually, they managed to park, and as they walked to the pier Roger reminded her that a couple of his most important Jersey-based clients would be there and could she please, if it wasn't too much trouble, make a particular effort with them, laugh at their jokes and so on, and not look so bloody bored like last time.

In the end, the evening was better than expected. There were plenty of hot canapés in addition to the sushi, Roger had taken full advantage of the drinks being proffered every few minutes, and it was just mild enough for many of the guests to stay out on deck, relishing the opportunity to knock back unlimited champagne that someone else was paying for. When Eleanor looked across at Roger to monitor his mood, it seemed to her that he was looking a lot less grim. He was talking and laughing with his clients, laying his hand on a blonde woman's arm in that annoying proprietorial way he had with younger women, but she didn't seem to mind. Eleanor began to feel more cheerful. The last couple of days had been barely tolerable, with her dreading the scraping of his key in the lock, the heavy thud as he slammed his briefcase down on the hall floor, the theatrical sigh if she wasn't there poised in the hallway ready to take his coat.

At the end of the evening, they returned to the car and Eleanor began to chat animatedly about how beautiful the river had looked with the lights sparkling on the water and how delicious the canapés had been after all, and—

'Yes, I was there, remember? Is my presence so unimportant to you that you didn't notice that I was also at the party? There's no need for you to replay the entire evening for my benefit, is there?'

Stung, Eleanor simply shook her head and concentrated on driving.

In her mind, Eleanor pictured dealing with the Cloud as like tiptoeing one's way across a minefield. It was, hypothetically, possible to navigate a safe path and make it through to the other side, she knew, and yet only very rarely had she managed to do this. Usually, sooner or later, she had said the wrong thing, or failed to exhibit enough wifely compliance and obeisance, and then it had got worse, with Roger harrumphing around the house and the two of them chewing through supper in stony silence, every mouthful – every exactingly prepared mouthful – like ashes in her mouth.

Over the years, she had become more adept at acting pre-emptively. It was easier to try to keep the Cloud at bay, after all, than it was to shift it once it had hunkered down to settle in. It had become a habit, deferring to Roger when it came to matters of preference, whether it was where and when they choose to go on holiday, or even over very minor matters, such as which path to take on a country walk. Often Roger would ask her, 'Which way do you want to go, darling?' For years, she had interpreted this sort of question as being a genuine enquiry; Roger was seeking her opinion. But then she might say something like, 'Let's go that way. It looks lovely up there.'

'But it's all in shade with so many trees. This way is more open. It's so gloomy that way.'

'Well, I don't mind. Let's go this way then.'

And it wasn't that she really minded whether they went that way or this way, on the whole, but she would have preferred it if Roger had said at the outset, 'Let's go this way,' or had simply led the way so that there was no illusion that she had any say in the matter. It was like being offered a plate with a choice of cakes and, as you reached out to take your favourite, the waiter just choosing one for you and dumping it on your plate.

29

NOTHING ELSE IS

1979–1982

Conrad writes to her – sometimes an outpouring of everything he feels about her, every thought fizzing through his teeming brain, and sometimes no more than a sentence: 'Today I saw a striped apron in a shop window as I rushed past and I thought of you wearing yours, completely naked underneath, stirring soup.' Writing to her helps to leaven those grey days when he cannot get away to see her. If email had existed back then, perhaps he'd have written more often. He returns to love poems he had read years ago, realising that he had never properly understood them before; or, rather, of course he had understood them intellectually, but not here, deep in his gut, his heart. From Donne...

> **She'is all states; and all princes, I,**
> **Nothing else is.**

'Yes!' He strikes the headboard with his hand. 'That is exactly how it is. When I'm with you...' He slows down now, and turns to pull her on top of him so he can look into her eyes. 'When I'm in bed with you, my love, really – *nothing else is.*'

* * *

'You *are* funny,' she says.

'Am I? In what way?'

'Well, because you're so clever and precise and articulate and... hmm – rational, I suppose – but then there are all these other facets you don't see at first: your playfulness, and sweetness. You're more sensitive... and tender... and kind than one would expect. When I first met you, I thought you were rather stiff and formal. I mean, I could see you were incredibly attractive, but you just seemed so self-contained, so controlled that I couldn't really imagine you ever showing your feelings or being wild and rude and delicious in bed...'

'Ah, but that's your influence.'

'Is it? I'm glad then. Yes, you were rather shy the first couple of times, weren't you? I think I shocked you the first time I used the word "fuck". Now you've become so direct. I love it.'

* * *

Talking and talking and talking; laughing and talking, and touching and talking. He can say anything to her – anything! And when they disagree – about a particular painter, or the design of a building, even politics – they argue vehemently, fiercely, but it doesn't dampen their feelings for each other; if anything, the friction adds an exciting crackle of static, and makes him want her even more. There is no one else with whom he can be so relaxed, no one else with whom he knows it is absolutely all right to be himself.

And so it continues, each carving out a larger and larger slice of their lives to encompass the other. She has had other lovers before, of course; he knows that. She's no simpering ingénue; quite the contrary, in fact. He does not like to think of the others who came before him, but he thinks they must have been fools to let her go. How awful must their lives be now? Grey, devoid of the spark, the passion, the deep joy that surely only she could bring.

Sometimes, as they lie in bed talking quietly, they discuss the difficult things, his other life. She tells him she would make a hopeless wife.

'You could well sit there all day waiting for breakfast. I'm a bloody awful cook, you know.'

'Then I'd do it. I don't care anyway – I wouldn't want breakfast.' His hand curves over her waist once more to linger on the irresistible place where her back swerves outwards to her beautiful bottom. 'Rather have the extra time in bed.' Pulling her close now to kiss her again, slipping his hand down between her legs, the thrill of hearing her breathing quicken once more.

'And supper?' Her voice blurry now.

'Sandwich. Takeaway. No time to eat anyway when I need to carry you off to bed at every opportunity, my love.'

'You do,' she says. 'That is your official job now. Bollocks to the British Museum, say I. Tell them you can only pop in there once a week for half an hour as I am extremely demanding.'

Afterwards, she scoops herself against him, her head resting on his shoulder, her soft hair tickling his cheek.

'See how perfectly you fit, my love.' He tucks her hair back behind her ear. 'This is where you belong. I just need to...'

'I don't want you to feel pressure from me. I would never ask you to leave.'

'I know. I know you wouldn't.' He kisses her once more. 'You're the most incredibly unselfish person I've ever known. It's just difficult. The boy is a constant worry. And she – she indulges him. I have to be there to – to – steer the ship a bit.'

'I know.' She kisses him and strokes his cheek very softly. 'I will wait, dear heart, I will wait. For as long as it takes. Just...' She stops.

'Just what?'

'Just never stop loving me, OK?'

'Never, my love,' he says. 'Never.'

30

EN ROUTE FROM A TO B

For their second date, Andrew and Olivia went to see a film. They held hands in the darkness, teenagers again. Afterwards, he drove her home and they kissed on her doorstep once more. This time, she invited him up for coffee, with a warning that her ever-present sister might also be in. When they got upstairs, Madeleine was indeed hanging out in the open-plan kitchen-cum-sitting room with a gaggle of her friends, eating pizzas and knocking back vodka shots.

'Hey, Liv, come and join us! And you've got the boyf with you, too!'

Andrew said hello and stood there awkwardly. He really didn't want to sit there stone-cold sober with a load of pissed twenty-five-year-olds; he'd feel like their sodding chaperone.

Olivia drew her sister aside and said something very quietly to her. But then Madeleine practically shouted in response: 'Go to your bedroom, why don't you? God, chill out! It's not as if we're all going to listen to you while you're at it.'

Her friends laughed and erupted into a series of whoops and fake orgasm crescendos. Olivia flushed deep red. She took Andrew to her room but left the door wide open.

'I'm so sorry – that was *so* embarrassing. She's awful when she gets drunk.'

'Don't give it another thought. It's OK.' Andrew drew her closer.

'You know, I do really like you, but I'm not ready to... I mean, I didn't ask you in to lure you to my bedroom, I just wanted to...'

'No need to fret. Really. There's no rush.' He kissed her lips softly.

At that moment, Madeleine walked past to the bathroom and said loudly: 'Why have you got the door open, Liv? Are you wanting us all to come and watch?'

'Oh, shut up, Mads. Give it a bloody rest.' Olivia crossed her arms.

'I think I'd better go.' Andrew kissed her again. 'But see you very soon, yes?'

'Yes, please.'

'Shall we go out for supper again next week? Maybe somewhere easier to talk?'

'That would be lovely. That's the trouble with going to a film – people kind of frown on it if you talk all the way through.'

* * *

'So, how are things going with your parents?' Olivia asked as she sat opposite him for supper on their next date a few days later.

'My parents? Fine.' Andrew smiled, then stared back down at his food. Olivia was looking so lovely this evening, he was worried he might just sit there gazing at her in a sort of dumb trance. Hurrah – he'd made it to a third date. This was brilliant. And, my God, she was so different from Vicki – and entirely *good* different.

'I mean, you are still staying there, right?'

'Yes, just for a visit.'

'A visit? Ah, I thought you were living there? Did I get the wrong end of the stick?' She stopped eating and looked at him.

'Drop more wine?' He picked up the bottle and topped up her glass, then did the same with the water. Reached for his own water glass, took a sip.

'It's not a trick question.' She smiled. 'I'm not trying to catch you out or anything.'

'No, course not.' He tried to look at ease. 'Well, strictly speaking... I suppose I would have to say that – *technically* – I am currently staying – living – at the house where my parents also live... in the short term.' The mangled sentence sounded awful to his own ears so God knew what it sounded like to her.

'You were living with a girlfriend before, you said?'

At least that sounded less pathetic.

Andrew nodded enthusiastically.

'Yes, that's right, but the relationship had... um... pretty much run its course so we decided to call it a day. It was all very civilised and amicable.' That sounded grown-up, mature. No way was he telling her Vicki had chucked him out. He was about to ask her what she was reading at present, but it was too late.

'Sorry, I don't mean to be intrusive, but if you knew you were leaving, why didn't you arrange to rent somewhere else to move to?'

'Well, yes, I could have done that, obviously. Yes.' He gave a small sniff as if he considered it a rather conventional suggestion that he'd sensibly avoided. He took a sip of his wine, and nodded appreciatively.

'But?'

'But I decided that... in the end... it seemed sensible... ah, simpler... to... to have this brief – very brief – ah, transition period... at my parents'... you know to... to... ah, take stock... and... and... so on. As it would be for such a short time.'

'Transition period?'

'Mmm.' He nodded again, wondering how on earth to get off this bloody subject and onto safer ground. 'You know, just like a – a – brief stop at the service station to refuel and have a quick coffee when you're en route from A to B.'

Olivia raised her eyebrows.

'I see. And may I ask how long this... refuelling stop has taken so far? You've been there... how long?'

'Oh, really not long, not long at all. Couple of weeks. Who's counting?'

'Sorry, but hadn't you already been there a while when I first met you? And that's about a month ago.' Her head was tilted to one side.

'Well, not *literally* a couple of weeks. Obviously.' He laughed airily, showing that he was really very relaxed about the whole topic, and took a deep swallow of his wine. 'I mean, do you want the exact date? Wow, I didn't expect the Spanish Inquisition!' He saw her expression change and hated himself for being the cause of it, but why couldn't she just

stop, for God's sake? So, he'd been there a bit longer than he meant to...
a few weeks, so bloody what? Big deal. 'I can check my calendar if you
need to know the precise day and hour, for some reason?' He took out
his mobile and jabbed in his PIN.

'Come on, Andrew, you know what I'm getting at. I'm sorry, I didn't
mean to make you uncomfortable.'

'You didn't. It's fine. I mean, obviously, I don't plan to be there *for
ever.*'

'No.' She frowned. 'Of course not. I wasn't implying that.'

'But in the short-to-medium term...' He paused, thinking: who talks
like this? Not me. I sound like such a prat. 'It merely seemed the expe-
dient thing to do – a simple, practical solution.'

'Mmm,' she said.

'And, you know, there's a lot to be said for it, in fact. It's handy for the
tube, it's comfortable, and—'

'The thing is, Andrew, I don't want to be rude, but I'm kind of a bit
old to be with someone who's still living at home. I can't see myself
tiptoeing up the stairs to get to some guy's bedroom because otherwise
his parents might hear, you know?'

'I'm not *still* living at home. I have *temporarily* moved back for a brief
stay. Big difference.'

He could feel himself flush. And why did she have to say 'some guy'
as if she were talking about some random person rather than him.

'And anyway, you wouldn't have to tiptoe. My parents are very
welcoming, in fact. You'd barely be in the door before my mother would
have pressed tea and biscuits on you.'

There was a pause. Olivia glanced at him, then looked down at her
food, moving it around the plate with her fork, but she had stopped
eating.

'Anyway, you can talk! You *still* live with your sister – and in your
mum's flat! Let he who is without sin, etc.' He drained his wine with an
air of triumph and reached for the bottle.

'Er, my mother doesn't live in the flat, Andrew, as you know. She
owns it, yes, but we pay her a fair rent, and we don't live with her; we're
not even in the same postcode. Big difference.'

He shrugged.

'Hmm, you say that, but it's essentially the same thing.'

'No, it really isn't. It's not the same thing at all.'

He avoided looking at her. Why did she insist on dwelling on this? Now, he could see that she was upset and he didn't know how to make things all right again.

'Well, I think a psychologist would judge them to be basically equivalent – your mother's flat, my parents' house – at least I'm planning to move out very soon.'

'What on earth's a psychologist got to do with it?' She sighed. 'How soon, may I ask?'

'*Soon.* At a time of my choosing.' Stop it, Andrew, stop sounding like such a total arse.

Olivia set her knife and fork together and reached into her handbag.

'Look, I'm sorry,' said Andrew, 'I didn't mean to be rude. I'm merely pointing out that we are basically in the same situation, that's all.'

'OK. I'm really not in the mood to argue about this. I don't believe you seriously think that sharing a rented flat with my sister is the same thing as living with your parents, but if you think it is, then fine, it's exactly the same thing.' In a single movement, she deposited some notes on the table for the meal and stood up, scooping up her coat from the back of the chair.

'You're not going? No, don't go.'

'I'm sorry, I think you're a lovely man, I really do, but clearly there's not much mileage in this and we'd do better to call it a day now before I – before we – one of us starts taking it seriously. I have to go now. Look after yourself.'

'No – I... Hang on. Please don't go.' He signalled frantically at the waiter for the bill, while trying to shove the table back so that he could get out. The wine bottle toppled over and smashed onto the floor before he could catch it. Andrew swore and waved at the waiter again. By the time he'd paid the bill and got his coat and dashed out onto the street, there was no sign of Olivia. He took out his phone and stared at it. He would call her and say he was sorry. He would tell her he was going to start looking at flats tomorrow. No – tonight. He could make a start online, right now, the moment he got home. Not home – his parents' house. He'd... he'd... No, he'd text instead – much better – less desperate, more casual.

He tapped in a brief message:

Sorry about that. Hope you're ok. Are you at bus stop? Can I come and meet you? A x

She responded quickly:

I'm OK thanks. Already on bus.

No kiss. Oh well, give her a bit of time then. She'd call him tomorrow, probably. Or he would call her in a day or two. Still, why did she have to make such a big thing of it? Plenty of people moved back home for a bit if they needed to. It didn't mean he was defective. It wasn't as if he'd moved in permanently. An image of the new packet of striped pyjamas positioned on his single bed popped into his head but he shoved the thought away.

* * *

He would call the next day, he definitely would. Or maybe wait a day or two, give her time to forget what a fool he'd been. He would call and say he was sorry. He wouldn't babble or sound like an idiot; he would be calm and composed, keeping it light just in case she said, no thanks, not interested, bugger off.

The thought gave him pause. Perhaps he should email instead, then he could compose exactly what he would say without getting flustered or thrown off-track if she was dismissive? After four attempts – too jokey, too heavy, too desperate, back to too jokey again – he abandoned the idea. Better to send a text. That way, it would be completely casual and, if she didn't respond, then so what? It was only a text. He'd probably barely even notice whether she replied or not.

Over breakfast on Sunday morning, with Mrs Tyler safely upstairs, changing the beds, his dad asked, 'Everything all right, son?'

'Mmm.' Andrew sawed through his grilled tomato and shoved a piece into his mouth.

Ron rested the paper on the table and raised his eyebrows.

'Want to say what's up?'

Andrew shrugged.

'A girl, is it? Was it the one who came about the tree? You liked her, didn't you?'

Naturally, he hadn't told his parents about Olivia. If he'd confided in his mother, she'd be asking him about his progress morning, noon and night and he didn't think he could stand that. His father was a different matter, and Andrew would have liked to tell him, but he knew it would make Dad nervous to have information in his possession that his wife wasn't supposed to know.

'We went out a couple of times, but... I don't know. I messed up, Dad.'

Ron sighed. 'Don't go giving yourself a hard time, Andrew. I'm sure you didn't do anything daft. These things aren't easy.' He cast a nervous look towards the door. 'Have you tried talking to her, like?'

'I didn't know what to say.' Andrew heard his own voice crack and suddenly felt on the verge of tears. He took a bite of his toast and picked up his tea so he could mask his face behind it for a moment. 'Anyway, it doesn't matter. It's over. I'm used to it. Just another woman who got sick of me. Big bloody deal. It's such a regular occurrence, I barely even notice it any more.' He stood up abruptly to clear away his plate and cup.

'Finished, Dad?' He hovered by the table, waiting for his father to finish up his breakfast so he could take his plate.

'In a minute.' Ron laid his hand on Andrew's arm for a moment. 'Sit for a second?'

'I can't. I have to go out, Dad. I've got things to do.'

'I know you have, son. It's just...'

'*What?*'

'Maybe give it another try, if you can, eh?'

'Why? I'm fine. Plenty more fish in the sea, as Mum always says.' Andrew stuffed his hands down into his pockets and started to head for the hallway.

'Maybe so, but they're not all the same fish, son, are they? I just...'

'What? I have to go now.'

'It was good to see you looking so happy for a while, that's all.'

31

THE INVISIBLE WOMAN

The next morning, Sarah called while Eleanor was at work, saying she happened to be nearby Eleanor's office and would she be free to come out for a cup of tea or an early lunch?

Eleanor met her at a café round the corner.

'Are you OK?' Sarah was one of the very few people on this earth who seemed to have some sort of finely tuned radar when it came to Eleanor, sensing when all was not well. Eleanor had occasionally confided in Sarah about the Cloud and how hard she found it to live with. But she had not said anything of late, partly because she knew Sarah was not exactly Roger's biggest fan in any case, and she didn't want to give her further reason to dislike him.

Usually, Eleanor would say she's fine, it's fine, everything's fine, but somehow, today, she felt... weary, defeated. She wrinkled her nose and looked round to check that no one she knew was seated within earshot.

'The Cloud,' she said, without further comment.

'Oh, for fuck's sake! That man is such a spoilt child. Eleanor, why on earth do you pander to him? It's ridiculous. I know what you're like, spinning round bloody Planet Roger in faithful orbit as if you're just a service satellite. Honestly, if it were me, I'd tell him to stop being such a grumpy old git.'

'Well, no two marriages are alike...'

'It's nothing to do with that. Look, I realise you're a lot more patient than I am and that's admirable, but no one's handing out medals for stoicism.'

'I'm not asking for a medal.'

'I know that, I'm just saying. If Mark's pissing me off, I usually just come straight out with it and tell him. And when I'm in a strop, he teases me out of it.'

'But you two have always been so straight with each other.'

'Yes, of course.'

'There's no "of course" about it. And I can't change tack now, can I? If I suddenly say to Roger, "Darling, I find your black moods really hard to live with – is there any chance you could fucking snap out of it?" he would go ballistic.'

'Would he? How do you know? And, frankly, so what if he does? That might be easier to deal with than having him glowering about the house for days on end.'

Eleanor silently shook her head. 'Anyway, to be fair to Roger, it was partly my fault. I failed to wash the cafetières the other day and he was seriously pissed off because he had to clean one himself in order to have coffee.'

'What?'

Eleanor repeated her explanation.

'Can you actually hear yourself?'

'What do you mean? I'm just explaining.'

Sarah reached for her friend's arm and looked into her eyes.

'You are blaming yourself. You "failed" – your word, not mine – to wash Roger's sodding cafetières! You don't even drink coffee, for God's sake. Why can't he wash one himself once in a blue moon? What's happened to you, El?'

Eleanor looked down at the table, unable to speak. She bit the inside of her cheek to stop herself crying.

'El, I'm sorry.' Sarah patted her hand. 'I don't mean to give you a hard time. It's not for me to tell you what to do.'

'It's OK. I'm fine.'

Sarah clattered her cup down into the saucer.

'No, you are *not* fine. You're clearly not fine. For God's sake, will you please stop saying you're fine.'

'Don't have a go at me!' Eleanor's voice snapped out much louder than she had intended and the people either side of them suddenly looked round.

'Sorry – but still, why can't you stand up for yourself like that with Roger?'

Eleanor shrugged. 'I don't know. I never have, I suppose, and now I don't know how to start.'

'You didn't used to be like this, you know. You had some *grit*. Every time I see you now, you seem to be growing fainter and fainter. There's more and more Roger and less and less Eleanor. It scares the hell out of me to see you like this. Soon I won't be able to see you at all.'

'You mean you won't want to see me any more?' Eleanor was struggling desperately not to cry. Her chest felt tight and full, as if had been packed full of sharp stones; her voice rasped in her throat.

'No, silly, not like that. I mean you're becoming the Invisible Woman. A sort of shadow in your own life, letting Roger have his own way about everything.'

'I don't really. Perhaps I was making too much of it. You know how much I hate arguing and often it's just easier to go with the flow and let him have his way. And once he's emerged from a mood, it's really not so bad at all. I know I'm very lucky: I have happy, healthy children, a lovely house, no money worries.' She shrugged. 'I should be grateful.'

Sarah said nothing.

'What?'

'Is "really not so bad at all" your idea of a happy marriage?'

'Oh, I don't know. I'm sick of thinking about myself. And how many people have a really happy marriage, after all? I don't think my parents were especially happy, but they rubbed along OK most of the time. Maybe it's not a realistic thing to want?'

'That's ridiculous. And I don't give a toss about other people and their marriages, I care about *you* and whether *you're* happy or not.'

'Well, thank you, I love it that you care, but you honestly don't need to. We're just having a bit of a bad patch at the moment because things have all been shaken up by Hannah's going away, I think, but we'll settle down soon and then everything will be fine.'

'It'll all be fine?'

'Yes.'

Sarah shook her head slightly then set down her cup.

'El, it's not good for you to be like this, and it really can't be good for Daniel and Hannah to see their mother being so consistently eroded by their father, can it?'

'But they're both away from home now, at least.'

'Oh, well then, in that case you might as well lie down on the floor and let Roger wipe his feet on you.'

'That's not fair! I'm *not* a doormat!'

'No, Eleanor, exactly. You're *not*. So why the hell are you acting like one?'

'I'm *not*. Don't give me a hard time. I'm bloody sick of everyone having a go at me and blaming me when I haven't done anything wrong.' Eleanor rose to her feet and tugged out some cash from her pocket and slapped it on the table.

'Of course you haven't done anything wrong. I'm not saying that. Come on, El.'

'I have to go.'

She left the café quickly and ran along the pavement. She was dimly aware of people turning to look; women in smart coats and office shoes didn't run in the street with tears streaming down their faces. Breathless now, she ducked into the park. To one side was a dense thicket of rhododendrons the children had loved to hide in when they were little, and now she plunged into a narrow gap between the shrubs. Branches clawed at the cloth of her coat, snagged at her hair, yanked her to a halt. She unhooked herself from their clutches, then suddenly felt completely overwhelmed. She crouched down on the damp earth, her vision blurred by tears, losing herself in the gloom, the silence, the barrier of branches, knowing she would be completely obscured from view, invisible.

32

DOING THE RIGHT THING

1982

That bloody boy will be the death of him. He's gone too far this time. Conrad can feel the anger engulfing him, an unstoppable wave surging into every blood vessel, so he is just a repository for rage, with no room for anything else. If the boy were here now, he'd give him a jolly good shaking. He slams the flat of his hand down hard on the desk. He'd... he'd... what would he do exactly? Shouting and railing at Benedict has never achieved anything. The boy laughs in his face when he tries to be strict, and gets away with murder when left to his own devices. When Conrad turns a blind eye to his son's behaviour – the stealing, the drinking, the skiving off school – the boy merely pushes it further. Marcia, never the most relaxed of creatures even at the best of times, has become as taut as a wire, holding her breath for the next crisis while doing nothing to avert it other than pleading with Benedict to please try a little harder and slipping him money so as to try to stop him stealing.

Conrad slumps into his seat, defeated, sinks his head into his hands. It is *his* fault, he knows; he has failed, not the boy. For Christ's sake, man, what the hell were you thinking? You're a father! *You* might as well have died when *he* was seven, for all the bloody good you've done the boy.

His legs are shaking uncontrollably, his knees pumping up and down like pistons, and he sets his hands on them to try to steady them, thoughts, images buffeting each other in his head. When it came to the children, he let Marcia have her way: with Eleanor – well, she barely seemed to need more than the odd parental steer now and then, a bit of help with her maths and science, the occasional lift home; she was almost scarily self-reliant. He once came down in the morning to find her laying the breakfast table, folding cloth napkins, setting out the cups just so, frowning in concentration in her intense need to get it right. She was *eight*. So, with Eleanor, it was different. But the boy... Marcia has been not just indulgent, it is more than that. He shuts his eyes, trying to picture his wife with their son, turning the image over in his mind as if it were some challenging puzzle. The way she looks at him, the way she smooths his hair back from his face or straightens his tie just before he goes off to school. It is oddly... intense. When he gets into trouble at school, she makes excuses for him: it is just a phase, or he's been influenced by some other boy, or the teacher is known for being unduly harsh. It has got worse, though, much worse, the last two or three years.

Conrad shoves those thoughts to one side: too easy to blame his wife. He is to blame, he can see that now. He has let himself be distracted from his duties and responsibilities as a parent, as the head of the household, devoting himself only to work and... and to *her*, of course. Yes. He has been selfish – so selfish! And his family have suffered. Benedict is like a highly-strung stallion and he needs someone firm and strong to train him, not soft words and a yielding hand. He has been given free rein, and it has made him impossible.

Enough. No more. For now, at least, they would need a cracking good lawyer or the boy would end up confined in a borstal and come out as an unthinking, unfeeling criminal in all probability. In his mind, Benedict looks at him with disgust and Conrad feels a deep stab of shame. He could not let that happen to Benedict, his own flesh and blood, not if he can do anything to prevent it.

He calls Geoffrey, their family lawyer, for advice and explains the situation as it stands. Benedict has been caught driving on an A-road. Drunk. No licence, of course. Who knew he could even drive? He's only fifteen. Good man, Geoffrey – he will know what to do. Benedict would hardly be the first lad from a decent family who has gone a bit haywire, after all. No one was killed, at least. The car was a write-off, but Benedict was in one piece and, though his friends had injuries – one with a broken leg, the other cuts from broken glass – they would be all right. Then he must leave to meet Marcia at the police station to collect Benedict. She was barely coherent on the phone, though he managed to extract the salient facts from her disjointed phrases between sobs. He will come at once, he said, as soon as he's spoken to Geoffrey to set wheels in motion. In the meantime, sit down, take deep breaths and for God's sake don't tell a soul – not your mother, not a friend, not a neighbour. With any luck, they might still be able to hush it up. Marcia, snivelling uncontrollably, at least saw the merit in that. 'Daddy will be so cross,' she said. 'What on earth will I tell him?' Fuck *Daddy*, Conrad thought, why don't you care what *I* think, for once?

There is a knock at the door while he is still on the phone to Geoffrey. Bloody hell, he can't deal with anything else right now.

'Come!' he commands.

The first sight of her face, her hair, brings him to silence for a moment, as it always does. She is here, here in his office. She is never here. The two parts of his life touch, spark intriguingly for a second, then collide awkwardly. She looks odd here, shorter than usual, and her clothes strike him as positively peculiar rather than interestingly bohemian. He winds up the call, after agreeing to meet Geoffrey at the police station in one hour.

Now he turns to her, explains briefly, and tells her he will see her tomorrow at her flat, as usual. He speaks to her for a minute, then says goodbye.

He will not go tomorrow, of course, he knows that. It is just to get her out of there. He cannot deal with tears and upset, not now. He will call her later or tomorrow. She will understand. He sags in his seat, defeated. It is not to be thought of now, living without her in his life. No. Not to be thought of.

He stays there for a few moments, deep in thought. She has never simply turned up here before. She knows that people might wonder who she is, that it could be awkward. So now he wonders if she came to see him for a particular reason. She didn't say so, but still... Well, no matter. Weightier business is pressing on him now. And, after all, she knew he was married when they first... got together, so he is sure it will not come as a huge shock, even though it has been more than an affair, yes, so much more. Do not think of it. Of her. At least not today. You will not, he tells himself, I forbid it.

But – he reaches for his briefcase as he must get going – she will be all right. As he puts on his raincoat, a thought pushes into his mind – a line from *their* poem:

Nothing else is.

33

FRAGMENTS FROM THE PAST

The girls were up at the top of the house in Cecilia's studio, allegedly decluttering, though so far this seemed to have involved multiple trips back down to the kitchen by Madeleine for wine, crisps, something to nibble, something else to nibble, more wine, and chocolate or anything sweet but please not the 'Ursuline' biscuits that tasted of sawdust. Cecilia suspected that, as ever, Olivia was doing the bulk of the actual work, while Madeleine fetched refreshments so as to avoid doing any sorting or tidying, her two least favourite activities. Occasionally, shrieks of hysterical laughter reached Cecilia here, reclining on her chaise longue, resting. It was ridiculous. How was it that she'd been managing to work on her mermaid mosaic perfectly well for weeks, halfway up a ladder without so much as a wobble, but then, yesterday, tripped over an uneven paving slab in the middle of the street? She'd twisted her leg badly as she fell. Her knee was swollen and her ankle was still throbbing. She refused to go to the doctor as she could never be bothered with all that unless it was really unavoidable, but she had at least submitted to enforced rest with her leg raised on cushions and ice packs on her knee and ankle (courtesy of Olivia), a glass of red wine and a trashy novel by her side (courtesy of Madeleine). When Olivia was not keeping a beady eye, Cecilia took the opportunity to shove the ice packs off because they felt pretty unpleasant and she was sure it would all mend in a day or two. At least the mosaic was almost finished.

Periodically, one of the girls appeared, bearing some 'mysterious relic' that required Cecilia's judgement. Was she really going to have this broken lamp repaired or could it be... um... recycled... perhaps? Madeleine brought down a cardboard box containing 'The National Collection of Moth-Eaten Scarves', many of which were perfectly fine and were just waiting for Cecilia to find a few minutes to embroider over the holes something small but pretty – a tiny heart or star, perhaps a little bird. Olivia bore a small sample of 'enough fabric scraps to make a patchwork tea cosy for St Paul's Cathedral'. Just when exactly was Ma realistically planning to take up patchwork again, given that she hadn't done any for, ooh, fifteen years? Cecilia was aware that sometimes her daughters smuggled items out of the house to charity shops, recycling or even – God forbid – into the rubbish. Usually, she put her foot down and insisted on keeping whatever it was that her spoilt offspring dismissed as junk: pillows with just a couple of coffee stains on; perfectly serviceable lamps with slightly wobbly fittings or shades; plastic food containers temporarily missing their lids; chairs with broken cane seats that she was planning to mend as soon as her friend Thalia had time to show her the complex weaving pattern to do it...

She fancied another coffee and could toy with one of those incredible dark chocolate ginger biscuits that Olivia had brought if the girls hadn't laid waste to them completely. Cecilia swung her legs down and attempted to stand up. Pain, intense and sudden, shot up her leg as if she'd been struck by a poisoned dart. She slumped back down immediately, feeling sick and faint, and laid her head back on the cushion. Bollocks, bollocks. She hated having anything wrong with her. She was not old, for Chrissakes! Refused to be old. Anyone could have fallen over that bloody wayward slab – anyone of any age. But if you fell over at her age, people were so bloody nice and sympathetic to you. They helped you up and called you dear and offered to see you safely home. Olivia had borrowed a walking stick from someone and there it was, leaning against the end of the chaise longue, just behind her so that Cecilia could reach it if she chose to but didn't have to look at it if she preferred not to. It was the kind of very particular thoughtfulness that was Olivia's defining characteristic. Madeleine would probably have left the stick miles away on the other side of the room or immediately in front of her mother so that she would fall over it the moment she got up. Not that

Madeleine was selfish, exactly; she could be extremely generous – would offer you her jumper if you were cold, her toast if you were hungry – but she didn't think beyond the next few minutes, just like a child.

At that moment, the pair of them suddenly appeared, looking decidedly shifty. Presumably they had broken something. With any luck, Olivia would make some more coffee. Cecilia wasn't in the mood for wine this early; it wasn't even six o'clock yet. She hated having to ask for things. And if she asked, Olivia would realise just how painful her leg must be and would start fussing over her and nagging her to go for an X-ray. She ostentatiously drained her already empty mug.

'That was lovely coffee. I wonder if there might be any more left in the pot?' Even though she knew they'd finished it.

'We found something,' Olivia interrupted.

'Stuck at the bottom of the plan chest. Must have fallen down behind the drawers,' Madeleine added.

They both looked furtive. Or embarrassed perhaps? Olivia passed over a bundle wrapped in a piece of red material with white polka-dots, bound in a length of dusty black velvet ribbon. Cecilia's mouth grew dry. She took the bundle as tenderly as if it were a bird with a damaged wing, ran her fingertip over the spotty cloth – a man's cotton handkerchief. God, even now the sight of it brought tears to her eyes. Automatically, she pulled the ribbon loose, peeled back the hankie. His letters. Notecards really – each one a single thick, creamy card in an envelope. His handwriting – that confident, sloping script in fountain pen. She thought they were lost, had hunted everywhere for them. In the past, before they disappeared, she used to get them out once a year to reread them on their anniversary. Anniversary! No champagne, no cake, no toasts, no kisses – it was a poor cousin of an anniversary – just Cecilia alone with her letters, thinking of him and wondering if, somewhere, he might for at least a few moments be thinking of her.

'You didn't read them?'

'No, of course not!' Madeleine said, at exactly the same moment as Olivia confessed: 'Yes. Just a couple. Sorry.'

The girls looked at each other.

'They're private.' Cecilia's voice was quiet. She looked up at them, waiting for some sort of explanation.

'We couldn't help it.' The words tumbled out of Madeleine, never one to keep silent. 'The bundle was loose when Olivia dragged it out and then we – we – fought over it. We were just messing about, and I grabbed it and the letters flew all over the place and so – so – we just took a tiny peek, really, while we were picking them up... just to see... what sort of letters they were, and – and—'

'We picked them all up and tied them back together properly in date order using the frank marks, I promise,' Olivia said.

Cecilia snorted with impatience.

'Do you think anyone binds up harmless holiday postcards in this way?' She held the bundle up in her cupped hands. 'For goodness' sake, you've seen love letters before, surely?'

'Well, no, actually. I haven't.' Olivia's voice was barely above a whisper.

'No, never. Who writes letters any more?' Madeleine made a face. 'I've had some pretty rude texts before now. Do you remember that guy Micky? He was really—'

'Mads! Getting away from the point here.'

'Oh, yeah. Sorry.'

'You're always going on about your love life and how many lovers you've had and all that, so we didn't think you'd mind.' The expression on Olivia's face was curious, unreadable.

'Madeleine, I'd be grateful if you could put the kettle on and make some more coffee, please.'

'Why me? I'm hopeless at anything domestic, you know I am.'

'Only because you're lazy.' Olivia sounded angry rather than teasing. 'Three heaped scoops of coffee. Add boiling water. Stir. Even you can manage that, surely?'

Madeleine stomped through to the kitchen.

'Ma? Are you OK?' Olivia's voice sounded hoarse and cracked, as if she had a cold coming.

'I'm sorry.' Cecilia looked up at her. 'Could you both give me a few minutes? I need... it's just... on my own, you see.'

'We were about to pop out to get some emergency chocolate anyway, weren't we? Come on, Mads. Leave the coffee.' Olivia manhandled her sister towards the front door and there was a flurry of whispers that Cecilia didn't even attempt to hear. 'Actually, I ought to be making a move anyway so I'll be off.' Olivia waved from the door and left.

Cecilia stroked her thumb across the top envelope. Took out the notecard. It was the first one he'd ever written to her:

My love,

When your fingers first brushed against mine, it was like a distant sound heard in a remote part of a house. A house where, you remember, with shutters stuck with paint, it was so very dark as well as silent. Your smile shot through to me like sunlight into a forgotten cellar, and then there was the gaze of those jewel-like eyes. Surely this must be happening to someone else...?

She clutched the bundle close and let her head rest back against the cushion.

* * *

The test is positive. She is six weeks pregnant. She feels as if her stomach is doing loop-the-loops inside her. She is horrified and thrilled at the same time, one moment sheer panic edging into the lead, the next a sensation of pure excitement shoving all else brusquely aside.

'Are you all right?' the nurse asks, leaning over her. 'Is it... good news for you?'

She feels herself flush – she, who is embarrassed by nothing on this earth, not nudity, not sex, not shitting, nothing. She nods quickly, inexplicably timid.

'I think so.'

The nurse's face lights up into a smile.

'Well, congratulations then! Remember now – go and see your GP and book your scan, OK?'

She comes out onto the street and into a different world. Look – that bird! What is it? She tilts her head back as it flies up then settles into a tree. Perched on a branch, its shape is now unmistakable. It is a pigeon. She laughs at herself. An image swims into her head of herself holding her baby up, dancing round and round. Her skin feels as if it is buzzing, a tiny sensation of current thrumming across her. It is as if she has been seeing the world through a murky glass screen for her whole life, and now, suddenly, someone has wiped it to make it sparkling clean and clear. The leaves on that tree – the purest, fiercest golden yellow she has ever seen; the outline of the branches against the cloudless sky. She wants to draw it, paint it, drink it all into her.

She knows she is his love, and when she thinks of him, which is so often that it becomes as unconscious as breathing, she thinks of him as Dear Heart. In bed, those are the words they use. The rest of the time, perhaps the precious intensity of those old-fashioned terms of affection – Dear Heart, My Love – seem too far removed from the ordinary world around them, and so they have abbreviated them to initials: he is DH; she is ML.

Ever since that first time when they lay in bed together, still light outside with the curtains half drawn, they stayed there as long as they could. She has had no shortage of lovers. In fact she has been to bed with men whose names she could no longer remember. They called it screwing back then, but now, here in the half-light, she hates that word. That is not it at all – not for this, not for the slow, dreamy, delirious joining of him and her that has transported them both. He is hers and she is his – that is the way it is. When they are together, he looks at her, not even smiling, just completely absorbed in her – her eyes, her hair, her voice. He traces the curve of her cheek with his finger as if he has never seen a woman before, never felt skin before.

'My Love,' he says.

Her eyes suddenly fill with tears.

'Dear Heart.'

'You are crying, my love. What is it?'

She weeps properly then, tears running unchecked down her face, her neck, onto her breasts, trickling onto the sheet beneath.

She shakes her head.

'I don't know. It sounds crazy. I think I've never been so happy.'

She laughs at herself and he kisses her eyelids and gently, so, so tenderly licks her tears away with the tip of his tongue.

* * *

But now, the thought of him gives her pause. Will DH be pleased? His own children are teenagers, it is true; soon they will be grown up. Who could ever have imagined they would have lasted together this long – over three years? They are at once thrillingly different but unexpectedly extraordinarily alike in some ways. With him, she is gentler, more patient. Talking with him, being with him, makes her feel not just more alive but more like her best self.

There is no doubt in their minds that they want to be, must be, together. They have talked about it many times. Once his son turns sixteen, he will ask for a divorce and he will be free. Less than a year to go. And she will wait. The idea of being with anyone else now is utterly repellent to her. She would wait a lifetime if she had to.

But it is different now. He will see that. It will have to be sooner. Surely he will see that? It is his baby, too. Their baby. She clutches the thought to herself, hugging it. *Our* baby.

She wants to see him, is suddenly desperate to see his precious face, to see the way his rather stern expression softens the moment he sees her, the way his eyes brighten. She wants to lean into him, look up at him, be wrapped in his arms and never let go.

She ought to call first, but she cannot wait to see his face when she tells him. And, really, it is so near. Already, she finds she is walking that way without knowing what she is doing.

She passes through the wide gates with a throng of others. The main entrance and the stairs are full of people coming and going. No one gives her a second look. She takes the lift up to the third floor. Goes behind the section of wall with the huge Michelangelo *Epifania* cartoon that hangs there, knocks on the door and waits to be let in.

'Please,' she says, trying to cover her excitement, wanting to run to her Dear Heart, wanting to call out for him right there in the lobby, 'can you tell me which room is the Keeper's Office? I need to see him. I need to see Conrad Marriott.'

She knocks.

'Come!'

She peeps her head round the door. Conrad is alone but on the phone. He looks very surprised to see her, but beckons her in.

'Got to go now, Geoffrey. Yes, please do that. Thank you. 'Bye.' He puts down the phone.

'How extraordinary.' He gestures for her to take the chair opposite, on the other side of this desk, though he remains standing. 'I was literally just about to call you. Are you all right? I'm so sorry but I'm afraid I really have to dash – right this minute.'

'Yes, I'm fine. Was it about tomorrow?' They have plans to meet tomorrow afternoon. She looks across at him. She is desperate to tell him about the baby but it will have to wait until tomorrow when he comes to her flat; he's clearly distracted and in a rush; now is not the time.

'No. It's Benedict. He's had a car accident – been found half off his head, driving on the wrong side of the road with his similarly bloody useless friends. That fucking idiot!'

She jolts back at the intensity of his anger but says nothing.

'He's in police custody.' Benedict is only fifteen so has no driver's licence. 'I had no idea he could even drive. At least it was my car he took, otherwise we'd have a theft charge on top of everything else.'

'Is he hurt?'

'No, thank Christ. Unbelievably. That boy has the luck of the devil.' Conrad strikes the desk with his fist. 'I'm sorry, I have to go right now. I'm meeting our lawyer at the police station.' He squeezes her arm firmly. 'I'll call you later, dear. I really must go.'

She rises unsteadily to her feet. He called her 'dear'. He never calls her 'dear'; even in a café or a park, where he does not call her 'My Love', still it is ML or nothing. When your world is just the two of you, why do you need a name?

She has never even met Benedict, but she hates him, *hates* him with an intensity and fury that shocks her. Clearly, he has been indulged his whole life and he's done nothing but abuse it and cock everything up. She drifts out of the Museum, not looking where she is going, and walks all the way home.

Conrad doesn't call her that day, but the following day, half an hour before he is due to come to her flat, he calls. As soon as she hears his voice, she knows he is not coming – not just today, but ever again.

'I'm sorry,' he says. 'I have to be at home more. I have to sort the boy out. Make him knuckle down somehow, make him work, get some qualifications so he can get into university – no, unlikely, a polytechnic maybe – any one that will take him, frankly. Keep him off the booze, the drugs. If I don't then one day they'll find him dead in the gutter.' His voice cracks and he stops speaking. A strange, choking sound reaches her ear and she realises that he is crying.

'No, Dear Heart, don't cry. Please don't. I cannot bear it if you cry. It's

OK. I will be OK.' She reassures him because he is in pain and she loves him more than anything and so what else would she do? 'I know you need to do this,' she says. She pushes her feet down hard into the floor, clenching every muscle to hold herself together or she will shatter into a thousand splinters.

Then he gathers himself and his voice returns, though it is so freighted with pain that it barely sounds like him.

'You know how much I love you. I have never loved anyone like this. I cannot bear it.' He stops again. 'I'm so very sorry. My Love.'

And he is gone.

* * *

Cecilia brought the letters up to her face, hoping for the faintest trace of his smell that might have lingered on his cotton handkerchief, but there was nothing there now but dust and age and regret. She leafed through the envelopes slowly, looking for that last one, back again. Shifting from her reverie to a state of alertness now. Checking the faded frank marks for the dates – the last one, the last one, months after the others, where is it? Telling herself that it must have just slipped down inside the plan chest, that's all. Later, she will crawl up the stairs and look for it. It must be there. The alternative sits in the middle of her head, a solid block of stone: the girls have taken it. Dear God. *Olivia*.

34

THE LAST STRAW

Andrew received a text from Vicki. Ah-ha! He knew it. She'd seen that Ian was nothing but an orange-hued, decking-obsessed creep and was begging Andrew to reconsider and take her back. Hmm, now that he thought about it, he wasn't at all sure that he would. The image of Olivia stole into his head, but he was determined to ignore it. No point letting himself wallow in self-pity. He might consider taking Vicki back, but it wouldn't do her any harm to sweat a bit first. He opened the text:

Hi. Can you pick up your last few things this weekend please? Sorry about you-know-who. Didn't know how to tell you. V

Yes, down on bended knee, begging to have him take her back, clearly. Where the hell was he supposed to fit all his stuff? His parents didn't have a garage and the shed was the one space his dad could actually call his own. Although in theory it was just where he worked on little DIY jobs or potted up his cuttings for the garden, Ron had a comfy chair in there and a radio and a small heater, and it was as close to a sanctuary as he could manage.

Hi.

Andrew never said 'Hi' normally but he wanted to match his tone to hers – casual, offhand.

Sure thing

He never said that either.

Sat a.m. Who's you-know-who??

That last sentence was ridiculous, obviously, but why couldn't she just say the bastard's name, tell it like it was without attempting to gloss over it: sorry about shagging Ian behind your back. Didn't know how to admit I'm a lying, two-timing cheat.

Another text:

Sat fine. Around 10 if poss.

* * *

Saturday, 10.25 a.m. Andrew was not usually late, but, of course, now that he was a devil-may-care single man, he couldn't be expected to be at Vicki's beck and call. Being late implied that he was so busy he could barely fit in this tedious, unimportant little errand, and it suggested that he had been out the night before – out with the lads, waaaay-heeey! – drinking and getting his end away with any number of hot women and had probably only just now dragged himself out of the tangle of sweaty sheets and soft, sleepy limbs to vroom up to Whetstone. He gave a long, impatient ring on the doorbell as if he had already rung it a couple of times with no answer.

Vicki came to the door. She was wearing grey velour tracksuit bottoms and a too-large fleece, plus flat, fluffy slippers, similar to the kind his mother wore, rather than her usual high-heeled mules. Andrew was struck by her outfit because it was so unlike Vicki ever to wear anything remotely baggy. She was proud of her trim figure and perky bottom, so always favoured fitted tops and tight trousers or skirts that showed off her slim form to advantage.

'Hi. How've you been keeping?' she asked. 'Please, come in.'

'Brilliant. Couldn't be better, in fact. Yes, indeed.' He nodded vigorously and entered the hall. 'You?'

'I'm fine, thanks.' Actually, she looked rather pale and tired.

'And how's the gardener?' Andrew drew himself up tall and sauntered towards the patio doors at the rear of the house.

'The gardener?'

'Yes, Whatsisface. Sutton.' God, that felt good. No wonder Conrad had used his surname. It felt like such a put-down while not ostensibly being rude or deliberately offensive. 'I see the decking's not been laid yet. Is he slacking?'

'Oh, Ian. He's very well, thank you.' She folded her arms and looked away. 'He's been very busy with the takeover and everything.'

'Takeover? Ah, has his tiny little firm been eaten up by some corporate giant, then? Shame. Still, difficult times I suppose...' He rocked back slightly on his feet and puffed out his chest.

'*He's* taking over another firm. A web design company. He's been wanting to expand for ages. I'm going to be in charge of that division, actually, after–' She looked down for a moment. 'Later on.'

'Well,' he said, trying to read her face, 'that's good. Congratulations. Anyway, better crack on.' Now he really was sounding like Conrad. He could see that this brigadier mode had quite a lot going for it in the right situation. 'Now, boxes, boxes. Let me at 'em.'

'It's just one more box plus a few awkward things that wouldn't fit.'

There was his wok and his tall reading lamp, the one they'd bought together. Well, he had paid for it, in fact, so he supposed it was more his than hers, but she had helped pick it out.

'Sure you don't want it?'

She shrugged. 'You know I'm not much of a reader, am I? Not like you.'

'Well, OK then. Thanks.'

He felt perhaps he should say something else, as this was clearly it. It would be useful to have a manual for this kind of thing: *Useful Phrases for Awkward Situations*. To give himself a few moments to think, he bent down and opened up the box. It contained his few remaining books, his sturdy walking boots in a plastic bag, plus his old green fleece. Almost the same colour as Olivia's coat, he thought.

They stood in silence for a few seconds, then Vicki reached into her pocket and stretched out her hand towards him.

'And there's this, too, of course.' It was a ring he had bought her. Not an engagement ring, as they had never officially become engaged. It was an eternity ring, with alternating diamonds and sapphires all the way round in a gold setting.

'But I bought it for you.'

'I know, and I love it, you know I do. But...'

He closed her fingers round it.

'It's yours,' he said. 'What am I going to do with it anyway? It'll only sit in a drawer, gathering dust.'

'You could always give it to another girlfriend?'

'No. I chose it for *you*. Please keep it. It doesn't have to mean anything – it's just a pretty ring for a pretty woman. Have it.'

'Well, thank you then, if you're sure.'

He nodded then picked up the box to put it in his car boot; came back to fetch the floor lamp and the wok.

'Well, goodbye, then.' Should he kiss her? It seemed weird to leave with just a wave.

'Andrew?'

'Yup – what?'

She looked very small suddenly, waif-like even.

'I need to tell you something, OK?'

'Vicki, look, if it's about Ian, I know. It's OK – I get it. You and him. Personally, I think you're too good for him but I'm not exactly impartial. I wish you well, really I do.' He rested the lamp down again, holding it by its stem.

'Thank you.' She looked down and away, focused on the garage door for a moment, then back again. 'Erm... it's kind of awkward...'

'Come on, you can tell me anything, you know that. Whatever my shortcomings,' he puffed out his cheeks, '– and I accept that they are numerous – at least I hope you know there's nothing you can't say to me. What is it – you're getting married? You're having triplets? You're moving to Alaska to hunt seals? I can handle it. I'm a big boy now.'

'Yes,' she said.

'Yes to which bit?'

'Not Alaska.'

'Getting married then?'

She nodded.

'Pregnant?'

Another small nod. Andrew clutched the lamp more tightly, as if it were a crutch.

'With triplets?' Keeping his voice light.

'No, luckily.'

'Well, congratulations. Take care of yourself, OK?' He dipped forwards to kiss the top of her head.

'You, too.'

He attempted to slide the lamp into the body of the car, then looked at her sideways.

'How far along are you? Just as a matter of interest.'

She stared down at the drive and said nothing.

'Vicki, it makes no odds to me now anyway. Tell me,' he said, wedging the lamp with an old blanket.

'Nearly five months.'

Well, that explained the need to chuck him out so speedily, at least.

'I see.' He stood upright and turned to face her.

'Don't be upset,' she said.

He shook his head, unable to speak for a few moments. Then he got into his car.

'Upset? Why would I be upset? Cheers for that. Have a brilliant Christmas.' He slammed the door and drove off.

35

DING-DONG MERRILY ON HIGH

'Do you realise that this will be the first time since the children were born that neither of them will be home for Christmas?' Roger pointed out to his wife a couple of weeks beforehand, as if she could possibly have failed to notice this appalling fact.

Hannah would be away until the beginning of March, and Daniel had pleaded to spend Christmas with his girlfriend, Alice, at her parents' home in Wales. He promised to pop up for a visit before Christmas, but he'd have to go back to Bristol for New Year as he'd been offered extra shifts of bar work and would get good tips at this time of year.

'I'm sure your dad would give you some money for Christmas if you —' Eleanor had said on the phone.

'Nah, Mum, let's not go over this again.'

'I understand. Of course it's better if you'd rather earn it yourself.'

'You know what he's like. If he does anything for you, even if it's only passing the salt, he makes you feel so obligated it's just not worth it. And if you dare to disagree with him, he gives you that look and we all have to deal with the bollocky Cloud for days.'

'Come on, Dan, he's not that bad.' Eleanor tried to laugh it off.

'No, he *is* that bad, Mum. You've just become so used to it that you've convinced yourself that it's normal. It really isn't. Alice's dad is like a totally different species. Last time we went there I had this heated argument with him about Welsh devolution and then I panicked because I thought he'd go all freaky weird and awful like Dad does. But you know what? He was *fine*. It just didn't bother him. When I told Alice about Dad, she thought I was hyping it up ridiculously to make her laugh.'

'Well...'

'Except it's not funny. Yeah, I know.'

'Anyway. Never mind. Tell me more about their place in Wales...'

And then, as promised, Daniel had come up to London last week for a visit, though only for two days in the end as he and Roger had clashed again and it had all become rather fraught.

So now Eleanor had the prickly problem of what to do about Christmas Day. If she didn't rope in some additional guests, then it would be an extremely Unholy Trinity of Roger, her father, and herself – hardly a winning combination, even for an hour, never mind an entire day. And it would be ridiculous to cook a whole turkey for just the three of them, but Roger would never sanction an alternative. One year, she had made beef Wellington for a change, and Roger was so enraged by this unfathomable provocation that he'd exploited every opportunity to take pot-shots at her. Could she pass the cranberry sauce? Oh no, there wasn't any because you only serve it with turkey... Where was the stuffing? Oh, of course... And no little sausages wrapped in bacon, then? What a shame that beef was so rich and heavy – now he didn't have any room for her homemade Christmas pudding...

Until she'd had to excuse herself and dash to the loo, where she had cried and fantasised about Roger's keeling over at the table from a heart attack, falling face down into the beef Wellington. She could picture his face smacking into his plate, fragments of pastry and mushroom *duxelles* spattering out in a two-foot radius across her best damask tablecloth.

It wasn't exactly that Roger and Conrad didn't get on. Actually, yes, it was exactly that. It was odd really as there were certain ways in which they were not unalike. They were both rather precise, good on detail, prone to pedantry, rather poor at seeing things from someone else's point of view – maybe that was why they rubbed each other up the wrong way? But in other respects, they were incredibly different. Roger could not compete with Conrad for intellect or erudition; her father was unquestionably far more learned, more articulate, and better read. He outranked Roger in every regard other than wealth and it was that, no doubt, that put Roger on edge. He liked to feel he was indisputably the most important man in the room, the unchallenged alpha male, but if Conrad were there, he wouldn't be.

* * *

'I wonder if it might be nice to invite a couple of extra guests for Christmas lunch?' Eleanor had suggested once Roger was safely well into his second glass of wine over supper. She always made suggestions in the form of very tentative questions as Roger did not like being 'bossed around'.

'Whatever you like, darling.' Roger waved his knife about expansively. 'Christmas has always been very much your domain, hasn't it? Happy to go along with whatever you think is best.' The idea of Roger's 'going along' with any decision made by his wife was so preposterous that Eleanor had to crush her napkin against her mouth for a moment to stifle a laugh. 'Let's ask Peter and Maggie. It's always lonely for them since their son emigrated to Australia.'

'Mmm, though they probably have other plans by now.' Oh bollocks, she'd walked straight into that one. Eleanor tried to keep a smile fixed in place. Peter and Maggie Harris could bore for Britain, but they had been friends of Roger's for many years.

'And maybe a couple of neighbours?' At least she could hope to dilute them with other guests. 'Jane? Her husband died earlier this year.'

Roger sniffed. 'I suppose we ought to, then.'

'And Freddie, the guerrilla gardener? He's on his own, too.'

'Ye-e-e-e-s, I suppose we could.'

She tried to think of some way of diverting onto a different path now but, inevitably, Roger then said through a mouthful of potato: 'And Mum, obviously.'

'Mmm, of course. Super.' She never used the word 'super'. It was like a flag of insincerity waving above her head. She looked down at her plate. Please, please, don't make me drive her. I can't bear it. Can my Christmas present just be that I don't have to endure being stuck in a car with Joyce? That's all I ask for.

'I'm happy to go and pick her up in the morning while you're cooking and fiddling about with the turkey.' He paused and she knew he was waiting for her to offer to take his mother back to the care home where she lived, an hour's drive away.

'More wine?' She quickly picked up the bottle, desperate to head him off at the pass. 'Do you like this one, darling?'

She could feel him looking at her, then he sniffed and said, 'Then you can take her back in the evening, can't you?'

'Why doesn't she stay over in the guest room? And one of us can take her back on Boxing Day?'

'No, you know she only likes to sleep in her own bed.' There was no evidence to support this but, equally, it was impossible to disprove. Roger seemed to be fond of his mother but not to the extent of wanting to be in the same building as her for more than a couple of hours at a time; he would find her presence at breakfast the next day irksome. 'You'll have to take her late afternoon or evening on Christmas Day. You can do it straight after we've had tea and Christmas cake.'

'Mmm, but then I wouldn't be able to have more than one glass of wine if I have to drive... which is a bit of a shame. I know you put so much thought into planning which wines to serve.'

Roger sighed, as if having to deal with his wife's alcoholic tendencies was a daily trial.

'You'll have to drive your father back, anyway, won't you, so what's the difference?'

'Actually, he insisted that he'd be happy to walk. I'll nip down and pick him up in the morning so he doesn't have to walk both ways, but you know how he loves walking.'

'Over five miles? In the dark?'

'He walks that most days anyway for pleasure and to keep fit. I did offer to drive him back, too, of course, but—'

'Good. Well, you won't mind taking Mum then, will you?'

'Fine.' She got up, cleared their plates from the table and switched the kettle on to make Roger his coffee.

It wasn't just that Roger's mother was mean-spirited and never had a kind word to say about anyone (other than her peerless son, of course, even though he was the one who had carefully chosen a care home an hour away so that he wouldn't be able to visit her too often); Joyce never read a book or watched a film or visited a garden or wondered about the world or formed a view about anything interesting. Her topics of conversation – and conversation was not really an apt word as she had no feel for the warp and weft of an extended exchange of views and thoughts – were restricted to tight-lipped pronouncements on her preferred TV programmes, how well Roger was doing at work and in life, and how lucky Eleanor was to have landed a catch like Roger as he was so successful and well-paid, and it must be lovely to have such a big house and live in the lap of luxury and not even have to do your own hoovering. *She* wouldn't have known what to do with herself if she'd had servants at her beck and call day and night, that was for sure and certain...

Eleanor had always managed to bite her lip and not point out that one cleaner once a week hardly meant that there was no housework to do the rest of the time, and did not constitute twenty-four-hour hot and cold running staff.

36

THE LAST LETTER

Cecilia could no longer kid herself that all was well. Olivia hadn't been to Sunday brunch with Madeleine for three weeks; she rarely missed a week unless she was away. Nor had she made an impromptu visit with a thoughtful treat – flowers, fresh-ground coffee – the way she often did. Cecilia had left messages on her elder daughter's landline and mobile, saying her knee and ankle were fine now, and asking Olivia how she was. She even dug out her own mobile, which the girls bought for her last birthday and which she never used because the buttons were too small and fiddly and she forgot to charge it. Painstakingly, she attempted to compose a text message. It was ridiculous. How could she possibly say all she needed to say in a stupid, truncated little message? It reminded her of the old joke about how many elephants could fit into a telephone kiosk. There was so much she wanted to say, should have said a long time ago. She had always meant to, once Olivia turned eighteen, but then she was so excited to be going off to university, spreading her wings, that Cecilia hadn't wanted to weigh her down with heavy talk about the past. And she'd told herself that perhaps there was no need after all. Olivia would surely ask when she wanted to know more, and Cecilia would be brave then and tell her the unadulterated truth and it would all be out in the open. But then Olivia had never asked.

With Olivia not there, Cecilia and Madeleine trudged through rubbery scrambled eggs and flaccid bacon without an ounce of pleasure.

Neither of them was even consistently successful at making toast. Once again, a slice had somehow become folded and trapped in the slot of the toaster and begun to burn. The smoke alarm went off and Madeleine leaped to her duty, grabbing a tea-towel and madly flapping it at the alarm until it stopped, while Cecilia tugged out the mangled toast with a pair of wooden chopsticks and plonked it on her plate; no point in wasting it.

Olivia's absence sat in the kitchen with them, a palpable ghost. They tiptoed around the Olivia-shaped space, sticking to topics that would have had her stealthily reaching for the Sunday papers if she were there – an out-of-the-way shop with divine wools and threads; the latest creations of Cecilia's determinedly eccentric friends; where exactly the dividing line sat between turquoise and aquamarine – but every mouthful of joyless food, every sidestep in the conversation to manoeuvre around her, served only to remind them of her.

Cecilia pushed away her half-eaten plate of food.

'Has she said anything to you, at least?'

Madeleine wrinkled her nose. They had trod this ground more than once before.

'Almost nothing.' She met her mother's gaze so Cecilia was sure she must be telling the truth.

The girls were so different in temperament. Madeleine didn't just wear her heart on her sleeve; she ran her feelings up the flagpole and waved them in the breeze for all to see. Olivia, by contrast, tended to bottle up her feelings. Outwardly, she might seem completely calm, revealing not the tiniest clue that she was upset, then she'd suddenly dissolve into tears, or flame into anger when you were least expecting it, like a wild creature rearing up from the depths of a beautiful still loch.

'She just said she was upset about something but didn't want to talk about it.'

'And it's not boyfriend trouble, you think?' That would be so much easier to deal with, after all. Cecilia rested her chin in her hands. 'I would ask, but I know she thinks I'm too intrusive and don't respect her boundaries enough. She should be glad. My own parents were completely uninterested in me, though, goodness, I remember this one time when I had to climb in the window naked because I—'

'*Mum*. Not now.'

'Sorry. I just want to know my girls are happy, that's all.'

'I know. Look, do not, not, *not* let on I told you, but she did have a couple of dates with this guy. You might even have seen him yourself; he lives round here. You know those people who were whingeing about your apple tree before Olivia got it pruned?'

'Not that timid little man who came round? He's much too old for her, surely? Well, perhaps he has hidden charms...'

'No, not him – the *son*. He's thirty-something. And not little. Average. Not bad-looking, I suppose, but not my type. She said he made her laugh and he was clever, too. Right up her street.'

'So... hmm... this man became her lover, and then he dumped her, you think?'

'Oh, gross, Mum. Don't put it like that. I don't know if she even slept with him. Probably not, knowing Liv. She always waits ages. Anyway, after their first couple of dates, she was all glowy and beautiful – you know what she looks like when she's really happy?'

'Completely radiant.'

'Exactly. And she was always hovering over her phone and they were texting like teenagers. But then the next time – afterwards, she was crotchety and mean: telling me to pick up my wet towel and not to leave the milk out, blah blah, and being all bossy and big sister-ish. And I said, have you had a row with your boyfriend and she said, "He's *not* my bloody boyfriend, OK?" and then she finished off the honeycomb ice cream and didn't save any for me.'

'Maybe it's just man-trouble then.'

'Maybe...' Maddy shoved aside her plate. 'You could call her?'

'I did. Several times. But it went through to the message thingy each time.'

'Voicemail. Use my phone if you like. Then she won't know it's you.'

'Isn't that a bit sneaky?'

Madeleine shrugged. 'Do you want to speak to her or not?'

Madeleine selected her sister's number then handed over her phone.

'Mads? Hi. Aren't you still at Mum's?'

'Olivia? It's me.' Cecilia's voice sounded false and bright. 'Mummy,' she added.

'Oh. Why are you on Mads's phone?'

'I just borrowed it for a minute to – to—'

'What do you want?'

'Well, nothing special, really. I was wondering if you might be joining us for brunch, that's all.'

'It's nearly noon. Bit late for brunch.'

'Well, lunch then. Or come for coffee.' Now that she had her on the phone at last, she was suddenly nervous, eager to backtrack. 'Not if you're too busy, of course.'

'I don't know. I'll think about it.'

'It would be nice to see you.'

'Mmm.'

'You'll try then?'

'OK.'

'You'll come?'

'Sure. Why not?' Olivia's voice sounded flat and colourless, as if all expression had been steam-rollered out of it. The call disconnected without Olivia's saying goodbye.

Maddy took back her phone and went to put on her coat.

'You're not leaving?'

'Yeah, I'm seeing friends down in Peckham for lunch and it takes ages to get there.'

'But Olivia said she's coming over soon.'

'So? It's not as if I won't see her later anyway.'

'But...'

'Oh, *Mum*.' Madeleine laughed. 'She won't bite you. Don't be such a noodle!'

'No, of course not.' Cecilia forced a small laugh. 'It's probably nothing anyway.'

Cecilia made an effort to tidy up as she knew her elder daughter found the mess irritating. She scooped up a teetering stack of paperwork – unfiled bills, receipts, fliers, etc. – from the old leather armchair and walked around the ground floor with it, looking for a new home. Eventually, she transferred it to another chair, but one that was tucked into a corner so was less noticeable. She loaded the dirty plates and mugs into the dishwasher and wiped the crumbs from the kitchen table into her cupped palm rather than straight onto the floor as she usually would. As an additional gesture, she inspected the interior of the fridge for elderly inhabitants and removed a crusty tub of taramasalata and deposited it in the bin. She refilled the kettle and rinsed out the coffee pot, feeling nervous yet excited, almost as if she were going on a date.

The doorbell rang – a long, insistent ring: not a ring to be ignored. Not an Olivia-ish ring. Please, not God-Squadders wanting to save her soul again. All that time and energy wasted on proselytising when they could be helping the poor, growing vegetables or knitting blankets for refugees… it was such a waste. A little unnerved, she put the chain on and opened the door a couple of inches. It was Olivia, after all. She breathed out, relieved.

'Oh, it *is* you. Did you forget your key? Hang on, the chain's on.'

She let off the chain and Olivia swept in past her – no hello, no how are you doodling, Ma? No kiss.

'It's lovely to see you,' Cecilia began. 'I've missed you—'

'See, what I want to know is, when exactly were you planning to tell me who my father really is? On your deathbed? Because many people might argue that it's my right to know who the fuck I am.' Olivia stood there, tall and imposing, eyes bright with rage. She tugged off her woolly hat and her red hair flamed out loose and wild, crackling with static.

'But when you found the letters, you dashed off in such a hurry. And then I called you, but you—'

'I wasn't in the mood to listen to any more lies. Can you blame me?' She pulled out the cream envelope from her bag and flung it onto the kitchen table. The letter. His last letter.

'You did have it then.'

'Yup.' She crossed her arms. 'What do the initials stand for? *DH*. David? Donald? *Derek?*'

Cecilia subsided into a chair and pulled the envelope towards her.

'*Dear* Heart.'

'He *is* the one, isn't he?' Olivia remained standing but leaned over to tap the frank mark with her finger. The date, though faded, was still decipherable. Cecilia was well into her pregnancy with Olivia by then.

Cecilia nodded. 'I'm sorry, I really am. You know I wasn't close to my own father—'

'Why does everything have to be about *you*? Can't you, for once in your life, just think of someone else for a change? How is that even remotely the same thing? So you weren't close! So what? He was in the house, you grew up with him, he was there every day, he kissed you good night. I *never* had that with my real father.' She stopped. 'I'm not criticising Dad – Phil. This is a completely separate thing.'

'You read it?' Cecilia stroked the writing on the envelope with a fingertip.

'I think I was entitled to, under the circumstances. Don't you?'

Another nod.

'That is not a letter written after a casual fling.'

'No.'

'The man was clearly off his head over losing you.'

'But I didn't receive this until—'

'Did you love him, too?'

'Yes.' Cecilia looked up at her daughter. 'You can't imagine how much I loved him. I've never loved anyone else like—'

'Quite so. I can't imagine. Nor should I have to.' She folded her arms across her chest. 'You see, I do think that any normal woman might have told her child that, actually, she had loved the child's father very much, don't you? One has to wonder what kind of person pretends it was a casual fling if it wasn't. I know your disregard for convention borders on the compulsive, but surely even you must struggle to see the logic in your actions?'

Cecilia tried to marshal her words but it was so hard to explain. At the time, she had been so sure that she was doing the right thing, but now...

'Well, I thought... I thought... ' She covered her eyes with her hand for a moment. 'I thought that if you knew how it was – that we had loved each other so much... as we did.' She paused. 'As we truly did – then you would never be able to understand *why*.'

There was a silence.

'So, just to be really clear because I'd hate to be in a muddle about this – unimportant though it seems to be to you – when you said that you'd got pregnant with me as a result of a fling in Boston, that was a lie?'

'I was trying to protect you—'

'It was a lie?'

'Yes. It was. I'm sorry.'

'And when you told me it was all tremendous *fun* but that the guy didn't matter to you and so shouldn't matter to me, that was a lie?'

'I didn't want you to—'

'That was a lie?'

'Yes, but I—'

'And when you said you couldn't even remember the man's surname so couldn't have tracked him down even if you'd wanted to, *that* was a lie?'

Cecilia gave the smallest of nods, then stole a look up at her daughter. Olivia's eyes, so like her own, stared back, unreadable.

'God knows, you're always rattling on about your ex-lovers – how this one was a great fuck and that one you shagged on the floor of an art gallery, never giving a toss about whether we actually want to hear all this stuff – but the one guy – the *one* guy it sounds as if you really cared about – who actually mattered to you – you never mention! You make out you're so chilled about sex and you masquerade as this laid-back, arty chick who has no hang-ups, but what about *love*?' Olivia suddenly made a gulping sound and started to cry. 'That's... *that's* the thing you... you can't deal with.'

Cecilia remained silent for a few moments.

'I'm very sorry,' she said. 'Please won't you sit down, Livvy?' She never shortened her daughter's name and, even to her ears, the chummy tone sounded fraudulent and out of place. 'Come sit by me and let's talk about this prop—'

'No – *let's* not anything.' Olivia roughly rubbed away her tears with her coat sleeve. 'How *dare* you? How dare you lie to me my whole life when you knew all along? You could have told me about my real father – even if – even if he wanted nothing to do with us – with me – you could have told me what he was like – what you loved about him. You could have given me that, at least. But you *chose* not to. What on earth is the matter with you? You always have to be special, don't you? To be unconventional and all that posturing, self-conscious crap. You got off on being the martyr, stoically raising your abandoned baby and marrying someone you didn't love so you could waft about being an artist and feeling noble and interesting. But it's all bollocks. You could have gone to him and said, 'Look, I seem to be up the duff – what are you going to do about it?' But that would just be too normal and, by your lights, therefore dull and boring, yawn, yawn, what a drag. Well, for fuck's sake,

Mother – guess what? Sometimes doing the normal thing is actually the best thing. Ever thought of that?'

'But I was only—'

'No. Enough. I'm going.' Olivia yanked on her woolly hat again.

'Please don't—' Cecilia started to rise.

'You don't get it, do you? You *lied* to me – not to protect me, but selfishly – to protect yourself, because you did something so appalling that even you could see that you had fucked up and that I might never forgive you, so you kept on with the lie, for years and years – and to him, too, by not telling him.' Tears pooled in her eyes again. 'I really, really don't want to be around you right now.'

'But just let me try to—'

'You know what? You've had thirty years to explain and you didn't. Take another look at that letter! He clearly didn't have a clue you were pregnant. You didn't tell him, did you?'

Cecilia slumped back into her seat and said nothing.

'*Did you?*'

'No.'

'Then we have no idea what he might have done, do we? Look at the letter. The poor man sounds half crazy, searching for you. Maybe he's looked for you since. Who knows? You moved, you changed your name, for crying out loud, while he could have been looking! He might have done the right thing!'

She turned away, towards the door.

'I know you're upset, I understand that—'

'*Don't!* Don't you dare patronise me and give me all that you understand how I feel crap! You *don't* understand. You *don't* have a fucking clue what this feels like. Everything is horrible. The ground has turned to quicksand beneath my feet and I can't even stand up any more. You act as if I'm the uptight one because I don't always like to talk about my private life or my feelings – but look at *you*. Maybe you just threw him aside once you got bored? Or maybe you didn't really love him at all?'

'No, it wasn't like that.'

'I don't believe you. I'm going.'

'Olivia, please stay.'

'Goodbye,' she said. 'Look after yourself.'

'But – but what about Christmas? You'll still come for Christmas, won't you?'

And then she was gone.

Cecilia took the envelope and pulled out the handwritten card. She had not read it for perhaps six or seven years. He had sent it to the art school where she sometimes used to pose as a life model, but it had taken months to reach her and by then, she had married Philip, moved house, and Olivia was born. Her gaze travelled over the words, her fingers relishing the half-forgotten feel of the thick card once more. She read it silently to herself:

Forgive me. Forgive me. Forgive me! I cannot bear this... I move through the days on auto-pilot – unthinking, unfeeling – without joy or purpose. Before I knew you, I had lived my whole life believing – telling myself – that love was just some silly notion conjured up by poets so that they had something to write about... a kind of idea that people could spin stories around – like magic – an enchanting concept – but not a real thing. Not something that anyone might experience every single day. You opened my eyes, ML, and now I cannot close them again. It is unbearable. I do not even know if you will get this. I came to your flat but the mad woman who lives downstairs told me you had moved and claimed not to have your new address. Where are you? Come back to me, My Love.

SYDH???

Still Your Dear Heart???

She held it up to her closed eyes, kissed it with dry lips and, at last, at last, began to weep.

37

MOCHACCINO

Andrew slathered his face in shaving foam and picked up his razor. He looked in the mirror. How odd it was that he did this every single morning. Who decided that this was a normal, sensible, reasonable thing to do? To smother your face in slithery crap made of God knows what, then use a dangerous blade to slice off your entirely natural facial hair, which was just attempting to fulfil its mission, become a beard. And that was just the shaving. Then there was teeth-brushing. Even worse because it was twice a day. It would be better if teeth could just *stay* brushed. When you mended a tear in a piece of antique paper, there – it was done! The tear was fixed. You had implemented an action that had brought about a tangible improvement. But when you shaved, showered, brushed your teeth, got dressed, it didn't stay done – none of it. You had to keep doing the same tasks, redoing them, on and on, day in, day out, for years, decades... until you died. Only then could you say well thank fuck for that, I can rest here in the dark, quiet earth and not have to shave any more. Alleluia and Amen, thank you and good night. All the tedious, God, so mind-numbingly tedious, routine maintenance you're supposed to do to make believe you're a civilised man in a civilised world just stops. How do people not go completely mad, overwhelmed by the complete pointlessness of it all? It was just futile. All of it. Absolutely fucking all of it.

Andrew ran his flannel under the hot tap and scrubbed at his face with it. Downstairs, he shoved his feet into his shoes, put on his long overcoat and scarf – getting colder now – grabbed his current book from the hall table, silently opened the front door, then quickly called out goodbye to his parents. He was not in the mood to sit and eat breakfast to the soundtrack of his mother's running commentary on the goings-on of every household in their postcode, relentless as a truck with busted brakes – powering on and through, crushing any stray, precious moment of silence in her path. And his father, sitting there, relishing the refuge his newspaper offered each day, breakfast the only meal at which he could legitimately escape, spinning it out, reading every inch: the foreign pages, the business section, even scanning the share index as if he might be considering having a chat with his broker. For God's sake, his father, who had worked his whole life as a postman. The business section might as well be written in Aramaic for all the relevance or meaning it could have for his dad.

On the tube, Andrew crunched himself into a corner, no seats free as usual, and burrowed deep into his book, at once freed from the crush around him, a woolly, sweaty, stressed mass of people, pressed close enough to each other to be lovers, carefully avoiding eye contact. The stench of generously applied perfume and after-shave was making him feel slightly queasy. Now he regretted that he hadn't grabbed at least a quick slice of toast as he was running out the door, but there was no grabbing a quick anything in his mother's domain. Breakfast must be taken sitting down, thank you very much. Cereal and a choice of fruit juice (orange or, if you are having trouble, you know, then prune), followed by toast as an optional – i.e., not very optional – extra. Full fry-up on a Sunday. You must eat properly, Andrew, or however will you get through the day? As if he were hard at it, sweating down a coal mine or digging holes in the road rather than sitting at a table, cleaning and restoring prints and drawings with painstaking care.

His walk from the tube to the British Museum took him past a small café where he sometimes bought a sandwich at lunchtime. Perhaps he would get a takeaway coffee, like other people do? London was now thronging with people walking along while drinking coffee out of a cup through a little hole in the lid, like in a toddler's beaker, but it had never appealed to him. The first time Andrew had seen someone doing that – a woman in a smart black suit and high heels, slurping at this ridiculous sippy cup while texting one-handed on her mobile, click-clacking along the pavement, he had actually laughed out loud at the bonkersness of it. But now it had become a perfectly acceptable thing to do.

He entered the café and looked up at the long hot drinks list on the wall. On a whim, he ordered a mochaccino. He had never had one before, but it sounded promising. It was the kind of thing other people ordered: smart, professional people such as... such as himself. Well, like himself only more... more what? More fashionable, maybe. More trendy. More... his shoulders sagged. More grown-up.

'And one of those, please.' He pointed at a Danish pastry. He hadn't had one for ages. Suddenly it looked irresistible, with plump raisins peeping out from its curves, oozing crème pâtissière.

Andrew carefully pulled up the little flap in the lid so that he, too, could drink while striding along. He smiled as he held open the door for a woman coming in as he was going out. She looked him up and down and gave him an intriguing sort of half-smile. Today he felt different. He *was* different. Women were noticing him. The image of Olivia's face as he last saw her swam into his head, the way her smile had disappeared so completely. Well, no matter! He was a single guy. The world was his oyster. He walked on to the museum, took a confident slug at his sippy cup.

'Jesus fuck!' He said this out loud and three or four passers-by turned to stare at him. Why was it so bloody hot, for God's sake? Did he order a sodding mochaccino or a cup of molten lava? He wiped his mouth on his coat sleeve and stomped upstairs to the conservation room within Prints and Drawings. It looked as if he was first in, even earlier than usual today as he had skipped breakfast. He sloughed off his coat, set the Danish down on his table, the mochaccino next to it. He'd feel better once he'd had this; just feeling a bit low-blood-sugary, that's all it was. Then he could start work.

The Keeper of P and D's door was closed, he'd noticed. Douglas, the Keeper, was in Madrid overseeing the transfer of an exhibition to the Prado there, but Conrad would no doubt be in already to cover infor-mally. Any excuse.

Lucy, the assistant conservator, arrived next.

'Good morning!' he heard her call brightly from the area by the coathooks where they left their coats and bags. She came in, then stopped a few feet away.

'Andrew?'

'Yes, Lucy.' He half-turned in his chair towards the sound of her voice. 'Good morning. Good morning to you today! And how are you? Feeling good?'

Lucy stood there, not moving. She looked at Andrew, then at the Danish and coffee in front of him, then back at him. She did not speak.

'I have here in my possession a mochaccino.' Andrew playfully tappety-tapped the lid with his fingertips. 'It is – apparently – some kind of coffee and hot chocolate combination. Combo, I should say, no doubt. And it is, I have to tell you, surprisingly yet considerably less nice than either – a horrific hot-drink chimera, if you will.'

'Are you... are you OK?' Lucy looked at him again, then away towards the closed door of the Keeper's office.

'I am not just OK, I am okey-dokey, tip-top, absolutely fantastico, thank you.'

Lucy said nothing. She stood there for a few moments, then crossed to the Keeper's door, knocked firmly and – without waiting for an answer – went in.

After a couple of minutes, Conrad emerged and entered the conservation room. Andrew was sitting at his work-table in his dressing gown and pyjamas. One side of his face was shaven, the other not. In front of him was a disposable cup and the remnants of some sort of Viennoiserie, Conrad deduced. There were flaky, buttery crumbs scattered in a wide arc radiating out from him. This table, which was meticulously, obsessively cleaned each day to remove the smallest particle of dust, the tiniest residue of oil or grease from an unthinking hand. This room, in which no form of food or drink, other than bottled water, was ever brought. Ever.

'Andrew?' Conrad pulled up another stool and sat down next to him.

'I bought a mochaccino,' he said.

'Yes.'

'I've never had one before.'

'No.'

'It's truly unpleasant.' He looked at the cup with loathing. 'Too sweet but then bitter, both at the same time.'

'I see,' Conrad said. 'It's all right now.'

'It's just –' Andrew turned his palms upwards, helpless. 'It's just – all – too difficult, you see. All of it. The teeth-brushing. And the shaving. And the dressing. Over and over. It doesn't stay done. None of it... it never stays done...'

Conrad awkwardly patted his arm and, suddenly, Andrew crumpled against him. Silently, he cried, his head making little jerks against Conrad's collar-bone and his tears leaching through Conrad's shirt. The older man held himself stiff as a lamp-post at first, but then, at last, put his arm around Andrew.

'I know,' he said, squeezing this trembling form the way a father might comfort his child awoken from a nightmare. 'I know.'

38

THE PAINTING

1982

'Marriott.' Conrad answers the phone in his office at the BM.

'Hello. It's Philip Herbert here.'

For a few moments, Conrad cannot place the name or the voice.

'The painter. Your painting is ready. You can come and collect it. Or I suppose I could deliver it to you if you're not miles away...?'

The painting. Oh dear God, the painting. She swims into his head again, though she is never absent for long.

'No, no, I'll come and fetch it. Tomorrow. Remind me of your address.'

Conrad has been there only once before, at the first sitting for the portrait. Commissioning it was entirely his idea but she recommended a painter, a friend she described as 'overburdened with talent'. Conrad pulled her onto his lap then, and traced the curve of her cheek with his fingertip.

'But he's bound to fall in love with you – sitting there gazing at you for hours while he paints you. I wish I could paint.'

'He won't. Trust me.' She kissed him, gently sucking his lower lip between her teeth. 'He's gay.'

'Gay? Oh, queer, you mean?'

'Oh – *you*.' She pinched him playfully. 'You can't say "queer" any more. It's perjorative and intolerant. Besides, it makes you sound about a hundred.'

'In my day, gay meant jolly. "We had such a gay time at the village fête", that sort of thing.'

'Well, it doesn't any more. You have to keep up.'

'Why have you stopped kissing me?'

'I haven't. I was merely pausing to reprimand you.'

'Reprimand accepted. Resume kissing.' His hand moved over the soft swell of her breast, and he started to fumble at the buttons of her satin blouse. Suddenly, he rose to his feet in a single movement, lifting her in his arms easily, and carried her back to the bed.

'Again?' She laughed. 'I thought you'd have tired of it by now.'

'Never.' His voice low and rumbling as he nuzzled the soft hollow of her throat. 'Never, never.'

* * *

Philip Herbert's studio is surprisingly orderly for an artist, Conrad thinks. He recalls that she had teased him – Philip – about his neatness; they were very chummy and relaxed with each other, a little like brother and sister; he had noted a pang of envy in himself. He had no friends with whom he could be so completely playful and at ease.

That earlier visit, Conrad looked at a few examples of Philip's paintings. He was clearly exceptional. He thought about the pictures on his walls at home – Christ, how tame they were! How polite. How fucking dull. These were like some completely different species: technically extremely fine but also fizzing with a curious sort of intensity and depth of colour that made them compelling. Mostly portraits but also some rather beautiful cityscapes, with buildings in extraordinary colours.

Philip wanted to begin at once and directed her to the window seat, telling her to find a position in which she could be comfortable for him to start his preparatory drawing.

Conrad looked round for a chair where he might perch and watch Philip work.

'You're not *staying*?' She sounded half-amused, half-horrified.

'Well, I rather thought I might.' Conrad cast about him again, but the only potential seating other than the peculiar three-cornered stool on which Philip was sitting was a wooden chest with a brass-studded lid, which looked far from comfortable. There was a divan at the far end of the room but it would be hard to see from there.

'No. Sorry – I can't have people in the room while I'm working.' Philip didn't even look at him. 'It's distracting.'

'I'd keep completely still.'

'No. It's out of the question.'

Conrad paused for a few moments, wondering whether to face up to the man. He was the client with the cheque book, after all. Philip had turned away and was poking about in a nearby plan chest for something. Conrad looked back at her. She looked at him with such love and tenderness that he felt something inside him give. She flicked her head in a tiny gesture towards the door and smiled. Conrad strode across and kissed her full on the lips.

'Shall I really go then?' He murmured close to her ear.

'Yes, Dear Heart,' she whispered back. 'Call me later?'

'Will do.' Another kiss. He straightened up. 'I'll be off then.' A curt nod at Philip. Bloody cheek of the man. Still, Christ, he could paint. What a thing to have a talent like that.

And then Benedict pulled his little joyriding stunt and that changed everything, forced him to face up to his responsibilities. He is managing without her. Not well, of course, but he is surviving by taking one day at a time and by immersing himself in his structured plan for Benedict, which involves checking Benedict at agreed half-hourly intervals while he does his homework, and working to a rigid timetable. When Benedict does well and completes the homework he has been set, he is allowed a small glass of beer with supper or to have a friend over at the weekend but they must both stay within sight and earshot. Benedict has been given an extremely stern talking-to by the family lawyer and does at least seem to have grasped that he was within a hair's breadth of ending up in a youth custody centre.

Night-time is the worst, for it is then that she comes unbidden to his mind, his thoughts – her voice, her body, her glorious laugh. Then he thinks he will go mad, that he cannot live without her. Sometimes he slips silently out of bed, careful not to wake Marcia, goes down to the study and sits at the desk, looking at the sole photograph he has of her – one she gave him a couple of years ago. He keeps it in his desk, tucked inside an envelope, secreted inside a second envelope, in a small stack of old correspondence in a box file, somewhere no one would think to look. He leafs through an old, red spiral-bound sketchbook of hers he'd asked to keep: a few of the pages are covered with sketches of himself – reading, just sitting, looking rather stern, a study of his hands, one half-dozing in bed, and another of him in three-quarter profile – 'always the hardest,' she said. He found it most peculiar being drawn, the way she looked at him so intently but as if she had never seen him before. It is all he has.

He replays his memories endlessly, tormenting himself by picturing her in every possible situation – walking in the park, standing naked by the stove stirring a saucepan of tinned soup, that intense earnestness when she was arguing about something, or the way she'd tease him when he was being pompous or didactic, and he would suddenly see himself through her eyes and laugh at himself. He was a better *him* with her, no question. Most of all, he conjures up what she was like in bed – her face on the pillow next to his, the transported look on her face as she comes, or when she is lying on top of him, her hair loose, a curtain around her face, around his – enclosing their own private world. He has written to her, begged her to take him back, but there has been no answer. If he doesn't hear from her soon, he is minded to go round there and pound on her door until she will see him. But then what would he say? Nothing has changed. He still loves her, but he cannot leave. Not yet, at least. She would understand, surely?

He trudges up the many steps to Philip Herbert's studio. Depressing stairs covered in brown linoleum with dirty white strips defining the edges. The hallway lights have timed switches, set to click off just before you have reached the next switch so you are suddenly plunged into darkness. He knocks on Philip's door. There doesn't seem to be a door-bell or even a knocker. Philip lets him in, nods hello and waves him towards the painting, sitting on an easel in the middle of the room.

And there it is. There *she* is. He hasn't seen her for well over a month, the longest break since they first met over three years ago. But here she is now, right in front of him, captured and captivating. It is the most extraordinary thing. He thought that maybe he would just pay Philip but tell him to keep the painting or give it to her, that he wouldn't be able to bear it if he has this reminder in his house. But now that he is here looking at it, he knows at once that he needs it, that he *must* have it. If he has to survive without *her*, at least he can have *this*. It has caught her expression absolutely – that look she has where you can't tell if she is looking at you with love or a sort of half-suppressed assessing amusement or a strange kind of wry pity.

He stands there, lost in another world, until Philip coughs.

'So... erm... it's OK, right? I mean, do you like it?'

'Hmm?' Conrad surfaces from the depths.

Philip nods towards the picture, a question.

'There is not a single brushstroke you could improve upon.'

'Oh. Right. Thanks.' Suddenly, the man looks quite boyish. 'Yeah, I'm pretty pleased with it.'

'It is...' Conrad pauses, '... absolutely *her*. I... I—' He cannot speak, turning away then to take out the money to pay him, looking down to count it out. Clears his throat, straightens up. 'Have you seen her lately?'

Philip makes a non-committal movement that conveys nothing, then says, 'I guess you haven't seen her yourself?'

He knows then.

'No. It's – ah – been difficult.' This is such a preposterous understatement that he wonders he could even say it out loud.

Philip nods. 'Sorry to hear it. I guess love is never easy, right?'

'Right.'

'You do still want the painting, though?' Philip's hand closes around the wad of notes. 'I mean, maybe you'll work things out?'

'Mm, maybe.' Conrad hears the over-cheerful note in his voice, as if he is wishing that the weather will brighten up. He hates himself when he is like this. He does not know how to be *him* any more unless he is with her. He has become the way he used to be, a competent, stiff parody of a human being. He watches himself from the outside, functioning, talking, making decisions, a dry husk of a man.

'And, yes, I want the painting, of course. Do you have some paper to put round it?'

'Sure.' Philip retrieves a roll of brown paper from a cupboard and some packing tape. 'And let me point you towards a decent framer, if you want one? It's really not far.'

Conrad nods. Yes, he will have it framed; he can take it straight there now. It deserves a good frame and it will give him a little more time to think about how he might have come by the painting. Marcia has been somewhat attuned to his movements in the last few months, asking more questions about his whereabouts in a way she never used to. These last few weeks have been well-timed, in fact, as he has been coming home promptly straight after work and is unmistakably present around the house at weekends, keeping an eye on Benedict and making him earn his allowance by doing his homework, helping in the garden with the digging or washing the car. Marcia has even made some no doubt well-intentioned remarks about it: 'I'm sure having you actually in the house as you should be is making a world of difference to Benedict, you know.' And the school is pleased, at least.

Eleanor notices everything but says very little, only commenting once as she kissed him good night, 'I like it when you are here for supper. So I have someone to talk to.'

39

A WOMAN WHO COULD MAKE HIM HAPPY

Andrew let himself in as silently as he could, keeping on his coat but shucking off his shoes to secrete them neatly in the understairs cupboard, as dictated by High Decree. The front door wasn't double-locked so she, or both of them, must be in. Bugger. He stifled his jangly keys and slipped them back in his pocket, rather than hanging them on the keyboard on the back of the cupboard door.

He wouldn't put it past his mother to have installed some sort of laser-beam crossing the hallway, which would alert her to his presence. But then why go to such unnecessary expense when her own inbuilt radar could detect the sound of a coffee mug being set down not on its assigned coaster from two rooms away?

Today, he really wasn't in the mood for her. He told himself he was being unkind, ungrateful, but still he craved just a few glorious minutes of peace and silence to himself before he could face her and the rat-a-tat fire of questions that would surely follow. If he could just go and sit in his room, maybe lie down for ten minutes, he'd feel better then, and could come down and sit at the kitchen table and ask about her morning and just listen without trying to curtail her account of the minutiae of Summerlee Avenue: who had walked their dog ten minutes later than usual, who had come back from the shops laden with bags clinking with bottles, who'd had a visitor spotted sneaking out at six o'clock in the morning. He would sit, sip his tea, and say 'mmm', just like his dad did, like a good son should.

But not now this minute. He wanted to slip into the silence like a pool of glorious cool water on a sweltering day. He set his foot on the bottom step, glancing along the hallway towards the closed kitchen door. He could hear the TV on in there, so that was a help. Dad would no doubt be filling time in his shed, keeping busy and out of Herself's way. Second step. Skip the third as it creaked. Take it easy now. Resist the urge to rush. Four, five. Six – scoosh to the left as it was dodgy on the right. Half-landing. Breathe out. Tiptoeing up the rest. Yes! Victory was his. A fleeting moment of smugness was replaced by a stab of self-loathing: God, you sad bastard, is this really your idea of a triumph: getting upstairs without being detected? What are you – eight years old? He tucked himself quickly into his bedroom and quietly shut the door. Breathed out, then lowered himself onto the bed. The bedsprings be-doinged in response. He stood up immediately and tried the chair. It was bolt upright, white, with an elongated, narrow back, the seat uphol-stered in olive-green Dralon. Andrew disliked it intensely, even more so now that he came to sit in it and realise just how uncomfortable it was.

Maybe he'd pop to the pub for a quick pint? He checked his watch. It wasn't even 10.30 a.m. yet. The café, then. He could go for a coffee and read the papers. Maybe go to the pub later. He could call one of his friends and arrange to hook up, have a pint or two, go for a Thai or a curry; yes, go out like other blokes of his age, have a drink, chat up some women. Why not? Because most of them are married and half of them have kids, you prat – that's why not.

Out of boredom, he opened the top right-hand drawer of his chest of drawers. His underpants, neatly arranged in staggered layers by colour: navy, grey, black. He'd thanked his mother innumerable times for doing his laundry but she was deaf to his insistence that really, she could just dump his washing on his bed and he'd put it away. It was no bother, she said, she was putting everything else away anyway, why shouldn't she do his, honestly she didn't mind. She was not attuned to subtle hints so either you'd have to be blunt and say, 'DO NOT put my washing away, it creeps me out and I'm not five or an invalid, so please, for the love of God, please STOP' – and risk leaving her with that wounded face and your feeling as if you'd kicked a puppy, or you'd learn to live with it. And, of course, she was doing something nice, so you should be grateful and not keep trying to circumvent her when she meant no harm by it. In his sock drawer, the socks were not just balled roughly into pairs, as he would do, but flattened and perfectly aligned, possibly – he shuddered – even ironed. His work socks were on one side of the drawer, his casual socks and 'comic' socks – given to him each year by his mother at Christmas, with golf-playing Santas or ice-skating reindeer or drunken snowmen cavorting on them – on the other. It was like a scab now that he couldn't resist picking, relishing the deep irritation he felt at her.

He opened the drawer below. Inside was a pair of brand-new pyjamas, still in their crackly plastic packet, that she'd put on his bed weeks ago, before that date with Olivia when it had all started to go so horribly wrong. Brown and orange stripes, his two least favourite colours. They were the sort with buttons down the front, the sort his father wore, the sort, Andrew realises, he is inexplicably wearing now this minute, though these ones are a sort of drab olive-green check, unpleasant in a different way. Did he really go in to work dressed like this? It seems very unlikely now, not the sort of thing he would do at all. A sudden memory of Conrad's putting his arm around him flitted into his vision and he shut his eyes and covered his face with his hands for a moment.

Then he batted the thought away and focused back on the pyjamas, took them out and slumped on the bed holding the packet. When he was living with Vicki, he used to wear just a plain cotton T-shirt with pyjama bottoms, but somehow, since he moved back in with his parents – he corrected the thought – since temporarily coming here to stay for a brief period while he sorted himself out – he'd taken to wearing the old-fashioned sort that men under the age of sixty hardly wore any more. It was the great generation divide: never mind which TV programmes you watched or how you chose to vote – did you wear matching pyjamas with buttons or mismatched casual ones? Over sixty. Under sixty.

He was a young man in old-man pyjamas, pyjamas that in every aspect of their being – colour, fabric, design, detail, buttons – were woman-repellent. What woman on earth would want to slip her hand inside there to reach for your cock? That's what it came down to. These were not pyjamas in which you might feasibly have an erection. In fact, your cock wouldn't even be a cock any more. It would be a willy, like a little boy or an old man has, good for weeing and nothing else. Say goodbye to your sex life, Andrew. There couldn't be a woman on the planet who would fancy a man wearing these. What sex life, you sad tosser? He made a conscious effort not to count back how many months it had been since he'd last had sex, while being unable to stop himself working it out. Four... five months? No, because Vicki had suddenly fallen asleep unexpectedly when they were about to... So... six months? He leaned back against the wall and looked round the room, letting his mind roam onto something, anything else. Funny, really. Aside from a single row of books on the narrow desk in the corner – all the rest were in boxes up in the loft – his alarm clock, and his laptop, there wasn't a single thing visible in this room that indicated that it was his. Of course, he'd only been here a month or so... five weeks, was it? He thought back, remembering the Saturday when Vicki had thrown him out. But that was early October and it was nearly Christmas now. No, that couldn't possibly be right, could it? He suddenly covered his face with his hands. Over *ten* weeks ago. He lowered his head between his knees, feeling sick and faint.

In five years, ten years' time, he would still be here, living out his days in this small and sexless room, helping his mother with the shopping at the weekend, occasionally going out for a pint with his father to the pub two streets away – whoop-de-whoop! – doing little jobs around the house when his dad got too old to do them any more. God! Then his father would see his chance and seize the opportunity to die – peace at last – leaving Andrew with the short straw of looking after his mother.

He would look in the Classifieds, go online, find a flatshare, a room to rent, anything – yes, at the weekend. He would take some time to find somewhere suitable and not too far out. There'd be time at the weekend. He would do it right this minute only he was so tired, so very tired, he just needed a little time to rest—

A sudden, sharp knock at the door made him jump. Then his mother swept in before he could respond.

'Oh, it *is* you! You gave me the fright of my life, Andrew. Whatever are you doing home at this hour of the day? I said to myself that's a funny noise, is that Andrew I can hear creeping about upstairs, but I said no he's not long gone to work and anyway he'd come say hello, of course he would, so then I'm wondering is that Dad back from the garden centre, but what would he be doing upstairs when he's been that desperate to get out into the garden the second it stopped raining? Your father's been back and forth to that garden centre I don't know how many times he'd forget his head if it weren't screwed on poor love. He's never sat down for more than half an hour before he's having to dash off on another errand, a five-inch pot for this or a reel of wire for that you'd think he'd rest up a bit since he retired but he's never been so busy, what with his allotment and the bowls club and his computer and now he's all of a sudden minded to take up fishing he's barely home. But what are you doing home, Andrew, you've never gone and got the sack have you, love?'

'No, of course not.' Andrew felt sick, his mother's words pounding against his head like a sudden storm of hailstones. He was praying she wouldn't look down and spot his pyjama-clad legs beneath the hem of his winter coat, but Mrs Tyler, while blind to many things in this world, could be relied upon to notice the one thing you most hoped she might miss.

'Andrew! You never went to work in your pyjamas? Oh my Lord, no wonder they fired you!'

'They haven't fired me.'

'Oh, but they will. They're bound to! It's a museum, Andrew. You can't just turn up in jeans – or – or – pyjamas – or whatever you like, you know. Whatever were you thinking?'

The idea that wearing pyjamas to work might be somehow equivalent to wearing jeans was suddenly amusing and Andrew covered his mouth and converted the emerging laugh into a small cough.

'It's dress-down Friday. We all came in like this.'

'But it's *Tuesday*.' She hesitated for a moment. 'I know it's a Tuesday because Dad put the bins out last night for the dustmen this morning.'

'It was for charity. Wear Your PJs to Work Day!'

He could see confusion writ large across his mother's face. She was struggling to fit the apparently conflicting pieces of the puzzle together.

'Tell me you've not been fired, Andrew? I said to Dad last night something was up with you. A mother can always tell.'

'Mum, I haven't been fired, I promise. I just wasn't feeling well. I had a terrible migraine all of a sudden. I came home to rest, and I've just now changed into my pyjamas this second, OK?'

'But you said it was for charity. You said the others were doing it.'

'I was joking, Mum. Sorry. It was just a joke. A pretty feeble one.'

'A joke. Oh.' Her face struggled to decide between smiling and frowning, and settled on a disconcerting combination of the two. 'Oh, I see.'

He saw her looking at his coat.

'And I put my coat back on because I suddenly felt a bit shivery.'

Mrs Tyler blinked several times, possibly trying to find some pattern of sense. She peered more closely at his face.

'Will I pick you up a packet of new razors when I'm at the chemist?' she said.

Andrew removed his coat and his mother took it from him, eyeing him with suspicion as if he were a broken teacup that had been glued together but not quite well enough so you could still see the cracks. He wanted to say, 'I can't do this, any of it, not any more, I need to lie down and go to sleep and never wake up. Go away, leave me alone and let me be until I am either cured or dead, I don't care which.'

'Will you have a lay-down then? Will I bring you up a cup of tea? It's no bother.' She was being kind and there was nothing he could tell her that would make any sense, so what was the point?

'I'll have a lie-down, yes. No tea.' His shoulders slumped. 'Thank you, Mum. I just need a bit of a rest, that's all. Think I've caught some sort of bug.'

He got into bed, lay on his back and pulled the covers up to his chin. He wished he weren't such a pathetic coward. A braver man than he would go and jump in front of a train or hurl himself off a cliff. He thought it would be a relief to die, now, if he could just slip away with no pain and no worry that he would be traumatising the train driver or that some poor sod would have to clean up his splattered remains. If he could just sink into blackness and be no more, he would do it. A single tear crept out of the corner of his eye and made a cautious journey across his cheek. He closed his eyes, slowed his breathing, and waited for sleep to take him away.

* * *

At some point, Mum came in and announced, 'Tea's on the table in five minutes. It's gammon steak, Andrew, your favourite, with all the trimmings.'

He could hear his own voice saying thanks, no, he wasn't hungry, but she said he must keep his strength up, she'd sooner die than see her men go hungry, and Andrew suspected she meant this literally rather than as a figure of speech. He pulled on his dressing gown and the effort felt as if he were hefting sacks of coal. He tottered downstairs on wobbly legs, watching himself from the outside as if he were weak and disembodied with flu. On the table were two oval platters for him and his dad, each piled high with a mound of chips and a shovel-load of peas alongside a great slab of pink meat, topped with a grilled tinned pineapple ring, quite the thing in 1973 – his mother had no time for the vagaries of fashion when it came to cooking – and a plate of white bread and butter on the side. All of Andrew's trousers were getting tight. Now, when he took them off at night, they left a red ring incised into his belly. Maybe he should get some of those slacks his father always wore, with an adjustable fastening to allow him to breathe after ingesting one of Mrs Tyler's considerable portions? Even these pyjamas were feeling very snug.

'See, love, your favourite.'

It wasn't his favourite, not even in his top one hundred, but once his mother had made her mind up about something, it was hard to disappoint her by introducing reality into the proceedings. It was better just to nod and say, 'Mmm, delicious.' He felt queasy. His dad shuffled in and asked if he were feeling any better.

Andrew looked down at his plate. The pineapple stared back at him, a yellow-ringed pink eye. 'Sorry, I don't feel so good.' He pushed back from the table and rushed to the downstairs toilet, opened the door and fell to his knees to vomit into the bowl, his body lurching in deep spasms. He flushed the loo, then stayed like that for a few minutes, waiting in case there was more, wanting to purge himself of this horrible, deadly weight that had lodged inside him. Then he stretched over and slid the bolt across and let himself slump sideways onto the floor, feeling the comforting softness of the peach fluffy pedestal mat around the base of the loo. Slowly, he lowered his head to the floor and lay there, stroking the bathmat gently as if it were a trusty old pet that was too tired to go for walkies any more, letting his tears trickle down his face.

When his dad tapped on the door, Andrew said he must be coming down with something, a stomach bug, a virus, that's all it was, he'd be out in a minute. He kneeled back by the loo and stayed there a little longer, clinging on to the cold ceramic like a lifebelt.

He flushed the loo once more and sprayed the Fruits of the Forest air freshener all around the room. Then he trudged back upstairs, brushed his teeth, and slid beneath the covers again.

* * *

Andrew lay in bed, an undrunk cup of cold tea beside him on the bedside table. He had no idea how long it had been there. Although his mother did not usually permit food or drinks in the upstairs rooms, she had definitely brought it to him and set it down on a coaster, saying, 'I've popped a tea there for you, love.' She had paused with her hand on the door handle. 'Should you call your boss to let him know you're... that you're... um... still not well?'

'He's a she, but I can do it. Thanks, Mum.' He reached for his mobile by the bed and waited for her to leave.

'Or maybe Dad could call, if you'd rather? He's just popped out for a lightbulb but he'll not be long, he said, though why he didn't get it when he went out for the paper first thing I don't know. I hope he's not getting that Alzheimer's what-have-you that everyone's getting these days. My friend Yvonne says it's the government putting fluoride in the water that's doing it.'

Andrew nodded and agreed that yes, indeed, it certainly was quite common.

'Give me a shout if you need anything, love.' She bent down and kissed his forehead.

He didn't want to talk to anyone, didn't know what he could possibly say that wouldn't sound pathetic or as if he were skiving. He emailed the Head of Conservation, saying he seemed to have come down with gastric flu and was likely to be off work for a day or two. He remembered Conrad at the BM. Being so kind. It seemed unlikely now. Conrad was many things: scarily clever and articulate, keenly observant, with astonishing powers of recall, but he wasn't the first person you would turn to if you were looking for kindness. And yet he *had* been kind. Unquestionably. Andrew ought to – to – acknowledge it, at least. And he was sort of in charge of P and D while the Keeper was away; not officially perhaps, but certainly he was the person everyone went to if there was a problem. He half sat up and emailed Conrad, thanking him for his concern and for paying for his taxi home, which he would reimburse him for when he next saw him.

* * *

The hours rolled by in a blur of dozing and murmurings from below, the periodic clinking of crockery and, oddly comforting for a change, the whine of the hoover, the small thuds as it bumped against the skirting board on the landing. A couple of times, Dad tapped on the door, then hovered in the doorway and asked him how he was feeling. His mother came in often, to take away the old tea and replace it with a new one. She'd even allowed a biscuit upstairs as she was worried he was wasting away – a garibaldi, presumably because it might produce fewer crumbs than most biscuits. The squashed raisins stuck to his teeth like tar, the dry biscuit clinging to the roof of his mouth. He swilled it down with cold tea.

He slid further down beneath the covers and rested his chin over the top edge of the duvet, the way he used to when he was little and thought the Dust Men would slide under the door to come and get him. He'd once overheard his dad talking about the dustmen but he'd pictured them as the Dust Men. He imagined the horrible way they could slip beneath doors, a creeping, silent layer of dust, then would reshape themselves into men once they were on the other side, to come and take him away to their horrible dusty lair. He was warm and safe now, here in this little room. There were no Dust Men, no horrors. Being a grown-up was an overrated pastime, he considered. Now, back at home, he was like a kid again. Plenty of men would love to live back at home, he was sure – having your washing done, hot meals every night, big fry-up on a Sunday morning, the loose button on your shirt re-stitched as if by magic. He didn't have to remember to buy more loo paper or pay the electricity bill or have the boiler serviced or keep a beady eye on his bank balance. And, if he helped out with any small household task – mowing the lawn, say, or helping his dad sort out the shed, or shifting the sofa so his mum could hoover behind it – they were so appreciative. He was valued here. He *mattered*.

He'd thought briefly – with Olivia – that maybe something might come of it… that he liked her and she seemed to like him, hadn't she? Well, it wasn't to be. Again, her face swam into his vision, and he forced himself to think of something else. No matter. And anyway, clearly he had no judgement when it came to women because he'd thought he'd be with Vicki, hadn't he? And look how that turned out. Relationships were too tiring. He was always trying to second-guess what the other person wanted, running in circles to keep someone else happy the whole time. What he wanted was a woman who would try to make *him* happy. Yes! And he had that now. His mum was being a real treasure, making him a packed lunch most days now, hoovering his room, bringing him tea, looking after him. Yes, he was a very lucky boy really. He rolled over and let himself doze off again.

* * *

There was a light tap-tap at the door. Perhaps he could pretend to be asleep? So tired, so very, very tired. Even his bones felt tired. If he lay here long enough, maybe he'd somehow become part of the bed, the bed part of him, conjoined twins, alike in their deep love of being horizontal and immobile.

'Mmm?' he murmured.

'It's me.' His dad opened the door a little way and stuck his head round. 'Mum sent me up. How are you feeling?'

Andrew shrugged.

'It's early to be in bed, son.'

'Is it? What time is it?'

'Not yet half nine. You could come down and watch *News at Ten*, if you like?'

'What's the point?'

'See what's occurring in the world, like.' Ron looked down at the carpet.

'Maybe.'

The door closed again and Andrew listened for the muffled tread of his dad's slippered feet padding down the stairs, but there was no sound.

After a minute, there was another light knock and his head reappeared round the edge of the door.

'We don't have to watch the news. Why not come down, eh?'

'I'll only have to come back up again. I'm tired.'

'Come on, son. Come and sit with us for a bit.'

Andrew stifled a sigh and drew back the covers.

'All right then. I'll be down in a min.'

'*There* you are, Andrew, love.' His mother gave him what he realised was meant to be an encouraging smile as if he had just managed his first few steps after a period of paralysis. 'There's fresh tea in the pot.'

A tray of tea-things, with a plate of biscuits and three paper napkins, each folded twice into a perfect little triangle, was on the largest of the coffee tables, its smaller sidekicks still nested beneath it. He chose two custard creams and a Viennese shortcake while his mother presided over the teapot. He took a bite of his biscuit.

'Crumbs, love. Take a serviette.'

'Thanks. Sorry, Mum.'

He took the proffered cup of tea and settled back on the sofa. Directed his gaze towards the television, losing himself in the flickering screen, letting it distract him from other, unwelcome thoughts. What was the point in fretting about life, after all? You couldn't control it anyway. You thought you could – people were always rattling on about being the architect of your own destiny and being proactive – but it was all a load of crap, wasn't it? You could dash about, captaining the ship and attempting to steer a course between the rocks and the whirlpools, but in the end you were only a chunk of flotsam that would get shoved this way and that by the current, and you might as well give in and go with it. The sooner you stopped resisting and followed the flow, the easier life would be, surely?

He picked up another custard cream and dunked it into his cup of tea and counted slowly to three.

40

THE DEATH OF MARCIA

Conrad sits beside the bed, staring into space. Eleanor is holding her mother's hand. They are blank and drained, having spent the last couple of days and nights scrunched awkwardly in uncomfortable chairs, taking it in turns to doze and keep watch. Marcia floats through the hours in a haze of morphine and music: Schubert, Brahms, Bach. Then, in a moment unnoticed by either of her sentinels, it is over.

The nurse says, very softly, for she has delivered this statement many times before, 'She is gone now.'

Conrad remains seated. He shakes his head.

His first thought is something that, even now, more than five years later, still chills him when he thinks of it. He has never told anyone, can barely recall it himself without shame and self-loathing, but still he knows he felt it absolutely keenly, fiercely. It was the truth: *Damn you – why couldn't you have died back then?*

He weeps. Eleanor, who has only ever seen her father cry once before, long ago, looks at him with such tenderness that he cannot bear it, her pity and affection are so undeserved. She loops her arms round him and simply holds him – Eleanor, who, like him, has little time for displays of emotion. She does not speak, does not attempt to frame these raw, jagged feelings into neat words, just holds him while his tears turn to sobs, proper sobs. And he could not say, 'No, no – do not comfort me, I do not deserve it. Give me nothing, nothing.' For he does not weep for the loss of his wife and he knows it. He is undone by the thought of the life he might have had, wishes he'd had with his love – if he had been given the chance, if he had seized the chance. But it is all too late now, years too late. And though he has told himself a thousand times that it no longer matters, that he did the right thing, that in all probability it would not have worked between them anyway, still he weeps for the love that he had so longed for... and it is hard to bear.

* * *

Marcia's will states that she would like a church service followed by cremation rather than burial, 'so that no one would feel obliged to visit my grave once a week'. It is a characteristically Marcia-ish statement. She had a way of making a sidelong criticism of something you had failed to do when the opportunity had not yet even arisen for you to fail to do it, leaving one feeling at once resentful of her assumptions and ashamed of one's own shortcomings. Marcia had a gift for anticipating the numerous ways in which you might fall short and about which she might graciously appear not to mind, bearing it all with admirable stoicism.

Naturally, Eleanor has made all the arrangements, assuming her father would be too distraught to handle them. She asked if there were any particular readings or pieces of music he would like to hear, but he said 'no, no, you decide, I'll leave it to you.'

Benedict travels in the principal mourners' car with them, so clearly Eleanor has been at her most persuasive or possibly even bribed him; usually, the boy could barely stand to be in the same building as his father, never mind the same vehicle. She sits between them on the wide back seat, a UN Peacekeeper set between warring factions, ready, no doubt, to dispense soothing words or a sharp tap on the wrist to either side if need be. The journey is brief, thank the Lord, as both father and son sit there without saying a word. Eleanor punctuates the cold silence with thoughtful observations about who might attend and the timing – whether cousin Julia might come down from Edinburgh, how long has been allowed for music, readings, the eulogy and so on. Roger is taking Daniel and Hannah separately in his car.

When they enter the church, Benedict hangs back a moment and waits for his family to choose a pew, then makes a distinct show of going to sit on the other side of the aisle from them. Eleanor leans in to her father and quietly suggests they cross to join Benedict, but Conrad refuses to move. Why should they? Roger, who has elected to sit in the pew behind with the children, is in agreement with his father-in-law, for once. They should stand firm. Head bowed, but whether out of deference to the occasion or embarrassment it is unclear, Eleanor quickly crosses the aisle and slips in to the opposite pew alongside her brother. Conrad watches her out of the corner of his eye, wondering what she would say and why she bothers. Benedict is quintessentially Benedict, a law unto himself. Is she appealing to his better nature? Does he even have one? For crying out loud, Conrad thinks, can't you just pretend to be a decent, civilised human being for an hour, sit with your family rather than trying to humiliate us? Conrad watches for a minute more, as if observing an intriguing experiment with detachment.

He sees Eleanor's shoulders slump then, and knows that even her considerable diplomatic skills are of no use here. Then there is a... hesitation perhaps? Eleanor shrinks from any kind of drama or public display. She does not willingly poke her head above the parapet. But she is always sensible of doing what is right, what is fair and just. Her sense of honour is deeply entrenched. Surely she would not leave her father sitting here alone? Would that outweigh her presumed reluctance to return across the aisle, unquestionably drawing attention both to herself and to the fact that her brother and father are sitting on opposite sides? Silently, she rises to her feet once more, and with a gentle parting hand on Benedict's shoulder, she moves with small steps back to the pew where Conrad sits, her face flushed with mortification at having made such a show of herself as if she has tap-danced clickety-click-click across the hard tiles, singing and waving, rather than flickering across like a candle flame. She slides along the pew and, without speaking, simply lays her hand over her father's. There is no need to explain: Benedict is Benedict; one might as well try to shift the church itself as to move him.

During the service, Conrad spends some time looking round, both at the church interior and at the gathering of mourners, rather more in number than he had expected, perhaps forty or fifty, certainly a respectable amount. He notes the extremely fine stained-glass window high above the altar and the considerably less fine paintings of the

Stations of the Cross that progress around the walls. Conrad considers churches to be interesting from a historical perspective and, of course, many have distinct architectural merit or interesting interiors, but he finds many of the rituals of religion – while perhaps useful in providing cultural and social insights – as essentially baffling and embarrassing. Why on earth would fully grown adults imagine they were engaged in some form of meaningful communication with an entity they could neither hear nor see? Nor, for that matter, establish a single piece of irrefutable proof of His/Her/Its existence? To his mind, there is not a whisper of difference between that and a five-year-old's writing a letter to Father Christmas or putting a tooth under the pillow for the Tooth Fairy. Harmless, possibly even mildly charming, in a child, but extraordinary in anyone over the age of ten.

It is a very English funeral: no wailing or sobbing, no rending of garments. Dry eyes or a few polite tears for the most part, the sort that could be dabbed away with the corner of a handkerchief rather than streaming down one's face, a river of grief. Marcia was not a regular church-goer but, unlike her husband, she attended services several times a year at key points in the Christian calendar. Conrad accompanied her once a year only: to Midnight Mass on Christmas Eve, saying he was interested to observe the English in the act of affecting a degree of spirituality when, as must surely be clear to even the simplest fool, the true religion of England was nothing to do with God; it was Sport. He drew analogies between the two, warming to his theme as his wife tutted and turned away – football being Low Church, of course, cricket clearly High Church; rugby, with its passion, gusto, and acceptance of physical violence as part of its creed, well, that must be Catholicism, surely? In sport, the congregants' intense devotion and interest were unequivocal and entirely sincere. At church, by contrast, Conrad judged that there were perhaps no more than a handful of people deriving any kind of spiritual succour from the experience. The rest were divided between those endeavouring to adopt a pious expression, while stifling their yawns and glancing surreptitiously at their watches, and those who were simply there for the singing or the company or whatever other reason might compel an otherwise sound-minded individual to quest forth on a cold, dark night to go and freeze in a damp church for the privilege of singing about a baby born over two millennia ago to a teenage mother who claimed to have been made pregnant by an angel.

Conrad was only there as an observer, of course, and to accompany his wife so that she would not have to come home alone at one o'clock in the morning. And yet... and yet... there were two or three carols which, when he sang them in his deep, velvety baritone voice – 'In the Bleak Midwinter', 'Adeste Fideles' , 'It Came Upon the Midnight Clear' – gave him an unfamiliar feeling inside, a strange swelling of the heart that he attributes to the resonance of the organ in the great vaulted space, but for which, truly, he cannot account.

Now, Marcia's oldest friend reads a passage from the Bible:

Who can find a virtuous woman? for her price is far above rubies.
The heart of her husband doth safely trust in her, so that he shall have no need of spoil.
She will do him good and not evil all the days of her life...

Conrad bows his head, his face a mask. Then Eleanor gets up to read a poem. She had asked him if there was anything in particular he would like, or to read himself, but he had said no, no, you choose. He cannot do it – for all sorts of reasons – and after all these years his daughter knows better than to try to draw him out if he chooses not to be drawn.

'I apologise if people find this poem too familiar,' Eleanor says, her voice clear and steady, 'It is often chosen for funerals, but none the worse for that, I think. I find it very beautiful and very sad. It's by Christina Rossetti.'

At her words, Conrad closes his eyes and sinks back into the pew. For once, he lets the words come into him, rather than assessing them with cool detachment as he usually would when confronted by poetry.

Remember me when I am gone away,
    Gone far away into the silent land;
    When you can no more hold me by the hand,
Nor I half turn to go yet turning stay.
Remember me when no more day by day
    You tell me of our future that you plann'd:
    Only remember me; you understand
It will be late to counsel then or pray.

Yet if you should forget me for a while
    And afterwards remember, do not grieve:
    For if the darkness and corruption leave
    A vestige of the thoughts that once I had,
Better by far you should forget and smile
    Than that you should remember and be sad.

Her voice cracks towards the end, but this serves only to make it more poignant. Conrad covers his eyes with one hand for a moment, then glances up to meet his daughter's gaze. He wonders if she is thinking that it is not especially apt for Marcia, but still a very moving poem, and offers comfort to those left behind. The intriguing volte-face, turning from 'Remember me...' in its opening to the tender resignation of 'Better by far you should forget...' is a fit for Eleanor's taste, and for her father's. Marcia, by contrast, would not have wanted anything other than for her mourners to think of her morning, noon, and night, whether waking or in dreams. And if the words conjure up memories of another whom he had lost – and now he fumbles in his pocket for a handkerchief and blows his nose, suddenly loud and shocking, almost comical in that solemn space – who is to say he is not so very moved by thoughts of his dear wife?

* * *

After the service, they drive in slow, stately convoy to the crematorium. Some well-meaning idiot at the funeral director's – where do they find these people? – has glued a grotesque 'gold' plastic cross onto the coffin and it is all Conrad can do not to wrench it off with his bare hands. Marcia would have been horrified by its tackiness. Some Bach is played, chosen once more by Eleanor. Benedict has refused to be involved in any of the arrangements, Eleanor reported, other than to say, 'Don't get lilies, El. You know how peeved she used to get when the pollen dropped on the carpet.'

Here, the proceedings are very simple and brief. Marcia's brother says a few words, then the music strikes up, some Schubert, one of Marcia's favourite pieces. Yes, that *is* fitting. The coffin sits on the catafalque and, as the curtains draw themselves, as if pulled by an unseen hand, the coffin starts to glide towards the gap as if exiting a stage.

Suddenly, there is an awful, high-pitched, keening sound. For a moment or two, Conrad wonders if it is the machinery of the conveyor, desperately in need of oiling, and he turns to scowl at the officiant who had pressed the button. But Eleanor swiftly crosses the aisle to where her brother was sitting, once again apart. Conrad cannot see him at all. Eleanor is hunkering down now. Her father cranes forward a little way to try to see, suddenly understands, faces front again, straight and stiff as a pillar. Benedict is on the floor, curled up tight in a ball, emitting this extraordinary, unbearable noise. The other mourners near him shift and turn and whisper, looking from Benedict to Conrad and back again. Eleanor kneels and wraps her brother tightly in her arms as if he is a small child and is speaking to him in a low voice, though her father cannot imagine for a moment what she might say, what on earth do you say to someone who is... behaving like that?

He observes them, then looks away again, knowing that it should be *he* who is taking care of his son, offering comfort and understanding. If he does, Benedict would no doubt tell him to fuck off, shout it unashamed in front of everyone, tell them all what a fucking hopeless apology for a father he really is. And no matter how easy it is to dismiss Benedict's rants, his rage, his abusiveness – to tell himself that Benedict is a wastrel, a loafer, a drunkard good-for-nothing – the keen, rational part of Conrad's mind, which so rarely takes a moment off from sitting in judgement, especially on himself, knows that the accusation would not be without a horrible grain of truth.

41

THE VISITOR

There was a loud knocking at the front door. The hoovering stopped and Andrew could hear the front door being opened. A deep voice then – authoritative, oddly familiar yet hard to place. He couldn't quite hear what was being said, only the alternating different patterns of sound: his mother's flustered chirrupings, then the confident tones of someone born to command, slightly military, Andrew thought, as if giving orders. Good God. *Conrad.* Here. He looked round his room, at the green fringed lampshade above him on the ceiling, at the mean little wood-effect wardrobe, the busily floral curtains, the candlewick bedspread. He imagined what Conrad would make of such a room, thinking he would judge it the same way Andrew himself did, disparagingly, snobbishly, thinking honestly, who had rooms like this any more?

Conrad took the stairs two at a time, Andrew could tell by the rhythm. God, the man must be fit, nearly ten years older than his father but he'd never heard his dad climb the stairs with anything other than a shuffle and a sigh. Why the rush?

A sharp knock. Andrew tried to sit up a bit, then thought it might be better to look ill. He slunk back down and said to come in.

'Andrew.' Conrad surveyed his prostrate form with a small nod. 'How are you?'

'Fine, thank you. I mean, not fine, obviously. Not well. I – I'm –' He paused. 'It's hard to say. It's a surprise to see you here.' He thought that perhaps it sounded rather inhospitable. 'A nice surprise,' he added.

'Well... I wanted to check that you were all right, making a speedy recovery and so on. You've been off for three days.'

Three days? No, it was only this morning that Conrad had escorted him to a taxi outside the museum, wasn't it? And even pressed some notes into his hand to pay for it. Andrew tried to think back but his head was muzzy. It might have been yesterday.

'May I sit down?' Conrad gestured to the chair and set a brown paper bag of – presumably – some sort of fruit on the bedside cabinet without comment.

'Please do. But it's very uncomfortable, I should warn you.'

'No matter. I wanted to come and see you.'

Andrew steeled himself for a telling-off. He was a shirking, good-for-nothing layabout, loafing about in bed and eating custard creams while his colleagues were having to manage his work as well as their own. Maybe Conrad had been sent to fire him? His department head was too nice, too sympathetic; perhaps Conrad had even volunteered for the task? In his heyday, he'd probably fired tons of people. He looked as if he would manage it with equanimity, possibly even while sharpening his pencil at the same time. Oh, well. Andrew didn't care any more. He would quite like to be fired really; then he wouldn't have to keep getting up and getting dressed and going out in the cold.

'I have an apology to make to you.'

'What?' Andrew was baffled. It wasn't like Conrad to apologise for anything. This was a man who never made a mistake so it was never necessary. He turned his head slightly towards Conrad, then simply waited in silence.

'I am... not good... at this... this sort of thing.'

'That's OK. I promise not to mark you out of ten.'

Conrad emitted a short snort of laughter.

'The painting. You did a very good thing there, you see.'

'Thank you. But you already thanked me. And paid me. Why should you apologise?'

Conrad inclined his head. 'May I finish?' As ever, he was at his most scary when he was being exceptionally polite. His voice was like steel.

'Sorry.'

'You did something that mattered a great deal to me. And then...'
Andrew watched Conrad out of the corner of his eye. Conrad pressed his
palms down against his legs. 'And then you asked me, perfectly civilly,
about the provenance of the picture you had so painstakingly
worked on.'

'I was interested.'

'Naturally. It's what we all do, isn't it? Any conservator or curator
wants to know, where did this come from? Do we know the date? Who
created it? It's second nature to you, as it is to me.'

'Yes.' Andrew nodded. 'I hadn't thought of it that way but that's absolutely right.' He started to lever himself up in bed a little way. 'I felt really
quite desperate to know – even when I could see I was making you
uncomfortable.'

'And I was rude to you and became obstructive.'

'Well, I'm a big boy now – I coped. That's not what sent me... you
know.' He gestured vaguely at his prostrate form in the bed. 'It was just...
other stuff.'

'I understand that. Anyway, I thought, if you would still like to know,
then I will tell you because I have never told anyone and it has been a –
well, I should not say a burden when other people have far greater
crosses to bear – but difficult, shall we say? But I do not want to disturb
your rest if you are, um, truly unwell?'

'Tell me.' Andrew turned his head towards him. 'Please. I'd really
welcome the distraction.'

Conrad nodded, then he leaned back in his chair, and began to
speak.

'Many, many years ago – over three decades ago now – I met and fell
in love with... aah...' An unfathomable expression came over his face, as
if he were basking in glorious sunshine for a moment after a long, harsh
winter. 'An incredible woman. She was beautiful – no, she was *radiant* –
but that was the least of her. She was highly intelligent, with a sort of
intense curiosity, talented, astonishingly frank and forthright – not like
anyone else I'd ever met before. And she... we... well, she loved me. *Me!*
Baffling. And she seemed to understand me: all of me – the good aspects
and the not so good aspects and the truly awful, darkest pits and
crevasses of my peculiar psyche. She *knew* me as I had never been
known before, never been known since. Yet she loved me anyway. She

loved me without judgement, without reservation, without equivocation. Perhaps you have been loved like that?' He sat forwards and turned to Andrew.

Andrew shook his head.

'Well, it's uncommon, I suspect. It's an extraordinary feeling. Anyway, we planned that, once my younger child reached the age of sixteen and so was well on the way to increasing independence, that I would exit my marriage and we would be together. I had no doubt in my mind at all that I would do this and I believe the same was true for her.'

'But you didn't, did you?' Andrew prompted.

'No.' Conrad exhaled loudly. 'When he was only fifteen, my son, Benedict, was caught driving – drunk, quite off his head – with two friends. Thank God it was my car and luckily he drove it into a ditch without seriously injuring himself or anyone else.' He paused. 'Though one of the boys had a broken leg, and it was clear it could have been so much worse. Benedict, as ever, emerged without a scratch on him.' Andrew could hear him swallow. 'My son had always been something of a tearaway – no, that suggests he was amusingly mischievous when it was never amusing. He was always in trouble at school, hanging out with other no-hopers, never doing any work, then he was suspended for accidentally, or probably not at all accidentally, setting fire to the cricket pavilion. And there were numerous incidents of this kind. His mother, my wife, Marcia – she indulged him, made excuses for him and I... I... '

'It's OK.'

Conrad blinked but carried on.

'I neglected the boy, you see. It was my fault. I didn't understand him and I was too preoccupied with what I understood to be my real life: the Museum, my work, the collection, my books, and My L— this woman I loved. I left it to my wife to raise him, even though it must have been clear to me that he was too much of a handful for her. I turned a blind eye much of the time and would then weigh in heavily to no good effect. But he and I – Benedict – we had no relationship, no nexus of communication. We could have had, perhaps, if I had only worked harder at being a better father to him earlier on. But I didn't.

'And then came this joy-riding episode and we were very much afraid that the boy would end up in youth detention. My wife became completely hysterical.' He stopped and bit his lip, bowed his head for a moment. 'God knows what they would have done to him – the boy with the posh voice and angelic looks. They'd have crucified him. He'd have been beaten up at the very least... knifed... buggered. I – I couldn't consign my child to that, not if it was in my power to prevent it. The received wisdom back then was that these places would turn your average juvenile delinquent into a junkie, psychopath or hardened criminal.'

'I believe it. So, what happened? Did you manage to get him off somehow?'

'Yes. I shelled out for an extremely expensive lawyer and he came up with character references from a couple of local worthies who owed him a favour. We tidied it up, swept it under the carpet. But part of the agreement was that I would drive Benedict to school every day and his mother would pick him up and that I would supervise his homework and know his whereabouts every moment of the day that he wasn't in school.'

'And did you do that?'

'I did.' Conrad nodded slowly. 'The alternative would have been to wash my hands of him, leave him to his fate.' He pressed his palms together and looked for a moment like a man in prayer. 'I cannot kid myself that I was a good father. I was barely even an adequate one. There comes a moment in every person's life when one must face one's flaws full on in the mirror in the cold, harsh light of day. Looking at my own was a very sobering experience. And I made a decision to take responsibility in the way I should have done years before. I had at least to give him a fighting chance, you see?'

'Yes,' Andrew sat up further in bed. 'I see. And what about your, um, mistress?'

Conrad turned suddenly.

'Don't use that word, please. It sounds sordid. Cheap. She was... ah... *everything* to me. You have no idea. Can have no idea unless you have ever felt like that. The sex was the least of it, in a way. She was *my love*. Really she was.'

'Ah. The initials then? M.L. My Love. Of course. But why in quotes?'

'I don't know. My guess is that she must have asked Philip, the painter, to put the initials there, and in quotation marks because she was "My Love", not his, perhaps – but as a little joke for me really, presumably before I... ended things between us.'

'When was it painted?'

'I commissioned it not long before we parted – 1982, it was. The painter was a very talented friend of hers. She wanted to get him some work, I presume.

'Anyway, Philip rang me up to say it was finished and I went and collected it and had it framed and brought it home and there it hung in my study for decades – a daily reminder of the woman I had lost.'

'But didn't you get in touch with her later? After your wife died?'

'No. I never found her.'

'But the internet – you can find anyone...'

'No. I tried that, of course. My Pauline Barnes wasn't out there. Presumably she got married and became Pauline something else. She may well have grown-up children and, I hope, a more deserving husband than I could ever have been.'

'Still, I bet she is out there somewhere. Perhaps she still thinks about you?'

'I worked at the BM for over thirty years, I will remind you, Andrew. *My* whereabouts were hardly a secret.'

'I suppose so, though if you had ended things, perhaps her pride prevented her? I can imagine that. And what about Benedict? Did it make a difference, do you think? Were you glad that you chose to stay?'

Conrad snorted and leaned forwards with his head in his hands.

'I don't know if it made a blind bit of difference really. I think he just became more devious, more adroit at hiding his vices: the drink, the drugs, screwing any half-sentient being of either sex.' He slumped further down. 'I suppose I got him through school, at least. Not college – his reports were so bad that no university would touch him. He took casual work when he could get it and I subsidised him too. I'd give money to his older sister, to Eleanor, and we'd pretend it was from her so he'd take it. He wouldn't accept it from me, not as a gift. He'd steal it from my wallet, or from his mother's purse, but he wouldn't accept anything that might make him feel any sense of obligation or duty towards me.'

'And what about now? You said you hadn't seen him for a while?'

'I have no idea. We haven't seen him since his mother died over five years ago. We do not say it out loud – Eleanor is rather similar to me in this regard – but I know we both suspect he may be dead or a junkie living in a squat somewhere. He could be abroad. There's no trace of him in the UK.'

'I'm sorry,' Andrew said. 'Really sorry.'

Conrad batted the words away.

'It's just that the... not knowing is... difficult at times.'

'It must be.'

'And...' Conrad paused for a long while and Andrew turned towards him. 'The thing is, you see, that....' He seemed to subside then, and shrink a little. 'I stayed, yes, and I told myself I was being noble – honourable – doing my duty, doing the right thing – but, oh God! How I resented them. It was my choice to stay, but it was my family who had to live with how unbearable it must have made me. I stayed, but only as an empty shell of a man, a physical presence, and not much more. And my son...' He suddenly covered his face with his hands. 'How I hated him for being the reason I had lost her. I *loathed* him. Have you any idea how it is to go through life, existing – not living – day after day after day, torturing yourself by thinking about the woman you have loved and lost and resenting your own child? Have you any idea?'

Andrew shook his head. 'No.' His voice was barely audible.

Conrad sat back again and subsided into the chair.

'I apologise. I'm amazed I haven't bored you to sleep by now, you poor fellow. I must get off and leave you to rest.'

'I'm fine.'

'I understand things are... difficult for you at present, but do you think you could face coming in on Monday? The department does need you, you know. And it's Christmas soon enough. You can have a break then.'

Andrew nodded.

'It is rare to come across someone with your skill and deft touch. I've been around a long time, you know. I am not easily impressed.'

'I know you're not. Thank you.'

Conrad rose and stood by the door.

'The world comes knocking at no one's door, Andrew. You must get out there and seize it by the scruff of its neck.'

'I suppose so.'

'No! Do not *suppose* so! It *is* so.' Conrad punched his fist into the palm of his other hand. 'Take it from me. Life is short. A cliché, of course, but true. It is tragically, unbearably short. If you don't choose to *live* – and I mean *really live* – squeezing every drop of joy you can out of this peculiar existence of ours, grabbing real love and never letting it go, if you should ever be such a lucky bastard that you happen upon it you will merely be breathing in and out, using up oxygen that might be better employed by others more willing to take risks. No one ever won a medal for passing up the chance to be happy.' He sighed then and shut the door behind him.

Andrew heard his fast tread on the stairs once more, then the sound of the front door opening and closing, and he was gone.

* * *

His dad sat down on the puny bed next to Andrew. He sat facing straight ahead, not looking at his son.

'So.' Dad clasped his hands together. 'What's occurring then?'

'It's all a bit crap, Dad.'

'I know, son. You're not wrong.'

'It's not Vicki even, not really. I don't even miss her, if I'm honest. But I miss *belonging* to someone, having someone I need to call if I'm late, someone else to consider, to care about. I met this woman – Olivia – and I thought – and she was lovely – really lovely, Dad – but I cocked it up. I was an idiot. Anyway, I guess she realised I wasn't up to much.'

'Don't say that, lad, that's not true.'

'Well, she's wonderful. She could have any man she wanted.'

'She'd be lucky to have you, Andrew. You're a decent man.' Ron started counting off on his fingers. 'You're kind, you're honest, you're clever as they come, and you're probably not a bad-looking fellow at all, though I don't know about that kind of thing, and what girls are wanting these days, I suppose, maybe a flash car and a big, fancy house.'

'She's not like that. At least I don't think she is.' Andrew paused, wishing he'd had the chance to get to know her better, suddenly deflated at the thought that, in all likelihood, he never would now. 'I don't mean to sound ungrateful. I know it was good of you and Mum to have me back for a bit.'

'Don't be daft. Always here if you need us, you know that. Though we might not be any good at saying that sort of thing, about feelings and all that.'

'It's OK. You don't need to. It's just... I'm worried, Dad. Actually, worse than that. I'm – I'm scared...' He tried to think how to say it, and his father waited, just sitting in silence as if he had all the time in the world.

'I'm scared that if I stay too long, then...' He shrugged, turning his hands palms up.

'I know. You don't want to be some sad, middle-aged so-and-so trotting along the front at Bournemouth with your sodding crumbly parents on your holidays, do you?'

'Well.' Andrew gave a small laugh. 'No, not really, I guess.'

'Now, you know I've never been one for telling you what to do and all that.' There was a long pause. 'That's more your mother's way of thinking. I hope I've always let you find your own way, make up your own mind, but I will say this.' Ron blinked hard and sat up a little straighter. 'You're not old, but you're no spring chicken either, Andrew. It's not good to be cooped up with your ruddy mum and dad, you know it's not.' He stopped again, then nodded, as if giving himself permission to carry on.

'It's been good having you here.' He suddenly fumbled at his side and patted Andrew's arm. 'But you're not to stay.' There was a catch in his voice, then he cleared his throat loudly. 'I won't allow it. So, I'm giving you your marching orders, son. You've got exactly one week from today then I'm changing the locks and I'll not let you in. I'm not kidding. Rent a room. Kip on a friend's floor, if you have to, but for crying out loud, get out. While you can.'

Andrew registered out of the corner of his eye his father's bowed head.

'I've got quite a bit put by in a separate account if you want to put it towards a flat, and I'll give it you and be glad to do it. I've no need of it myself. Not now.' He stopped again. 'Ah. Your mother doesn't know about it, though, and I'd be glad if you'd not mention it.'

'Course.' Andrew nodded, as if it were completely normal for his father to reveal that he had a stash of money kept secret from his mother.

'Don't be getting anywhere too nice, mind.'

'What? Why's that, then?' Andrew turned at last to look at his father properly.

''Cause then I'll be round to kip on your couch and you'll not get rid of me.'

Andrew snorted with laughter and suddenly his dad was laughing too and he didn't know why it was funny. Really, nothing could be less funny than that all these years his father has been imprisoned here, squirrelling away money just in case, just in case, but now, in that moment, the preposterousness of it, of their lives, of these two grown men and their obeisance to the despotic reign of Mrs Tyler was ridiculous and what else could you possibly do but laugh?

42

A VERY LUCKY WOMAN

There was always a magical hour or two on Christmas morning when the house was silent and still. Eleanor put on the radio quietly so she could listen to carols while she drank her tea and finished preparing the turkey, smothering it with homemade herb butter and swaddling it carefully in foil.

She cut a thick wedge of panettone for herself, her favourite treat for Christmas morning. Then she sat down at the kitchen table to allow herself a few minutes' idleness before embarking on peeling a mound of potatoes. One year, she had made the mistake of being too organised: she had prepared everything – all the vegetables, set the table, etc. – the day before, with the result that she had been all too obviously free and available all morning and had to sit in the sitting room with her husband, attempting to make lively conversation until Daniel and Hannah got up. Now, she paced herself with a steady succession of tasks that would regularly demand her attention.

Roger's heavy tread on the stair. Eleanor shoved her plate of panettone to one side and picked up the potato peeler.

'Happy Christmas, darling!' She jumped up and went to kiss him.

'Happy Christmas!' He bobbed his head to kiss her. 'Good Lord, what a vast number of spuds! I thought we were only eight for lunch, not eighty!' He laughed.

'There's some panettone, if you'd like, for breakfast?'

'No, no!' He waved it away with an expression of mock-horror, or possibly actual horror. 'I can't understand people wanting to eat cake for breakfast.' Roger sat down at the table at the other end from the potatoes.

'Well, it's not really a cake, it's more like—'

'No, it's far too rich for me. Perhaps I'll just have something light – some scrambled eggs, darling. With a bit of smoked salmon on the side. And a single slice of toast. That'll do me.' He sat back and picked up yesterday's paper, which she had left folded by his place setting.

She suppressed a sigh as she abandoned the potatoes and went to the fridge to get out eggs, milk, and smoked salmon.

'What time are you off to fetch your mum?'

'Not till around ten.' He glanced at his watch. 'Any coffee?'

'I can make some.' Honestly. It wouldn't kill him to get off his arse and make himself a coffee, at least, while she was cooking his bloody eggs. She'd almost bought him a coffee-maker as his Christmas present – one of those ones with the little capsules or pods you slot in and it does it all for you – but she had recalled that some months ago Roger had gone on about how there was no substitute for proper, fresh-brewed coffee and he was certain it couldn't possibly be in the same league.

'Good, good.' He peered at her over the top of the paper. 'Now might be the perfect moment to give you your present.'

'Really?' She half-turned, while stirring the eggs. 'Before lunch?' Roger had always maintained that presents should never be opened until teatime, when one might open them at a leisurely pace while having tea and Christmas cake, a delay that had driven the children near-crazy with bottled-up anticipation when they were little, until Eleanor had hit on the idea of making them outsize Christmas stockings; then she could stuff most of their presents inside and, of course, even Roger had to accept that it was usual to open stockings first thing in the morning.

'You're going to love it, I know.' He smiled with a worrying glint.

Eleanor turned from stirring his eggs and attempted a smile. Her husband's confidence about what she would and wouldn't love was often misplaced. She had emailed him, at his request, a few infallible suggestions, including links to the exact part of each website to make it as fuss-free as possible, but sometimes he was determined to go off-piste, as had happened on her birthday.

'I can't leave the eggs now, though, or they'll burn.'

'After breakfast then. I can wait for mine till later.'

* * *

'Close your eyes, darling!'

Oh God, that didn't bode well. She hoped it wasn't another ruddy hoover, not like three years ago. Or a bloody food processor.

'You can open them now! Dah-dah!'

'Wow!' He had to be kidding surely? 'Goodness!' What the fuck was she supposed to say? It was a Nespresso coffee-maker, not wrapped, but bound with a huge red satin ribbon.

'It's marvellous.' Roger patted the box as if it were a much-loved pet. 'The coffee is excellent and there's plenty of choice with all the different pods – Colombian, Costa Rican, etc. I was rather sceptical at first, but Alan recently got one for his office so I've tested it numerous times and it's really very superior quality. I defy you to tell the difference between this and fresh-ground beans. And – best of all – there's no mess! No coffee grounds for you to get all het up about, darling!'

Was he serious? Perhaps it was just some bizarre, rather expensive joke? Surely not even Roger could be so wrapped up in himself that he had somehow forgotten he was married to a person who didn't drink coffee?

'Gosh!' She pretended to study the box. 'Yes, I had heard they were good. Funnily enough, I had considered getting *you* one for Christmas but thought you didn't like them.'

'That would have been funny. I knew you'd be thrilled. I can set it up for you later.'

Was her face really conveying 'thrilled'? She was tempted to dash to the mirror in the ground-floor loo to check.

She flicked the kettle on to make herself a cup of tea, partly so she wouldn't have to look at him.

'I don't actually drink coffee, though,' she said over her shoulder.

'I think it does mocha. It may even do tea – who knows? It'll say on the box, I should think. Or in the booklet thingy.'

Clearly, she was supposed to be grateful that it might do tea, even though she was pretty damn sure that it didn't. Even if it did, how would that help? Anyone who had known Eleanor for more than five minutes would know that, for her, half the pleasure lay in the ritual of tea-making, the anticipation, the enjoyable delay: warming the pot, spooning in the leaves, the soft clink as she set the strainer on her cup.

'Oh. Right.'

Roger's fork clattered onto the plate.

'Oh, don't say you've gone into a huff about it just because you don't drink coffee that much yourself? Honestly, Eleanor, don't be so selfish! It's not like you at all.'

'I'm not being selfish. It's just that I don't drink coffee. Ever. As you know.'

'Nonsense. You do sometimes. I've seen you so you can't deny it. You had a cappuccino in a café that time. When we were on holiday.'

'About once a year, tops. In Italy. If I feel like it.'

'Well, you'd be bound to have it much more often if you had a fancy, posh coffee-maker right here in your own kitchen, wouldn't you? And it'll save you washing out the cafetières each time, which you always make such a song and dance about. I was thinking of *you*.'

Her shoulders sagged. What was the point?

'Sorry. I'm sure you were. Thank you.'

'Well.' He sniffed. 'I suppose I'd best get on and fetch Mum. See you later.'

* * *

A glance at the table settings confirms that, unsurprisingly, Roger had ignored his wife's suggestions and placed his mother next to her, with Jane on his mother's other side, thus depriving Eleanor of the one guest she'd most like to talk to and giving her the one she'd like least. Though, to be fair, this was more likely to be due to his own desire to have both his mother and Jane as far away from himself as possible, sitting at the other end of the table. On her other side, she would have her father, at least, though again this was simply because Roger didn't want him at his end. Freddie, another neighbour, was on Conrad's other side. Eleanor quickly swapped Jane and Joyce's name-cards around and hoped that

Roger either wouldn't notice or wouldn't want to make a fuss in front of guests.

Roger carved. Of course. He was old-fashioned in this respect, believing that there was something inherently wrong about a woman's carving. In fact, as Eleanor was still attending to things in the kitchen, she was happy to relinquish it to him. Also, she did not like to witness her husband carving. There was something unpleasantly slow and surgical about it that she found disturbing; it had the same deliberate quality as when he excised the final page from one of her novels, so it made her feel sick even to watch him. And he would say, inevitably, 'Light or dark?' to each guest, instead of 'Leg or breast?' If it were up to her, she would carve plenty of slices of each and place them on a serving platter in the centre of the table for people to help themselves. It would be faster, too. With Roger's way, the first person was left sitting watching their food go cold while they politely waited for every other person to be served. Also, he always cut off the outer slice and set it to one side to save for himself. Roger liked the skin, and the way the flesh was smooth and perfect beneath it on that slice only, rather than cut.

'Not quite as good as last year, darling,' he pronounced on her home-made cranberry sauce, 'but still superior to the shop-bought product, I'm sure.'

'It's the best *I've* ever had,' Jane said. 'It's all so delicious.'

'What are all these bits in the gravy, Roger?' his mother hissed, not even slightly lowering her voice. 'Did she not sieve it?'

'It's just a bit of onion, Mum. Fish it out for her, will you, darling?' Roger bellowed at his wife from the other end of the table. He frowned, presumably suddenly noticing that she wasn't sitting next to his mother after all.

'I always used to run mine through a sieve.' Joyce turned to Jane. 'That way, there are no lumps, you see.'

'It's really very good, you know. Those pieces are caramelised onion – they're delicious. Do try them.'

Eleanor smiled at Jane and reached for her wine. God, she'd nearly finished her allotted single glass. She'd meant to spin it out slowly, but every time her mother-in-law spoke, she found herself reaching for her glass. Maybe she could pretend she'd run out of petrol – silly me! – so Roger would have to take his mother back. Or Joyce would have to stay over, which would be awful, but at least then she could have more wine. But Roger would be bound to check, knowing him. He'd never take her word for it.

'Do you know why you cry when you chop onions?' Conrad asked the table at large. Sometimes her father could be like a twelve-year-old boy, wanting to regale you with facts; it was fine, but didn't always help the flow of conversation.

'No, do please tell us,' Jane said.

'If you must,' Roger added.

Conrad launched into an explanation of how cutting the onion ruptured the walls of numerous cells, thus releasing a volatile sulphur compound, syn-propanethiol S-oxide, which irritates your eyes, stimulating the lachrymal glands to produce tears to wash away the source of the irritation.

'How very interesting,' Jane said.

'I always wear my snorkel-mask when I'm cutting onions,' said Freddie.

'The best thing with gravy is to sieve it,' Joyce said, pushing her glass towards the wine bottle so that someone would top it up.

They pulled crackers and read out jokes and, all in all, it was no worse than Eleanor had expected. Oddly, she found she was rather looking forward to clearing up and loading the dishwasher and tackling the pots and pans later on. Roger always stayed well away from the kitchen then, presumably for fear he might be expected to assist in some way. She could turn on the radio and even sing along if Roger were listening to music in the sitting room via his headphones.

After tea and cake and presents a little later, Roger turned to his mother and said, 'Well, that really was a very good feed, wasn't it, Mum?'

'I've never been keen on marzipan.' Joyce's slice of cake had the marzipan picked off and laid round the rim of her plate like gobbets of unpleasant gristle.

'No, but you liked the cake bit, didn't you, Mum?'

'*I* used to make a very good Christmas cake.'

'Yes, you did. I remember it well.'

'I don't bake now,' she announced. 'I've not got the facilities. But everyone said that *my* cake was the best cake they'd ever eaten.'

'It certainly was, Mum.' Roger rose to his feet, to indicate that the party was now over, at least for his mother. 'Eleanor's going to drive you back now, so let's go and get your coat on, shall we?'

She slowly shuffled out towards the hallway and Eleanor could hear her saying, 'Can't *you* take me, Roger?'

'I'd love to, Mum, you know I would, but I'm afraid I've had a drop too much wine. Better safe than sorry, eh?'

Eleanor turned to her father.

'I can drop you back first, then take Roger's mother – if you're tired, Daddy? It *is* a long walk.' She suddenly felt a swell of affection for him, and wished it could just be the two of them. 'Or come with me while I take her first, then we can talk on the way back to yours?'

'It's completely the opposite direction,' Roger pointed out. 'Mum needs her rest, you know.'

'Isn't her abode an hour's drive away?' Her father's face was impassive but she knew the prospect of being cooped up in a car with Roger's mother would seem like the eighth circle of Hell to him.

'Well, yes, but there'll be barely any traffic. We might well do it faster than that.'

He dipped to kiss her cheek and whispered a brief sorry in her ear.

'I do need the exercise,' he said aloud. 'Thank you very much for lunch. You are a superlative chef, daughter-dear, and it was kind of you to include me.' Conrad turned to Roger and shook his hand. 'Roger. Excellent wines. Well chosen.' And with a wave and a 'Merry Christmas!', he was out the door with an annoying spring in his step.

Eleanor settled her mother-in-law in the passenger seat and fastened her seatbelt for her. She paused a moment, seizing a tiny breath of solitude before the hour ahead. Come on, she tried to rally herself, she's not that bad. And it *is* Christmas – try to be kind.

'You know, if you soak the dried fruit in tea overnight then your cake won't be so dry.'

'Really? I must remember that.'

'Roger prefers a cake that's nice and moist.'

'Rightio. Good to know.' She put on her headlights and set off. 'Let's have some music.' Eleanor didn't wait for a response but put on the music she'd been listening to: Chopin.

'I don't like classical music.'

'You're welcome to select something else if you like on the radio.

Please, be my guest.' Eleanor gestured at the controls, knowing that Joyce wouldn't attempt to tackle anything 'technical'. Discreetly, she increased the volume slightly on her steering wheel control.

Joyce sniffed – it must be a family trait – and clasped her handbag more firmly on her lap as if Eleanor might attempt to steal it at any moment.

'Roger says he's taking you on a luxury cruise. You're very lucky.'

'Hmm-mm.'

'Yes, you're certainly a very lucky woman. Roger could have had his pick, you know.'

'Mmm-mm.'

'My husband never took me on a cruise.'

'Shame.'

'Of course I've not got the knees for it now. Too many steps.'

'Uh-huh.'

Soon they would be there, and Eleanor would park and unload her mother-in-law with tremendous patience and care, rather than shoving her out of a moving car as she'd like to. She would escort her inside and then possibly skip back to her car. Yes, she would skip so that Joyce could see her. On the way home, she would have an hour to herself, possibly more if there were traffic, which she had a feeling there might well be, and she would put on something loud – the soundtrack of *Oklahoma!* or *West Side Story*, maybe – and sing her heart out.

* * *

Eleanor had nearly finished the clearing up when Roger came in from the sitting room where he'd been sitting with his e-reader, savouring another glass of port.

'Early night tonight, I think, yes?' He put his hand on her waist and deposited a kiss on the back of her head.

Their seasonal sex schedule always included some room for manoeuvre in case Eleanor happened to have her period or if they were travelling. They hadn't 'made love' on Eleanor's birthday for that reason, and had had to delay it until Sunday evening, she remembered, after they'd returned from that weekend in Suffolk. Roger called it 'making love', but when he said it, which was not often, Eleanor pictured the words in quotation marks, as if he were repeating some odd expression he had heard elsewhere and was merely reporting it to her for her information.

* * *

Upstairs in the bedroom, Roger removed his trousers and inserted them precisely into his trouser-press: 'Shall we, then?' he said. He unbuttoned his shirt and dropped it into the laundry hamper in their en-suite bathroom. 'It all went off rather well today, I thought.'

'Mmm, yes it did.' Suddenly, Eleanor felt slightly sick and shivery and tugged the duvet up higher around her. 'But I'm rather tired, what with all the cooking and clearing up.'

'Well, just a quick one then.' He stripped off his underpants and padded back from the bathroom naked except for his black work socks.

Eleanor flipped back her side of the duvet and got out of bed.

'I must just get some water.'

'You can get it afterwards.'

'I really won't be a minute.' She ran downstairs. In the kitchen, she poured herself a glass of water and stood by the sink in her bare feet, shivering in her thin, sleeveless nightie. She gulped the water down, then topped it up. Beneath her feet, the tiled floor was hard and cold. She thought for a moment of the sheepskin slippers Roger had given her for her birthday. Very practical really; this floor was always cold, even in the height of summer. She sipped her water and looked into the shiny whiteness of the deep enamel sink. She was very lucky to be married and have a lovely house and a lovely sink. Really very lucky, as Joyce had reminded her. She should be grateful and not always thinking of... imagining... other things, a different kind of life. Not helpful. Not at all. Slowly, she climbed the stairs again and set her water down on her bedside table.

'Oh, sorry, did you want one?' she said, starting towards the bedroom door at once. 'I can easily pop down again.'

'No, I have a glass here.' He patted the bed and Eleanor slid beneath the covers next to him.

He kissed her closed, dry lips briefly with his own, then gave the smallest of nods to indicate that she might begin. Awkwardly, she twisted towards him and reached down beneath the covers. Roger closed his eyes and sank back against the pillows.

'Lovely. Yes, just like that.'

After a few minutes, his breathing grew thicker and he instructed, 'Don't take me too far.'

She carried on for another minute.

'You'd better stop there, I think. Are you ready?' he asked.

'I'm not sure.' She knew she wasn't.

Roger heaved himself on top of her and pushed his way in with a satisfied grunt.

His eyes were squeezed shut. 'That's good.'

'It's a bit uncomfortable.'

He opened his eyes and dipped his head to deposit a kiss on her lips. 'Women of your age often have this sort of problem, apparently. It's very common.'

'Yes,' she said. 'I suppose so.'

Yes... very common. She should face up to it... accept life as it was and stop pointlessly yearning for something else when she didn't even have a clue what that something might be. *The untold want*, she thought, a line from a poem flitting into her head.

Roger had shut his eyes again and was concentrating on the task in hand. It shouldn't take too much longer now. Eleanor looked across to the window. Those curtains were starting to look a little faded and sad now; perhaps she should order some new ones... fabrics and colours unfurled in her head... something with an unobtrusive pattern, perhaps, or richly textured... with maybe—

'Darling?'

'Mmm?' She looked up at him.

'Are you OK?'

'Mmm, yes, of course.'

'OK. You seemed distracted.'

'Sorry. No. I'm fine. Really.'

Roger pressed deeper inside her and she winced.

Roger's breathing grew louder and thicker as if he were pounding away on a running machine with the gradient set too high.

I don't want to be here. The words appeared in her head all at once. No, don't think that – you mustn't think that – never, never. She tried to shove the words back down, then opened her eyes to look at Roger's familiar face, his features clamped tight in concentration and effort. She shut her eyes again to take herself somewhere else...

Roger grunted to a halt and lowered his full weight onto her for a few moments before rolling off with a sigh back onto the pillows. He turned towards her briefly to aim a kiss in the general direction of her mouth.

'Thank you, darling,' he said. He lay there for half a minute, then got up and went through to the bathroom. She could hear him running the water in the basin, getting it nice and warm so that he could wash thoroughly before returning to bed for the night.

I don't want to be here. The words came again, this time in colour... iridescent... the shimmering blue metal of an exotic butterfly's wing. The words curled and twined around her mind, circling and turning in an irresistible dance. *I don't want to be here.*

43

A HABIT WORTH CULTIVATING

Of course, Olivia may well not be there. It isn't her nearest café, after all. But she did say that she went there a lot, almost every weekend. Besides, Andrew ought to pop in to see his parents, as he's not seen them for a few days since Christmas. He could give his dad a bit of a breather, and act as a buffer for an hour or two, absorb his mother's energy like a human shield.

And if Olivia's not there, then what? He could call her or email her or drop a note round to her flat, though he didn't want to come across as some crazy stalker. He could stroll casually up and down her mother's street on a Sunday morning, when she often visited. And if he did bump into her, then what? What could he say? What possible reason could he have for loitering in that street when she knew his parents lived around the corner?

Why does it matter so much? he wonders. Why pursue Olivia? Why not simply start again with someone else who doesn't already know you moved back in with your parents for three months at the age of thirty-five? Someone who might think you're a proper, together sort of guy? Because... because... she is who she is – sharp yet soft, beady yet kind, clever but with no need to show off, beautiful but couldn't be bothered to spend more than five minutes getting ready. It wasn't just that being with her made him feel excited yet peaceful at the same time. Even on that first date, he found himself gazing at her, wondering what it would be like to wake up next to her day after day, grow old with her, go scuffling the rustly autumn leaves in the woods with her into their seventies and beyond.

He enters the café, scanning the room. Bugger – not here. Still, she might come. As he looks round, a woman gets up from the coveted corner seat on the sofa and smiles at him. Automatically, he glances behind him; presumably she is greeting someone else. But no, she advances a step.

'I'm just going, if you want my seat?'

'Thanks very much. I may sub-let it, of course, as it's such a desirable position.'

She laughs loudly, as if he has made a hilarious joke rather than a mildly amusing quip. Still, he is cheered by it. He occupies the space, colonising two seats' worth with his jacket because what is the point if one can't at least try to act with some hope?

He orders a cappuccino and a cinnamon Danish. Usually, he would have a banana muffin but he is making a point of trying new things, even when the new things seem too small or trivial for it to matter one way or the other. He read about trying new things, in one of the papers. He can see there might be some merit in it – that it is hard, perhaps impossible, to make huge strides every day but that sometimes tiny baby steps are still worth making, so that you do not become a person who is nothing but predictable routines and safe places.

The door opens again and he looks up. No. Dear God, his heart is pounding. If he has to endure too much more of this, he might drop dead of the strain. He grabs a newspaper and keeps his gaze fixed on it. Do not look up every time the door opens, do not.

'You're here,' she says. 'In my café. Are you stalking me?' But she has that look on her face, that look he loves, with a smile poised on her lips, one eyebrow tilted slightly in question.

'Absolutely. I've been camped out in this corner for weeks, waiting for you.'

'No, you haven't, because I checked frequently and you weren't here.'

'Metaphorically camping, not literally.'

'You knew I couldn't survive without an almond croissant for long.'

'I did. Your weakness has been your undoing.' He gestures for her to have the corner seat.

'Really? Are you sure? You could sub-let it for an extortionate amount, you know. You don't want to just give it away.'

'Well, it's on the market with a few lettings agents, but there's a lull at present if you want to try it out.'

She subsides into the sofa beside him and he helps her off with her coat.

They sit in silence for a minute, then both turn towards each other at the same moment.

'Andrew...'

'I've moved out.' He looks at her, scanning her face for a response. 'I'm not saying you give a toss one way or the other, I just need you to know that I'm not completely pathetic, that's all. It took me longer than it should have done, I know that, but I've done it. I moved just before Christmas. I've rented a flat not far from here and signed up with agents to buy somewhere.'

'No one thinks you're pathetic.' Her expression is hard to read.

'Well, I did.'

'Well, I didn't.' She smiles then, but it is a sad sort of smile, barely a dim ghost of the real thing. 'But, it seemed to me that perhaps you had... um... some problems that you needed to sort out yourself. And, just from a practical point of view, I didn't want to be like a teenager again, trying to sneak out of some boy's room so his parents wouldn't hear.'

He nods. He wants to take her hand but cannot bear the thought that she might shake her head sadly and dump his hand back in his own lap.

'I'm really glad you've moved out from your parents.'

'Me, too. I love them, but God, they were driving me crazy.'

'How was your Christmas?'

'It was all right. Too much bad television, too many mince pies, you know. How was yours?'

'Completely horrible. I went to a friend's because I... well... I had a huge falling-out with my mum, but it just made me miss her so much, even the things that normally drive me mad about her. Anyway... moving on...'

The waiter zooms up with her tea and croissant at that moment and Andrew registers how the man's face lights up as he basks in her smile. Yes, that's how I feel when she looks at me, how anyone would feel when she looks at them like that. Maybe she's seeing someone else? She's hardly going to be waiting about for long, is she? He wants to know but cannot bear to know. Better to live in ignorance. Fuck it, he has to know.

'So...' he takes a sip of his coffee, 'are you meeting someone here?'

'Yup.' She nods.

'Your sister...? Or...?' He starts to reach for his jacket, then he can just get up and leave if he has to. He will not sit there like a lemon while she bestows that smile on some other lucky tosser.

'Nope. A man.'

He nods. Yes, of course. Well, what did he expect? He fumbles in his pocket for cash so he can get the bill and get out of there.

'OK. Jolly good.' Why did he say that? Stop being such a twat. 'Well, have a good one.' What did that even mean? A good what?

'I'd better be off, in any case.' He stands up very suddenly. 'Though I will expect commission if you plan to sub-let my corner to someone else. Obviously.'

'Andrew?' Olivia tugs at the hem of his jumper. 'Will you please sit down and stop being a twat.'

'What?' He remains standing. Looks down at her.

And then she smiles. Ridiculously, he knows he is on the verge of crying. And he can see her eyes start to pool.

She clasps his hand.

'You said you were meeting someone. I don't want – I can't – OK? I'll be fine, but not yet. I mean, I'm very happy for you and all that, but I need to get going.'

'I'm meeting *you*, you noodle.'

He sits down.

'What?'

'Andrew, I've come in here every Saturday morning for the last month, hoping to bump into you accidentally – gosh, fancy seeing you here.' She looks at him, then away. 'I didn't know if you'd gone away for Christmas or were avoiding me or what.'

'But why didn't you just call me?'

She looks at him again, brows lifted in question.

'Why didn't *you* call *me*?'

He shrugs.

'Because it's hard.'

She nods.

'It's *hard*. It feels impossibly hard to call someone and say, "Hey, I miss you," because of course you think the other person will just say, "Oh, sorry, I've got along fine without you, keep well, 'bye now."'

'Yes.'

'And I'd dropped enough hints when I first met you about coming to the café almost every Saturday... so I kind of thought... but then you didn't come.'

'I was moving, getting the flat straight, and buying bed linen before my mother inflicted brown polycotton on me.'

She smiles and he takes her hand without thinking, draws her towards him. She meets him halfway.

'This isn't like us – kissing in public,' she says.

'I know. Still, I think it could be a habit worth cultivating.'

'Mmm.'

* * *

They stand on the street outside the café.

'Are you dashing off or have you got a bit of time?' He knows he must be grinning like a fool. He doesn't care. If he is a fool, at least he's a happy one for now.

'No rush.'

'Well, would you like to do something now? Go somewhere? Walk? Bookshop? See my new flat, though it's so small, we may have to take it in turns to actually be in it. Not that I would be trying to lure you to my bedroom or anything.'

'Flat, please,' she smiles. 'I'm terribly nosy – you should know that about me. And I do want to check that your sheets are definitely one hundred per cent cotton, not polycotton, as you've been so snooty about it.'

'Good. It's important to be certain about these things.' He takes her hand firmly and they start to walk along the street.

'And will you show me some more of your work, too? I'd never really thought before how all those pictures have to be looked after or cleaned or mended.'

'Of course, if you're really interested? But I don't keep them at my flat.

The British Museum rather frowns on the staff's taking items from the collection home.' He turns to look at her, drink her in.

'Really? They mind if you bring back a Hogarth print with a teensy smear of ketchup on it? God, how *fussy*.' She smiles and squeezes his hand. 'The ones on your phone, I meant, like you showed me that first time at supper.'

'Oh, was it the tempera painting? Of the woman in green? Was that the one I showed you? I loved working on that one.'

'I don't know – you didn't say. I never saw the whole thing. You just showed me before and after pics of one corner and you told me you'd had to clean off blood spots, so of course I was intrigued.'

Andrew opens up his photos file and starts to hunt for the picture as they walk along.

'Do you have the whole image? Or just close-ups of the parts you worked on?'

'Both. Hang on. Here it is.' He taps on the picture. 'God. That's so weird. How on earth did I not spot it immediately?'

'What? What is it?'

Andrew passes her the phone.

'No wonder I thought you looked familiar the first time I saw you. Take a look. How bizarre is that? She's a dead ringer for you.'

Olivia looks down at the screen, at the beautiful woman in green, her red hair flaming around the pale moon of her face.

'It's not bizarre at all,' she says. 'That's my mother.'

44

A BREAK WITH TRADITION

For the last four years, Roger had accepted – without consulting his wife – an invitation to a New Year's Eve dinner party held by his friends Peter and Maggie Harris, and he now regarded it as an unbreakable tradition.

'It'll save you having to cook, darling!' Roger always said, as if bestowing a wonderful gift on her, never having understood that Eleanor enjoyed cooking and would always prefer to be a host than a guest.

There was no aspect of the evening that failed to fill her with dread – the food, the people, the banal conversation, and the long drive there and back again. Maggie would insist on poking platters of canapés in her face every three minutes with a chirpy, 'Go on, Ellie, be naughty! Have another! We can start our diets tomorrow!', even though Eleanor had no need to diet and was only reluctant to take another because how could one choose between quails' eggs boiled hard as bullets, some form of rusk lurking beneath an oil slick of black tapenade, or 'cheesy surprise parcels' – 'surprise' rarely a welcome word in the context of food.

Each time, Eleanor hoped that surely there would at least be some interesting people to talk to, but then her heart would sink as each couple arrived: the same guests as last year, all apparently extruded from the same moulds: the men, grey of skin, attired in smart-casual slacks, shirts without ties (living on the edge...) and Germanic metal-rimmed spectacles; the women, with false nails and surprised eyebrows, carrying their astonishingly expensive handbags to the fore as if brandishing shields. Like the other men, Roger always 'dressed down' for the occasion, too, but he only ever looked at home in a suit. In casual clothes, he resembled a mannequin that might come to life at any moment if only a magic wand were waved over him. He reminded her of those photographs of the Prime Minister 'chillaxing' with his wife and family while on holiday – 'Look, I'm just an ordinary guy!' The men talked too much, apparently believing that they were very amusing, while the women spoke too little, which made Eleanor feel she had to work too hard to maintain any sort of conversation, as if desperately trying to bale out a boat with a gaping hole in it.

The thought of spending an entire evening at the Harris's was making Eleanor feel sick, but she couldn't see how she could possibly get out of it. She'd feigned illness last time they were due to go there for lunch, so she definitely couldn't try that again. Well, she would simply say that she doesn't want to go. How hard could it be? Then she remembered how difficult Roger had been about the cruise and put off raising the topic once more.

In the dull, dead days between Christmas and New Year, Eleanor occupied herself by cleaning and tidying the children's rooms, and looking out and pressing any clothes that might be needed on the cruise. As she dusted the bottom of Hannah's wardrobe, she reproved herself yet again for being such a coward. You're forty-seven, for crying out loud – don't be such a mouse! What's the worst that can happen? Say you're not going. Go on – do it. Do it *now*.

Roger appeared suddenly behind her.

'Shall we take champagne to the Harris's tomorrow, do you think, darling? Or maybe a bottle of that nice Fleurie Beaujolais?'

Eleanor backed out of the wardrobe on her knees and looked up at him, thinking: I don't care, I don't care, I won't be able to drink it anyway as I know you're going to land me with driving home.

'Well, perhaps the Beaujolais then? You know you love it and you're not always sure about Peter's wine choices, are you?'

'Hmm, that's true.' Roger nodded. 'But a bit of fizz is always festive, isn't it? And perhaps people expect it at New Year?'

'True.'

'Good, good. Let's take the champers then.'

'Good.' Why did you ask me? Why ask me at all? Eleanor turned her attention to the wardrobe once more. She was tempted to climb inside it and shut the door behind her, the way she used to sometimes when she was a child, just to savour the solitude and the sense of being secreted somewhere where no one would think to look for you.

'Think I'll zip to the gym for a quick workout, then, if you don't need me?'

'Roger?'

'Yes?'

Eleanor delayed coming fully out of the wardrobe, thinking maybe it would be easier if she could at least start what she wanted to say from the safety of the cupboard.

'Um, I wonder...' she said over her shoulder, 'would you mind very much if I gave the dinner a miss tomorrow evening?'

'What?' Roger laughed. 'Nonsense, darling. Don't be so silly. We can't pull out now. It's far too short notice.'

She emerged from the wardrobe and kneeled back on her heels, looking up at him.

'I'm not suggesting that *you* miss it. You could go without me.'

'On my own? What on earth's the point of being married if one has to turn up to parties alone, looking like some hopeless loser, Eleanor?'

'No one thinks you're a loser. It's just that I'd really prefer not to go.'

'Why ever not? It's not ladies' trouble? What reason can you possibly have for not wanting to go?'

'I just don't want to – that's all.'

'That's not a proper reason, is it, darling?' He laughed and shook his head at her funny little foibles. He removed his glasses and sucked at one stem as if he were a judge assessing the evidence.

'It is to me.' At last, she stood up. Straightened her shoulders. 'I find them and their guests rather...'

'Rather what, Eleanor? Spit it out.'

'Rather boring, then, since you insist. Frankly, I'd far rather stay in and read or watch a film, if we're not going to a proper party.'

'It *is* a proper party.'

'It's ten people.'

'Well, I'm sorry if the Harrises aren't offering sufficient excitement for you.' Roger sighed. 'I must say, I tolerate your friends without complaint. It's part of marriage. It's called *compromise*.'

Eleanor was speechless for a moment, then dug her fingernails into her palms and looked him in the eye.

'Who do you have to tolerate then?'

'Sarah and Mark, for a start. I have to endure entire weekends with them.'

'But you said you liked Mark.'

Roger sniffed.

'He's all right in a wishy-washy sort of way. But Sarah's extremely aggravating – always with a bee in her bonnet about human rights or greedy bankers or women's this, that and the other. It's so tedious.'

'I'm sorry you feel that way. You should have said. I'm always happy to see them on my own. I have no wish to make you spend time with them if you don't want to. Look, why don't you go tomorrow and have fun? I'm quite content here by myself.'

'And what on earth am I supposed to say to Peter and Maggie about your absence? Really, darling, this last-minute messing about is very inconsiderate. It's most unlike you. I wonder if there's something wrong with you? Is it the change of life coming on?'

It was all she could do to not clonk him over the head with the can of furniture polish in her hand. She clutched it tightly.

'Very possibly. Say I'm not well, if you'd rather.'

He sniffed again.

'I might say you're suffering from a temporary brainstorm.'

'Whatever you like.'

Roger turned to leave the room.

'Oh, did you remember that my father is coming over at teatime tomorrow, by the way?'

'Of course. You note that I am prepared to put up with your relations and associates, Eleanor, without complaint?'

'It's very good of you. Your patience knows no bounds.' Surely even Roger must be able to clock such grinding sarcasm? 'Anyway, he'll only be here for an hour or so, so we can Skype Hannah in Thailand and Daniel in Bristol all together.'

'I am wholly aware of the purpose of his visit.'

'Fine. Hannah said she'll spend the evening with her friends at this bar and internet café right on the beach everyone goes to. I thought it would be better if we use the big desktop computer rather than trying to huddle round a laptop.'

'Yes, Eleanor, thank you. I do understand the advantages of a large monitor. I'm not an idiot.' He sighed loudly. 'And how is your father intending to get home afterwards, may I enquire?'

'He was planning to walk or take the bus, but I can drive him as I won't have to get ready for the Harrises.

'Suit yourself. Clearly, I have no say in anything in my household any more.' He looked back at her. 'I seriously think you need to buck up your ideas, Eleanor. If you're really going to be this bolshie all the time, I rather regret spending so much of my hard-earned money on the deluxe cruise. I trust you'll try to get yourself into a more amenable frame of mind before we depart. Well, you'll have the house all to yourself for two days while I'm in Jersey. Did *you* remember that I have to pop over there to finish up the contracts for Alan?' He paused, jingling the coins in his pocket, then sniffed. 'Do a bit of thinking about your attitude, eh?'

45

AFTER MARCIA'S FUNERAL

2007

Afterwards, the mourners are invited back to the family home. Some sit in the large, elegant drawing room, while others drift out through the French windows onto the terrace, or down the steps onto the lawn. It is late spring, and a rather fine day, Conrad thinks. The guests stand around, awkward and uncomfortable in their dark, hot suits, commenting stiffly on how lovely the garden is at this time of year and how good the sandwiches are – the English, as always, desperate to avoid any mention of death at a funeral. Tea is brought round by motherly Irish women in white blouses and black skirts, overseen by Eleanor, who with her customary unshowy efficiency, is making sure that elderly guests are seated in comfort, that everyone has a drink, some food, someone to talk to. Conrad watches her gliding from person to person, dispensing kisses and – rarely – hugs, laying a gentle hand on an arm there, nodding and listening, saying the right thing, doing the right thing, as Eleanor always does. She proffers crustless sandwiches, slices of cake, tea, a small whisky perhaps? Until one of the Irish ladies puts an arm round her and guides her to a chair next to her father's, and tells her not to worry herself, it's all in hand. She sits for all of two minutes before spotting some wrinkle in the proceedings that demands her attention and she is up and off again.

Conrad is aware that she is also keeping an eye on Benedict, but, like him, from a safe distance. No doubt Eleanor cannot help but assess just how many whiskies the boy is imbibing. It is an impossible challenge: not to let Benedict have too much, but not to get into an embarrassing confrontation with him either. The scene at the crematorium comes back to him. He knows he should feel something for his son – pity, perhaps? Regret? Compassion? Love, even? – but mostly all he feels is dislike. He shucks the thought away in shame and folds an egg sandwich whole into his mouth, tamping down the feeling.

One of the waitresses comes up to him with the bottle of whisky and a small tumbler.

'You'd have a small taste, wouldn't you now?' she says.

'Well, perhaps then. Thank you.' He sets down his half-drunk tea. He is not usually a lover of whisky, but now the thought of its peculiar tingling sensation and haunting aroma seems tempting. 'Um,' he says, gesturing for her to stop pouring. 'The whisky?'

'Sure, there's another bottle,' she says. 'There's no worries there. It's grand.'

'No. It's... You see – I wonder if...'

The woman waits.

'My son.' Conrad detests inarticulacy; he has always relished his own ability to express himself with great clarity and precision. He can talk about anything – anything! – well, anything he can understand. 'Over there.' He nods towards Benedict, who is pacing to and fro by the herbaceous border, taking deep drags on his cigarette as if trying to fill his entire body with smoke. Now he stomps over and hurls himself into the ancient net hammock, which sags between two apple trees. His weight sinks it almost down to the ground. He lies there, looking up at the sky, smoking. 'He – it would perhaps be the wiser course of action if he weren't to be offered...' Conrad nods at the bottle in the woman's hand.

'He's just lost his ma so.' She means well, he can see that, but she doesn't understand, you see, not about Benedict. No one does, other than Eleanor.

'Yes, of course. But it's really not good for him, you see.' Conrad straightens up in his seat. 'He has a medical condition and so it's really better not. I'd appreciate it greatly if you'd direct the others accordingly. Keep the strong stuff away from him.'

She nods and gives a small, tight smile, then moves away.

Conrad takes a sip of the whisky – Christ, who'd drink this stuff because they liked it? – and watches Benedict, now swinging manically in the hammock like a child. God, he remembers: the boy playing pirates, up in his crow's nest of the upper branches of the apple tree there, spying through his treasured antique telescope, the only present his father had ever given him that he'd truly loved. He used to leap from way up in the tree into the hammock – once he missed completely and broke his arm. Or he'd spring out at anyone who happened to be passing by and lunge at them with his wooden sword, playing, yes, but always in the end pushing it too far, so you'd be winded by the blow or thanking your lucky stars that he'd just missed taking out your eye.

Suddenly, Benedict lurches out of the hammock once more, tipping himself out onto the ground. His suit is covered in green marks, lichen from the hammock, and cobwebs. Still, it's not as if he needs it to go to work in. Presumably, it's his only suit; it seems unlikely that he would need one to do the odd jobs that float his way from time to time: weeding people's gardens, clearing out their garages, short stints as a motorcycle courier, a hospital cleaner, a waiter, a gravedigger until, inevitably, he pushes it too far and is hours late once too often, or tells the boss to go fuck himself and is fired. Who knows what he does these days? Conrad is pretty sure that Eleanor must give him money now and then, otherwise no doubt the golden boy sponges off whomever he's living with. Benedict no longer asks his father for cash but whether it's because he hates Conrad too much even to stand that brief contact with him or because even he – insensitive oaf that he is – knows that he is certain to be refused, Conrad doesn't know.

Benedict looks absolutely awful today – an angel fallen from grace: scrawny and scruffy, his face unshaven. His eyes, though the same intense blue as his father's, are bloodshot and puffy; his hair, though a rare golden blonde like his mother's, is greasy and in need of a cut. There is little sign of just how devastatingly handsome he is on a good day. Conrad watches him head off around the corner of the house, where the whisky-bearing waitress has just gone. Eleanor is flitting round the garden, attentive to the guests once more, like a keen gardener tending her plants, and he strives to catch her eye, motions towards the empty hammock with a nod.

There is no need for explanations. They are as one in this regard. At once she comes over to her father.

'I can't see him,' she says.

'I suspect he's gone to waylay the waitress with the—'

'Of course.' They approach the corner of the house and peer round as if playing a game. No sign of him. 'Maybe down where the old shed used to be?'

Benedict used to smoke down there, of course, at the far end of the enormous garden. Conrad can't face it.

'Perhaps you could check there? I'll start in the house.'

He ventures into his own house with a degree of caution, as if he fears a prowler might be hiding behind a door ready to leap out.

'Benedict.' He does not raise his voice, does not want to cause a scene. He wants just to separate his son from the whisky bottle and persuade him to go and sleep it off, that is all. He hopes to God Eleanor finds him instead; she is much better at this sort of thing, and with that thought shuffling awkwardly at the back of his mind, he ambles rather than quests about the house, taking cursory checks into the spare bedrooms, ignoring the cellar, the laundry room and other more likely, out-of-the-way spots. Finally, with a sigh, he slinks into his study, craving just a few moments alone in his sacred space, where he can look at *her* image and let it soothe him, as it always does.

He opens the door. It is as if a whirlwind has spun through the room. The floor is covered in his papers. Books lie scattered and spread-eagled everywhere. And there is Benedict, sitting in his father's old captain's chair, with his earth-smeared shoes up on the desk, resting on the freshly printed-out latest draft of Conrad's book, which he'd been planning to proofread the following day. Benedict is swigging whisky straight from the bottle. He looks at his father.

'I've rearranged your study for you,' he says, his voice blurred at the edges.

'So I see.'

Conrad is not a man of violence, always preferring the pen to the sword, but the urge to grab the whisky bottle and smash it over his own son's head is frighteningly strong. He clasps his hands behind his back and breathes deeply.

'Get out.'

'Really?' Benedict smiles, that long, lazy smile that seems to send everyone else to their knees in helpless adoration. 'Not in the mood for a cosy father-son chat, Pa?'

'I rather think we're past that point, don't you?' Conrad looks round the room at the sea of academic essays, articles, notes and print-outs now strewn across the floor. It will take an age to sort out. He takes a covert glance at the painting. Unharmed, still on the wall. He breathes out. 'And I do not sanction the presence of vermin in my study, so I would welcome your imminent departure. It will be aided by the toe of my boot, if necessary, believe me.'

At the word 'vermin', Benedict's face contorts into a sneer.

'Get out. I'm not kidding.' Conrad stands firm.

'Really, that stern patriarch posturing is a fucking joke. You don't give a fuck about anyone or anything other than your fucking tedious prints and books – that pile of dusty crap you spend your life wanking over in the British Museum. You make out you're some pillar of the Establishment because you strut about in your jacket boring everyone shitless about eighteenth-century *chiaroscuro* or the heyday of copper engraving, but you don't give a toss about people – not me, not El, not even your dead wife, you absolute bastard. You only mind about Mum dying because it's dragged you away from obsessing over your great work for a day.'

He grinds his muddy heels into the manuscript, then kicks it off the desk as he swings his legs down and staggers to his feet.

'You're a cold-blooded, unfeeling prick and as far as I'm concerned you could drop dead tomorrow and I for one would smile and sod off to the pub and toast your demise. Fuck you, you desiccated old git.'

So, Benedict could be articulate enough when he chose. He steps closer and lifts the whisky bottle as if in a toast.

'Here's to your extremely sad and lonely old age, Pa. Christ knows, you deserve it.' He takes a slug from the bottle then pushes past his father and leaves.

Conrad stands there trembling, white and rigid with shock. He seems quite unable to move and so he is still there when Eleanor finds him several minutes later, standing in the doorway like a resident of Pompeii caught in a moment of horror.

They have not seen or heard from Benedict since.

46

A SPADE IS A SPADE IS A SPADE

New Year's Eve. Eleanor made a rich ginger cake to serve for tea, enjoying the simple, predictable process, the heady smell as she poured the molten butter and sugar onto the ginger and mixed spice, stirring the batter with a wooden spoon, enjoying the feel of it, the sense of being in charge of at least this one small thing.

While the cake was baking, she popped up to her studio. She'd barely been up here for weeks. If she went up while Roger was at home, he usually came harrumphing up the stairs to find her or kept bellowing questions from downstairs – Where was his newspaper? Had she moved the coffee? Why wasn't the remote in its proper place? – until she gave up and came down. His presence in her room never failed to set her on edge, like a cat whose fur has been stroked the wrong way. It was such a lovely, peaceful space, the only room in the house that was entirely to her own taste. It was painted a soft grey-blue, with Roman blinds of grey tweed and a faded, well-worn blue rug on the bare floorboards. There were proofs of her best prints pinned up on a board, and, in a plan chest, a modest number of each print she'd ever made. She kept the original woodblocks themselves in a glass-fronted cabinet. The most recent print, of the woman stretched out in the park, was in the centre of the pinboard. As she passed it, she automatically reached out and tapped the corner with her fingertip, as if it were a good-luck talisman. She had made two prints to have framed so that she could give one each to Sarah and to her father as Christmas presents, and been almost moved to tears by their response, although they exhibited their enthusiasm in such different ways. Sarah told her she intended to march her round to some galleries to show her portfolio of engravings as this one was 'the best, best – definitely the best you've ever done – I completely love it!', while Conrad had nodded and looked at her with one raised eyebrow, then pronounced: 'This, daughter-dear, is in another league. I rather think you have come of age.'

Eleanor plucked out the sketchbook she had used the last time she was in Suffolk. There had been that intriguing view she had made a start on – the way those trees leaned out like arms reaching for something. She'd love to work on it some more. She leafed through, looking for it. Hmm, the sketch was a bit scrappy – she'd only been drawing for a few minutes when Roger had interrupted her, saying, 'Come on, my little da Vinci! Can you possibly stop doodling for a few minutes as the table at the pub is booked for one o'clock.'

And she had stopped at once, mid-line, and tucked the sketchbook away, hoping she'd have a chance to return to it later, but then inevitably there hadn't been time.

* * *

The place in Thailand where Hannah was now staying was seven hours ahead, so Eleanor had arranged to speak to her at around four thirty p.m. UK time to wish her a Happy New Year. Conrad arrived at three forty-five, on the dot as usual, and they ate smoked salmon sandwiches, tea and cake, accompanied by conversation in fits and starts. Roger had hunkered down into the Cloud, infuriated at his wife's refusal to join him for festivities at the Harris's, and was barely speaking other than the occasional offering of some sort of criticism – of her, the tea, the weather, the Government, people in general, the world. Conrad, in response to his daughter's prompting, told them about the progress of the enormous new extension at the BM, still under construction. To be fair, although brevity was not his forte, he made his account very interesting, including amusing asides about the finances and the shenanigans and the key players involved.

Shortly before four thirty, Roger said they should go through to the other room to gather round the computer, where he had arranged extra chairs, and Eleanor texted Hannah to see if she was ready. Roger made the Skype connection and, suddenly, there Hannah was on the screen.

'Hey! Happy New Year!' She looked brown and happy and relaxed, suddenly rather grown-up. Hannah turned away for a moment to call her friends over to come and say hello. It was difficult to hear because of the background music and it looked pretty packed, with young people talking and dancing behind her.

'I've met so many cool people here, Mum, it's amazing. Joe, Joe! Come over!'

A young man dressed only in a tie-dye T-shirt and swimming trunks appeared and looped his arms around Hannah from behind.

'Say hello to my parents and my granddad. This is Joe. He's my – he's a friend.'

Joe waved at the webcam and said, 'Hey, guys.'

'Is there some reason he's not wearing trousers?' Conrad queried. 'Or should I not ask?'

'The place is right on the beach, Dad. Hannah, what's the bar called?'

'Benny's Beach Bar – it's like totally cool. It's in all the budget travel guides so it's always buzzing. That's Benny over there.' She waved towards the long bar down one side of the room. 'Hey, Benny, have you got a sec?' she called out. 'Come say hi to my mum and dad?'

The man waved towards the camera from a distance.

'No, come over! Please, *please*, Benny? Come show them your cool beard.'

Benny, blond, with a pronounced paunch that made him look heavily pregnant, and wearing a brightly coloured shirt covered in loud flowers, flip-flopped towards the webcam.

'See, Mum, isn't Benny's beard like the most fab beard you've ever seen?'

He was sporting a tiny goatee, secured into a miniature ponytail by being threaded through a large blue glass bead.

'Hey, Hannah's folks!' He waved at the screen.

And then Eleanor looked properly at his face. And he looked back.

She heard a deep sort of moan from her father at her side and she reached for his hand.

'El?'

'*Benedict*? Is that really *you*?'

'What?' Hannah turned round towards him.

'Hey, big sis! How's tricks? This is *awesome*.'

'Good God.' Roger drew a little closer. 'That's not your brother, Benedict, surely?'

'Oh, Roger. You're still... there. Hi. And is that my father with you too? Shit. I mean, wow. This is amazing, man. It's like totally doing my head in.'

'You're not my uncle Benedict?' Hannah turned to him. 'No way! Wow, we all thought you must be dead. But you look so *different*, I can't believe it. You're so...' Her voice tailed off.

'*Benedict*.' Eleanor's voice, suddenly clear and unusually loud. Her heart was hammering in her chest as if she'd plunged into icy water.

'Sis. Good to see you. So, this is little Hannah! I can't believe it. Hey, she's all grown up and everything. She was just a scrap of a kiddo last time I saw her. Hold fire – you should see mine.' He called to someone at the back and a tiny Thai woman and even tinier boy, aged only two or three, came towards the camera. 'This is Arisa, my wife, and the little one is my son, Chatchai.'

The diminutive duo waved and smiled, though it was clear they had absolutely no idea what was going on. Benedict turned and spoke to them briefly in Thai and they waved again and wandered off.

Benedict turned towards the webcam once more.

'You're looking well, er, Father. Um. Dad.' There was a pause. 'You know – I'm very sorry about everything.' Benedict shrugged. 'The past and all that. I guess I was a real pain in the arse. I know I didn't make life easy for you and Mum.'

Conrad's eyes were shining and he tugged out his cloth handkerchief and briskly wiped his nose.

'It doesn't matter, my boy.' Conrad stretched out a hand towards the screen, and touched it for the briefest of moments, then withdrew it. 'I'm very relieved to see that you're all right, really I am.'

'*FOR FUCK'S SAKE!*' Eleanor's voice exploded out of her.

'Eleanor! Language! Really, is that necessary?' Roger clamped his hand tightly round her arm.

'Mum!' Hannah looked shocked.

'Benedict! For over five years, Dad and I have been worried sick about you. You *disappeared*. We thought you must be lying dead in a gutter somewhere. But now, here you are and—'

'But I'm fine, El. Look at me – lovely wife, great kid, my own business. Take a chill pill. You always were such a worrier. But there's no need – I'm *fine*.' He smiled and gave her a thumbs-up sign.

'Exactly. You're *fine* and *fuck* anyone else. All this time, you've been absolutely fine but you didn't give a thought to letting us know that. How about a phone call, Benedict? Or a postcard? How *dare* you? How dare you be perfectly all right, you selfish, selfish bastard? It's so completely typical of you. You could have made a thirty-second call but you didn't. I don't fucking believe it.' Eleanor stood up suddenly, knocking her chair over.

Roger clutched her arm again.

'Eleanor,' he hissed. 'Calm down. You're upsetting Hannah with this embarrassing display. Will you control yourself?'

She yanked her arm away from him.

'*Control* myself? *Control myself*! I've controlled myself since the day I was bloody born and what good has it ever done me? Has it made me *happy*? Is that what they'll carve on my headstone – "At least she always controlled herself"? I've never won a fucking medal for it. I'm sick to the back teeth of controlling myself and doing the right thing and saying what I think other people want to hear. I'm sick of being told what to do and what to wear and what to read and how to read it. I'm sick of being told what to think and how to behave – sick of trying to second-guess how other people want me to be. For God's sake, I have no idea what *I* want or what I even *think* any more. I've spent so long acting out some twisted idea of how I imagine I'm expected to be that I don't have a bloody clue who I even *am*.'

'You're being over-emotional.' Roger picked up the fallen chair and set it to rights. 'You're feeling tired, clearly.'

'NO, I'm not. *Don't* tell me how I feel. You have *no* idea how I feel.'

'Now, now, Eleanor, you don't mean that.' Roger grasped her elbow, directing her towards the chair. 'Come on, have a little sit-down here and then—'

'Don't patronise me. *Fuck you*.' Eleanor suddenly grabbed the chair and hurled it across the room. There was a glorious splintering of wood as it broke, and a resounding crash like the triumphant clash of cymbals as it careered into a side-table, knocking off a horrible floral vase that had been a gift from Roger's mother.

'Eleanor!'

She bolted from the room, grabbing her bag and a coat as she charged out of the house.

Eleanor ran along the road, half-holding, half-dragging the coat behind her. No doubt Roger would regard her outburst as yet more evidence that she was mad and menopausal. She slowed her steps for a minute to tug on the coat, realising after a moment that it was her father's dark wool overcoat rather than her own. It came right down to her ankles, making her feel like a child again, small and powerless. She stamped along the pavement as if she could grind Benedict and his flowery shirt and his preposterous, creepy beard under her boots. God, but it had felt so good to break that chair! Roger must be seething – it was one of the set of eight from the dining room. Poncey repro bollocks that he had insisted on buying a few years ago. Eleanor had never liked them anyway.

The surge of volcanic rage started to boil up inside her again and, as she passed the end of an unlit alley, she struck a large wheelie bin hard with the flat of her hand. Her palm stung satisfyingly. God, how she wanted to punch someone, break something. She faced the bin and, clutching onto one of its handles, suddenly gave it a bloody good kicking, ramming her suede-clad foot into it again and again – bang, bang, bang! – until her foot hurt. Breathless, her heart racing, she looked around for something else on which to vent her anger. There – a stray lone beer bottle. Eleanor picked it up, weighed it in her hand for a moment, then she turned and chucked it as hard as she could down the alleyway. From the depths of the darkness beyond, there came a scintillating smash as it hit the stones.

Her mobile rang, vibrating in the back pocket of her velvet jeans: 'ROGER'. She ignored it and shoved it back in her pocket. Fuck Roger. Fuck everyone.

Eleanor strode along the road at a cracking pace, thoughts shoving each other in her head. *Benedict.* Tears sprang to her eyes and she wiped them away roughly with the edge of her sleeve. He was all right. It was hard to believe. All those years of his being such a complete and utter fuck-up. Even before he'd done his disappearing act, he'd caused them all a lifetime of worry – and Eleanor had suffered too. Benedict was like some horrible black hole, hauling in everything, all the attention – both positive and negative – in the household, leaving almost none left for her. Christ, but wasn't he the most selfish git on the entire planet? Why on earth hadn't he picked up the phone for a minute, just to let them know he was OK? She exhaled loudly. Because... because he was Benedict, that's why. It wasn't in his nature to make that kind of empathic leap, to understand that his family deserved at least to know that he was all right. The thought struck her then that Hannah might be worrying, too. Eleanor never normally swore in front of her daughter; she'd barely even lost her temper in her presence before. She quickly sent Hannah a text to say she was very sorry and that she was OK and would call her tomorrow. She'd give Daniel a call later on this evening.

And Daddy... She paused in the street for a moment, remembering, then walked on but more slowly than before, letting her thoughts and her footsteps slow down a little. It was surprising. Surely, he should be absolutely furious too? Benedict had always driven him up the wall, though he'd strived to contain his temper. But he didn't seem to be faking it. He just seemed genuinely relieved.

Her mobile rang again: 'ROGER'. She ignored it; not in the mood to talk to him this minute. He wouldn't leave for the Harris's until six thirty. She texted her father to say sorry for taking his coat and to ask him to hold on so she could give him a lift, though he often had his phone switched off. A brief text came back immediately:

Still here. Are u ok?

She smiled. The 'u' was a silly joke for her – because they were the only two people they knew who never usually resorted to text-speak. Conrad would begin a text 'Dear Madam' if he could, and Eleanor hated homophonic abbreviations – 'How R U?', etc. She needed a bit more time by herself to walk it off, then she'd be calm enough to drive. She responded, saying she'd be back in twenty minutes. Her father would understand this need for time on her own. Roger would be puzzled, inevitably. Well, tough shit.

Eleanor walked to the fish-and-chip shop on the high street, bought herself a portion of chips and slathered them in salt and vinegar. She hadn't eaten chips on the street for an age. Roger didn't really approve of eating on the street as he considered it 'common'. The chips were delicious, all the more so because the air was bitingly cold; she dipped her nose into the bag to grab a whiff of heat and vinegar. Amazing how restored you could be by something so ordinary. Benedict. And that hilarious beard! She laughed briefly. And he was so *fat*. No wonder Hannah hadn't recognised him. He looked like an old hippy, an entirely different species from the golden fallen angel he'd once resembled. She dug in for another chip and turned her steps towards home.

* * *

On the way to her father's flat, they talked about Benedict.

'I do see why you were so angry,' Conrad said. 'Roger was distinctly... unsettled by it, however. I imagine he is unused to seeing you lose your temper?'

'Well, I never do normally, as you know. I just bottle it up in the great English tradition, and walk around seething with rage and resentment. A shrink would have a field day with me.'

'With all of us, no doubt.'

'But were you really not cross, Daddy? I thought you would be. You worked so hard with him, you tried so hard – and he let you – and me – think he was dead.'

'You know, I doubt if he gave it that much thought. It probably didn't occur to him that we would worry so much. Benedict was – perhaps still is – a narcissist. He is not in the habit of putting himself in someone else's shoes. I imagine he didn't think about us much and so assumed it would be the same the other way round?'

'Perhaps. I'll call Hannah tomorrow and no doubt she'll have found out more. Hannah has the gift of managing to be nosy yet charming at the same time.'

She parked near the entrance to his block and turned off the engine.

'Won't you come in for some hippy tea?' He laid his hand on hers briefly.

'Thank you, yes, I'd like that.'

Upstairs, she curled up on the green chaise longue and let her father make the tea, for once. He came in with two mugs and set hers down on the side table next to her, then paused for a moment and left the room again. When he came back, he had a blanket in his hands. Without speaking, he draped it round her like a shawl, and tried to tuck the two ends together rather ineffectually. This rare gesture of tenderness brought tears to her eyes. Conrad took his seat by his desk as usual. Silence filled the room, stretching into the space and the corners, waiting.

'It is not, of course, any of my business, Eleanor, but are you... dare I ask... are you... happy?'

Eleanor waved a hand as if shooing away a small insect.

'I'm fine.'

'That's not what I asked.'

'No one expects to be happy all the time. I'm a grown-up. Well. Of sorts. How many people skip about delirious with joy all day long?'

'Again. That's not what I asked.'

'Stop being so Conrad-ish all the time.'

'*Mea culpa.*' He held up his hands.

'Well then, I suppose it depends on what you mean by happiness...'

Conrad sighed. 'Do not lead us down the diverting path of philosophical discussion, daughter-dear, when we both know exactly what I mean. A spade is a spade is a spade. I repeat – are you *happy*?'

'Yes, of course I am.' Eleanor looked down at her hands, then tugged the blanket around herself more tightly. 'Well,' she added, 'not every minute of the day, of course not.'

Her father said nothing.

After almost an entire minute of silence, she looked up and met his eye. Her father, the most dismissive, judgemental person she had ever come across, apotheosis of reason and logic, who usually had no time for emotions other than as a curious topic one might occasionally dissect with the keen scalpel of derision, was looking at her, his own eyes oddly shining as if he might be on the verge of tears himself, an unfamiliar look of – what? Yes... compassion softening those determined features.

'No,' she said at last, looking down again. 'I'm not.'

Tears leaked from her eyes and coursed down her face. At first, she emitted a funny little sound, like a hiccup, and began to weep, her eyes clamped shut, as if to barricade out the wave of pain. But it was too big now, vast and overwhelming, and, at last, at last, the dam could hold no longer. Eleanor released a wail of despair, a raw sound of absolute desolation as of a tree being wrenched apart in the fury of a thunderstorm. She sobbed, her body convulsing in spasms. Quietly then, her father came to her, sank onto the chaise, let her subside against him. He held her trembling form close, speaking softly.

'My dearest girl, my dear, dear Eleanor...'

At last, she sniffed herself to a halt. He handed her the crumpled cloth handkerchief from his pocket – who used cloth hankies these days? – and she laughed a little and wiped her face.

'I don't know what to do,' she said.

'Perhaps you could talk to someone who might help you?'

She turned to look at him. 'You mean a therapist? Or a divorce lawyer?'

Conrad shrugged. 'Either? Both?'

They shared a smile.

'He's not really a bad person, you know. Despite dropping your picture.'

'I know.'

'And it's not as if he beats me or anything awful. I don't have a proper reason.'

'One might argue that being unhappy is very much a proper reason.'

'But what if it's all me – that I'm incapable of being happy, no matter how perfect the other person might be?'

He sighed.

'Well, by that logic, all the more reason for you to consider living on your own, perhaps. One could say that you're being selfish, a dog in the manger, hoarding Roger for yourself when you don't really want him, whereas there might well be another woman out there who would be completely happy with him. Perhaps it would be kinder to free him to be with someone else?'

This was a typical line of argument from Conrad, and Eleanor knew it wasn't what he thought, not really, but that it was a reasonable premise. You could never win an argument with her father, but you could enjoy the journey, the hills and troughs and unexpected switchbacks.

'It's just that I hadn't really thought about the future – allowed myself to think about it – how it might be once the kids grew up. It snuck up on me. One minute you're still having to hunt for their school shoes every morning, the next they're swanning off round the world and sounding blasé about backpacking through the Far East. I hadn't realised – not properly – that...' She sank into silence for a minute.

'What?'

'That they would really *leave*. And that it would just be the two of us. I mean, I knew it – of course I did – but intellectually, not here, in the *core* of me.' She clamped both hands to her stomach. 'I know I'm being ridiculous. Everyone else just knuckles down and gets on with it, don't they? Plenty of couples stay married for decades – and they don't all still love each other or are – are – desperate to talk to each other at the end of each day...' Her voice faded. 'But they manage. They stay together. What's wrong with me?'

'Eleanor.' Conrad took her hand in both his own. 'Staying together when you no longer love each other is something... something people of *my* generation did.' He bowed his head for a moment. 'Your generation wants more. Expects more.'

'We're never satisfied, you mean.'

'No. I'm not talking about silly celebrities who get married for two months then divorce because the gilding gets a little chipped. If you still love Roger, and want to make it work, fine – go and get a decent marital therapist. Work it out.'

'But I don't love him.' The statement sounded calm and matter-of-fact, as if she had been offered chilli sauce in a restaurant, and was politely declining it. She had never said the words out loud before, perhaps had not even allowed them to take shape in her head.

Conrad nodded without enthusiasm.

'How long?'

'I don't know.' She shook her head, gazing blankly into the room as if blind. 'Years. Years and years. I cannot even remember what it felt like to be close to him... connected. Sometimes he comes into the room and I am surprised to see him there, as if he were someone I knew long ago who had unexpectedly wandered back into my life. When I hear his key in the door each evening, I feel sick. Just a sense of absolute *dread*.' She rested her chin in her hands, half-turned towards him. 'I don't know what to do.'

'It's not for me to tell you what to do. All I will say is this. I think...' His eyes met hers for a moment, then he looked away. He glanced towards the painting then looked towards his desk, '... being in a marriage where you do not love each other is a very, very lonely... *desperate* place to be. Far more lonely than living alone. Truly.' He gestured briefly at his study, his flat, his space. 'It is possible to find a good deal of peace and contentment on one's own.'

There was silence for a few moments, then she said: 'But you – you stuck with it.' This was turf onto which she had never dared tiptoe before.

'I did.'

'You regretted it?'

He said nothing but the lack of denial was enough.

'Oh, Daddy.' Now she squeezed his hands in her own. 'But were you never in love? No, don't answer that – I don't mean with my mother, let's not go there – but with someone else? When you were younger? Or – or...?'

Her father was looking at the painting once more.

'With *her*? You *knew* her?'

He nodded. 'I commissioned it.' He stood up then and walked over to the painting. 'For thirty years, it's all I've had of her.'

'But how on earth have you borne it... if you still loved her? *Love* her?'

A crumpled laugh escaped his lips.

'Badly,' he said.

There was so much she wanted to ask him: How had it ended? What was the woman's name? Was she still alive? Did he try to get her back after Marcia died? But now was not the time. Perhaps one revelation was enough for now.

'Back to you, I think.' He stood by the painting, now with his back to it.

'I don't know if I'm brave enough.' She looked down again.

'To leave?' He removed his glasses and held them up to the light as if they were smeared. 'You do it every day. You open the front door and leave. It's just that you go back again. Find somewhere for *you*. Rent a flat for three months to give yourself time on your own to think, at least. Do you have enough money to do that? I can help if you need it. You know how much was left after I sold the house. Take it. Put it towards a place of your own.'

'I have enough for a while.' For a decade or more, she had kept her own separate savings account 'in case of emergency'. She had never defined to anyone, least of all to herself, what that emergency might be, but – now that she let herself own the thought – she realised that she had known for a very long time.

47

RESTORATION

There was a small tapping at the door. Honestly, some days it was impossible to get anything done. If it was those bloody people about the tree again... She'd already had some branches lopped off to appease those barbarians – what more did they want? Cecilia slipped her coat on. Her friend Lilian had advised her always to put her coat on when answering the door, then she could say she was just on her way out if it was someone she didn't want to waste time on. Rather a good idea really.

Olivia was standing on the doorstep, looking small and waif-like in her thick woollen coat and outsize scarf. The white oval of her face peeped out from the mossy green of her hat and coat, a shy flower hidden among leaves.

'Are you all right? Will you come in?' Cecilia was tentative, as if inviting in a rather formal guest. 'I've been so worried about you. Christmas was horrible without you.'

'Mads told me you went to Ursula's?'

'I did. She made something grim and grey out of what appeared to be budgie food and mushrooms.'

Olivia grimaced and shuffled in.

'Can I make some tea? It's freezing out there.'

'Of course. Shall I do it? Let me make it for you.'

Olivia usually preferred to make her own as she was fussy – no, particular – about the way she took it. Now she shrugged. 'But can you leave the bag in, please?'

'Yes, I know you like it strong.' Cecilia looked at her daughter. 'You look chilled to the bone. Where are your gloves?'

'Mads nicked them. I'm OK.'

Cecilia reached out to feel her hands.

'They're like blocks of ice!' She held Olivia's hands between her own to warm them, but Olivia withdrew them slowly and tucked them into her own coat pockets.

Cecilia bustled about in the kitchen in a fluster, over-filling the kettle then tipping half of it out again and hunting for the better teabags that Olivia herself had once brought. She took down the teapot, thinking it would be nicer, friendlier somehow, if they shared a pot of tea together, even though she usually drank coffee.

'What I wanted to know...' Olivia's eyes shone with tears. 'I only wanted to know what he was really like. And how you felt about him.'

Cecilia reached for her daughter's hand but she gave the smallest shake of her head and withdrew it.

'I know you had all those lovers... and we make jokes about it and all that... but you've never sounded as if you loved any of them, not really. I mean, I do believe you loved Dad – Philip – but not in that way...' Her voice tailed off.

Cecilia gently guided her to a chair.

'Philip was your father in all the ways that matter most, you know that. He was there when you were born, holding my hand, poor sod. That nearly killed him, he's so squeamish.'

'Ma.'

'He *adored* you. Adores both of you. You know he does.'

'I know that.' Olivia exhaled loudly and unbuttoned her coat a little way. 'Look, I'm not complaining about Dad – I love him to bits – but this is not about him. It's about me. I've always wondered about him... my father. I know it's just his DNA, but it still *matters*.'

'But you hardly ever asked anything.'

'Because you were so dismissive about the importance of it!' She covered her face with her hands for a moment. 'Don't you see? Oh, it was just this guy, great screw, so tall, so clever and handsome... You never told me you *loved* him.'

'I found it too painful to talk about him.'

'But it was selfish, Ma.' Olivia seemed to scrunch down inside her overcoat. 'You were thinking of you, not me.'

Cecilia nodded but said nothing.

'And why marry Philip at all? You must have known he was gay, even back then?'

'Yes, of course. The only people who didn't know were his parents. They were completely in denial.'

'But it wasn't the 1950s or 60s – were people really so hung up then, in 1982?'

'God, you have no idea. His parents were uptight like you wouldn't believe. Do you remember them from when you were a child? Ultra-establishment, rich, upper-middle class, terribly anxious about what other people might think, conservative with both a small and a large C. Honestly! You can't go through life fretting about what other people think all the time!'

'I remember Grandma took us out for tea at Fortnum & Mason and you dressed us up in our party frocks and you did my plaits so tight, I could barely move my head. And she told me off for reaching across her to get the butter.'

'Quite. And among arty people, you're right, no one cared about the gay thing. If anything, we thought it was pretty cool. But Philip's parents were a completely different kettle of fish. He said if he'd told them, they would have disowned him. And you have to understand that people were already very jittery about AIDS. By then, there had been so many deaths in the States. The tabloids were calling it "the gay plague". Suddenly, it seemed to be acceptable to be openly homophobic again. And Philip's parents were constantly throwing parties and dinners to introduce him to eligible women – he hated it. But he was over forty by then and they were extremely antsy about the fact that he showed no sign of getting married.'

'And then what?'

'And then I – I became pregnant.'

'With me?'

'Yes, my darling. With you. But I was... alone... and frightened. And completely broke. And I didn't know what to do. I was getting more and more panicky as the weeks went by. Then Philip happened to call me and I burst into tears and he rushed round and said "Look, sweets, let's get married." He offered to support me and the baby, and said his parents would buy us a house – a *house,* for God's sake! – and mostly leave us alone and... and I didn't know what else to do... and I thought it would be better for you to have some sort of daddy around, at least, so I said yes. We were both desperate in our different ways, I think.'

Olivia nodded, then looked down.

'Did you want to get rid of me?'

There was a silence.

'The thought crossed my mind. God, you have no idea how desperate I was before Philip. But I couldn't. I was nearly thirty-seven by then. And I thought maybe I would never have another chance to have a baby – and even though I was scared – really scared – I thought that, if I did, then I would hate myself sooner or later. Even without Philip, I would have gone ahead and managed on my own somehow.' She looked at her daughter. 'And I've never, ever regretted it, I promise you.'

'And later you had Mads? She's not *his,* is she?'

'No. I did conceive her during a casual fling, just as I said.'

'And you said the same thing about me.'

'Yes. When you were little, you called Philip "Daddy" and it never really came up till Maddy was born.'

'But then you got divorced anyway, a few years later.'

'Well, it was inevitable. Philip fell in love with someone and moved out, but by then his father was terminally ill and his mother moved to Florida and just turned a blind eye to the whole thing. Philip gave me the house and carried on supporting us until my mosaics started to do so well, and seeing you girls often. Even later on he was always around, popping in and out, as you know, until he moved to the States.'

There was a pause.

'Are you hungry? Shall I make you something to eat?' Cecilia got to her feet.

'No, thank you.'

'Really nothing? I think there might be some of Ursula's wholemeal mince pies left over somewhere. They're really not too bad.' Cecilia rootled in the cupboards.

Olivia shook her head and hunkered down into her coat.

'But, Ma?'

'Yes?'

'I need to know, why didn't you tell him you were pregnant?'

Cecilia turned and faced her daughter. 'I – it's hard to explain.'

'I want to know the truth, that's all. Please don't try to fob me off with, you thought it was for the best, or you didn't want to make him leave his wife in case he regretted it later. Why didn't you tell him?'

'I can't... you don't understand.'

'Exactly. I really don't. And I want to. You owe me.'

Cecilia stood there, staring into space, shaking her head.

'Please. Think back. Remember – I *know* you – reason has nothing to do with it. Nothing rational: you were trying to let him do the right thing by his family, or any of that. How did you *feel*? That's how you make decisions.'

Cecilia moved a few steps and sank onto the edge of a chair. She shook her head again, wordless.

'I need to know.'

'It's just – so – awful.' Her face crumpled, eyes squeezed shut, and, when at last she spoke, her voice cracked.

'I was afraid.'

'Because?' Olivia's voice was cold.

'I—' Cecilia tried to meet her gaze but, abashed, looked down again. 'Please.'

'I was afraid that – if I told him – that...' Cecilia caught her breath. She had never given voice to the thought, barely allowed herself even to glimpse it for a moment when it slithered, dark and reptilian, into her dreams. But now, here with Olivia, she could no longer hide from it. 'He – he—' She started to cry then, curling into herself, giving in to it. After a minute, she felt the pressure of Olivia's hand on her shoulder and heard her voice.

'I do see it's hard, Ma, but please try. Don't you think I have the right to know?'

Cecilia straightened herself up as best she could and nodded.

'Yes, of course you do. I'm sorry.' She cleared her throat and took a breath. 'I was scared that I would tell him about the baby – about you – and that, even then, he might not choose me. That he would tell me to get rid of you or want to keep me on the side for ever, visiting us in secret – like some horrible, shameful thing. I was afraid that he would still choose to stay with... *her*... with them. From wanting to do the right thing, the honourable thing.' She shook her head. 'His fucking honour! But that's what he was like. I could bear it for me but not for you – not if he knew about the baby, yet still chose not to leave his marriage. I couldn't bear that.' She covered her face with her hands.

'So, if you never told him, how could you possibly know what choice he would have made?'

Cecilia shook her head, unable to speak.

'Perhaps he would have chosen you? Us.'

'I don't know.'

'Well, we'll never know now, will we? Because you never gave him that choice – a real choice. You should have given him that choice. It was a terrible, terrible thing to do – not fair on him, not fair on me.'

'I know.' Cecilia stretched out a hand towards her daughter's but Olivia kept hers on her lap. 'I am truly sorry. Can you ever forgive me?'

Olivia shrugged, as if she had been asked a question to which she did not know the answer and did not care that she did not know it.

They sat in silence for a minute.

'Tell me what to do to help make it better. What can I do?' Cecilia got up again and crossed to the kettle to boil more water.

'Build a time machine to turn the clock back?' Olivia scraped her chair back over the floor then stood up. 'Not so easy to repair the past, is it, Ma?'

'Do you want me to try to contact him?' Topping up the kettle at the sink, she spoke over her shoulder. Dear God. What the hell would she say? Often she thought he might be dead, though even the idea of it made her feel sick. Better by far not to know, not to try to find out. 'I have no idea if he's even still alive.'

There was a pause then Olivia spoke.

'He *is*.'

'What?' Cecilia dropped the kettle and it crashed into the sink. She swung round. 'What do you mean – how do you know? My God, have you *seen* him?'

He was *alive*. Tears sprang to her eyes once more and she swept them away with her hand. *He's alive.*

'No, of course not. I only found out who he is very recently. My...' She paused for a moment. 'My boyfriend, Andrew, works at the British Museum. He sees him there all the time.'

'At the BM? But he can't possibly still work there? He must have retired ten years ago.'

'I don't know.' Olivia shrugged. 'Andrew says he's working on a book and is there two or three times a week. In Prints and Drawings.'

'I can't believe it.' Cecilia sat down again. She used to go to the museum sometimes, long ago, taking her sketchbook so she could draw, but really just so she could feel near him even though they were apart. Once, she had met his daughter by complete chance, sat side by side with her drawing in companiable silence, unknowing. Then, when Cecilia had realised who the girl was, she had thrust her own sketchbook into her hands as a gift, wanting somehow with this strange gesture to feel connected to her in some way. The incident had given her pause, made her see that maybe it was the right thing after all, that his children still needed him.

'If you didn't refuse to have a computer like every other soul on the bloody planet, you could easily have found him yourself. You could have Googled him. He's written three books. Articles for specialist journals. He gives lectures. He's right *there*.'

'But – but – he might have forgotten all about me by now. It's thirty years ago. Anyway, no doubt he's still married to that uptight twit.'

'No. His wife died a few years ago, Andrew told me.'

'She *died*?' Cecilia sank back into her chair.

So he was free but hadn't come to find her. Maybe he had tried? No, she would not kid herself. He had made his decision back then and she knew what he was like. He would rationalise it, tell himself it was the right thing to do, then live with the consequences, no matter how awful it was.

'And when did you discover all this?'

'A couple of days ago.' Olivia looked embarrassed. 'Just before New Year.'

'Why didn't you come and see me at once?'

'That's rich, coming from you.' Olivia sighed. 'Look, I didn't because I'm not like you, OK? I needed time to take it in as I was pretty freaked out about the whole thing. I've been spending time with Andrew and he's been telling me all about my – about him.' She gave a small smile. 'It's been *good*, Ma.'

'But how on earth did you make the connection?'

'Andrew's a conservator there and he restored a painting for him. For *Conrad*.' Olivia paused for a moment. 'And he showed me a photo of it, then was gobsmacked because he clocked that the woman in it looked so like me. It was you, of course. Painted by Dad. Philip.'

'That painting? I can't believe he still has it. I assumed he'd have hidden it in the back of a cupboard or sold it, or given it away by now.'

'It clearly means a lot to him. It was damaged somehow, and Andrew says he was creeping about the Conservation department for almost a whole year peering over people's shoulders before he asked Andrew if he would work on it to restore it. And then when Andrew asked him about where it came from, he clammed up and went all weird on him.'

'Weird? What kind of weird?'

'I don't know. I wasn't there, OK? He just said he was touchy about it.'

'But what can I do? I can't just show up at the BM. I'd give the man a heart attack. He's over seventy.'

'Well, all the more reason to hurry up before he pops his clogs and it's too late then.' Olivia picked up her bag. 'It's not for me to tell you what to do, but you do need to do *something*. Send him a belated Christmas card, why don't you? Pop in a PS saying there's one teeny thing you forgot to mention before.'

'You're not going now?'

'Yes. I have to. I need to be by myself, Ma. I'm still upset. I'll be all right; just give me a bit of time, OK?'

'OK.'

Olivia wound her scarf round and round and buttoned up her coat again.

'Do you – do you still think about him sometimes? Didn't you wonder what had happened to him?'

Cecilia looked at her daughter as if the question were nonsensical.

'Of course. Every single day.'

'Do you still have feelings for him, then? After all this time?'

Cecilia smiled then. The relief at being able to say it out loud at last.

'I've never stopped loving him.'

48

AT LAST...

January 2013

It is a fiercely cold day, the wind abrading Conrad's cheeks and making his nose run and his eyes water as if he is an old man. Bugger it, he *is* an old man, he reminds himself. He is nothing but a ridiculous, foolish old man. And this is a fool's errand, no doubt. She will not be there; she may barely even remember him. And how old must she be now – dear God, the woman could well be senile, a toothless wreck covered in drool. No, no, *she* is not old – don't be ridiculous. She is... he thinks... sixty-six or sixty-seven... yes, sixty-six. Her birthday falls in February, so nearly sixty-seven. He checks his A-Z once more. It is only a few minutes' walk from the bus stop.

As he gets nearer, he grows more nervous. What on earth was he thinking of? He should have called first, or written a note – something fairly light-hearted, nothing too weighty or overblown. But how will he even address her? Back then, he called her – the thought brings a flush of pleasure to him even now – 'My Love'. And she was. It was as simple as that. On the phone, he used to say 'ML', the initials. She hated her given name, Pauline, so much that she couldn't bear for him to use it ever. So, it turns out that she has changed her name. Well, of course – she always said she would. He could have checked the records, but did not think of it.

Could he have done more to find her? Yes. So, why hadn't he? Pride, for one thing. After his pleading letter went unanswered, he retreated into himself – his books, his work, always a refuge – and told himself it was better this way. Benedict flunked most of his exams but at least he stayed out of serious trouble. No college would touch him, of course, but at eighteen he managed to get some casual work, helping out in the kitchen at a local restaurant. The hours were a good fit for Benedict. No need to stir himself before lunchtime. Go in to work in the afternoon, work till late, go out with the other staff at midnight when the place closed. It was an odd sort of life but he seemed, for a brief time at least, to be more stable, and Conrad could tell himself that he had done the right thing.

She could not have wanted to find him. He has to accept that. He has worked in Prints and Drawings at the British Museum for some thirty years, and even after his retirement, he continues to go in at least twice a week, so an enquiry would reach him almost immediately. Two minutes on the BM's website would track him down. Even now, his face is as familiar to the curators, the security guards as the Rosetta Stone.

This is the street. He glances down at the scrap of paper in his hand on which Andrew has written down her address, though he has committed it to memory. Andrew passed it to him in an envelope with no comment. On the paper are just the address and phone number and the words: 'The woman in your painting: now called Cecilia Herbert.'

This is the door. *Her* door. He stands in the street, unable to lift his hand and knock, unable to turn away – go back, back to his calm, familiar life, the life he has told himself is a good life, an honourably lived life. It does not do to think of what might have been – too easy to conjure up a fantasy. Perhaps, after all, they would have made each other horribly unhappy. She would surely have been driven mad by him – his stiffness, his lack of spontaneity, his linguistic pedantry? She was a crea- ture of impulse, of passion. What, in the end, would she have wanted with a stodgy academic such as himself?

He swallows. The door is dark green with dull brass fittings. He stands well back from it as if standing too close might cause him to be sucked in and he would no longer have a choice. What if...? What if...? For over thirty years, there has not been a single day when he has not thought, What if? What if I had allowed myself to seize that chance, to choose at least the possibility of happiness – even if only for a handful of years before she tired of me? Eleanor would have been all right either way, in all probability. Eleanor could always be relied upon to be all right. Had staying made a real difference to Benedict? It was impossible to know. Perhaps, if Conrad had left back then, the boy might even have been forced to pull up his socks and grow up a bit? Still, look at him now. Alive, married, with a child, a business – even happy, by the look of it. He nods. The boy is all right, thank God.

He turns to go. He cannot do this. Let sleeping dogs lie. He is not equal to this sort of thing, doesn't have the vocabulary for it. And she is bound to be changed, of course. The thought that she could have tried to cling to youth, might be tarted up with heavy eyeliner and vermilion lipstick in a gruesome parody of the beautiful woman she once was makes him feel sick and trembly. But what is he now? An old man. His hand reaches up automatically to smooth back his thinning white hair, once so thick and dark. He squares his shoulders. Well, come on, man, are you doing this or not? Come along now! Say hello, have a cup of tea, reminisce for half an hour, trot off back to your study, ghosts laid to rest. Yes.

He steps forward, two long strides, lifts the knocker and raps sharply twice before he can think any more. He has done so much thinking; his whole life has been devoted to the intellect, to the cultivation of the mind, and it has brought him deep satisfaction, fulfilment. But not much joy.

And then, suddenly, she is there – here – before him.

There is so much he wants to say, is desperate to say, but he does not speak. Conrad, who has lived his entire life through the medium of the written word: writing, reading, studying, lecturing – Conrad, for whom words have been as gods, at last has no words.

He takes a hesitant step towards her, cautious as if she might flee at any moment. But still she stands there, though he sees she is trembling. He had forgotten – almost – how small she is. She doesn't even reach to his shoulder, yet she makes him feel powerless as no one else on this earth could do.

'You have come,' She looks up at him, and he sees that her eyes are shining with tears. 'At last.'

'I have come.'

All his life, Conrad has taken charge, made decisions, led the way, but here, in this moment, he is unequal to it. He wants to draw her to him, to wrap her in his arms and hold her there where she belongs. Perhaps she hates him for pushing her away, for choosing Benedict, his wife, his safe existence over her. Or perhaps – worse? – she didn't care much at all and thought herself well shot of him? He does not know how to do this, any of it. There is no text to turn to, no footnotes, no appendices to shed light on it.

He has pictured this moment so many times over the years – what he would say, how he would declare his love or, when he was feeling angry with her for having disappeared and left no word, he imagined being cool and imperious with her, showing her he didn't care any more, that she was as nothing to him.

Her face crumples then and he steps forwards and folds her in his arms, cupping her precious head against his solid chest, his hand stroking her still-soft hair.

His chin rests gently on top of her head and he stands there, holding her, letting her weep into his shirt, feeling her soft body melt into him.

'I can't believe you've really come,' she says into his damp shirt.

He speaks into her hair, his voice low, catching in his throat: 'It would have been a hell of a lot sooner if I'd known where you were.'

'Really?' She looks up at him then, her green eyes glistening.

'Really.'

He looks down at her, at her hair – now faded, a quiet copper colour – but still in its single plait, snaking over her shoulder. The sight of it stirs him and at last he says what he needs to say.

'There has not been a single day when I have not thought of you.'

She nods. It is the same for her.

'I heard you still have the painting? Maybe you should have got rid of it. Then you could have forgotten me.'

He shakes his head.

'It would have made no difference.' He taps his head. 'You were always in here.'

'And here?' She rests her hand on his chest, feeling his heartbeat.

He lays his own hand on top of hers, pressing it closer.

'Sole occupancy.'

She takes his hand and draws him into the hallway, then into the sitting room, where she stands before him. She curls her own small hand into the larger frame of his.

She looks into his eyes and at long last whispers the words he has dreamed of for years, for decades.

'Dear Heart,' she says.

He enfolds her in his arms, looking down at her upturned face:

'My Love. My Love. *My Love...*' Rocking her, holding her, now looking down into her eyes. God, those eyes, that look that first found its way into the cold, dark cavern of his heart and lit a flame there, that smile that has stayed with him all this time.

It is so long since he has kissed a woman with love, with affection, with desire, that he is not sure he remembers how. But still, it is her face, her lips – long-remembered, as familiar as if he had kissed them every night for all these past years. At last then he kisses her and she loops her arms up and round his neck. At last.

Nothing else is.

49

NOW, VOYAGER...

Eleanor is packing. She is good at this. If she were to keep an updated CV, she would be tempted to include 'Packing' under 'Additional Skills'. There is something rather satisfying about the process, the containment of separate items into an orderly whole. She packs her husband's case first. The habit of putting him first is so deeply ingrained after over twenty years that the idea of doing anything else flits through her head so fleetingly as barely to be noticed.

She coils his belts tightly to tuck them into his shoes. Flattens his pairs of socks – Roger does not like his socks to be balled because then they look 'lumpy and untidy' – and counts out enough of each type: navy to go with his new deck shoes, tan or burgundy to match his pairs of loafers, black for evening. He has instructed her to pack enough for 'two-point-five weeks' so that they will only have to avail themselves of the ship's laundry service twice during the voyage. She interleaves his shirts with white tissue to minimise creasing, as a good wife does. Roger is a man who prefers everything just so, you see; he likes order and stability and predictability. He expects his wife to be exemplary in every way: to pack perfectly, to ask about his day, to show concern when he is tired or fretful, to soothe him with soft words and considerate actions: a perfect cup of coffee, a beautifully cooked meal, a shoulder rub, an endless capacity to listen, to absorb his woes and worries like a sponge so that he can be free of them.

She digs out an extra pair of cufflinks – little gold anchors once given to him by a client – and pops the box in next to his bow tie. Roger would like those for a cruise, she is sure. She can imagine him trying to be chummy with the captain and dropping random bits of nautical know-how into every conversation to show that he is not a 'landlubber'; the thought makes her smile.

Roger will take his beloved e-reader, of course, but Eleanor decides to pack a few books for him as well in the second case, where there is plenty of room – 'physical books', as he has taken to calling them, a phrase that makes her want to hit him over the head with the heaviest 'physical book' she can find. She pops upstairs to her studio to fetch the ones she hopes he will find time to take another look at. As an afterthought, she adds her birthday slippers.

Both cases are heavy. Well, no matter; Roger's invaluable PA, Linda, has, as ever, pre-empted the problem by arranging for a courier to pick up the two large cases this afternoon and they will be delivered directly to the cruise ship in dock at Southampton so that Eleanor would not have to struggle with hefting them on and off the train on her own. Like Roger, Linda is marvellous at that sort of thing – logistics, timings, arrangements. Roger's plan was for Eleanor to take the train down to Southampton in the morning – plenty of time as the ship wouldn't set sail until the afternoon. Roger is currently away for work in Jersey again for a couple of nights, so will fly back from there direct to Southampton tomorrow. Pointless to come all the way back to London, then have to slog down to Southampton again. Roger would meet his wife in their luxury suite an hour or two before the ship departs. It is all arranged.

In a holdall, she carefully places her wood-engraving tools and materials and, in a small portfolio, a sheaf of her favourite Japanese handmade paper. She would love to take her press, too, but it is impossibly heavy and needs to be bolted into position. For now, she can manage without. Several years ago, when she had first studied engraving, her tutor had showed them how to make a reasonable proof – a test print – from a woodblock they had carved without using a press at all, just by pressing the paper onto the inked woodblock with any kind of heavy weight. This trip is really a gift, she thinks: so many weeks of time and space to draw, to read, to think, to work. Engraving is a slow and painstaking business. Her tutor said – making them all laugh – that you needed to be 'a finicky fucker' if you were going to be good at it. She is endlessly patient and, yes, a finicky fucker when it comes to something that is a labour of love for her. She likes the absolute absorption that comes when she is working on a woodblock, the way each groove she makes feels beneath her fingertip, the moment of revelation when she peels the paper away from the inked block to see those grooves transformed into the print. That last one she did was good and she is rightly proud of it. And she will do more.

The courier rings the bell and Eleanor checks the luggage labels and hands over the two large cases with a smile. So, it is done.

Night-time. Eleanor cannot sleep. Although she is anxious about the trip, she is also beginning to feel excited. It is a strange, unfamiliar feeling, pawing at her like a cat desperate to get out and explore. After a couple of hours, she gives up and goes downstairs. By her handbag is a new novel – out in full view instead of secreted in a hiding-place. It is a hardback, a glorious piece of self-indulgence. It is thick and heavy, solid and comforting in her hand. She opens it and dips her nose briefly into the silent centre of it, then runs her fingertips lightly over the words. Irresistible. She curls up on the sofa under a blanket, opens the book to her favourite part, the final page, and begins to read... slipping into the words and... at last... into sleep.

* * *

She wakes very early, unfurling slowly from her soft cocoon, a butterfly emerging into the first hour of its first day. It won't be light for at least another hour or two, but no matter. She is wide awake and tingling with anticipation. A quick shower, clean clothes, tea and toast, and she is ready. From her jewellery box, she picks out a couple of pieces given to her by the children: a pair of moonstone earrings from Hannah on her birthday, a jade pendant brought back by Daniel from his own gap-year trip, a simple silver bracelet, some sparkly crystal beads. She darts round the house, doing a final check, setting various lights on timers, making sure the window locks are secure, leaving a note and payment for the cleaner, who will pop in regularly to keep an eye on the house.

She takes out her mobile and rereads the email to Roger over which she deliberated for so long. The drafts became longer and longer until, in the end, she gave up attempting to explain, accepting that there was no point. No point in offering reasons, no point in heaping blame upon him or on herself, no point in wallowing in apologies. It is brief and to the point:

R

I am not coming with you on the cruise. I hope it gives you time to rest and relax.

I do not want to be married to you any more. No animosity, no blame, no apologies. We can discuss matters on your return. I will not be reachable in the interim.

Bon voyage.

E

Whatever she says, it is unlikely that Roger would understand. For now, the email will stay in her Drafts folder and, shortly after the ship's departure, she would press 'Send'. She will stop en route to call the children to tell them. Roger will no doubt rant and rave and tell everyone she is having a mid-life crisis, she must be menopausal, she must be mad. Frankly, she couldn't give a flying fuck.

In the hall is everything she needs for now: her son's old backpack with her clothes, her warm, waterproof jacket, her walking boots, the holdall and folio with her tools and paper. Sarah said that they barely use the Suffolk cottage at this time of year anyway. She can have it for as many weeks as she likes. She transfers the bags to the boot of her car, takes one last look around the house. It *is* lovely, she thinks, yes, but largely because *she* made it that way. In the end, it is just a building.

Later, there will be the difficult part, she knows, but she will manage, as she always does. Now, at last, she is no longer afraid. Solitude holds no shadows for her. She does not need to be Satellite Eleanor any more. She is not even sure she can blame Roger entirely for pulling her into his orbit because, after all, she is a grown-up, and she allowed it to happen. It is a very sobering thought, an uncomfortable one, one she will have to take out and look at many times, she knows. But, for now, while she is feeling brave, there is this journey to make, a new trajectory. If she thinks about it too much, she knows she will never go. If she pauses too long, she will order a taxi to take her to the station and get on the train to

Southampton and all will be as it was before. She will meet Roger in the cabin and have cocktails on the balcony and she will smile and listen and say she's fine when she isn't. But it is time. The clock has stopped on her old life and sometimes that is just how it is. She cannot do it any more.

Eleanor takes a last look around the hallway, slips out into the world, and shuts the door quietly, finally, behind her.

Some people like to begin at the end.

ACKNOWLEDGMENTS

Writing a novel is a long and largely lonely business, so I would like to thank the following for their support and guidance:

The British Museum, especially past and present staff of the Prints and Drawings department and Conservation and Scientific Research: Western Art on Paper, who showed me round and answered my innumerable questions.

David Gentleman, a legend in his own lifetime, who patiently answered my questions about wood-engraving, showed me his studio, tools, printing press etc, and also checked the passages on engraving after I'd written them.

My dear friend and fellow writer Sarah Monk, who read the first draft in progress and always came up with particularly incisive and wise insights, and also special thanks for valuable help and inspiration from my other good writing friends Lucy McMaster and Renee Knight.

The members of my former writing group, for their encouragement and constructive comments on early chapters of the first draft, which they had to read out of context and out of sequence.

Sophie Wilson and Richard Skinner, for their professional expertise.

Luci Eyers, who provided me with technical information on painting with egg tempera and checked the relevant text.

Richard Carvalho and Angus Walker, for their continued faith in me despite the lack of reasonable supporting evidence.

My editor and copy-editor at Boldwood Books, Sarah Ritherdon and Yvonne Holland, for their great attention to detail, to designer Alice Moore for a wonderful cover, and to the diligent proof-readers Sue Lamprell and David Boxell.

My agent, Charlotte Robertson, for her unflagging encouragement and support, keen editorial instincts, and innumerable breakfasts.

My friends, who help keep me sane, especially Luce 'W', Janine, and Sarah.

Larry for his continued enthusiasm and support, in spite of everything.

My sister, Stephanie, always my favourite writer.

BOOK CLUB QUESTIONS

• The novel tells us about the lives of four people in an intertwined narrative. Why do you think the author opted to tell the story that way?

• Each chapter is seen from one character's viewpoint, though written in the third person (he/she) rather than the story being told by a more distant, single, all-seeing narrator. Do you find this draws you into the story more?

• Are there times when you found yourself feeling angry with the heroine, Eleanor, and wanting her to stand up for herself more? Why might the author want you to feel angry as well as sympathetic?

• There are different marriages held up for examination in the story – not just the main one of Eleanor and Roger, but also Eleanor's friends, Sarah and Mark, Andrew's parents, and – in flashback, Eleanor's parents. What makes the marriage of Sarah and Mark so different from the others?

• Do you think Marcia was a good mother to either Benedict or Eleanor, or both? What do you find odd about the way she is around Benedict?

• In the beach scene, when Sarah shouts at Eleanor to come back, why is she so panicky, and is she right to be so?

• Eleanor is someone who can seem all right on the outside, while on the inside being actually wretched. Do you think we all, to a greater or lesser degree, mask our deepest feelings?

• Do you think a man like Andrew might be treated quite badly if he ended up in an unhappy relationship? Why do you think he struggles to be assertive? What do you think would happen to him if he didn't leave his parents?

• Cecilia seems like a free spirit, but one can imagine that she might be quite annoying in real life. But are there things that someone like that could teach the rest of us?

• Cecilia's daughters, especially Olivia, seem more grown-up than their mother at times. Why do you think they are like that?

• Some readers might feel no sympathy at all for Conrad – after all, he's unfaithful to his wife and doesn't know how to be a good father to his son. But he has a key moment of redemption that makes us warm to him even if we hadn't before. What is it and why does it matter so much?

• Sometimes there are funny moments, even in the darkest scenes. Does that correspond with your own experience of life? Do you think humour can help us deal with difficult times?

MORE FROM CLAIRE CALMAN

We hope you enjoyed reading *Growing Up For Beginners*. If you did, please leave a review.

If you'd like to gift a copy, this book is also available as an ebook, digital audio download and audiobook CD.

Sign up to Claire Calman's mailing list for news, competitions and updates on future books.

http://bit.ly/ClaireCalmanNewsletter

ABOUT THE AUTHOR

Claire Calman is a writer and broadcaster known for her novels that combine wit and pathos, including the bestseller *Love is a Four-Letter Word*. She has appeared on BBC Radio 4's Woman's Hour and Loose Ends.

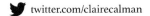 twitter.com/clairecalman

ABOUT BOLDWOOD BOOKS

Boldwood Books is a fiction publishing company seeking out the best stories from around the world.

Find out more at www.boldwoodbooks.com

Sign up to the Book and Tonic newsletter for news, offers and competitions from Boldwood Books!

http://www.bit.ly/bookandtonic

We'd love to hear from you, follow us on social media:

facebook.com/BookandTonic

twitter.com/BoldwoodBooks

instagram.com/BookandTonic

Printed in Great Britain
by Amazon